THE GOLDEN CUP

Also by Marcia Willett

FORGOTTEN LAUGHTER
A WEEK IN WINTER
WINNING THROUGH
HOLDING ON
LOOKING FORWARD
SECOND TIME AROUND
STARTING OVER
HATTIE'S MILL
THE COURTYARD
THEA'S PARROT
THOSE WHO SERVE
THE DIPPER
THE CHILDREN'S HOUR
THE BIRDCAGE

For more information on Marcia Willett and
her books, see her website at
www.devonwriters.co.uk/marcia.htm

THE GOLDEN CUP

MARCIA WILLETT

McArthur & Company
Toronto

First Published in Canada in 2005 by
McArthur & Company
322 King Street West, Suite 402
Toronto, Ontario
M5V 1J2
www.mcarthur-co.com

Library and Archives Canada Cataloguing in Publication

Willett, Marcia
The golden cup / Marcia Willett.

ISBN 1-55278-483-5

I. Title.

PR6073.I277G65 2005   823'.914   C2005-900583-1

Jacket photograph: *Gettyimages*
Design: *Stephen Mulcahey/TW*
Printed in Canada by *Webcom*

10 9 8 7 6 5 4 3 2 1

To Clare Foss

ST MERIADOC – FACT AND FICTION

First, the facts:

Meriadoc was a wealthy Welshman who lived in the fifth or sixth century. At some point, he gave all his money to poor clerics and his land to the needy. Setting aside opulence and the purple silks he loved to wear, he dressed in rags, ate simple food and lived in complete poverty. He came to Cornwall, where he founded several churches, before crossing over to Brittany to continue his ministry. Elected to be Bishop of Vannes, he accepted the post with great reluctance and continued to live a life of abstinence. To this day, he is remembered in both Cornwall and Brittany – the parish church at Camborne is dedicated to St Martin and St Meriadoc, a miracle play in Cornish still survives recounting his legendary exploits and there is an infant school named after him. His feast day is 7 June.

'Poverty is a remover of cares and the mother of holiness'
St Meriadoc

Now for some fiction:

St Meriadoc's Cove, the well (there is no known well ascribed to the saint) and Paradise are fictional, as are the osteopathy practices in Bodmin and Wadebridge. The cove is 'situated' on the north coast of Cornwall between Com Head and Carnweather Point, overlooking Port Quin Bay and almost directly north of Polzeath. There are two lanes leading down to the cove, one from the east is disused and leads directly to the house: 'Paradise'. The other, from the west, drops down to the head of the cove, passes the old boatyard and 'The Row', crosses the stream that runs down from the well and divides to the left, leading to 'The Lookout', and to the right, to Paradise.

PROLOGUE

The two figures, leaning together beneath the bare boughs of an ancient beech, were barely distinguishable in the fading, wintry light. They stood quite still, a smudge of darker grey against the high granite wall that separated the sheltered garden from the sloping meadow. As he stared across the frosty grass he heard the arched, wrought-iron gate open with a clang and saw a girl pass through, closing the gate carefully behind her. He straightened, recognizing her from the brief glimpse he'd had earlier when he'd called at the house. A soft plaid was wrapped about her shoulders and she wore green gumboots beneath the long, knubbly-textured skirt.

The donkeys plodded to meet her with their familiar head-dipping gait and she spoke quietly to them, holding out her hands, bending down so it seemed as if she might be kissing their suede-soft muzzles. He hesitated – longing to call out to her, to make a connection with her – but his courage failed him. Instead, he pictured her as he'd first seen her as she'd come in through a door half hidden in the shadows at the back of the hall: a straight, uncompromising glance from beneath dark, level brows, her arms crossed over something that she held to her breast – a book? or a box? – and an air of wariness. She'd paused, watching, listening, and then had vanished through another door, leaving him with the older woman who'd smiled with such sweetness and sympathy.

'I *am* sorry. It would be quite impossible for you to see Mrs Trevannion today. She's got this wretched chest infection on top of everything else. If only we'd known that you were coming.'

'I wrote Mrs Trevannion,' he'd answered quickly, unable to hide his disappointment. 'I sent a copy of a photograph with the letter. I think – I'm really hoping – that she knew my grandmother's sister way back during the war. She emigrated to the States in 'forty-six, my grandmother, and then they just lost touch. We were so excited when my mother found the wedding photograph, all four of them together, the names on the back of it clear as clear. Hubert and Honor Trevannion . . .'

'I'm afraid she's been too ill to answer any correspondence. A broken ankle, you see, and now this infection.' She'd frowned a little, crushing his enthusiasm kindly but firmly. 'Perhaps in a week or two . . .'

'I'm only here for the week,' he'd told her, dismayed, 'staying over at Port Isaac. I'm working in London for a spell and taking the opportunity to follow any leads I've managed to find while I'm over here. But I've been interested in this for a long time now and the photograph was a real find . . .'

Once again, at the mention of the photograph, he'd sensed a faint withdrawal.

'I don't see how we can help you at the moment.'

He tried a different tack. 'What a magical little valley this is; so secret and so green. And what a great name for a house. "Paradise". You really do have strange names in Cornwall, don't you? Indian Queens. Lazarus. Jamaica Inn.' He shook his head as if in amused puzzlement. 'And then there are all these

Saints. But I love "Paradise". And it certainly looks like it is one.'

'We think so too.'

Her courtesy was as blank as a stone wall and, in the end, he'd given her his card and she'd promised to contact him, smiling farewell, closing the door quietly. The sense of anti-climax was almost overwhelming and, walking back down the drive to the narrow lane, he'd felt oddly hurt, thinking that she might at least have offered him a cup of tea. As he stood at the five-bar gate watching the donkeys he tried to be more rational, persuading himself that Honor Trevannion was probably very ill; that the older woman and the girl were too concerned with her wellbeing to have time to spend with an unexpected stranger hunting for an ancestor. He hunched his shoulders against the chill of the evening and rested his arms along the top bar of the gate. The shadowy group at the far side of the meadow was hardly visible now as the twilight, creeping across the grass and thickening beneath the trees, blotted away the glimmerings of sunset and dimmed the last bright reflections slanting from the west. He frowned, still thinking about the interview. Had he imagined that slight tension? A reluctance to discuss his letter and the photograph? He shrugged. More likely she hadn't a clue what he was talking about and was too worried to be interested.

He heard again the metallic clang as the gate closed: the girl was gone and the donkeys had moved into the small open-fronted barn. Frustrated, but still driven by curiosity and a determination to follow his lead through, he walked on to the disused quarry where he'd parked his car and drove away.

PART ONE

CHAPTER ONE

The grassy track from the meadow twisted between rhododendrons as tall as trees, whose woody arms, stretching along the hard, bare earth, were supported and propped upon deep-rooted, knuckly elbows. The tough, lance-shaped leaves shivered in the chilly, gently shifting air and, at the edge of the path, clumps of snowdrops gleamed dimly in the gathering shadows. Light shone suddenly from an upstairs room and a figure stood with arms wide-stretched, pausing briefly to look out, before the brightness was quenched by the sweep of curtains drawn swiftly across the windows.

By the time the girl had reached the garden door, kicked off her boots and crossed the hall to the drawing-room, Mousie had come downstairs and was piling wood onto the open fire.

'So there you are, Joss.' There was an odd note of relief in her voice. 'I wondered where you'd disappeared to. Were you putting the donkeys to bed?'

'I took some apples.' She sat on the wide fender, curling her toes in their thick, cosy socks, relishing the warmth from the flames that licked with greedy yellow and orange tongues at the rough-sawn logs. 'How is Mutt?'

'Sleeping peacefully. I shall take up a tray of tea and sit with her for a while. Would you like to join us?'

Joss shook her head. 'I'll go up later and read to her. She gets restless after supper and it distracts her. Who was that man who was here just now? What did he want?'

Mousie hesitated, as if making an effort to formulate an accurate answer. 'He's an American tracking down a relative. He seemed to think that your grandmother might have known his great-aunt during the war. Something like that. Not a particularly suitable moment, I'm afraid.'

'And does Mutt know her?'

'I haven't asked her,' answered Mousie crisply. 'Do you want some tea?'

'I'll come and get mine in a minute, just leave it in the pot.' Joss smiled at the small upright figure, whose high-necked jersey was slung about with several pairs of spectacles all mixed up on long pieces of cord. 'You know I can manage perfectly well if you want go home, Mousie.'

'I know that, my darling.' Mousie relaxed visibly, tension flowing from her shoulders and smoothing away the lines of anxiety: her slate-blue eyes were bright and warmly affectionate beneath the unruly crest of soft white hair. 'But perhaps just one more check to make sure that she's settled. This new antibiotic . . .'

Joss chuckled. 'Hopeless,' she said. 'It must be all those years of nursing and being in charge. Old habits die hard. I'm qualified too, you know. OK, I know I'm not a *proper* nurse, but I can lift Mutt and I promise you that some gentle massage will really help now that her foot is out of plaster.'

'And you also know very well that I am *not* prejudiced against osteopathy,' said Mousie firmly. 'I have no anxiety about you looking after your grandmother; I'm just rather worried about the chest infection. And she's in a rather confused state, although that's mostly due to the antibiotics.'

Her eyes were anxious again and, watching her, Joss had no

desire to tease her further but felt instead a stomach-sinking fear.

'We have to give her time,' she said. 'It was a bad break and this horrid infection isn't helping. She'll be fine, Mousie.' It was almost a plea for consolation and Mousie swiftly responded to it.

'Of course she will, my darling. Thank goodness you can spend some time with her. Having you here is the best medicine she could have.' She smiled mischievously, her sense of humour and natural resilience returning. 'That and the massage, of course.'

Left alone, Joss drew her feet up onto the fender, rested her chin on her knees and began to think about the good-looking American. She'd been attracted by the eagerness that had informed his gestures and expression, and was already regretting her own wariness. How simple – she told herself now – to have joined in the conversation; offered him some refreshment. She'd seen him standing at the field gate but this newly acquired reticence – so foreign to her character but necessary to protect herself – had made it impossible for her to call a friendly greeting. She'd been surprised, however, at Mousie's uncharacteristic caution and the guardedness with which she'd parried his enquiries, although, under the circumstances, it wasn't terribly surprising that Mousie was preoccupied.

Now, as Joss gazed into the bright heart of the fire, she imagined a different scene: a scene in which she'd strolled forward, smiling in response to his friendly glance, saying, 'Goodness! This sounds fascinating. What's it all about?' They might have had some tea together and he could have shown her the photograph of his long-lost great-aunt. She felt frustrated by this new constant need for wariness that clamped her tongue and inhibited her gestures, although, she reminded herself, she was at least able to remain open and confident with her patients.

This was because they rarely asked about her private life and so there was no need to be on guard. If the dreaded questions – 'Are you married? Do you have a boyfriend?' – *were* to be asked, she was able to deal with them more casually with patients than with those she loved. Relationships with her family had become more complicated since she'd moved out of the bed-sit in Wadebridge to stay at Paradise whilst she renovated the tiny cottage at the end of The Row. Yet how could she have foreseen that a childhood friendship would flower so abruptly into a love that must be kept secret?

'Tea's made,' Mousie called on her way upstairs.

Joss went out into the hall, pausing to revel in the atmosphere of this house that she loved so very dearly. It was such a perfect little place, elegantly proportioned with high sash windows, and she'd sometimes imagined tilting back the roof and looking down inside as if it were a doll's house. Mousie's voice could just be heard, murmuring comfortingly beyond the closed bedroom door, and Joss wondered whether her grandmother had once known the American's great-aunt, way back when they'd both been young. She understood his interest in this vanished relative, dimly recognizing in him a need for security that is centred in family. Her own heart was much more at home here in this tiny valley of St Meriadoc, where her mother's family had lived for centuries, than in her parents' house in Henley or the London flat where her father spent most of his working week.

She decided to ask Mousie if she might see the photograph, hoping that there was some connection that would encourage the young man's quest. Still thinking about him, she poured tea into a mug and carried it back to the fire.

Upstairs, Mousie removed the tray, saw that Mutt was dozing again and looked about the room. A small but cheerful fire burned in the grate, safely contained behind a tall meshed guard, and a pretty painted screen had been set so as to shield the elderly woman in the bed from the brightness of the tall lamp set on a gate-leg table near the window. It was at this table that Mousie kept her vigil and it was piled with books, newspapers and the paraphernalia of letter-writing.

She stood for a moment, her back to the bed, tidying the bulky newspapers, squaring the loose sheets of a letter she'd been writing before folding them into the leather blotter, collecting stray pens and a pencil and putting them into a blue and white ceramic jar. Presently she slid the print from beneath the blotter and stared down at it. It was evident that it had been recently copied from an original photograph itself, rather than from the negative, and it bore the marks of scratches and creases. Nevertheless she'd recognized it at once: in 1941 her cousin Hubert had sent an identical print all the way from India to his aunt in Portsmouth.

He'd written:

I was deeply horrified and sad to hear about Uncle Hugh and the loss of HMS *Hood*. But I am so pleased that you're going to St Meriadoc to be near Mother and Father. . . I can't wait for you all to meet Honor, she's a darling. Give my love to Mousie and Rafe . . .

Even now she could remember the shock and misery she'd felt at this news coming so soon after the death of her father. From her earliest memories she'd loved Hubert with an overwhelming devotion, willing herself to grow up quickly, imagining the glorious, much-dreamed-of moment when he would see her as an adult and realize that he'd loved her all the time. It was Hubert who had given her the nickname 'Mousie' and, though he had teased her, he could always make her laugh: there was no-one else like Hubert. She'd gazed at the face of Hubert's new wife, mistily smiling beneath the charming, silly hat slanted over one eye, and had silently, bitterly, hated her. As the war dragged on, news had filtered back to St Meriadoc from India: Honor had given birth to a son, Bruno, and, three years later, to a daughter, Emma. Mousie was seventeen when they'd heard that Hubert was trying to book a passage to England for his wife and children in an attempt to protect them from the riots and upheaval of partition. He'd planned to follow them when his discharge came through, later in the year, but he had died of some kind of food-poisoning days before his family were due to sail and Honor – whom Hubert had nicknamed Mutt – and the children had come back to Paradise alone.

Mousie slid the photograph beneath the blotter and glanced across at the bed. Mutt was lying on her side, watching her with calm intelligence. Mousie concealed the tiny shock that these switches from feverish confusion to brief moments of lucidity caused, and smiled.

'I'm afraid that tea must be cold by now,' she said. 'Would you like some more?'

Mutt made a faint negative shake of her head on the pillow and Mousie moved back to the bed, sitting in the low up-holstered armchair so as to be nearly on the same level as the sick woman in the high bed.

'Poor Mousie,' the words were barely stronger than a breath and Mousie had to bend closer to catch them. 'What a nuisance I am.'

'Not a bit of a nuisance.' She took Mutt's weakly out-stretched hand and held it warmly between both of her own. 'You're getting better by the minute. And Joss will be up soon to read to you.'

There was a little silence whilst the logs crumbled together in a soft ashy explosion of flames and the shadows streamed across the ceiling.

'Odd, wasn't it,' Mutt murmured, 'both of us being nurses?'

'It was all Hubert's fault,' Mousie answered lightly. 'You know how he was my hero when I was small. Once he'd qualified as a doctor I was determined that I would train to be a nurse. I was always foolishly pleased that he knew I'd started my training before he died. It was as if it made some kind of connection between us.'

Mutt stirred restlessly, turning onto her back and pulling herself higher up the bed.

'I might try to sleep again,' she said.

The tranquil moment had passed, although there was no sign of fever, and Mousie watched her thoughtfully for a moment before putting the handbell beside her on the quilt, and going quietly away.

CHAPTER TWO

The Porch Room, given its name because it was situated directly above the front door, looked south across the secret, sheltered garden to the lane and the hillocky, gorse-edged little fields beyond. A sturdy wisteria grew beneath the window, so that in early summer the scent from its grey-blue flowers drifted into the room through the open casement. Here Mutt had placed a wicker chair at an angle from which, on a June evening, she could be ravished by the exotic crimson and white flowers of the rhododendrons and watch the full moon, egg-yolk yellow, rise above the distant thorn trees at the head of the valley.

As she entered the room later that evening Joss felt a sense of pleasure at its peaceful, elegant comfort, although, privately, she preferred her own room at the back of the house, which looked north towards the high rugged cliffs. At night she could hear the restless, rhythmic sighing of the waves, as they pried and dragged at the resisting rocks with foamy fingers, and tumbled hugger-mugger into the caves to carry out the grey shaley sand with them as they retreated. Now, the cold, frosty night was closed out behind thick, velvet curtains and

her grandmother's room was as quiet and self-contained as a
little space ship rocking on its way through a silent universe.

She glanced towards the bed and its motionless occupant
and, seized by sudden terror, moved quickly. Mutt opened
her eyes as Joss stooped beside her, feeling for the thin wrist,
checking the light, fast pulse. She grimaced, as though guessing at her granddaughter's momentary fear and mocking it.

'I'm still here,' she murmured.

'Yes.' Joss silently expelled a little gasping breath of relief.
'So you are.'

They smiled at each other, the deeply special love that
had defined their friendship from the earliest days flowing
between them. Mutt's frail grip tightened a little on Joss's
warm hand. Nothing now must harm her plans for this dearly
beloved grandchild: the natural inheritor of Paradise. She and
Joss had always been a team: occasionally defying the middle
generation and making their own fun. Joss touched the thin
hand lightly with her lips and smiled at her grandmother.

'It's nearly time for your medicine,' she said, 'but I
wondered if you'd like some massage first?'

'Mmm.' Mutt acquiesced readily, accepting what she recognized was an offering of love as well as relief and comfort. It
was she who had enabled Joss to heal – taking her side against
her father's prejudice and helping out financially – and now
she reaped the benefits. 'Did I hear the telephone?'

'You did.' Joss edged her carefully into position so as to be
able to treat the lower back and spine. 'Mum's coming down
tomorrow.' She took a small bottle from the bedside table,
tipped a little oil into the palms of her hands, let it warm for a
moment and then began to knead the muscles and soft tissues
with dextrous, confident gentleness. 'She'll stay down at The
Lookout with Bruno but she'll be up to see you as soon as she
can.'

Mutt showed no change of expression at this proposed
treat; her concentration was fixed elsewhere.

'Did someone call here earlier?'

Joss hesitated, wondering if her grandmother knew about the American and his photograph, realizing that she must have heard the ringing of the doorbell. It was not in her nature to dissemble, however, and she could see no harm in a truthful answer.

'There was an American here who's trying to trace his great-aunt. He has some idea that you might have known her during the war.'

She was turning her again, so as to deal with the lower leg, and saw a spasm of pain pass across the old woman's face. Joss paused, watching her anxiously.

'Did that hurt?'

Mutt shook her head, frowned and began to cough con-vulsively. Joss lifted her, cradling her thin frame in one arm whilst pouring medicine into a plastic measure with the other hand. Presently, the attack over, Joss laid her back carefully, supporting the injured leg on a pillow.

'I must wash my hands,' she told her. 'Shan't be long.'

Left alone, Mutt rolled her head on the pillow, staring across at the table where Mousie had been sitting just a few days ago; opening the morning post and reading, at Mutt's request, the messages and letters that she was too weak to deal with herself.

'Great grief!' she'd said, amused. 'There's a letter here from a young fellow who wants to know if you've ever met his great-aunt. He's enclosed a photograph.' There'd been a moment's silence and when she'd next spoken, her voice had been different, tender and hedged about with emotion. 'How extraordinary,' she'd said. 'Remember this, Honor?' and she'd got up and come over to the bed, holding out the paper.

The shock had been very great: to see her own youthful, merry face laughing out of that little group of friends, re-calling with a sharp twist of painful joy that happy day and the grief and fear that followed after – these sensations had deprived her momentarily of any rational thought. It was some moments before she'd remembered the letter Mousie had read aloud to her.

'I can't see him,' she'd cried apprehensively, cutting across something that Mousie was saying. 'I simply can't. It's all too painful, too long ago,' and Mousie had calmed her, agreeing that she wasn't fit enough yet for visitors, and had given her some medicine to soothe the wretched cough that racked her. Alone afterwards, she'd eased herself out of bed, making her trembling, uncertain way to the table, but neither the letter nor the photograph were to be seen and she'd had barely enough strength to climb back into bed.

Now, waiting for Joss to return, she thought of something else – a foolish, secret thing, long forgotten – and fear crept and tingled in her veins. Her muscles flexed involuntarily, as though she might rise from the bed, but the medicine was beginning to have an effect and, instead, she grew drowsy. She imagined she was in India again, visions and noises jostling her confused memory: the sounds of rumbling wheels and the carters' cries, shuffling footsteps and shrill voices; the pungent, acrid smells; brown bodies and bright bougainvillaea; soft, warm dust and the relentless heat.

The telephone bell shrilled suddenly, muffled but insistent in the hall below, and was silenced abruptly as Mousie lifted the receiver. Mutt mumbled and cried out in her sleep and Joss, sitting beside her, raised her eyes from time to time from her book and watched her.

'I've just been thinking whether I ought to stay up at the house,' Emma's quick, light voice was saying into Mousie's ear, 'instead of with Bruno. If Mutt really is, well, *really* poorly with this chill, Mousie, perhaps I should be a bit more available. It's just that I don't want to butt in on Joss. I feel it's *her* territory at the moment, not just because she's living there while she's renovating her little cottage, but also because she's actually been in charge since her grandmother broke her ankle. She and Mutt have always got on so well, haven't they?'

Mousie smiled to herself, picturing Emma hunched over the telephone, gesturing with her free hand: warm, scatty, lovable.

'You'll be fine with Bruno,' she assured her. 'Great grief! It's only ten minutes away and Honor isn't in a dangerous condition . . .' She remembered the doctor's words and bit her lip. 'Although, given her age, we should be prepared—'

'That's what Raymond's been saying,' Emma cut in, anxiously. 'That I should be with her. You know he doesn't have much confidence in Joss. He can't be doing with all that alternative medicine stuff and he feels that we're relying too much on you.'

Mousie's lip curled. She could well imagine that Raymond Fox would prefer it if his wife were to be very much on the spot at this critical time.

'Tell him not to get too stressed about Honor,' she answered drily. 'He can certainly rely on me to know my place on these occasions.'

'Honestly, Mousie,' Emma was almost breathless with a mixture of embarrassment and amusement, 'he doesn't mean to, dear old Ray, but he goes on a bit, sometimes. It'll be heaven to see you all. My dear brother is only *quite* pleased at the prospect of my arrival; he's wrestling with a tricky bit of the book, apparently, and I can tell by his voice that he's totally wrapped up in it. Never mind. It'll do him good to have a bit of distraction.'

'If you say so.' Mouse felt a fleeting sympathy for Bruno. 'I think you're very wise to leave Joss in charge here. You can assure Raymond that she's more than capable and Honor feels very comfortable and safe with her. This is very important just now.'

'Bless you, Mousie. I'll tell him. The trouble is that he can't take on board that she's grown up, and it's not as if she's a qualified nursing sister like you are, although I keep telling him that she's done brilliantly. But she was always such a caring, sensible child, wasn't she? Not like me at all. Of course, Father was a doctor and Mutt trained as a nurse so I expect she gets it from them. . .'

'Joss is fine,' said Mousie firmly, 'and Raymond should be proud of her. She's been to Truro Hospital to check Honor's X-ray results with the physio and she knows exactly what she's doing. I promise you, she's extremely professional.'

'You are such a comfort,' said Emma fervently. 'I'm hoping to be down in time for lunch. Give everyone my love.'

Mousie replaced the receiver with the familiar sensation that she'd been for a brisk run, and returned to the drawing-room. Two small, comfortable sofas were set at right angles to the fireplace and a third, longer, sofa made the fourth side of the square. Mutt's love for quiet, formal elegance informed each room in the house and nowhere more than here and in the small parlour where she sat to read or work. She was well known locally for her beautiful needlework and had received many important commissions; lately, however, her failing eyesight had made her reluctant to take on too much, although the tapestry in the small rectangular frame, which she stitched away at each evening by the fire, still lay half-completed on the rosewood table that stood behind the long sofa and on which she kept magazines and a few books.

Mousie sat down in the corner nearest the fire and leaned to open her big carpet-work bag. Carefully she drew out the photograph with its accompanying letter and looked at the four laughing faces: Hubert and his wife and another couple.

The American had written:

It was a double wedding because the four of them were such close friends. My grandmother remembered that both girls were nurses but thinks my great-uncle ran some kind of company in India. It's all a bit vague but my great-aunt's maiden name was Madeleine Grosjean. I know that the two sisters were very close, but shortly after my grandmother moved to the States there was a complete silence from the Indian end. From enquiries made at that time it seemed that Madeleine and her family had just disappeared. We suspect that they died during the unrest in 1947.

Perhaps, by that time, you and Dr Trevannion had already returned to the UK. It would be terrific to find out the truth and I hope you might spare me a moment if I were to visit next weekend, say on Saturday round three o'clock?

She folded the letter and stared ahead, remembering Honor's arrival at St Meriadoc. By 1947, Hubert's mother was dead, his father rather frail, but they'd all done their best to make the travellers feel at home: the small Bruno, so like his father, dazed by the events of the last two months, and sweet Emma, too young to understand what had happened but good-naturedly ready to embrace her new family. From the first moment Mousie had adored the children – but as for Honor . . . Mousie sighed regretfully. There had always been some kind of barrier between them, a reservation that Mousie had found impossible to breach. She'd feared it might be the result of her own love for Hubert, and had worked hard to overcome it, but she had never succeeded. She hadn't even been able to use the silly nickname that the children used: to Mousie she was always 'Honor'.

She heard footsteps on the stairs and bundled the letter and photograph back into the capacious bag so that by the time Joss opened the door Mousie was sitting with the newspaper open, apparently absorbed, relaxed and comfortable beside the fire.

CHAPTER THREE

Travelling the familiar road past Launceston, turning off at Kennards House, waiting for a sight of the distant, shining sea, Emma – bored with the radio and her tapes – talked aloud for company, encouraging herself: nearly there now, nearly home. Despite the very early start she felt alert, full of energy and looking forward to seeing her family – especially Joss and Bruno.

'And dear old Mutt,' she said aloud. She was anxious and miserable about her mother's condition but her anxiety sprang from the fact that she felt so useless with ill people: not like Mousie, who had the knack of being caring and practical without getting worked up.

'She looks terrible,' Emma had cried privately to Mousie, the last time she'd seen Mutt. 'She looks so frail and old.'

'She *is* frail and old,' Mousie had answered with her typically sharply humorous look that always comforted Emma. 'She's nearly eighty and she's had a bad fall. What did you expect?'

'She's always been so . . .' Emma searched for the right word, '. . . so independent.'

'True,' agreed Mousie wryly, 'but independence is tricky when you can't walk and you're in a very confused state.'

The thing was, thought Emma, as she drove through Delabole, that it had been much more than a shock to see the cheerful, capable Mutt confined to her bed and under sedation. It was as if a secure, reliable point of reference had been destroyed overnight and she'd found herself adrift, untethered. There was no question that Mutt loved her children but there was on occasions a strictness to her love and the odd thing was that she, Emma, always needed Mutt's approval. However old she grew, she felt a glow of pleasure when Mutt smiled that loving, warm smile of approbation upon her daughter.

'Crazy, isn't it?' Emma would cry over the years, down at The Lookout with Bruno, as she helped him to prepare a meal in his kitchen, getting in his way. 'I'm twenty . . . thirty-three . . . forty-two . . . and I still need to feel that she approves of what I do.'

At intervals in her busy social life – the daily round in Henley and entertaining Ray's business clients at lavish dinner parties in the London flat – it was always a bit of a relief to be with Bruno, to kick off her shoes – metaphorically speaking – and indulge in an orgy of unburdening: oh, what stories that strange stone house could tell.

She passed through St Endellion and Porteath, turned right into the lane that led down to St Meriadoc and pulled abruptly into a gateway. Opening the car door she stepped out into the pale sunlight, delighting in the familiar scene. Startled sheep with lambs at foot stampeded away over the field, their cries echoing in the cold, clear air as she gazed across rough, open land to the cliffs that ran north to Kellan Head and west to Rumps Point. By climbing a few rungs of the gate, so that she could stare down into the steep valley, she could make out the slate roof of the house surrounded by tall shrubs and trees; to its west lay the tiny, scooped-out bay with the disused boatyard and a row of cottages which, together with The Lookout perched on the cliff above it, made up the estate known as St Meriadoc. She realized that she was listening for the sound of the lark's song, although she knew it was far too early in the year. Mutt referred to this quiet, secret valley as 'the golden cup'; a phrase taken from George Meredith's poem about a lark, which she'd read to them as children. Emma could still remember a few lines of it:

> And ever winging up and up
> Our valley is his golden cup
> And he the wine which overflows . . .

She'd always loved to look down on it like this, coming home from school or, later, from London; this scene was one she carried in her memory.

'Why on earth do you want to stop?' Raymond Fox would ask impatiently, on visits during those early years of marriage. 'We'll be there in a minute.'

And there was no answer, she told herself. At least, no answer that she could give to *him*. Bruno understood that moment of glorious anticipation when, for a brief moment longer, you'd postpone the excitement of being a part of that scene below: looking down on all the promise to come.

'Never mind,' she'd mutter, acceding as usual to his will – Raymond was so mature, so sensible – and he'd reach to pat her hand or knee, unaware of her instinctive shrinking, her momentary absolute rejection both of his physical presence and of his values.

'Silly girl,' he'd say with patronizing affection whilst she'd press her own hands between her knees and pretend to be absorbed by something beyond the car window. Moments later, however, some deep-down early conditioning would be rousing her guilt and she'd be reminding herself of his sound qualities – a rather clumsy kindness allied to a natural tendency to protect, his ability to provide the necessary comforts whilst carefully husbanding his resources – qualities, Mutt pointed out, that were just as important as mutual passion. Twelve years her senior, good-looking and already successful, he'd seemed so glamorous to her inexperienced twenty-year-old eyes and his determined pursuit had been very flattering. Remembering, Emma made a little face; the point was that, once Bruno had announced his engagement to the waif-like gamine Zoë, a Juliette Gréco look-alike and photographer's model, Emma had felt rather left out of things. Zoë had a way of making her future sister-in-law feel gauche – clumsy and raw – and Raymond had been conveniently at hand to soothe this sense of inadequacy.

'You can't marry him,' Bruno had said flatly, after the first meeting with Raymond – and they'd stared at each other resentfully.

'Mutt really likes him,' she'd said stubbornly. 'She thinks he's reliable and steady.'

'*Reliable*?' Bruno had stared at her in disbelief, shaking his head. 'For God's sake, Em! Do me a favour.'

Now, still thinking about the ensuing quarrel, Emma climbed back into the car and drove down the steep, winding lane, slowing down when she reached the boatyard beside the row of cottages and, finally, pulling into the disused quarry opposite.

The cheerful tattoo, thumped out on the car's horn, roused Rafe Boscowan from his work and drew him to the window of his study.

'It's Emma,' he shouted to his wife. 'I'll go.'

Pamela continued to sit at the kitchen table, carefully peeling vegetables, a look of expectant pleasure lighting her face. She heard Rafe reach the bottom of the stairs, open the door and shout a welcome, and then turned in her chair as they came in together. She could smell Emma's flowery scent, felt her face taken between gentle hands and her cheek kissed: a little pause – and she instinctively knew that Emma was studying her closely.

'You look so good, darling. Such a pretty jersey – and a new haircut? I love the blonde streaks.'

Pamela's hands went straight to her head: how like Emma to notice the change.

'D'you approve? Rafe says it's good but I'm not sure I can trust him to tell me the truth. Olivia said I was looking dowdy so I decided to brighten myself up a little.'

Rafe and Emma exchanged a glance: the eldest of the Boscowan children was not noted for her tact. Pamela smiled into the tiny silence.

'No Slips,' she said with the devastating acuity that had developed with her blindness. 'I know that Liv can be out-spoken but she's quite right: I mustn't let myself go.'

Emma touched Pamela's shoulder; in the Boscowan family, the word 'slip' in that context stood for 'Sly Looks in Private' – meaning an exchange that Pamela could no longer see – and they all tried to keep to the rules that her blindness should in no way be exploited. Nevertheless, Emma couldn't quite restrain the irritation that Olivia's tactlessness so often called up.

'I promise you,' she said, 'that it looks really good. You know I'd tell you. I'd rush you over to Wadebridge and stand over the girl until she got it right. As it happens, there's no need.'

Rafe lifted the board of peeled vegetables away so that he could slice them and took some glasses from the dresser.

'You'll have a drink?' he asked. 'I told Bruno to come down and join us but he probably won't notice the time. He had that look of being in some other world. Mousie will be in soon. How's Raymond?'

He poured some wine, took a glass to the table and lightly placed Pamela's fingers around the stem. Emma wandered about happily: pinching a piece of raw carrot which she crunched, inspecting the latest photograph of Olivia's new baby, peering from the window, talking all the while. The row of cottages was only a few feet from the sea wall and the kitchen was filled with grey, watery reflections, giving a sense of light and space to the long low room with its heavily beamed ceilings and thick, stone walls. Emma sighed with contentment; just so had it looked when Aunt Julia had welcomed the small Emma with home-made fudge or Cornish splits, although now the old range was gone and the kitchen had been modernized so that Pamela could make her way about with confidence and freedom.

Watching her now as she moved carefully, opening drawers, laying the table, Emma was reminded suddenly of a younger Pamela, who'd flitted about carelessly, bending to deal with the small Olivia who tumbled at her feet, proudly pregnant with Joe. They'd joked, Pamela and Rafe, when Emma had visited them: speaking in broad Cornish, pretending to tug at forelocks. ''Tez the young lady come down from Paradise,' Pamela would call to Rafe. 'Where be yer manners, bey? Get the maid a chair.'

She'd never minded, in fact it made her feel rather special, although she secretly envied their easy companionship and readily demonstrated affection. It was evident that Pamela's blindness had brought her and Rafe even closer, deepening and strengthening their relationship, yet Emma was filled with sudden sadness for all that Pamela had lost.

Rafe's sister, Mousie, came in. She held out her arms, in welcome, and Emma went gratefully towards her, concealing the unexpectedly poignant sense of loss in the warmth of Mousie's embrace.

CHAPTER FOUR

Bruno emerged from his small, book-crowded study, glanced at his watch and grimaced guiltily: twenty past two – and lunch would be over down at The Row. Taking comfort in the fact that his family would understand, and suddenly aware that he was very hungry, he went to see what there might be in the fridge to sustain him. Nellie – the happy result of an unscheduled mating between a pretty Border collie bitch and a handsome golden retriever – who lay stretched on the cold slates of the kitchen floor, roused herself and looked hopeful.

'Lunch is a bit late today, old dear,' murmured Bruno, putting a large, half-full tin of dog food, some eggs and a piece of cheese on the draining-board. 'Sorry about that.'

Yet he felt elated by his morning's work, conscious of a sense of wellbeing that was the result of translating his ideas successfully onto paper – through the medium of his computer. Half a chapter had been written and, for once, he was content with the end product of those periods of mental anguish and long minutes spent pacing the cramped spaces of his cluttered study floor.

'Why?' visitors would ask, wide-eyed. 'Why do you work here when you could have that fantastic view?'

They'd stare disbelievingly at the stone walls, hung with huge squares of cork boards to which were pinned photographs, drawings, glossy-paged pieces ripped from magazines, yellowing newspaper articles curling at the edges; all relevant to the work in progress. A creeping tide of books oozed at the edge of the faded carpet whilst the trestle table, at right angles to his desk, was covered with scribbled-over shreds of paper and notebooks.

'Nothing more distracting than a view when you're trying to work,' he'd answer, encouraging them back to that amazing, central room with its curved window, so that they could stand in its great, swelling bay, looking down into the ice-green sea.

Built as a folly by a Victorian ancestor, Bruno found The Lookout to be the perfect place to write his books: a series inspired by his own family, historical faction beginning with a Trevannion who'd fought for the King during the Civil War. Since these books took two or three years to research he also wrote, under a different name, what he called his wolf-scarers: stories about the modern Royal Navy, the first of which had brought unexpected success when he'd written it just after he'd left the Navy in his mid-twenties. Today he was completely preoccupied with an engineering Trevannion who'd worked with the great Sir Joseph Bazalgette on the main drainage system for London.

It was fortunate, thought Bruno as he fed Nellie and grated some cheese, that the Trevannions of the eighteenth and nineteenth centuries had been so prolific: plenty more characters to keep him busy for a few years yet. Lucky, too, that his present family was so tolerant regarding his time-keeping. He was halfway through his omelette when Emma came in.

'You are useless,' she said, regarding him affectionately.

'Utterly useless. Where were you today? Mousie said that you were probably halfway down a sewer in Victorian London.'

'And she was absolutely right.' He stood up, reaching across the table to embrace her. 'Sorry about that.'

She bent to fondle Nellie's soft, floppy ears, happy to be in this place where she was most able to be herself. Bruno looked just as he always did: relaxed and comfortable in dark brown cords, a fisherman's navy-blue jersey and fraying sand-shoes. As a concession to the February chill he wore woollen socks and a red silk scarf wound around his neck. Emma had given him the scarf for Christmas but she suspected that he was wearing it today simply because it had been the first thing to hand at the precise moment he'd noticed he was cold.

'Love the scarf,' she observed brightly, testing him.

He inclined his head a little, accepting the compliment. 'So do I,' he answered blandly. 'Do you want some coffee or are you going up to see Mutt first?'

'I'm going straight up.' Her expression grew more serious. 'How is she? Mousie is doing that sort of guarded thing. You know what I mean? "We have to remember that she's nearly eighty but I'm sure she's going to be fine" stuff.'

Bruno forked up the last piece of his omelette and gave his plate to Nellie to lick. 'I saw her yesterday just after lunch,' he said. 'I usually go up about tea-time, just after I've finished work, but to be honest I don't feel qualified to make a judgement. Sometimes she's lucid, if frail, and at other times she's wandering. I think a lot of it depends on when she's had her medicine. Joss is wonderful with her.'

Emma's face brightened. 'I can't tell you how thrilled I am that it's working out. It's so good for her to be able to help with Mutt. Raymond's still utterly dampening about her work and they seem to have a row every time she comes home.'

'Not much change there, then,' observed Bruno. 'And how *is* Brer Fox?'

Emma shrugged, clearly torn between the luxury of telling

the truth and the tug of silent loyalty, and Bruno, knowing from past experience that loyalty would be temporarily abandoned, decided that now was not the moment for a heart-to-heart.

Such an unsympathetic hour, he thought: three o'clock in the afternoon, that dull, flat, desert stretching between those cheerful indiscretions induced by a long lunch and the after-supper intimacy with the wine still to hand, curtains drawn and a fire burning on the flat, stone hearth.

'Go up and see Mutt,' he said, not waiting for an answer. 'Stay and have tea with Joss and I'll see you later.'

She hesitated, anxious at what she might find up at the house, suddenly unwilling to leave the familiar comfort of The Lookout. He watched her thoughtfully, knowing how difficult she was finding Mutt's deterioration since her fall.

'Tell you what,' he offered casually, 'I need a walk – so does Nellie, come to that – we'll come with you over the cliff path. Or were you going to drive up?'

'No, no.' She shook her head quickly. 'That would be good. As long as I'm not taking you away from your sewers?'

'Bazalgette designed other things too,' he told her. 'Putney Bridge for one. But don't worry, you're not distracting me. I need to think out a few things and the walk will help.'

He shrugged himself into a jacket, changed his sandshoes for short sea-boots and, with Nellie rushing eagerly ahead, they all went out together.

Joss closed her book, paused to check that Mutt was sleeping soundly and slid quietly out of the room. She'd heard voices, kept low but still audible, the scrunch of boots on the gravel drive beneath the window, and had no wish for anyone to disturb her grandmother now that she was able to rest peacefully. As she reached the turn in the stairs she saw that her mother had come in and was taking off her coat in the hall below. The expression on Emma's down-turned face, the little frowning look of mingled worry and fear, checked Joss's step and she paused in the shadowy corner, fixed by a familiar mix of emotions: tremendous affection for her mother intertwined with occasional bursts of irritation at Emma's refusal to stand up for her own principles against her husband. Joss could not remember at what point in her life she'd become aware of her father's acquisitive, insensitive brand of morality but she'd soon learned that no-one outside his immediate family was allowed to benefit from, share in, or receive any portion of his – not inconsiderable – wealth. His patronizing smile bore down any attempt at protest; the large, spade-shaped hand, uplifted in schoolmasterish rejection, was ready to slap down a different point of view. Even when it came to Christmas or birthday presents, his jovial, 'And what did *that* cost, I wonder?' or, 'And does Mummy *really* want another scarf?' managed to spoil all the pleasure she'd had in saving for and choosing the gift.

Once, when she'd given her pocket money to a beggar, he'd read her a long lecture on the unwisdom of encouraging the idle and, a few days later, showed her a newspaper article that reported the story of just such a beggar who was able to run a BMW on his takings. He'd humiliated her in front of her school-friends by criticizing their parents' extravagant foreign holidays and, later, frightened away boyfriends by asking for financial credentials on their third or fourth visit to the house. It was such a relief, once he'd left for the London flat each Monday morning, to revel in four days free from his bantering criticism.

She suspected that it was these few days of freedom that enabled her mother to cope with those small humiliations in front of her close friends and his regular lectures on thrift. She had a wide circle of acquaintances, her bridge club and – despite his joking strictures on how it was spent – a generous allowance. For years after Joss had moved on to her next school, Emma had continued to spend two mornings each week at the primary school, helping those children with reading difficulties, and she was a member of the WVS. Emma had a naturally cheerful disposition but Joss sometimes found it hard to believe that she could be truly happy with her father.

'How can you bear it?' she'd cried to her mother, after he'd discovered that Emma had lent a very close – but unreliable – friend some money and Joss had witnessed the scene that followed. 'How can you stand his meanness?'

'He's been a good father to you, darling,' she'd answered with her usual loyalty. 'I know that he can be insensitive, which at your age can be particularly difficult to deal with, but you mustn't be too hard on him. He's made sure that we both have absolute security . . .'

'But everything he gives has a price tag. With him, nothing's unconditional, is it? He has to have a return.'

'Security is very important to him; you'll understand that better when you have children of your own. After all, Joss, everything he has will be yours one day. It's all for you in the end.'

'I don't want it,' she'd answered childishly. 'I'll earn my own money.'

How hard she'd worked to earn money during her training – refusing to take a penny from her father, who jeered at any kind of alternative medicine – taking on jobs in bars and cafés to pay for any extras. It was Mutt who'd believed in her: Mutt who had been such a support through those painful teenage years, opening Paradise to Joss and her young friends and making a haven from the humiliating criticisms and heavy humour that her father inflicted on them. Without appearing to take sides Mutt nourished and encouraged her grand-daughter and gave as much financial help as she could with an income deriving from her widow's pension, some shares and the rents from the cottages in The Row. Emma, caught between them all, worried for her daughter's physical ability to cope with her extra jobs as well as her degree, had begged Joss to be sensible.

'You'll kill yourself before you start,' she'd said. 'You look exhausted, darling. Why can't you just ignore him? Under-neath all that nonsense he's anxious for you. It's simply that he's incapable of seeing anything except from his own point of view. Look, let me help you . . .'

'I can't, Mum,' she'd said, hating herself for causing the misery on her mother's face. 'You must see that I can't. I shall manage. Other people have to. After all, that's what he's always saying, isn't it? That people should fend for themselves, get on their bikes, all that stuff.'

Bruno's generosity had been life-saving on occasions.

'I suppose Mum's been getting at you,' she'd say un-graciously once or twice – but his wry look always managed to call her own smile into being. 'Sorry,' she'd mutter. 'It's just I can't take anything from either of them when I know how much he despises what I'm doing.'

'Just take it, girl, and don't be so prickly,' he'd advise, pushing a cheque or some notes into her pocket or her bag. 'I promise you I hold no brief for Brer Fox's views, and my money's my own to do what I like with.'

'Why?' she'd asked him once – just as she'd asked her mother. 'Why did she marry him, Bruno? He's just . . . so *not* Mum. She's so warm and kind and loving, and he calculates everything. What did she see in him?'

He'd been silent for a while. 'You have to remember,' he'd answered at last, 'that, for women, marriage was much more important thirty years ago than it is now. It would be almost impossible for you to imagine the pressures put on girls to get married. Your father was a very good-looking, successful fellow and he was quite a bit older than Emma, which added to his glamour. And Mutt approved of him. She saw – with justice – that he'd look after her daughter and so she encouraged him. Emma had no experience to fall back on

41

and was rather flattered by his absolute determination to have her. You could say that he rather swept her off her feet but the fact is, Joss, that nobody can judge a marriage. However close you are to it, you'll never understand what makes it work or see the million tiny invisible strands that hold a couple together. Emma is very loving and very loyal – to both of you – and it's not for either of us to judge her. Just don't make it more difficult for her than you must.'

Now, standing in the shadowy turn of the stairs, Joss remembered Bruno's words and her heart speeded with remorse and love.

'Hello, Mum,' she said, hurrying down. 'Did you have a good trip?'

Emma hugged her child warmly. 'No problems at all,' she said. 'How's Mutt?'

'Sleeping. I was just going to have a cup of tea and then we'll take some up for her. How long can you stay?'

'Oh, for a few days at least. Ray's up in London at the flat, meetings and so on. You're looking very well, Joss. I thought you'd be feeling the strain. Mousie told me that you're being such a help to her. So, anything new?'

Joss's heart sank. This hopeful question, from Emma, generally referred to her love life and, as she followed her mother into the kitchen, she thought instinctively of the young American as a distraction.

'Actually,' she said slowly, 'rather an odd thing happened yesterday. Someone came looking for a relative. He was hoping that Mutt knew her out in India . . .'

Upstairs Mutt groaned, half waking, muttering long-forgotten names and turning restlessly on her pillows before subsiding again into a troubled sleep.

CHAPTER FIVE

'Who is Lottie?'

Emma stood with her back to the fire, leafing through the new paperback edition of Bruno's most recent novel. Receiving no answer to her question, she glanced towards the archway that led to the kitchen and raised her voice a little.

'Bruno? Did you hear me? Do we know anyone called Lottie?'

There was the noise of the oven door being shut, water gushed briefly, and when he finally appeared Bruno was drying his hands on a rather ragged towel.

'Sorry. Who did you say? Lottie?' He shook his head. 'Why do you ask?'

'Something Mutt was saying earlier.' She held the book up. 'Nice cover. Looks good, doesn't it? Very modern and exciting and lots of good reviews on the back.'

He took it from her. 'I'm very pleased with it,' he admitted. 'Apparently the backlist is going to be packaged in the same format.' A pause whilst he turned the book over in his hands, studying it. 'So what was Mutt saying?'

'Oh, she was rambling rather.' Emma kicked at a smoulder-
ing log and bent to take another from the big basket beside
the hearth. 'Joss mentioned it too. The medicine confuses her
a bit and I wondered if it might have anything to do with this
American who was here yesterday.'

Bruno put the book down carefully on the long table that
stood at the back of the room, facing the bay window.

'I haven't heard about an American,' he said. Rather mechanically he began to tidy the table, clearing a space ready for
supper. 'So what did he want?'

'He wrote, so Joss said, saying that he's looking for a
relative who might have been out in India at the same time as
Daddy and Mutt. He sent a photograph of this aunt, or
whatever, with the letter to see if Mutt recognized her and
then he turned up yesterday afternoon hoping to have a chat
with her.' Satisfied with the blaze, Emma perched on the arm
of the sofa and began to stroke Nellie, who was stretched out
on her back in a languorously abandoned position on the
old blanket thrown over one of the faded cushions. 'Joss
wondered whether it might have stirred up some memories
for her.'

Nellie groaned pleasurably and Emma chuckled, leaning
further over so as to reach the soft hair on her chest. 'You are
such a tart,' she said to Nellie. 'Look at you. You haven't a
single shred of modesty, have you? *Good* girl, then.'

'And did she?' asked Bruno, after a moment.

'Did she what?'

'Did Mutt recognize this . . . relative from the photograph?'

Emma shrugged. 'From what I can gather, Mousie's playing
it a bit low-key. She wouldn't let the young man actually see
Mutt but, from what Joss said, I think she'd told her about it
or read the letter to her. Joss said she called out the name
several times in her sleep. Lottie.' She frowned. 'It sounds odd
but it kind of rang a bell.'

She looked at him hopefully, brow furrowed in an attempt to cudgel her memory, but he shook his head.

'Not with me,' he said firmly. 'And if you want a bath before supper you'd better get a move on.'

When she'd gone, collecting up various belongings, pouring a glass of wine to take upstairs with her, Bruno sat beside Nellie on the sofa. He stretched a hand to the silky black-and-white coat – but it was an automatic gesture and his thoughts were elsewhere.

Emma is not yet four years old when she first asks that question. Halfway up the cliff, out of breath from the steep climb, they sit together on spongy, springy turf, staring over the silky surface of the bosomy sea that gently lifts and swells below them. Rounded rosy-pink cushions of thrift, honey-scented in the hot sunshine, cling to the rocky ledges where seagulls sit in rows. A fishing boat chugs north, heading towards Port Isaac, and Bruno gulps down deep breaths of delicious salty air, feeling the cool breeze tugging his hair. He looks sideways at Emma: her hair is fine and fair as candy floss and the sun shines through it so that she appears to have a halo. Her pudgy fingers pluck at the grass and her gaze is fixed, thoughtful, so that he knows that she is working something out, remembering.

'Who is Lottie?' she asks him. 'Lottie.' She speaks it carefully in two distinct singsong syllables – 'Lot-tie' – as if she is tasting the name.

Abruptly, Bruno allows himself to fall backwards on the turf. He closes his eyes, not only against the sun but also to keep the question outside. There were so many questions when they first arrived in St Meriadoc nearly two years ago.

'Goodness!' Aunt Julia cried, half amused, half shocked. 'Why do you call your mother "Mutt"? Does she allow it?'

He felt panic rising inside him as memories of that last dreadful week in India edged back into his consciousness.

And dear Mousie smiled at him – oh, how he loves Mousie! – and said, 'You're just like your father. He always gave people nicknames, do you remember, Mother? It was Hubert who called me Mousie.'

To Bruno's relief Aunt Julia nodded, although she wasn't quite happy about it. 'But "Mutt",' she murmured, 'it sounds so disrespectful,' and it was Mutt, herself, who said, 'Oh, I'm used to it now. It was his way of saying "Mother" when he was very small. Please don't worry him about it. He's been through quite enough, poor little fellow . . .'

As he lies in the sunshine, the sun hot on his face, Emma prises with her small fingers at his tightly closed eyelids. He rolls away from her, over and over, and she scrambles after him, shrieking with laughter, her question forgotten.

The smell of stewed fruit, spilling over the side of the saucepan onto the hotplate, brought Bruno back abruptly to the present. He cursed beneath his breath and hurried out to the kitchen. Nellie stirred, raised her head to sniff hopefully, and settled back with a disappointed sigh. No delicious smells tempted her from her comfortable seat: no noise of a tin-opener, which might indicate that her own supper was being prepared. Bruno, having gone straight from boarding-school into the Royal Navy, had never bothered to develop his cooking skills beyond pasta, stews and a delicious goose cassoulet; his friends and family knew exactly what to expect and, if they required variety, then they supplied the ingredients themselves. It was Emma who had come back from the house with the apples – picked in the orchard and stored away last autumn by Honor and Mousie – and had peeled them, chatting all the while.

Now Bruno snatched up the saucepan and dropped it hastily on the draining-board, opened the oven door to check the stew and turned the potatoes, which were baking in their jackets on the shelf beside it. All was well. Closing the door on his creation, he began to assemble knives and forks but he was clearly preoccupied: part irritated, part anxious. It was difficult, almost impossible, at this critical moment to detach himself from the world he was creating, to re-engage with reality, and part of him resented Emma's arrival and the need to entertain her. He longed to be alone: to be going back into his study to pore over old documents and books; to be weaving together those plain strands of fact between other brighter, fictional threads that would bring life and colour and shape to the fixed, historical part of the pattern. His own vividly imagined story must coexist alongside the true records of the time and it required concentration to listen to its rhythm as it developed: he needed to stride over the cliffs and along the secret, wintry lanes and hear it coming to life inside his head.

Yet it had seemed churlish to refuse Emma's request when Mutt was ill and Mousie already stretched in caring for her. Bruno paused, his hands full of clashing spoons and forks, his thin, clever face thoughtful, anxiety gnawing in his gut. Just how ill, he wondered, was Mutt? Unease edged his mind further from its own interior world; thrusting it towards sealed-off places and reminding it of voices long since silenced.

The gurgling and splashing of the bath water pouring away, the pattering of footsteps in the small bedroom above the kitchen, forced him to concentrate on the present. By the time Emma appeared, the table was set, candles were lit and Bruno was opening a can of dog food with Nellie in close attendance. Emma sighed contentedly and topped up her glass from the bottle on the long sideboard, looking affectionately at the familiar scene. A modern oil painting of the harbour at Port Isaac – with a bright Reckitts-blue sea and crimson-splashed fishing boats – hung on the whitewashed stone wall alongside a charcoal drawing of The Lookout, sketched strong and bold with its outflung window, clinging to the precipitous cliff. Another water-colour showed a row of terraced houses, squeezed together, toppling down a steep, cobbled alleyway to the sea. At first glance it was a charming scene, invoking times past; yet a second look showed something disturbing beneath the picture-postcard image. Beneath the high gables, pointy as witches' hats, small windows glinted – sly eyes, half-closed, winking at a shared secret – and narrow doors gaped like shocked mouths. It had a cartoonish, fairy-tale look and, like all good fairy tales, there was a sense of menace implicit in the pretty simplicity. Staring at it, Emma could believe that the big, bad wolf – or a wicked stepmother – lurked just out of sight, waiting.

She shivered a little, turning away to the huge, framed, black-and-white photograph, which hung over the sideboard, opposite the big granite hearth. It showed a Paris boulevard, passers-by stepping round the pavement café, a Citroën parked at the kerb: the girl's head was turned a little aside, chin up, but the long, narrow eyes looked straight at the camera; indifferent yet provocative. Her elbow rested on the small wrought-iron table, a cigarette between the fingers of the drooping hand whilst her companion, just out of focus, was bending towards her, holding a coffee cup.

Bruno came in carrying the casserole dish, saw the direction of Emma's gaze and hoped that they were not about to embark on a discussion of his ex-wife.

'Dinner is served,' he said cheerfully with a mock bow. 'Hang on, I've forgotten the potatoes. So how do you think Mousie is looking? Pamela and Rafe are on good form, aren't they?'

He lifted the lid and plunged a spoon into the lamb stew, used a threadbare linen napkin to put a hot potato on her plate. The warm room seemed to close in a little, leaning as if to listen, and Emma settled more comfortably in her chair, ready now for confidences and gossip.

CHAPTER SIX

Mousie woke early in her cottage at the end of The Row. The room brimmed with quivering sea-light and she lay quite still, savouring the cosy comfort of warm blankets, watching the milk-blue sky beyond the window. Except on those wild nights, when a north-westerly gale whipped the sea halfway up the cliffs and drove rain against the cold glass panes, she hated to sleep with the curtains closed. She might waken suddenly to the bright, white radiance of a full moon, boxing her bed with square black bars, or she could watch the softly twinkling points of starlight pricking out one by one on a midsummer's night.

This morning, by hauling herself up and propping a pillow more firmly behind her back, she could see past Com Head to The Mouls, whose rocky bulk seemed to float on the surface of the flat, silvery water. Still half asleep, she let her thoughts drift between the duties and pleasures of the day ahead: Joss would be off to Wadebridge, busy with her patients all day, so straight up to the house after breakfast; seize the opportunity of some time alone with Emma; write and post the birthday card for Tom, Olivia's eldest; a quick dash into Polzeath for some groceries; remember to book the MOT for her ageing little Fiat; check the donkeys. What a relief that Emma would be able to stay with Honor whilst she caught up with a few tasks. Poor Emma, so worried about her dear old Mutt . . .

It was odd, thought Mousie as she pulled the bedclothes more closely around her shoulders, that the arrival of the young American had filled her with such a strong sense of apprehension. After all, there was no reason why he shouldn't pursue his quest as far as he could, and the photograph was certainly an important lead. It was such a shock to see it again, after so many years, and it was obvious that Honor had been affected by it too. Remembering her cry: 'I can't see him. It's all too painful. Too long ago . . .' Mousie was pierced by remorse.

Why had she never quite been able to drift into the habit of calling Honor by the foolish little nickname? Though she'd been the first to agree that it was typical of Hubert to invent it, that there was no harm in the children using it, yet there was something that blocked such familiarity between herself and Honor. The shock of the news of Hubert's death, the sight of the numbed, bewildered little family, had gone a long way in subduing her jealousy of this beautiful, casually elegant woman; nevertheless she could remember how she'd watched Honor with a clear, cool eye – ready to disapprove.

After the long sea passage, Honor seems disorientated: confused by this homecoming to an unknown home, keeping her children close.

It is as if, thinks Mousie, Hubert's young widow has been silenced by her grief, made dumb by sorrow.

'She won't talk to me,' she says to her mother. 'Not properly. She's not interested in anything that happens here and she seems afraid to let the children out of her sight.'

The latter, at least, is true. Not yet two, Emma is too young to be given much freedom but Honor rarely lets Bruno go anywhere without her either: not that he shows much desire, at first, to be adventurous.

'Think back to how we were when Daddy was killed,' advises her mother. 'I know it's six years ago now but remember how we all clung together? They are suffering from shock and it takes time to recover from these dreadful things. And, after all, Honor is a stranger here. When we came back to St Meriadoc we'd looked upon it as a second home ever since you and Rafe were babies. Honor knows only what Hubert has told her. No wonder she behaves as if she has been hit over the head, poor child.'

And Mousie, ashamed of her jealousy, tries harder: inviting Honor to accompany her on walks, to talk about Hubert, but any encouragement to share the past is met with resistance. Honor, it seems, simply cannot bear to dwell on what she has lost. Yet Mousie notices that she spends long periods talking to Hubert's frail, elderly father. Occasionally, during that first summer, Mousie comes upon them sitting beneath the lilac trees in the Paradise gardens: Uncle James in his old steamer chair whilst Honor is half turned towards him, her face animated.

'He specialized in tropical fevers . . .' she is saying. 'He was quite brilliant. Everyone loved him . . .'

Bruno leans against her knee, his face bright, as if through her words his father lives again, whilst Emma staggers about the sunny lawn, wrenching pink-tipped daisies from the grass, threatening to topple into the waters of the pond where great gold and black fish dart beneath the weed. The old man watches Honor, a smile pulling at his lips. Only his hands, smoothing and rubbing one against the other as if he is continually washing them in invisible water, show his private emotions and, as Mousie watches, she sees Bruno reach out to take hold of his grandfather's hands so as to still the endless restlessness.

At her approach, the small group seems to solidify into

watchfulness. Uncle James peers towards her beneath the sweet-scented flowers and Honor instinctively holds Bruno close against her side. Only Emma is untouched, shouting with pleasure at the freedom of the garden after so many weeks restrained on the steamer, holding out her trove of daisies and blades of emerald grass.

Mousie crouches, taking the ragged bouquet, giving Emma a hug, but her eyes are still on the three under the trees. Honor breaks the spell: sitting back in her wicker chair, crossing her long legs, raising both hands to her hair, which she wears – gypsy-like – beneath a cotton square.

'Hello, Mousie,' Honor calls; she uses the nickname with no apparent effort or awkwardness, yet Mousie still feels ex-cluded from intimacy, and the moment never arrives when she is able to return the compliment. For some reason this makes her feel guilty and her only comfort is that, apart from Rafe, who is hardly more than a child himself, none of the rest of the family does either; only Bruno and Emma use the cheerful little name that links the three of them to the past.

The shrill, insistent bell of her alarm clock shocked Mousie fully awake and drove her from her warm nest, shivering into the bathroom. Her cottage was small and neat: no knocking through of rooms or building of extensions; just the right amount of space for someone who was positively Franciscan in her minimalist needs. It was because of this trait that Hubert had nicknamed her when she was a child: her liking for small nooks and odd corners, combined with her horror of excess – large portions of food, too many belongings – had inspired him. His son, taking up the tradition years later, referred to her little cottage as 'The Wainscot'.

Mousie grinned as she pulled on warm trousers and a thick jersey. Bruno was so like Hubert and she loved him very dearly: but then Bruno was so easy to love. Mousie sighed, regretting the readiness to criticize that had so defined her early relationship with Honor. Had she been too ready to judge her? Had she withheld love?

It is in judging others that we betray them most.

The words remained with her as she finished dressing and, still trying to remember where she'd read them, she went down to breakfast.

Next door, Rafe and Pamela clattered about, each interrupting the other as they discussed the exciting prospect of the arrival of their son, George.

'Just for one night.' Rafe picked up the postcard, received yesterday, and read the words out loud again. '"A quick dash to see you all. Penny and Tasha won't be with me." Let's hope he has a good run down.' He cracked eggs into a white china bowl. 'It's odd that he's coming on his own.'

'It's a bit of an upheaval just for one night,' Pamela rationalized her disappointment, excusing Penny, 'when you've got a tiny baby to organize. Perhaps Penny thinks it would be nice for us to have him to ourselves.'

She took the card into her own hands, running her fingers over the shiny surface, imagining the photograph of Dartmoor ponies on Yennadon Down, which Rafe had described to her. Penny often sent embossed cards so that Pamela was able to feel the shape of the scene: a flower or a little house. This was simply a picture postcard. She put it aside and began to make coffee, measuring and spooning from jars on which Rafe had stuck Braille labels so that she could 'read' with her fingers, wishing that she was able to see the faces of her grand-children. Mousie and Rafe did their best to describe them for her: Mousie was very good at it, painting in the tiny details of each child, remarking on the likeness to a parent or some other relative, until Pamela not only vividly recalled her own children at various stages of their development but was able to form an idea of the faces of the new members of her growing family.

'Olivia looks just like you did at her age,' she'd say, 'and little Tom is going to be just like his father. He's got those brown eyes set wide apart just like Adrian's. Now Joe reminds me very much of my own father, though you never knew him, of course, rather than Rafe. And George . . . well, George is exactly like his father, just as we always knew he would be.'

Pamela smiled to herself, admitting privately to herself that George had always been very special to her and Mousie, and suddenly had an idea.

'See if you can catch Joss before she goes off to Wadebridge,' she said suddenly to Rafe, switching on the percolator. 'Perhaps she could come in for some supper. I can smell burning. Is the toast stuck again?'

Rafe dealt briskly with the toaster, shared the scrambled eggs between two plates and carried them to the table, ducking automatically as he passed beneath the heavy beams. The two middle cottages of The Row had been converted into one larger dwelling and, when his mother, Julia, died, Rafe had moved back into it with his young wife and their baby girl. His view was that the quiet beauty of St Meriadoc more than made up for a higher salary and career opportunities up-country. Pamela, already pregnant with Joe, gazed at the cottage, the shining sea, the tumbling cliffs, and agreed with heart-felt gratitude.

'It's good of Mutt to let us have it so cheaply,' she'd said. 'The rent is terribly low. She could earn much more money letting it to holidaymakers. Or I suppose she could sell it?'

He'd shaken his head. 'Probably not. I don't know how Uncle James left the estate but I imagine it would have passed from Hubert into some kind of trust for Bruno and Emma. We don't come from that side of the family. Uncle James's wife was my mother's sister and they took us in during the war when Father died. Well, you know the story.'

'It's so beautiful here,' she'd said. 'I've loved being in Exeter – and I know you'll find sixth-form colleges a bit different from university lecturing – but, oh, Rafe, this magic valley is *such* a place to bring up children.'

'Mutt calls it "the golden cup",' he'd told her, 'from a poem about a lark. You just wait until you hear the larks up by the Saint's Well.'

Watching her now, as she reached for the toast, her fingers testing the side of one of the small pots of conserve for the raised shape of the orange – marmalade, today, rather than strawberry jam – he felt such love for her. He did every-thing possible to enable her, suppressing the early instinctive reaction to protect, quickly seeing how much could be done to give back some of the freedom this swift descent into blindness had snatched from her. They'd stride arm-in-arm together over the windy hills, plunging down into the sheltered lanes, pausing so that she could identify the birds – 'I can hear a robin . . . and there's a buzzard somewhere. Wait! There's something else. A yellowhammer?' – whilst he held his breath, willing her to succeed. He'd put a creamy crown of honeysuckle into her hand and watch her frown of con-centration smooth into delighted recognition as she held it against her face, breathing its heavy evocative scent, reliving long-ago sunny afternoon walks; the children racing ahead whilst they'd stroll more slowly, revelling in the wild hedgerows streaked with the bright, paint-colours of late spring: bluebells, campion, buttercup, rioting together beneath a blush of May blossom.

The light on the percolator glowed red and he stood up to pour the coffee.

'Odd, though,' her voice from behind him echoed his own secret thought, 'that George sent a card. I wonder why he didn't ring us?'

CHAPTER SEVEN

Mutt woke to confusion and a clutching fear. The letters must be found and there was something else . . . Joss was bending over her and, gazing up at her, Mutt seemed to be looking at herself when young; those same level brows, that short, straight nose and the widely curling mouth, these features had all been there in the photograph Mousie had shown her. Visions passed before her eyes – she could almost feel the soft, rich silk of her frock between her fingers, the pressure of the silly hat on her forehead; she heard Hubert's voice telling her to smile: 'Come on, Mutt. It's a wedding not a funeral!' – and she felt hot and weak but, despite the wave of weakness, dimly she perceived some kind of danger lurking: for herself and for Joss. She clung to Joss's hands as if she were her rescuer – or a fellow conspirator.

'The letters,' her voice creaked and cracked. 'My letters, darling.'

Her granddaughter's hands were blessedly cool, her short hair – cropped below her ears and falling over her hazel eyes – was brown and shiny as seaweed. The old woman in the bed was stilled briefly by the clean, calm beauty of her young face, untroubled and unlined, and felt herself soothed. She lay back on the pillows and tried to marshal her thoughts, breathing as deeply as she could whilst this terrible band of pain gripped her chest.

Joss watched her anxiously, concerned both by the wheezing sound that whistled between her grandmother's lips and by the pallor of her skin. She wished that Mousie would arrive and, still holding Mutt's hand, glanced surreptitiously at her wristwatch. Yet she maintained her outward calm and managed to smile.

'Mousie will be here soon,' she said rather cheerfully, as if it were to be a social visit. 'Would you like some cordial? I suppose we'd better get the nasty bit over first.'

She took the small plastic measure of medicine and held it to the shrunken, withered lips. Mutt swallowed obediently, choking a little, and relaxed against Joss's arm, studying her. She wore a loose overshirt in soft, mole-coloured needlecord and smelled deliciously of lavender. Mutt inhaled more slowly, her panic subsiding a little: she knew now exactly where her letters were. The temporary relief from pain brought a return of confidence along with the clearing of her mind.

'Will you do something for me?' She watched Joss pour the cordial. 'It's private. Just between you and me. Do you promise?'

'Of course.'

Joss's instinctive response was to comfort rather than to bind herself, but the old woman sensed this and struggled up a little. She sipped at the cordial impatiently, almost out of politeness, then held the glass away from her mouth with trembling hands.

'No more. It's important, Joss darling. A real promise.'

Joss stood the glass back on the tray. 'I'll do what I can, Mutt,' she said, puzzled by such urgency and aware that she might be taking rather too much on herself. 'But Mum will be here soon. Wouldn't it be better—'

'No.' She shook her head, vehemently. 'Only you.'

'OK. I'll do my best.' Joss sounded dubious. 'Is it to do with those letters you were talking about? Do you need something to go in the post?'

Her mind jittered nervously, full of scenes from Agatha Christie novels: a letter to her lawyer? a change in her will?

'Find them,' muttered Mutt. 'Don't tell anyone. Promise.'

The hand she stretched out was hot, and Joss nodded, frightened alike by her grandmother's terrible urgency and this descent into breathlessness.

'I promise,' she mumbled.

It was with great relief that she heard the front door click shut and Mousie's voice calling from the hall below. She shouted an answer and her grandmother opened her eyes again, fighting the familiar confusion, clinging to this new comfort. Joss had promised to find the letters . . . but there was something else; something she'd forgotten. Mousie was in the room and Joss was going.

'Don't forget,' she whispered as her granddaughter bent to kiss her.

'I won't. Stop worrying, Mutt, and get better.'

Now, she and Mousie were murmuring together, glancing towards the bed. In a new fever of anxiety Mutt wondered if Joss might tell – but no, no, it was clear from Joss's lightly blown kiss from the door and Mousie's warm smile that it was merely the usual changeover. Mutt sagged gratefully, submitting to Mousie's professional touch.

Half running down the drive, Joss felt unhappy and very anxious. Part of her was pleased that Mutt had not told her where the letters were: clearly she could do nothing without that information yet she had made the promise. Nevertheless, to obey Mutt's instructions whilst she was not in her right mind was a huge responsibility. Was it right to keep something private between them at this stage of her grandmother's life? What could it be that must be kept secret from her own children?

Joss forced herself to slow down, aware that she was trying to escape from her worries rather than hurrying towards her work. Out in the lane she gasped in lungfuls of freezing air, heard the iced-over puddles splinter beneath her feet. Such weather was unusual here on the coast and suddenly she felt as excited as a child at the unexpected sight of snow. The black hawthorn twigs were rimed with frost and, in the ditch, a rabbit's sudden flight crumbled last year's crisped, brittle leaves to powder.

At the field gate she stopped, climbing a rung or two, feeling in her big bag for the apples she'd bought for the donkeys, Rumpleteaser and Mungojerrie. These were the latest in a long line of animals from the sanctuary, who'd come to enjoy the peace of the meadow here at St Meriadoc. They came towards her, breath steaming, heavy heads nodding, and she spoke quietly to them, stroking their velvety muzzles and pulling at their ears. Dropping her bag, she swung herself lightly over the gate and crossed the meadow to the trough, smashing the thin layer of ice on their drinking water with the heel of her boot whilst they nuzzled at her pockets, hoping for more treats. Flushed with the exertion of pushing them off, laughing at their antics, she finally reached the quarry and her car in a much more positive mood.

Mutt was feverish, she reminded herself, away with the fairies: silly to get so upset about it. At the same time, she'd made a promise and Mutt was trusting her. Her heart contracted with love and fear.

'Don't die, Mutt,' she muttered childishly. 'Just don't, that's all.'

Across the road Rafe had appeared, calling from the door, and Joss turned quickly, fumbling with her keys.

'George is coming down,' he was saying. 'Did Pamela tell

you? Only for the night but she says that you must come in and have some supper.'

She nodded agreement, pointing at her watch and miming the need for haste, and climbed into the car: it was like sitting in a fridge but the engine started at the third go. Driving carefully, heading away from St Meriadoc, she grappled with this new complication. Even in this icy chill her cheeks burned hotly, her heart jumped. Her love for George was still the best-kept secret in the world. Only she and George knew of it and, though her instinct assured her that he loved her too, his marriage made it impossible for him to acknowledge it openly. Oh, how she loved him . . . Joss gave a tiny cry of fear as she pressed down incautiously on the accelerator and the back wheels slipped and swayed across a patch of ice.

Concentrate, she told herself. Forget Mutt. Forget George. Think about the morning ahead.

She liked to be at the practice early, at least half an hour before the first patient was due to arrive or the telephone started to ring: those anxious 'acutes' who were desperate for treatment and hoped that she might have a free appointment. Or they might be too acute to come in and she'd need to talk to them and give them advice. She'd quickly learned the importance of being able to reassure people who were in pain and, though she sometimes wondered if she'd ever be in the position to afford a receptionist anyway, she was deeply conscious of the need to be the first contact for these poor souls who were frightened.

At least by sharing rooms – renting a consulting room and a tiny waiting-room on the ground floor at a dentist's practice – she had the benefit of the place always being clean and warm, of having other personnel in the building, and even a share in the car-park which was a great boon during the busy summer months. The forty pounds a week she paid for these advantages was a rather worrying expense but she was hopeful that her practice would grow and, meanwhile, the income derived from working as an assistant to a well-established osteopath in Bodmin for two days a week helped with the bills.

Who was first on the list this morning? Joss took a deep breath and began to think about Mrs Tregellis; gradually the blessed solace of work and her innate professionalism distracted her from thoughts of George and Mutt and focused her mind on the day ahead.

Once Mutt was sponged down and resettled, Mousie went downstairs and put a call through to the surgery, asking if the doctor could call in later. She was anxious: the breathlessness and pallor might indicate that Mutt was going into heart failure. Once Joss had gone, she'd grown calmer, falling asleep quite naturally, but Mousie felt it best to take no chances. Joss had left the kitchen tidy – her breakfast things washed and upended in the plastic dryer, the dishcloth hung neatly over the Aga rail – and Mousie set the tray down and refilled the kettle. Whilst she waited for it to boil she piled sheets into the washing-machine, set it going and made a quick check to be certain that the house appeared suitably welcoming for Emma's arrival.

The drawing-room had a sad, secretive look, as if it were faintly affronted to be visited unexpectedly in the middle of the morning, and the ashes in the empty fireplace were dusty and grey in the bright slant of sunlight. Mousie noticed that the small basket that held kindling was nearly empty, swept the grate and laid the fire ready for the evening: tomorrow, Mutt's cleaner from St Endellion would come and give the house a thorough going-over so now there was time for a quiet moment with a cup of coffee before Emma arrived. First, however, she looked into the small parlour, unused since Mutt had tripped over and broken her ankle. Glancing about her – at the big roll-top desk, the beautifully worked screen, which stood behind the two small upright wooden armchairs,

the oval inlaid table covered with workboxes and silks –
Mousie was reminded of a scene that had taken place here
more than forty years before, just after Rafe had been called
up for National Service and gone away to Catterick.

Honor stands at the table, matching silks, holding up the
smooth skeins and laying them across a piece of canvas.

'Your turn now, Mousie,' she says.

'My turn for what?'

'Time to stretch your wings outside the valley.' Honor turns
a smiling glance upon her. 'Time to have some fun. You
mustn't become indispensable.'

'I don't know what you mean.'

'Don't you?' Honor makes a little face. 'You mustn't lose
sight of the fact that you have your own life to plan. Your
mother will rely on you even more heavily now that Rafe's
gone and it's best to make the break at once. What about that
job you were telling me about at the BRI? Bristol's not that far
away and Julia will manage without you. She's got old Dot
next door on one side and Jessie on the other. And me up
here at Paradise. We'll all miss you terribly but I'll look after
them, don't worry.'

'It just seems rather hard, with Daddy dying and now Rafe
going away . . .'

'Look, Mousie,' Honor drops the silks and comes round the
table. 'You don't want to spend your youth dashing home to
St Meriadoc on your days off from Bodmin Hospital. Get right
away, Mousie.'

Her intensity makes Mousie uneasy as well as defensive and,
as if she realizes this, Honor smiles.

'It's easy to get into a rut,' she says, 'and then it's too late.
Opportunities pass and never return. It's different for me. I
had plenty of fun before the war. I've lived abroad, been
married – and I've got the children to live and plan for. This
valley is a tiny piece of Paradise, I grant you that, but you need

to rough it out there for a bit before you can really appreciate it. Trust me, Mousie . . .'

As she stared about the silent room, Mousie remembered that she'd taken Honor's advice – and that it had been wise. She *had* looked after them all: extending Julia's cottage once Jessie had died and, years later, offering Dot's old home to Mousie at a ludicrously low rent.

'You're ready to come back now,' she'd said. 'Your turn for a walk to the Paradise gardens, Mousie.'

Remembering, feeling strangely moved, Mousie closed the door gently behind her and went to make some coffee.

CHAPTER EIGHT

'There goes Joss.' From the curved window of The Lookout, Emma could see across to The Row and the boatyard as well as far out to sea. 'The sun is just touching the roofs. Ray always says that it's a shame that we don't get much sun down here in the valley in winter.'

'Yes, I can well imagine that Brer Fox would blow up some cliffs or chop down a forest or two so as to make a place more attractive to the masses and earn himself a fast buck. It's impossible for him to appreciate the countryside unless it's in the terms of property development.'

Emma moved back into the room, hugging her long fleecy robe more tightly about her generous figure.

'He *is* rather tiresome at the moment,' she admitted. 'You know, talking about what he'd do if Mutt . . . well, when Mutt dies.' Her worried expression trembled into distaste.

'Do about what?' Bruno was sitting at the table, spooning porridge from a large bowl. The porridge was lavishly spread with clotted cream and brown sugar and he was clearly relishing it. 'He hardly ever sees her now. What difference will it make to him?'

During breakfast he'd been mentally blocking out his next chapter whilst Emma reviewed the day ahead but, once again, reality was forcing him into an anxious awareness.

'Well, not much,' she agreed, shrugging, 'but you know what I mean. Oh, I'm well aware of what you think about Ray but you'd have to be supernaturally disinterested not even to consider what would happen, wouldn't you?'

'I don't see why anything should change.' He put the bowl down for Nellie to lick and stood up. Anxiety battled with the overwhelming need to get back to his own internal world and he felt restless and edgy. 'Why are we talking about Mutt dying, anyway? She's broken her ankle and now she has a chill. Is it really serious? Mousie hasn't said so.'

Emma stared at him thoughtfully. 'Odd, isn't it?' she observed. 'We've been coming here all these years, me and Zoë,' she gave a little nod towards the photograph, 'and then Olivia and Joss too, whenever we've been in trouble. And you've sorted us out and got us kick-started again. But with Mutt it's like you just don't want to accept that she's old and frail and ill.'

'It's not the same at all,' he answered irritably. 'Good God! I didn't ask you all to come. This place was like an asylum for fallen women at times. And I wish you wouldn't make me sound like Voltaire's philanthropic Dr Pangloss type of character. Although I do happen to agree with him that, to be happy, man must work.'

'Oh, don't start that.' Emma made a face. 'You were always going on about work.'

'And I was right. If you or Zoë had had other things on your minds apart from love affairs and spending money you'd both have needed less kick-starting or whatever you called it.'

'Ray didn't want me to work. He liked me to be there for him. And anyway, there was Joss . . .' Her voice changed. 'Of course, it was rather different for Zoë.'

'Let's not get on to that one, shall we? Won't Mousie be waiting for you?'

Emma burst out laughing. 'Ten out of ten for subtlety, dear bro. But yes, I must get a move on. Are you coming up to the house with me?'

He hesitated. 'Will it be a bit much for Mutt? All of us at once? Tell her I'll be up about tea-time as usual . . .' He frowned, feeling guilty.

'And anyway, you want to work,' she prompted, grinning.

He grinned back at her. 'I don't have a wealthy spouse to support me. Only an ex-wife who still thinks it's my duty to bail her out of trouble at regular intervals.'

Emma's smile died, the old, familiar protectiveness aroused. 'She has absolutely no right to exploit your good nature. Why should you have to support her when she walked out on you? What about all those other lovers she's had?'

'Give it a rest,' he said, hands raised, palms outward. 'I'm not in the mood. Go and get some clothes on before Mousie phones up wondering where you are. Mutt's probably all keyed-up to see you.'

She trailed away, retying the belt on her thick, soft robe, her expression sulky and dissatisfied, resenting Zoë's presence in their lives.

The room seemed to settle and expand a little around Bruno now he was alone again. He strolled over to the window and, hands in pockets, stared down towards The Row and, beyond it, to the corrugated iron structure of the old boathouse. Under its roof, at the top of the slipway, was his old boat the *Kittiwake*, built in the yard before the war by the man who'd once lived here in The Lookout. She was clinker built, mahogany on oak, sixteen feet long, and as a child he'd learned to sail in her, taught by Rafe, who'd been barely more than a boy himself. Another smaller sailing boat sat nearby on a trailer. George owned the Enterprise, and Bruno wondered if there might be time for them to get out for a sail at some point while George was down. He glanced seawards: the sea, flat as a shelf, was banded with bars of silver, and there was no breath of wind.

He found that he was thinking about George: how he'd come upon him, standing with Joss one hot afternoon last summer, high up the valley beside St Meriadoc's well listening to a lark singing high above them. There'd been some tension between them that caught his attention: the way that, though not actually touching, they'd seemed to be drawn to each other. They'd smiled at him in a dazed kind of way, rather as travellers might greet a stranger – polite but not terribly interested – and he'd suddenly realized why, much to the whole family's puzzlement, Joss didn't get serious with her boyfriends . . .

'See you later.' Emma was waving to him from the doorway, her sunny good humour restored. 'Enjoy your trip down London's sewers. No, Nellie, you can't come this time. Sorry, old girl.'

She disappeared and Bruno began to collect the breakfast things together, relieved that the subject of his ex-wife had been avoided for once. From the very beginning Zoë and Emma had crossed swords and his loyalty to each had been severely strained. He piled the dishes beside the deep Belfast sink, let Nellie out for her morning potter in the valley and allowed his mind to flow back into its natural channels of creativity. However, now that he was able to return to his own world he felt that, mysteriously, it was closed to him. He tried the usual methods: conjuring up his characters, deliberately setting them in different situations, trying out conversational openings, but all he could think about was Zoë: bringing her home to Paradise and introducing her to Mutt before taking her down to show her The Lookout.

At twenty-three, just out of naval college and on fourth-year courses, he is well aware that Zoë is rather outside his experience: he cannot take his eyes off her. Conscious of his admiration she slightly exaggerates her movements, swinging her hips in the tight black mini-skirt, crossing her legs in long black leather boots. The severe Mary Quant bob suits her thick black hair. Zoë always wears black: she is sophisticated and sharply aware of her image. Not quite as famous as The Shrimp or Twiggy, she is, nevertheless, building up quite a portfolio and is much in demand for her Juliette Gréco type of sexuality: a waif-like gamine with an air of weary boredom; a black-eyed stare that challenges. There is nothing naïve about Zoë.

She is impressed, however, by St Meriadoc, lying in its sheltering valley, and though she makes no concessions to Bruno's people – no playing the sweet young *ingénue* for their benefit – the fact that, one day, he will inherit this charming little estate elevates him in her estimation.

'Nice, darling,' she says, wandering round the big room with its curving window, digging a crumpled packet of Sobranies out of her bag. 'You could have really fab parties here.' She gives him an admiring little glance: teasing, rather veiled. 'So this is your pad?'

He hurries to light her cigarette with the smart Dunhill lighter she's given him for his twenty-third birthday and she smiles at him, her eyes narrowing above the smoke, assessing him. She likes The Lookout even more than the pretty house: it lends itself to fun décor and promising weekends – although it's rather a long way from London.

'Yes,' he says. 'Yes, The Lookout is mine.'

That's how it's always been. 'You can have The Lookout,' Emma says, 'and I'll have Paradise,' although neither of them takes it too seriously. In his final year at school, Bruno works hard redecorating The Lookout so that his friends can come to stay. It's good to get away from the constraints of the house and have some fun, and Mutt is very understanding. She allows him to take down some unwanted furniture and discarded curtains, and she buys a few other pieces: enough to furnish it adequately. He celebrates his twenty-first birthday with a party at The Lookout, with his fellow officers from BRNC and Emma's seventeen-year-old school-friends.

'We had a ball,' he tells Zoë casually, not wanting her to think him inexperienced, thinking of those girls: smelling delicately of Elizabeth Arden's Blue Grass, rather self-conscious in their long, pretty pastel-hued frocks. Zoë wears a scent called Jicky and wouldn't be seen dead in bright, light colours. 'Drank too much and went swimming off the slipway at midnight.'

'Great,' she says indifferently, turning from the window, grinding out her cigarette in the hastily proffered ashtray, her eyes on his. 'So what's the scene upstairs?'

Though grateful for the experience gained on various runs ashore in Holland and Sweden, Bruno is almost relieved when they hear a door slam and Emma's voice echoing up the stairs. He mutters apologies, tucking in his shirt, hurrying down to meet her.

'Mutt said you'd be here,' she says. 'I can't wait to meet Zoë.'

'I was just showing her round upstairs,' he says awkwardly. 'She's just . . . um. You know. Powdering her nose. Ah, here she comes.'

Zoë descends the stairs slowly, aware of Emma's fascinated gaze, meeting Bruno's eyes with a secret smile. Whilst Bruno introduces them he senses antagonism on both sides: Zoë lets Emma see that she thinks her unsophisticated and of little account, that her arrival is ill-timed; Emma is knocked out of her stride by such sophistication coupled with barely concealed indifference. For the first time Bruno is caught between two women – between, on one side, strong physical desire and, on the other, deep affection and loyalty – but at twenty-three there is no contest.

'You can't marry her,' cries Emma. 'She's all wrong for you. Don't be confused by sex.'

But he *is* confused by it: confused, drugged and drowning in it. His oppos are wildly envious and his pride knows no bounds. Zoë is chosen to market a famous brand of cigarette and her image is to be seen everywhere: staring down from posters and out of the shiny pages of popular magazines. The photograph becomes an icon and he feels excited and over-whelmed each time he sees it. This woman, desired by men and envied by women, is his. She gives him the huge framed copy, which hangs in The Lookout, as a wedding present.

CHAPTER NINE

'Mutt looks better today,' said Emma hopefully. 'Don't you think so, Mousie? I don't quite know what it is but she seems calmer and her mind is surprisingly clear.'

She was busy at the ironing board, pressing and folding sheets with swift, economical movements, whilst Mousie sat at the kitchen table, peeling and dicing vegetables for soup; heaping the vegetables together in a bowl, saving the peelings for the compost heap. Although she understood that Emma's diagnosis was coloured by wishful thinking, nevertheless she was inclined to agree with her. Following that early attack of breathlessness and sweating, Mutt *was* less distressed; she was sleeping more deeply.

'The antibiotics are helping,' she said – yet she felt that it was something more than that: rather as if a burden had been lifted and Mutt had truly relaxed for the first time in several days. For the first time since the letter and the photograph had arrived . . . This unbidden thought had the impact of a sudden shock and Mousie looked thoughtfully at Emma, who was now carefully ironing one of Mutt's nightgowns.

'Did Joss tell you about our American pilgrim?' she asked lightly.

'Yes, she did.' Emma paused from her work, setting the iron on its rest and turning to look at Mousie, whose fingers continued to chop busily. 'A rather good-looking chap, I gather, who was trying to track down an aunt or something.'

'Great-aunt,' said Mousie, almost absently. 'Does the name Madeleine Grosjean ring any bells?'

Emma frowned. 'I don't think so. Was that her name?'

'Apparently. He said that she knew your parents out in India.' Mousie deftly scraped the last peelings into some newspaper. 'She might have been a nurse.'

'Oh, well.' Emma shrugged and turned back to her work. 'That's a closed book to me, you know. I wasn't quite two when we came home. I think I can remember things, sometimes, but then I wonder if I confuse them with stories Mutt and Bruno have told me. Do you know what I mean?'

'Mmm.' Mousie seemed to be distracted. 'Did you ever see any photographs? I know you all came away in such a hurry that you didn't bring much with you but I just wondered . . .'

'Hardly anything. And, of course, very little had been sent home. Mutt's got a few photos but those little black-and-white snapshots aren't very revealing, are they? Bruno and I were too young to go in for souvenirs, though we've each got a very nice cabinet-size photo of Daddy taken when he first went out.'

Mousie stood up, carried the vegetables to the sink, rinsed them and turned them out into a large saucepan containing a rich, meaty stock. Emma smiled at her with enormous affection. She liked being here, ironing whilst Mousie prepared some lunch, bringing life to this rather cold, functional room at the back of the house. Mutt had never been a kitchen dweller, preferring her little parlour or the drawing-room, and so no atmosphere pervaded it. However, since Joss had moved temporarily into Paradise, there were one or two signs of new life: two or three cards from her friends ranged along the window-sill; her plaid shawl flung over the back of a chair; a tiny bunch of snowdrops crammed into a small blue pot. Emma was oddly touched by these signs of her daughter's presence. Privately she hoped that, one day, Joss might live at Paradise, bringing up her own children here; re-creating those happy times when she and Bruno had been growing up together. She sighed in pleasurable anticipation.

'It's nice, isn't it?' she said spontaneously to Mousie. 'Being together like this, I mean. The clean smells of the ironing and delicious food cooking on the Aga, and having a good old gossip. Bruno would say that it all goes back to the hunter-gatherers. All those millions of years with women gathering and spending all that time together while the men were off hunting. He's got a thing about it.'

Mousie slipped an arm about Emma's shoulder and gave her a little hug but she was not distracted by Bruno's theory. An idea was growing in her mind but for some reason she was afraid of it: she couldn't get to grips with it, yet the shadow was there.

'Have you ever seen a photograph of their wedding?' she asked. 'Honor's and Hubert's? It was a double wedding, you know. Hubert sent us a photograph at the time. My father had just been lost with the sinking of the *Hood* and we came back to St Meriadoc. One of the cottages was empty so we were able to move in. You know all that, of course, but it was just at that time that Hubert got married and sent the photograph.'

'I love all these stories about the family.' Emma folded the night-gown and placed it on the pile of crisply laundered items. 'How terrible it must have been for you all, Mousie. I do wish I could remember more. Do you know I can hardly even bring Grandfather to my mind? But then he died quite soon after we got home, didn't he? Thank goodness we had all of you. It must have been such a comfort for Mutt to come back to a ready-made family, especially when she'd lost her own parents so tragically in the Blitz.'

'We were very lucky,' agreed Mousie. 'All of us.' A pause. 'So you haven't seen the wedding photograph?'

Emma looked at her curiously. 'Have you still got it?'

'Not the one Hubert sent to us. Or, at least, if we have I don't know where it is. I just wondered if Honor might have had one somewhere. The American sent a copy of it. It was very odd, seeing it again after all these years.'

'I'd love to see it,' said Emma. 'Joss didn't show me the photograph, she just said he'd called.'

Mousie went out of the kitchen, crossed the hall to the drawing-room, and picked up the large leather bag which was lying beside an armchair. She stood quite still for a moment, the photograph in her hand, before returning to the kitchen.

'There.' She laid the print on the table and Emma bent over it eagerly. 'Have you seen it before?'

'Never.' Emma was smiling. 'Those ridiculous hats! But don't they look happy and – good gracious, Mousie, doesn't Joss look just like Mutt at that age?'

'That's what struck me,' agreed Mousie. 'It was quite a little shock . . . Do you recognize the other woman at all?'

Emma picked up the photograph, holding it towards the light from the window.

'I don't know.' She looked puzzled. 'There's something about her . . . Isn't it odd, though, Mousie . . . ?'

The sound of Mutt's handbell sounded through the house and the two women instinctively tensed.

'I'll go,' said Emma. 'I'll shout if I think you should come up.' She dropped the photograph on the table and disappeared, running up the stairs. Mousie picked up the print and stared at it.

She thought: I wonder what happened to Madeleine Grosjean.

*   *   *

George Boscowan parked his car in the old quarry and sat for a moment, summoning up the courage required to break the news to his parents.

'You have to tell them,' Penny had said. 'No, I can't come with you. I just can't face them. Sorry, George. Anyway, it simply wouldn't work with Tasha screaming her head off or whatever.'

'Please, Penny.' He'd made another effort. 'Look, I don't have to stay in the Navy if you hate it that much. Of *course* I can imagine how much you miss your family, especially when I'm at sea. Look, we can all go to New Zealand. Why not? Make a new start together.'

'Are you crazy?'

She'd stared at him in such horror that he'd realized with a shock that the idea of him being with her in her own country, amongst her own people, was completely unacceptable to her. Mentally she'd already moved into a new life; a life where her lover, Brett Anderson, had usurped him. It was because Brett had broken off their engagement that Penny had come to England in the first place. Now he wanted her back.

'I think I must have been in love with him all the time,' she'd said pathetically, seeing the reaction on his face at her instinctive response, quickly trying to engage his sympathy and divert his anger. 'Only I *did* love you, George. I still do. Oh Christ! This is terrible. Can you love two people at once?'

'Yes,' he'd wanted to shout. 'Yes, you bloody can. I should know. But you can at least try to fight it.'

Instead, he'd grimaced bitterly, unable to hide his feelings but feeling betrayed by her readiness to break up their marriage at Brett's sudden reappearance.

'He left you before,' he'd said, 'he might do it again. And what about Tasha? She's mine too. How often am I going to see her with you in New Zealand?'

'You don't see her much now,' she'd answered unforgivably,

upset by his pain but determined not to give an inch, 'you're away at sea so much.' And then, seeing his expression: 'I'm sorry, George,' she'd said sadly but with finality. 'I just belong back there with my family and friends – and with Brett. I realize that now. Please don't make it difficult for me with Tasha. She needs to be with me. What sort of life could you give her? You'd have to put her into some kind of childcare so you could work, wouldn't you? After all, you could hardly expect your mother to manage, and you're away for months at a time. You couldn't put a three-month-old baby into someone else's care for months on end. Please George, if you really love her you'll do what's best for her.'

He'd felt so angry by this manipulation of his love for her and their baby that he'd been obliged to walk out: striding away from the little house on the edge of Meavy village, climbing up on to the moor above Burrator. An icy wind pinched, cold-fingered, at his face and passed on across the waters of the reservoir, shivering and splintering the reflections on the surface. Black-faced sheep, with tiny, jug-eared lambs pressed against their woolly flanks, huddled in the lee of humped boulders. The tall stately conifers at the water's edge made a dark green wedge of colour in this bleached, dun landscape; patches of bracken, rich and bright in the late-afternoon light, rusted on the slopes of Sheep's Tor where a scattering of snow iced the granite peaks.

Staring westwards, beyond Plymouth far into Cornwall, where the sunshine showered insubstantial shafts of dazzling gold upon the distant, mysterious hills, he'd thought of Joss – and felt the balled fist of guilt deep in his gut. It was Joss who'd listened whilst he'd talked, pouring out his worries that Penny missed her family, was lonely when he went to sea, wasn't managing too well with the baby: Joss, with whom he had fallen suddenly in love, between one glance and the next, realizing with a blow to his heart that his feelings for Penny were a dim reflection of this shattering experience. However, he'd been determined that it should not be allowed to affect his commitment to Penny.

This is what Penny feels for Brett, he'd told himself later, when Brett had reappeared and Penny was clearly being drawn back to him. George believed that they should fight for what they shared and for the security their marriage gave their baby. Yet, the moment Brett beckoned, Penny had been prepared to jettison it all without a backward glance: he could almost laugh at the irony of it all. The guilt was there, though: had he, in any way, allowed his feelings for Joss to colour his relationship with Penny? If he had never loved Joss in the first place would Penny have succumbed so quickly to Brett's overtures? And part of him, if he were truthful, longed to chuck it all in and turn with relief to Joss . . .

Now, he reached for his overnight bag, took a gasping breath to steady his nerves and climbed out of the car.

CHAPTER TEN

Pamela knew at once that there was something wrong. The postcard instead of a telephone call, his intention to come alone, these things had aroused her suspicions. Now, his physical presence confirmed them. Once she would have seen from his body language that there were problems here. Now she could only intuit these things from the tones of voice, the quality of the silences. Nevertheless, she smiled steadily into the darkness, waiting for him to come to her and kiss her; putting up her hands to clasp his broad shoulders, to touch his hair. His lips grazed her cheek, his 'Hi, Ma' was a warm breath in her ear, and then he'd moved away whilst her hands still sketched the empty, airy shape of him before they dropped to her lap.

'What a morning,' Rafe was saying cheerfully. 'You must have got away early, George. We weren't expecting you quite yet. Have you got snow on Dartmoor?'

Pamela could hear the sounds of coffee being prepared, the screech of chair-legs as George sat down, the exchange of pleasantries, and she tensed, waiting for the blow to fall. Already she'd mentally rehearsed the possibilities: financial difficulties? Well, they'd certainly extended themselves when they'd bought the cottage in Meavy.

'Penny thinks that she'd like to be in the country,' he'd told them, 'and especially now with the baby coming. With me being at sea so much I think she has the right to live where she's happiest.'

Privately, Pamela had feared that Penny might miss her friends in London, the bustle of the town, but she and Rafe agreed that Meavy was a delightful village and Tavistock only ten minutes away: a wonderful environment to bring up a family. Penny and George had got a good price for the flat but the asking price for the cottage was certainly on the upper edge of the limit they'd set themselves.

'We are simply so lucky,' Pamela had said to Rafe, when they'd seen the estate agent's particulars and gasped and rolled their eyes with shock at the price tag. 'Thanks to Honor we can live in this fabulous place for an almost silly rent. I simply don't know how people cope with these huge responsibilities. I hope they'll be OK.'

Listening to Rafe setting out mugs, she wondered if they hadn't been OK. Perhaps they'd come seriously unstuck and needed help. Her mind ranged to and fro, wondering how she and Rafe might raise money. With the onset of her blindness, Rafe had resigned from his teaching posts and worked instead for the Open University so that he could be at home with her. They'd managed to save a small amount over the years but, with three children, the sum wasn't going to stretch too far.

Perhaps Penny was lonely and asking George to resign his commission? The trouble with that was, what could George do outside the Navy that would earn him the same kind of money so as to support his family and the mortgage? And would George be happy outside? He loved his job and was doing well . . .

Pamela realized that an uncomfortable silence had fallen and grew instantly alert, listening: the kitchen clock ticked with an unnatural loudness, the sea whispered unceasingly from beyond the window, Rafe cleared his throat. A chair creaked suddenly and she heard the ring of spoon against china.

'Look,' George was saying, 'I expect you've both guessed that this isn't just a friendly visit. The thing is . . .'

She could hear him swallow, knew that his throat was dry, and was gripped with a spasm of pity and love for him.

The thing was, apparently, that he and Penny had decided to separate, things weren't working out; they'd agreed that it was the best way and that Penny would be returning to New Zealand.

Rafe murmured something – she could imagine his shocked expression – and she guessed in the pause that followed that George was gulping a reviving draught of hot coffee.

'Darling,' she said shakily. 'Oh, George, this is terrible. You've always seemed so happy. And what about Tasha . . . ?' Her voice trailed away uncertainly and, out of sight, her hands twisted together whilst her mind raced to readjust her ideas. Oh, how petty her former anxieties – so easily surmountable now, compared with the reality – had been.

Rafe was attempting to ease his son's path through the daunting thickets of explanation: perhaps Penny had been too much alone or had George . . . ? Might this be a temporary misunderstanding? One of those 'funny five minutes' that could occur in any partnership or marriage? Another silence.

Pamela pressed her lips together, resolutely holding back the questions that she wanted to shout at him, forcing herself to wait until he was ready. If only she could see his face, read between the lines. The tension was palpable, the air was thick with it, but there was something she couldn't quite grasp, some emotion just out of reach . . .

'Is there someone else?' she asked sharply – and heard George's swift intake of breath. She knew that Rafe and her son were looking at each other. 'No Slips,' she cried. 'Not now. This is much too important. What is it, George? What has happened to make you take this step?'

He was able to answer this honestly and did so.

'Penny was engaged before she came to England,' he told them flatly. 'The man, Brett Anderson his name is, broke it off and she came here to start a new life. Well, he's turned up again and she's decided that she's loved him all along and that she fell for me on the rebound. She says that her life is with him and her family in New Zealand.'

Pamela could imagine his shrug – a kind of relief that it was out in the open, a 'there you have it' kind of shrug.

'And how did you react to that?' Rafe asked the question almost diffidently, trying to probe the depth of his son's pain.

'I fought it.' He sounded almost truculent. 'What do you think I did? I suggested that we should all go to New Zealand. I know she misses her family and I can sympathize with that. We'd have managed if he hadn't come looking for her.'

'I can't believe that anyone would deliberately break up a family like that.' Pamela was listening for those tell-tale nuances. 'It's cruel.'

'Penny was invited to London to see some Kiwi friends,' he answered. 'He just happened to be staying with them.'

The bitterness was there in his voice; and something more than bitterness.

'But what will happen to Natasha?' Rafe was asking. 'Surely Penny can't expect you to give your child up so easily?'

His short laugh had no mirth in it. 'I'm between a rock and a hard place,' he said. 'I can't keep her, can I? How would I look after a three-month-old baby? And even if I could think of some way round it, would it be fair to her? Penny has a big family to support her . . .'

He stopped abruptly and Pamela, knowing why, felt quite unreasonably as though she had let him down.

'Oh, darling,' she said sorrowfully. 'I am so sorry. We're not much use to you, are we?'

'Don't be silly, Ma,' he said harshly. 'It's not your fault, how could it be? It's simply that we have to face facts. I haven't got anyone who could look after Tasha while I'm away at sea and I don't know what the hell I'd do if I came outside. Tasha is better off with her mother than with strangers, however wonderful they might be, and Penny says that we have to do what is best for Tasha.'

'Isn't it best for a child to be brought up by both its parents?' asked Rafe gently.

George's laugh, this time, contained a note of resignation but some of the tension had gone out of it. 'That's very old-fashioned, Pa,' he said. 'You're showing your age.'

Pamela was struggling with a variety of emotions: anguish for her son; despair at the thought of losing her grandchild; a momentary hatred of Penny, of whom she'd been so fond. Never had she regretted her lost sight more than at this moment. She longed to see George's face, to look into his eyes and watch his expressions whilst she talked to him. She knew that he was loyal, independent, straight-talking, yet something nagged at the back of her mind; something was missing.

'It must be really serious,' she was feeling her way, 'for Penny to react so drastically. Don't think I'm not on your side, George. You know I am. But Penny has been a good wife to you. She's supported you very loyally, although she's missed her own family and spent a great deal of time alone. She must feel very strongly to be doing this.'

'She does feel strongly,' said George after a moment. 'She says that she never stopped loving Brett, although she really did think she had. When she saw him again she realized the truth of it.' She sensed his shrug, heard his sigh. 'Well, I can understand that.'

She was on to it like a hound on the scent: *this* was what she'd been feeling for, this tone that indicated a true under-standing of Penny's dilemma. Oh, yes, there was bitterness, anger – but alongside those reactions ran a genuine sympathy: the very real sympathy of someone who actually knew the score and struggled with the same dilemma. She responded to it instinctively.

'I think George should take his things upstairs and then have a serious drink,' she said. 'We all need a moment to re-group.'

She waited, listening to George's departure, his footsteps on the stairs, and stretched her hand to Rafe who took it, holding it tightly, comfortingly.

'Telephone Bruno,' she told him urgently. 'Tell him to get hold of Joss and cancel supper. Tell him why if you have to. Hurry, before George comes back.'

CHAPTER ELEVEN

Bruno picked up the message when he left his study to make himself some lunch. He kept the telephone in the kitchen, permanently on answerphone with the bell switched off, and checked it at moments when he was unlikely to be distracted from his work. Now, he saw the red winking eye and pressed the Play button. Rafe's voice sounded odd: deliberately kept low, as if he feared to be overheard, but with a kind of compelling haste. Bruno listened, his brow furrowed with surprise.

George had a problem and it was best that Joss didn't come to supper: it wasn't likely to be a particularly jolly evening. Could he contact her and warn her off?

As he cut bread for a sandwich, gave Nellie a cuddle and fed her, poured a glass of apple juice, Bruno pondered on this message. He had an unwelcome premonition that he might have guessed the possible reason for George's problem and presently he checked his almost indecipherable address book and telephoned a number. Joss answered in the rather flat voice that indicated that she was with a patient.

'Sorry to interrupt,' he said. 'Message from Rafe. Supper

seems to be off for one reason or another. George isn't on form.' He heard her breathing rather quickly and imagined that narrow, focused look. 'Make sense to you?' he asked lightly.

'Yes,' she said shortly.

'I thought it might.' He hesitated. 'Want to come in on your way home?'

He could hear her thinking about it: a desperate, almost violent mental exercise with half her mind still on her patient.

'Could I?' she asked. 'Thanks, Bruno. Yes, I would like to. About six?'

'Great,' he replied. 'See you then.'

Nellie had brought her toy to his feet, a brightly coloured rubber bone with a tinny bell in it that Bruno detested. She looked from it to him, tail wagging, flopping ears pricked hopefully, and he kicked it across the kitchen. She leaped after it, paws scrabbling, seizing it with delight.

'Daft animal,' he muttered. 'No, take it away.' But she placed it beside him again, tongue lolling as if she laughed at him, and, unable to help himself, he laughed back at her.

'What is it about this place?' he asked her. 'A refuge for females in distress or what?' and he kicked the bone again, watching her skidding across the slates and fetching up against the larder door, remembering her arrival at The Lookout.

'She's the last one,' Mousie had said, standing just inside the kitchen one December evening, the puppy in her arms, rain dripping from her hat. 'The farmer found homes for the dogs but nobody wanted the bitch.'

Various apt retorts had risen to Bruno's lips, none of them politically correct, and she'd beamed at him, sensing capitulation.

'She'll be good for you,' she'd promised. 'Make you get out and exercise.'

'I walk miles every day, Mousie,' he'd said drily. 'Perhaps you just haven't noticed me about the place?'

'Walking's nicer with a dog,' she'd said, nodding sagely, clinching the argument.

'Then why don't you keep her?' he'd suggested. 'After all, you spend all day driving round from patient to patient. You get no exercise at all.'

'Oh, it wouldn't be fair to keep her in the car all day,' she'd answered, as if reluctantly refusing a treat. 'No, no. You must have her.'

She'd set the puppy on the floor where it had immediately crouched and made a puddle; in the tiny silence that followed Mousie hadn't quite met Bruno's eyes.

'Must dash,' she'd said brightly. 'Oh, by the way, I thought you might call her Nellie. It seems to suit her, don't you think?'

Bruno, slamming the door behind her with unnecessary vigour, had stared at the black-and-white bundle that was now cautiously exploring his kitchen.

'Welcome, Nellie,' he'd said, resigned. 'I hope you like sausages because that's all there is, apart from porridge. If you're going to live here you'll need to be adaptable.'

And Nellie had been adaptable. She was an easy-going companion, provided that she was allowed to share the sofa and was fed regularly, but she had an independent streak and enjoyed her solitary morning constitutional, pottering round The Row and visiting the Paradise gardens.

Now, after Rafe's message, Bruno decided that a walk would probably do them both good. The prospect of seeing Joss later was already distracting him from his work and once again the world of St Meriadoc was threatening to displace that other world where he most longed to be. With luck, a walk might start the creative juices flowing again. Anyway, he wanted to see Mutt.

*   *   *

Emma was alone at Paradise. Mousie had gone to Polzeath to do some shopping, she told him, and would look in later on.

'We are so lucky to have her,' she said. 'Joss is doing what she can but she has to keep her practice going and, after all, darling old Mousie is so experienced. Mutt seems calmer today, we both think so, though she's very weak. The doctor will be calling in a bit later. Go and talk to her.'

He went upstairs, relieved that he was able to have a moment alone with Mutt, wondering how he might broach a very difficult subject. He closed the door quietly behind him and stood for a moment, seeing that her eyes were closed. The sight of her, frail and tiny in the big bed, affected him powerfully. He realized now that he'd always seen her as a brave and gallant figure: watching over him and Emma, guiding them as she'd thought best. He remembered her as she'd been only a few months ago, at the end of the summer: still sailing with him in the *Kittiwake*, working with Rafe in the garden, walking over the cliffs and along the valley. Their scattered neighbours and friends had been very slightly in awe of her for, despite her natural warmth, she'd tended to hold them at arm's length. Yet he'd known another side of Mutt's character: a ready sense of humour, a vulnerability, and a deep, compassionate insight into human failings. She'd looked after them all, his grandfather and his Aunt Julia, as well as old Dot and Jessie Poltrue: Paradise and the valley would seem empty indeed without Mutt's presence.

Trying to conceal his emotions, he crossed to the bed and kneeled down beside her, kissing her soft, wrinkled brow. He took her hand, holding it tightly, and very gently shook it, as if to attract her attention. She turned her head slowly on the pillow and her eyes beseeched him for understanding.

'Everything was for you and Emma, wasn't it?' He leaned closer so as to hear her feeble voice. 'But now I want Joss to have Paradise.'

'Is that how you've left it in your will, Mutt?' he asked. 'I need to know this. Have you been explicit about the estate?'

She frowned as if remembering something, her lips mumbling a little, her eyes sliding away as if she could no longer meet his own. 'I've been a fool.' She took an uneven breath. 'Forgive me.'

Her withered lips shook with distress and he pressed his own together as he watched her struggle against the pain that dimmed her eyes, quite unable to question her further.

'Nothing to forgive,' he told her firmly. 'Remember how happy we've been, all of us. You kept us together as a family.'

Tears squeezed beneath her papery lids and she clutched his hand tightly. 'You'll look after them, I know that,' she whispered with difficulty. 'But I did so want Joss to have Paradise.'

He leaned forward to kiss her. 'I promise to look after Joss,' he said clearly, his lips close to her ear.

Before she could answer, the door opened and Emma appeared. Bruno sat back on his heels as she approached the bed and, releasing the thin hand, stood up and walked away to the window.

'I think she should rest now.' After a few moments Emma joined him, speaking in a low voice. 'I'll come and sit with her for a while but shall we go downstairs and have a cup of tea first?'

He followed her down to the kitchen but he knew that, in his present mood, it would be quite impossible to sit cosily over the teacups.

'Do you mind if I crack on?' he asked. 'Poor old Nellie needs a walk and I'd like to get a bit more work done, then we can have some time together after supper.'

She responded at once to the suggestion: those after-supper times with Bruno were terribly important to her.

'I might be a bit late, though,' she warned him. 'I don't

know what time Mousie will be back but I said we'd have something together here.'

'Doesn't matter,' he said, just needing to get away, to be alone to think things over. 'Whenever. Come on, Nellie.' But, at the door, he hesitated, suddenly conscious of Emma's fears and anxieties. 'Are you going to be OK?' he asked.

'Of course I am.' She was touched by his concern. 'To tell you the truth I rather like being here on my own. It's so peaceful and I like to listen to the silence. I know you'll find it difficult to believe,' she made a face at him, 'but I *can* manage an hour of my own company if pushed. Specially here. I like to think of Joss living here – well, she's doing that anyway at the moment – but Paradise is her natural home, isn't it?'

'Sure,' he said abruptly.

He stooped and kissed her cheek, turned quickly away, and she watched him stride off down the drive, surprised at this unusual display of affection.

She thought: He's upset by the way Mutt looks. I expect he wants to be on his own for a bit to come to terms with it.

And she went back inside and upstairs to her mother.

But Bruno wasn't thinking about Mutt. He was remembering how, thirty years before, Emma had introduced him to the young Raymond Fox. As he climbed the footpath to the cliff, Nellie already far ahead, he recalled her expression: pride mingled with anxiety – and a kind of 'anything you can do I can do better' tilt of the chin.

It is a warm evening in June and the big windows are open to the swelling sea, its taut surface skin gleaming and iridescent as a peacock's feather, its toothless mouth sucking and mumbling at the rocks beneath. The room is washed by golden light and full of sweet, fresh air. Fiddling with a dish of olives, wishing that Zoë would appear, Bruno checks his watch for the third time. It is at his suggestion that Emma is bringing

Raymond to The Lookout. Instinctively, Bruno has arranged this meeting on his own ground: Emma's descriptions of Raymond Fox, twelve years her senior, make him sound formidable. Already he is the junior partner in a company of City stockbrokers, he has inherited a highly desirable town house in Henley and owns a flat in London.

With his short-term commission ended and his first book attracting attention, Bruno need not feel overshadowed by such a reputation. Nevertheless, there is an air of contest here. Ever since his marriage to Zoë, it is as if Emma feels that she must match his status but the harmony between them is shattered by the two girls' antagonism. As he pours himself a drink he hears their voices: Emma's light and rather breathless – she's nervous, he thinks – and the pleasant baritone accompanying it, measured, calm, confident.

He lets them come in to him, Emma leading the way and calling out as they pass through the kitchen, and the next minute they are here. She makes the introductions, cheeks flushed with that odd blend of pride and defiance, whilst Raymond holds out a large square hand. His handsome face is oddly lacking in expression, as if it has been carved from brown, lightly pitted wood. There are already deep grooves between nose and chin and his light grey eyes are watchful. He exudes self-satisfaction and Bruno feels a childish satisfaction at being several inches taller.

'Nice little place,' Raymond says, strolling to the window. 'Damp in the winter, though, I should think, isn't it?'

'The whole of Cornwall is damp,' answers Bruno coolly, 'winter and summer alike. We have amazing varieties of fungus in the peninsula.'

He pours Emma's usual gin and tonic and holds the bottle questioningly towards Raymond.

'Got any Scotch?' he asks genially – as if he doubts that Bruno will be so sophisticated – and Bruno pours some malt whisky into a tumbler, his mouth compressed into a line of irritation. Emma hastens into speech, demanding admiration of the view, whilst Raymond smiles tolerantly but possessively upon her and Bruno writhes with embarrassment.

'Very narrow little cove, isn't it?' Raymond remarks, sipping his drink, peering downwards. 'Not easy to sail from, I imagine.'

'Not very,' answers Bruno. 'Apart from anything else there are very dangerous rocks right across the entrance.'

'Pity.' Raymond frowns judicially: already there is a black mark against St Meriadoc's viability.

'Not particularly.' Bruno comes to its defence. 'We know exactly where they are.'

'Mmm. Not very good for holidaymakers, though. And there's no real beach, is there?'

'We don't have holidaymakers here. It's a private valley.' Bruno can hear that he is being snobbish but cannot help himself. 'We live here.'

'Mmm,' says Raymond again. 'But you could make a nice little killing if you were to knock down that old boatyard and build a hotel . . .'

It is at this moment that Zoë makes her entrance, coming down the stairs, yawning a little, her black eyes taking in the scene. Her feet are bare, she wears one of Bruno's shirts and very little else, and she looks bed-rumpled and terribly sexy: in this company she is rather like a predatory, experienced tigress set down unexpectedly amongst a litter of domestic kittens. Emma's face grows sulky and cross, Raymond's hands go instinctively to his tie and Bruno begins to chuckle inwardly. He simply cannot help himself.

'Hello, love,' he says. 'All dressed ready for dinner, I see.'

Zoë's eyes wander over Emma's pretty frock and Raymond's London suit and, although she doesn't speak, Emma instantly feels frumpy and Raymond overdressed. He steps forward, however, undiminished by her glance and introduces himself.

'And I know who you are,' he adds playfully, though she has made no effort to tell him her name.

She turns away from him, reaching for the drink Bruno has poured for her. 'Everyone knows who I am,' she says indifferently. 'You didn't say we had to dress up, darling.'

Emma stares at her. 'You weren't coming up to dinner like that, were you?' She laughs, an artificial sound. 'Honestly, Zoë. Mutt would have a fit, you know she would.'

'Well, of course not,' Zoë says impatiently. 'But you're looking a bit formal for such a warm evening.'

She yawns, assessing Raymond, decides that, even for the pleasure of upsetting Emma, he isn't worth flirting with and makes a tiny bored moue.

'I'm going to have a bath,' she says, trailing away, carrying her drink, pausing to stretch on tiptoe so as to kiss Bruno. Bare-legged, the shirt only just long enough to be decent, she knows the picture it will make and cannot resist a backward glance to check out the reaction.

'Hurry.' Bruno pushes her towards the stairs, still amused at the performance, grateful for the distraction that has pre-empted a row between him and his putative brother-in-law. He sees trouble ahead.

'You can't marry him,' he tells Emma later.

'Mutt really likes him,' she says stubbornly. 'She thinks he's reliable and steady.'

'*Reliable*?' He shakes his head in disbelief. 'For God's sake, Em. Do me a favour.'

'What's wrong with being reliable?' she bristles. 'Why don't you like him?'

'Because he can't love properly,' he answers after a moment. 'There's no real warmth in him. You need to feel safe emotionally in marriage, Em.'

'You mean like you and Zoë?'

She can't resist the cutting retort: the taunt is bitter but well observed and he has no answer for it.

CHAPTER TWELVE

It was dark by the time Joss arrived back at St Meriadoc. She was later than usual, having fitted in an appointment at the end of her surgery hours: a farmer complaining of a low backache. He'd never been to an osteopath before and, as she'd welcomed him in, he'd looked faintly sheepish and rather wary. She'd sat him down beside the little desk, talking to him so as to put him at ease and, very gradually, in fits and starts, the facts had begun to emerge.

'. . . Did it ten days ago or thereabouts, diving for an old ewe . . . felt it go but couldn't stop . . . had a hot bath, not a bad night, bit uncomfortable . . . got a bit better but it never went away, then, yesterday, turned round in the Land Rover to grab my coat and, hey, the whole thing's worse again.'

She'd listened carefully to his story, asked a few questions: low backache on the right side, no pins and needles, no numbness, no radiation of pain down the leg, so probably not a disc problem. He hadn't been too happy about stripping down to his underwear and she'd gently explained that she needed to see his spinal movements but that he could put his shirt back on afterwards. She was able to work with one layer of clothing – no more – and, feeling happier, he'd soon relaxed enough to allow her to check the state of his soft tissue and joint mobility. As she worked it became clear that, as he'd lunged to the right to catch the sheep, he'd strained the lower lumbar segments and the muscles had gone into spasm to protect the area from further damage. At last, after massage, passive articulation to release the joint restriction, and then some manipulation, he'd felt a great deal easier.

His shyness had evaporated during this treatment. Joss had learned to talk as she worked, finding out more about her patients so that she could take a holistic approach to their healing. She liked to build up a picture of what kind of people they were, how they related to their environment, and so, if necessary, gently helping them towards a realization and acceptance of the need to bring their lives into balance.

This holistic approach was what had drawn her most powerfully to the work; that and seeing a young friend, almost crippled by a fall from a horse, restored gradually to health by an osteopath in Maidenhead. Joss's training – and now her practice – continued to confirm this belief and vitalize her; in her own way she was putting back into society what her father had taken from it in his lifelong meannesses and petty behaviour.

Now, driving down the narrow lane towards St Meriadoc, she chuckled as she remembered the farmer's reaction to the manipulation. He'd first looked alarmed and then laughed almost gleefully at the sound of the clicks, and he'd been very ready to make another appointment. He might need several more visits over the next two weeks but, if it had resolved itself by the next appointment, then all well and good. Joss often reminded herself of a phrase frequently used during her training: find it, fix it and leave it alone.

She parked the car and remembered with a shock that George was here. Anxiety replaced her sense of satisfaction with a good day's work and she slid silently from the car, closing the door as quietly as she could, lest Rafe or Pamela should appear. As she crossed the road and climbed the track to The Lookout, she told herself that it was foolish – that whatever might happen between George and Penny, she had done nothing of which to be ashamed – nevertheless, unease dogged her and she was glad to see the light shining out like a beacon from the great outflung window.

Bruno poured her a glass of wine and she sat down in the bentwood rocker, suddenly at ease, feeling exactly as she did in Mutt's bedroom: that they were cut off and freed from the day-to-day anxieties. She fetched a great sigh and stretched a foot to Nellie, who was lying on her back in front of the fire, looking as fluid and boneless as a bendy toy.

'Good day?' asked Bruno. 'Getting the hang of it now?'

She smiled up at him gratefully; he knew how anxious she'd been because, to begin with, she'd worked so slowly. Even after nearly two years, in her own practice she still booked an hour for each appointment, which allowed her the time to build up her picture of the patient – general health, occupation, family ties – to get down all the details before she began the examination and this way she didn't have to rush. As an assistant she was obliged to work more quickly so she felt that, at present, she was having the best of both worlds.

'I'm getting better,' she told him. 'Working a half-hour list at the practice in Bodmin is giving me confidence. One of the things I'm learning is the ability to shut down on the details of one patient before picking up on the next one. I think I'm getting a bit more efficient. I'm beginning to get a few referrals so I must be getting something right.'

Bruno sat down on the sofa and Nellie immediately leaped up gracefully beside him, curling against his side. Joss rocked herself, sipping with pleasure at the chilled Sancerre.

'You look content,' Bruno observed, raising his glass to her.

Joss thought about it. 'I am,' she agreed, sounding rather

surprised at this discovery. 'I just love my work, I suppose – why are you smiling?'

He shook his head. 'Nothing, really. Just a conversation I was having earlier with Em about the benefits of honest toil.'

'Mum didn't have much chance, really,' said Joss quickly, as if defending her mother. 'Married so young and Dad wanting her to be there all the time. There's always quite a lot of entertaining in London. Actually, I think Mum enjoys that bit.'

'I was remembering,' he said mildly, 'not criticizing.'

'I'm sure you weren't but there have been times when she's been . . . well, restless probably describes it best. And then I've wondered if it would have been better for her if she'd other things to think about apart from Dad and me.'

They sat for a while in companionable silence, watching the flames flaring and dying, whilst, in the background, Billie Holiday's husky voice singing 'No More' created an atmosphere of bittersweet melancholy. Bruno had a vast CD collection of female blues singers: Bessie Smith, Ella Fitzgerald, Lena Horne, Dinah Shore – he loved them all, playing them as he sat after supper, thinking about his characters and the worlds they inhabited, losing himself in their company.

Joss, listening to the gravelly, sexy voice, wondered why it was that, once you fell in love, it seemed that every love song might have been written for you personally.

'Since your supper plans have been cancelled,' said Bruno at last, 'can I offer you something or will you go up to the house and join Em and Mousie?'

'Oh, yes, I think so or Mum will wonder where I am.' Her face clouded. 'Sorry about that message, Bruno. You must have wondered what's been going on.'

He shrugged. 'Just a tad. Rafe sounded the least bit harassed. I gather that George has a problem. I imagine it's to do with Penny.'

Joss stared into the fire whilst he watched her consideringly: she made a rather charming picture, rather off-beat but very much her own person. From childhood her style had been eclectic: a blend of countrified bohemianism that appealed to Bruno. On anyone else the mole-coloured needlecord overshirt worn with a long charcoal-striped flannel skirt, embroidered at the hem, and the whole outfit finished off with leather ankle boots might have looked strange but Joss carried it off with her usual air of casual elegance and managed to look different and special.

'The thing is,' she said suddenly, 'that Penny wants to go back to New Zealand. She misses her family terribly and having the baby, instead of bringing her and George closer, has made that longing worse. She's been terribly depressed since she had Tasha and she just wants to be back at home amongst all the old familiar things. I can understand that, can't you?'

'Oh, yes.' Bruno answered readily. 'Home is always best when we're miserable or hurt. I suppose she and George haven't been together long enough for her to feel that that place is with him?'

'Well, he's been at sea quite a lot and they've only known each other for two years, anyway.' A pause. 'And then there's something else,' she added.

'Ah yes,' he said. 'I had a feeling there might be.'

She looked at him quickly. 'You guessed, didn't you? I wondered after that day you saw us up in the valley at the well but it's not like you might think it is.'

'I don't think it's like anything particularly.' Bruno emptied his glass. 'You and George have always been very close. Like we said just now, at times like these we turn to old friends, people we trust.'

'Mm.' She wasn't looking at him now and her voice was rather non-committal. Bruno waited, turning the empty glass between his fingers, feeling Nellie's warm weight comfortingly heavy against him. 'It's a bit more than that, though.'

Bruno smiled to himself, guessing that Joss's inherent honesty wouldn't allow her to dissemble. 'You don't have to tell me,' he told her gently. 'It's between you and George.'

'The thing is,' she said again, 'I love him. I do love him. I've tried not to but there it is. But I've never tried to influence him, if you see what I mean. I've just listened.' She looked at him anxiously. 'There's nothing wrong in that, is there?'

He grinned at her, quirking an eyebrow. 'Depends how you listened,' he said.

She laughed, as he'd meant her to, toeing off her boots, tucking her legs up on the seat and folding the soft material of her skirt round her ankles. Bruno recognized the gesture: he'd seen it so many times with Emma and with Zoë. It meant that it was confession time.

'You're utterly right,' she was admitting, combing her fingers through her shiny brown hair, her body relaxed by the wine, encouraged by the warmth and the compassion she sensed was flowing from him towards her. 'I tried to be absolutely fair but I admit that I was always on his side. We agreed that things are hard for Penny, that she needs time to adjust, that she's lonely when George is away but, underneath, I kept wanting to say, "If she really loves you, George, then she'll manage it somehow." I never actually spoke the words but it was implicit in my response to him.'

'And do you suspect George of transferring his attentions from Penny to you?'

She shook her head and then paused. 'I think George loves me,' she replied honestly, 'but he wouldn't have let it make a difference if Brett hadn't come back into the frame.'

Bruno got up, threw two logs on the fire, fetched the bottle from the table and refilled their glasses.

'You've lost me now,' he said, sitting down again. 'Who's Brett?'

Joss explained. 'And now Penny wants out. It's awful, really. Deep down inside me a tiny voice is shouting "Yes! Yes!" and punching the air because it means we can be together, but it's so complicated. What happens about Tasha? And Rafe and Pamela will be absolutely gutted. George is in a terrible position. He's told Penny that he's ready to move to New Zealand and try a new start but Penny is adamant. How can he let his baby go? But how can he keep her here?' She sighed. 'I suspect that Penny has finally pulled the plug and that's why George is here. Can you imagine anything more terrible than telling your parents this kind of news?'

She glanced at Bruno after a moment, saw that he was looking particularly sombre, and looked at her watch.

'Hell!' she said. 'Mum will be having fits. I'd better go. You won't say anything to anyone, will you, Bruno?'

'Don't be daft,' he answered impatiently, getting up to go out with her. 'Do you want me to come up to the house with you?'

'No, I'm fine. It's a fine, bright night, not properly dark at all. And thanks.'

She stood on tiptoe to kiss his cheek and he watched her walk away, swallowed up by the shadows, before he turned back into the house. Sitting down again, leaning forward to reach for the poker, it seemed that he heard other voices echoing in the shadows.

'I might as well tell you that I'm pregnant.'

'I'm going to have a baby, isn't it wonderful?'

The same news but oh, the different ways of telling it. Bruno stabbed so savagely at the logs that showers of sparks burst and exploded against the smoke-blackened stone of the wide chimney. Dropping the poker, leaning back into the sofa, he picked up his glass again and closed his eyes.

CHAPTER THIRTEEN

'I might as well tell you that I'm pregnant.' Zoë's voice is flat, and she huddles her dressing-gown around her as she sits in the rocking chair, one knee crossed over the other. Her black hair, usually so shiny, is lank, and her bare legs and feet look bird thin and sharp-boned.

Bruno sits down on the edge of the sofa, elbows on knees, his hands clasped.

'But that's wonderful,' he says, though he sounds tentative, reining in his own joy because of the expression on her face, the glum voice. 'It's fantastic.'

'Is it?' She raises his head and stares at him, her expression almost contemptuous. 'Wonderful for you, perhaps. Not for me.'

'Why not?' He longs to kneel beside her and put his arms about her but he knows Zoë in this mood. 'Why shouldn't it be wonderful for you too?'

It strikes him that she might be frightened and he is pierced with a sharp compassion for her. During the last year the gloss has been rubbed from the brilliant veneer of her popularity – the blonde British starlet, beloved of the late-sixties cinema, is now in the ascendant – and Zoë has adopted a protective air of almost insolent hauteur. It hasn't helped her pride that Bruno's second wolf-scarer has been received with great enthusiasm and it is beginning to look as though, in his own field of endeavour, he might become just as successful as she is. Unfortunately, Zoë doesn't view this likelihood with a great deal of excitement.

All these things pass through Bruno's mind as he watches her, wondering what he might say that won't affect her *amour propre*.

'Think of the effect you'll have,' he suggests. 'You'll be the first of your group to become a mother. Terrific press coverage, all the glossies will want an interview. It'll put all the others in the shade. The photographers will fight over you. After all, pregnant women are so sexy.'

He sees that behind her half-closed lids she is considering these images and he tries to think of other persuasive tactics that might comfort her. He rejects the more brutal: 'It might be a good idea for you to stay out of the limelight for a bit' or – the thing he really longs to say – 'Perhaps you might even enjoy being a mother. Stay here with me and give it a try.'

It has been impossible for Zoë to pursue her career from The Lookout so, for much of the time, they live together in their flat just off the King's Road in Cranmer's Place. Bruno, however, finds St Meriadoc a far more peaceful place to plan his books and returns to The Lookout to write. Zoë joins him regularly, relaxing from the London scene, although she often brings friends with her. It works very well to begin with but, just lately, he's begun to see a little less of her.

'Why don't you stay down here for a while?' he says carefully. 'Give yourself a holiday. We could have friends to stay. Give some pre-Christmas parties.'

He offers these entertainments, knowing that after a few days on the north Cornish coast in late November she will be bored and restless, silently cursing that this has to happen whilst he is in the middle of writing his latest book. Feeling guilty he edges forward so that he is kneeling in front of her and takes her hands.

'I wish you would, love,' he says. 'We could have fun.'

He leans forward to kiss her; her body is a frail cage of bones beneath his hands and he is moved by a protective tenderness. She responds for a moment and then draws back, smiling at him, reaching for the inevitable Sobranie.

'Pour me a drink, darling,' she says, and she curls back in the chair, staring into the fire as she lights her cigarette.

He pours some wine, wishing this could be simple, that they could both be celebrating with a shared joy. For a moment he allows himself to think about the baby: about being a father. His heart bumps with excitement and terror at the prospect and he wonders if either of them is ready for such a huge responsibility. His hands tremble as he sets down the bottle and lifts the glasses, and he is washed through with a happy pride. As he passes her the glass, he bends to touch his lips to her cheek, and she smiles again, veiling those cat-like eyes. She draws her feet up beneath the dressing-gown, threading her fingers through her short hair, and sips at the wine, flicking ash in the direction of the great granite hearthstone.

'The thing is,' she says, and her voice is full of confidentiality, 'I've been offered this part in a film.'

He watches her, trying to hide his dismay. He is not envious – merely filled with a sense of foreboding.

'What kind of part?' He is careful to keep his voice fairly neutral.

'It's the old marital triangle thing with a bit of a twist. It's very controversial stuff, actually. The man is really a homo-sexual and has a lover. The other woman is a camouflage, you see, but neither woman knows that. It's terribly sad and shows the impossible position of people who have to hide what they truly are, and it sets out to explore the prejudices and the misunderstandings that surround them.'

'It sounds good,' he says sincerely. 'I approve. And what is your role?'

'I would be cast as the other woman,' she answers, 'although it's very early days to be able to say too much about it. It's a very new film company but I think they're going places.' She hesitates, not looking at him. 'So you can see why the prospect of a baby isn't exactly a brilliant one just at the moment?'

He stares at her, disbelievingly. 'But need it make a difference? How far – ' he glances at her thin frame – 'how many months are you . . . ?'

'Two months.' She looks sulky and he is seized with fear. 'By the time we start filming it will be showing. These projects take ages, darling, you know that. I can't risk it.'

'What do you mean?'

She glances at his white angry face and looks away again.

'It's OK for you. Nothing need ever interfere with your career. I'm not ready to abandon mine yet. But I don't want to go to some back-street abortionist. You'll have to help me, Bruno.' Her voice changes, wheedling, persuasive. 'Please, darling, this means so much to me. I might never get another chance like this and we can have a baby any time.'

The row that follows is so deeply destructive that Zoë leaves for London early the next morning. Later, she tells him that the pregnancy was a false alarm but he hears through friends that someone has helped her to get rid of the baby. The film is never produced – perhaps it is too compassionate, too open-minded for the censorship board – and Zoë's career as a film star suffers the same fate as their baby.

Bruno never mentions it again but, as the years pass, and he watches Joss and George growing up, he thinks: My child would be five, seventeen, twenty-two.

When a few months later Emma says, 'I'm going to have a

baby, isn't it wonderful? Ray is out of his mind with pride,' Bruno feels as if something sharp is being twisted agonizingly deep inside him. Before the end of the following year Zoë has left him for the first in a long line of lovers.

By the time supper with Mousie and Joss had finished, and Emma reappeared at The Lookout, Bruno had moved on to Ravel's String Quartet in F major and was stretched full length on the sofa with Nellie asleep on the floor beside him.

'How was it?' he asked without getting up, raising a tumbler half full of whisky in a kind of salute, and then resting it again on his midriff. 'How's Mutt?'

Emma dropped her coat on a chair and sat down in the rocker. The tone of his voice alerted her to the fact that he was having a 'downer', as they both called it, and she wondered if he'd at last faced the fact that Mutt might not be much longer for this world.

'The doctor called in earlier,' she said. 'This wretched infection is pulling her down and she's rather weaker again this evening. The doctor says she might have some fluid on her lungs but he's convinced that the best place for her is in her own home with her family nearby.'

Bruno pushed himself upright. 'Should I go up to see her?' he asked anxiously.

'Heavens, no.' She was quite emphatic about it. 'After all, you had some time together, didn't you? She seemed very peaceful and happy once she'd seen you. Mousie will have settled her for the night by now and Joss has promised to telephone if she thinks it's necessary. I thought she was surprisingly lucid, actually. Did you find that? We had lovely little talks together through the day, just very short moments, but I was amazed at her memory for odd things. We'll go up together first thing in the morning.'

'OK.' He sat for a few seconds, staring at nothing in

particular. 'You must be very proud of Joss, Em,' he said at last. 'She's a great girl.'

She warmed to his praise but now knew what the trouble was all about. At regular periods he had downers when he thought about Zoë and the baby she'd refused to have. Her own pregnancy, coming so close on Zoë's, had caught him off guard and he'd told her about that evening and described the row that had followed his refusal to assist in the destruction of his own child.

Even now, Emma could remember the shock she'd felt and the way she'd instinctively closed her hands protectively over the new life within her: as if, in some way, Zoë's reaction had threatened her own baby. Seeing the gesture, Bruno had turned away, his face creased up with anguish, and she'd been unable to comfort him. Passionate and angry on his account, it had taken her years to see that bad-mouthing Zoë was not an answer: vilifying his ex-wife brought him no comfort. Bruno would point out that Zoë had to cope with the unfortunate character she'd inherited: once she was beyond her youth, she was unlikely to have a peaceful or happy life. Deprived of this natural outlet for her rage on Bruno's account, Emma tried to cheer him up in other ways but was unable to resist the occasional outburst.

'It must be hell to be Zoë,' was all Bruno would answer. 'Give it a break, Em.'

'You say things about Ray,' she'd grumble.

'You're right,' he'd say, grinning at her. 'It must be hell to be Brer Fox too.'

'He hates you calling him that,' she'd say. 'He thinks it's affected.'

'He expects me to be affected. He has his own preconceived idea of a man who writes novels and I don't like to disappoint him.'

Now, watching him, Emma was unable to think of anything that could be of comfort. Instead she said warmly, 'I'm terribly proud of Joss. It's lovely to see her with Mutt. I know I shouldn't say this, Bruno, but I have this dream of Joss living at Paradise. I keep hoping she'll meet someone special and settle down. After all, she could have her patients to the house, couldn't she? No neighbours to worry about, plenty of parking space, and she could use the dining-room as a consulting room. That old back road to the house could be reopened so that patients didn't have to drive through St Meriadoc.'

'I feel we're jumping the gun a bit, don't you?'

She looked guilty. 'Oh, I'm not wishing Mutt's life away. Of course I'm not. Anyway, it's just as much her dream as mine, I promise you.'

'Have you any idea what's in her will?'

Emma shook her head. 'But it was always settled, wasn't it? You have The Lookout and The Row and I have Paradise.'

'I suppose Mutt might have other ideas. You might get The Row and the boatyard.'

'God, I hope not,' said Emma involuntarily. She glanced quickly at Bruno but he'd leaned forward to stroke the recumbent Nellie and wasn't looking at her. 'It's simply that Ray would be a pain in the neck,' she said, laughing a little, making light of it. 'You know how he's always said that we should pull down the old buildings and build a hotel there.'

'But since that means destroying the quality of life for everyone in The Row, I imagine he'd see that it's not an option.'

'Oh, you know Ray. He thinks that Rafe and Pamela and Mousie would be just as happy in nice new bungalows in Polzeath.' She sighed. 'He has no idea. The trouble is he's such a juggernaut once he's got an idea in his head. Of course I don't agree with it for a moment and it certainly wouldn't improve our relationship.'

'He wouldn't want to sell Paradise?'

She hesitated. 'Probably not as long as he thought Joss was getting it. God, it does make him sound a bit of a shit, doesn't it? But you know Ray.'

'Yes,' he answered grimly, 'I know Ray. And, as I've said before, none of it is his to do anything with, either now or in the future.'

'I know that,' Emma said rather crossly, 'but it's simply not that easy. When he gets a bee in his bonnet he goes on and on until I'm worn down with it. This would be rather different, of course,' she added hastily.

'Of course,' Bruno agreed drily. He felt that it was time to change the subject. 'Have you seen George?' he asked casually.

'No.' She was distracted at once. 'But Mousie thinks that this isn't just an ordinary visit.'

'Really?'

Emma kicked off her shoes and tucked her legs up on the chair. 'Mousie has this idea that there's a problem between him and Penny . . .'

He let her talk but, although he nodded, raised his eyebrows, made all the right responses, his thought were busy elsewhere and his heart felt constricted with anxiety and dread.

CHAPTER FOURTEEN

Lying in bed, clasping each other for comfort, Rafe slept at last, whilst Pamela listened to his regular breathing, counting the steady beat of his heart. Her thoughts flicked to and fro, sharp as a needle through a tapestry, pinning a thought here, fixing a memory there. The evening had been an agony: the three of them agreeing that to discuss the problem any further – once every angle had been explored – was simply counter-productive and they'd attempted to talk of other things. Earlier in the afternoon George had taken himself off for a walk and she and Rafe had sat together in the kitchen, silent with shock and misery.

'What does he look like?' she'd asked.

'Preoccupied,' Rafe had answered after much thought. 'He's clearly distressed but at the same time he's holding himself very much in check.'

He'd paused and she could imagine his own focused ex-pression as he attempted to describe their son. Rafe had always felt it vital to communicate as much detail as possible so that she shouldn't feel isolated and, indeed, Pamela's blindness had opened up new vistas for him.

'Describe it,' she'd cry: the valley softly greening into its spring colours; the sea on a wild moonlit night; the sky in the early dawning of a summer morning.

'Well, it's a very pale blue,' he'd begin cautiously, 'with streaks of glorious colour. You know what it's like just before the sun rises? Those orange banners flaming across the sky? Although there's crimson and gold as well as orange now I really look at it. And there are some little puffy white clouds. Well, actually, they aren't just white, there's a kind of blue rinse to them and a greenish shadow . . .'

Gradually, the more he'd looked the more he'd seen and his stumbling tongue began to rise to the occasion, eloquently painting the scenes for her as she stood beside him, calling up her own memories, seeing them again in her mind's eye embellished by his descriptions. She'd become acutely aware of sounds, of the different textures beneath her feet; conscious of currents of air that indicated an open door or the feel of the sunshine as she passed a window. They'd learned, after one or two painful accidents, that doors must be left wide open or kept completely shut, that furniture must never be moved out of its familiar place. Food might be a lucky dip on the plate or what Rafe called 'clock-face'.

'Carrots at twelve, potatoes at three, meat at six, broccoli at nine,' he'd say.

The one thing she missed most was being able to see the faces of her family and, in his longing to help her, Rafe had worked hard to become her eyes on these occasions.

'He looked as if he was hating every minute of it,' he'd said, forcing his recalcitrant mind to identify his son's expression. 'Humiliated. And he looked angry . . .'

He'd paused, aware of his shortcomings, knowing that Pamela would have seen a million tiny things that he'd missed. She'd waited, not wanting to prompt him, waiting for confirmation of that clue she'd picked up on earlier.

'He looked,' he'd cried suddenly, on a burst of inspiration, 'just like he did when he was seventeen and Jeremy MacCann beat him by one point at that school quiz and won the ticket for the Twickenham rugby match. Remember Jeremy admitted that he'd picked his father's brains on one of the questions? And afterwards, though George was gutted that he'd lost because of that one answer and angry because Jeremy cheated, he said, "But I can't really blame him. I know how he feels about it. We'd all kill to get a ticket to see the Army and Navy match at Twickers." That's how he looked. Cheated and cross but with a kind of . . . compassion.'

Pamela had felt a surge of conviction, a similar reaction to her earlier response: that George, along with a natural sense of being hard done by, was feeling an unusual sympathy for Penny's dilemma. She'd tried a shot in the dark.

'I think we were right to put Joss off, don't you?' she'd asked, carefully keeping her voice neutral.

'Oh, yes,' Rafe had answered at once: his voice indicated that he had no suspicions here. 'It would be very uncomfortable, everyone trying to pretend that things were normal. Embarrassing for George.'

'You don't think Joss might know? She and George have always been very close.'

She'd listened to him considering this, tapping lightly on the table with the pencil he'd been using earlier to do the crossword.

'I suppose that's possible.' It was clearly a new idea. 'But even if she does I still think it's not the time for a jolly family supper.'

Pamela had been relieved by Rafe's answer. If George was having an affair with Joss she felt certain that even Rafe would have noticed something: severally and jointly Joss and George had been in and out of the house all their lives but Pamela believed in the old saying: 'Love and a cough cannot be hid.' If they'd become lovers surely one of them would have let something slip? And Joss and Penny were such good friends –

and Joss was Tasha's godmother. At the thought of her grandchild Pamela had been seized with fresh misery.

'Oh, what shall we do?' she'd cried. 'If Penny goes back to New Zealand with this man we shall never see Tasha again.'

'What we mustn't do is make it any harder for George than it is already,' Rafe had answered firmly. 'What choice does he have, poor fellow? The child must be with her mother – and it's no good feeling guilty because we can't offer her a home. It simply wouldn't be fair on Tasha.' A pause. 'I suppose she *is* George's baby?'

'Rafe!'

'Well,' he'd sounded irritable, not wishing to be accused, 'if Penny's been in love with this man all this time . . . George is away quite a lot, isn't he?'

'But surely . . . didn't you say that Tasha had a look of George?'

'I might have done,' he'd said crossly, as if she'd been trying to catch him out, 'but, let's face it, a three-month-old baby doesn't really look like anyone particularly, does it?'

Now, lying wakeful in the dark, she wondered if this thought had crossed George's mind and she felt a new sense of compassion for him. Exhausted by the emotions of the day, comforted by Rafe's rhythmical breathing and relaxed by the warmth of his body, she fell at last into an uneasy sleep.

Across the landing, George lay propped about with pillows, his legs stretched out, lacking the will even to undress and climb into the bed. It had been just as bad as he'd expected, probably because he felt most unhappily divided and was afraid that his mother might have divined his dilemma.

'Is there someone else?' she'd asked – and although he'd answered truthfully, it hadn't been the whole truth. Yet how could he have involved Joss when there was nothing more physical between them than a look, a sudden realization of belonging followed by a sense of overwhelming loss? That it should be Joss, his childhood companion, his second cousin, with whom he should discover himself in love! During the holidays they'd been inseparable and the adults tended to refer to them as if they were a unit. It was always 'George and Joss'; 'Joss and George'. Whilst his elder siblings had fought and shouted their way through childhood and adolescence – rivalling each other, vying for attention, determined to be best, first, strongest – George and Joss had pottered quietly on the sidelines: making play-houses up the valley beside the Saint's Well; riding their bicycles in the hot, sunken lanes; learning to sail the small Mirror dinghy in the rocky waters of the narrow cove.

George cursed himself for a fool: for not seeing what had been before his eyes. There had been a gap, he comforted himself, when he'd gone off to BRNC in Dartmouth and Joss was still at school, followed by her four years of training whilst he was joining his ship and going to sea. During those years they'd lost touch, childhood over and finished with but nothing yet to put in its place. The blow had fallen when he'd been helping her to clear out what had once been the store-rooms and offices for the boatyard. Her grandmother had agreed that Joss could rent this tiny end cottage, so long as she refurbished it and made it habitable, and he'd come to lend a hand whilst Penny, six months' pregnant, was next door having an afternoon rest, and his parents were clearing up after lunch. He'd reached to lift an old desk, carrying it with Joss to the door, and it had unexpectedly crumbled into pieces and crashed to the floor in a powdery, worm-ridden explosion. Joss had shrieked and clutched at him and they'd roared with laughter – and then looked at each other, still holding on, the silence lengthening. Shocked, they'd each turned away, working quickly, silently, until George had said that he'd better go back and see if Penny was awake and Joss, without looking at him, had agreed that he ought. For a while they'd avoided each other as much as was possible without arousing suspicion within the family, and it was not until after Tasha was born that he'd continued to confide in Joss; to be comforted by her unobtrusive presence in the background of his life. And now what . . . ?

George swore aloud, got off his bed and, with brisk, economical movements, began to undress.

CHAPTER FIFTEEN

With supper over and Emma gone off to The Lookout, Joss and Mousie cleared up together; Mousie washing whilst Joss dried and put away, talking over the events of the day together. Joss had got herself into a yawning fit, eyes streaming, and Mousie put a sympathetic arm about her shoulders.

'Go and run a hot bath and soak for a while,' she suggested. 'You look exhausted and I'm not surprised. You've worked a long day and there's nothing more tiring than people, especially people who are in pain. I'll go and get your grandmother settled for the night and then you can both get some rest.'

Shaken by another great yawn, Joss gratefully agreed to this plan, returning Mousie's hug before trailing away upstairs. Presently Mousie heard the bathroom door close and the sound of water gushing in the cistern. She finished tidying the kitchen and crossed to the drawing-room to gather her belongings together, pausing to put the photograph carefully at the back of her capacious bag so that it shouldn't be creased. After that initial look at the wedding picture Emma had been moved to fetch other albums of photographs from

114

the bookcase in the parlour and, whilst they'd waited for the doctor, they'd turned the pages together.

'Old photographs are so sad,' Emma had sighed. 'All that hope and innocence. And somehow much more poignant in black and white, don't you think so?'

Looking at a snapshot of Rafe and a youthful Pamela smiling at the baby Olivia, Mousie could only agree. She'd wondered if Emma might think to mention the wedding photograph to Joss, and had experienced an unidentifiable clutch of fear, but Emma had been more interested in discussing George's arrival, although Joss had looked too tired and strained to add anything to her mother's speculation. Now, as she picked up her reading spectacles and slung them round her neck, Mousie wished she could identify this anxiety that touched her heart with icy fingers and squeezed her gut: it was something that stretched back to those early days after Mutt's arrival at St Meriadoc, something to do with her silent wariness. Mousie drew out the letter from the young American and stared down at it. What had happened to Madeleine Grosjean?

The name had clearly meant nothing to Emma but it suddenly occurred to Mousie that Bruno might have the answer. He'd been not yet five years old when the small family had left India but old enough to remember a family friend; perhaps if she showed him the photograph it might jog a memory. Again, that tiny tug of fear. Of course, she could simply consign the letter and the photograph to the fire, and that would be the end of it, yet she had the feeling that they hadn't heard the last of the young American. She glanced at the signature at the foot of the page: Dan Crosby. She remembered the enthusiasm and hope in his face and the set of his jaw: he didn't have the appearance of someone who gave up too easily. Perhaps it would be more sensible to discover the truth as far as it was possible, so that they were ready for him.

She thought about Mutt. 'I think that time is short,' the doctor had told her privately. 'Though at this stage there's a borderline between getting better or worse and one can never quite tell – but she doesn't seem to be improving. Anyway, there's nothing more could be done for her if we got her into hospital and, in my opinion, this is where she needs to be – at home with her family nearby. Don't panic them – it could be a few more days – and keep her as quiet as possible. You can call me any time.'

Perhaps it had been wrong to allow Emma to go back to The Lookout but she hadn't wanted to frighten her or Bruno and there was nothing any of them could do for Mutt now, except to keep her comfortable and secure. Just as some instinct cast a shadow of disquiet across Dan Crosby's visit so now Mousie felt that tonight Mutt should be left in peace with her grand-daughter. Having made this decision she went upstairs and into Mutt's bedroom.

The fire had burned low and the screen shielded the bed from the lamp, so that the room was shadowed and peaceful, but Mutt was awake, stiffening eagerly as she watched the door open – as if she waited for someone. Mousie crossed to the bed and stood looking down at her, all those old instincts alive and pressing in upon her consciousness. Questions crowded to her lips but the sight of the elderly, frail woman aroused her compassion and prevented her from asking them. Instead she said: 'I'm going to give you your medicine and settle you comfortably and then I think I shall go home, Honor. Will you be happy with Joss to look after you?'

She saw a slight sagging of the thin, square shoulders, a relaxation of the old bones, as if Mutt were in some way relieved, and Mousie smiled mischievously as she held the small measure to her lips.

'Glad to see the back of me, are you? Well, I don't blame you.' She laid her back against the pillows and made certain that the ankle was supported. 'You've probably had more than enough of my bullying and fussing over the last six weeks.'

'No, no. Not that.' Mutt reached out a hand and Mousie took it. 'Nothing like that. Thank you for everything, Mousie.'

She hesitated as if wanting to say more and then shook her head, denying herself the luxury, but she looked distressed and the pressure on Mousie's hand increased. Mousie thought she understood: she and Mutt had never been overdemonstrative with each other and it would be difficult at this late stage for her to be effusive with her gratitude or affection. Nevertheless, she had a fleeting thought that Mutt was on the brink of some other disclosure and Mousie wondered if it should be encouraged.

'I should like to thank you too,' she told Mutt. 'Not many people would have been as generous as you've been, Honor, to me and all my family, letting us stay in our cottages at ridiculous rents. Don't think we're not grateful.'

She realized that there was a ring of finality in her words, as if she might not have the chance to say these things after this evening but, before she could decide how to proceed, Joss came in behind her. Mousie turned to her with relief, the difficult moment over, and explained that she was on her way home. She kissed Mutt, everything easy and natural again with Joss looking on, said goodnight and went away downstairs.

Left alone with her grandmother Joss felt a tiny thrill of fear. Oddly, the old woman looked quite serene yet Joss felt some kind of impending peril: she knew, even before Mutt spoke, the words that she would say.

'Have you found the letters, darling?'

Joss shook her head, praying for some kind of release from her promise, wishing that Mousie had not gone home.

'In my desk.' She closed her eyes. Joss hesitated and Mutt's eyes opened suddenly. 'Give me a kiss before you go.'

Joss touched the dry lips with her own, trying to hide her anxiety, smiling down at her grandmother.

'I'll be in later when I've found them,' she said. 'Ring the bell if you need me.'

'Bless you, darling. It's all for you, remember.' Mutt sounded drowsy and she appeared to sink further into her pillows. 'I want you to have Paradise.'

Joss paused at the door, but Mutt seemed to be falling asleep, and she went out, closing it quietly behind her. She descended the stairs slowly, shrinking from the task ahead, fearing what she might find, and crossed the hall to the small parlour. The kneehole desk, where generations of Trevannions had sat to write their letters, stood squarely beneath the window and Joss pulled the curtains across the black, cold glass panes before sitting down on the battered revolving chair. The bottom left-hand drawer was full of catalogues – Mutt had shopped a great deal by mail order in the last few years – but in the right-hand drawer were some battered brown files with the words 'School Reports' scrawled across in biro. The first file was headed 'Bruno', the second one 'Emma', and they were wedged rather firmly down in the drawer so that she had to tug at them to get them out. Beneath them was a pile of letters, some loose but with their pages neatly folded whilst others had been pushed into envelopes.

With her heart beating painfully against her side, Joss drew the papers out, piling them onto the desk, recognizing her grandmother's handwriting. Not love letters, then, unless they were Mutt's own, returned to her. Joss was struggling with herself, trying not to look at them, but knowing that she must at least see to whom the letters were written, although even this small act of curiosity made her hot with guilt. Yet they were a piece of Mutt, these letters: they contained her thoughts and were part of her history. Would Mutt want her to destroy them? To burn them, perhaps, on the fire in her bedroom? Joss began to realize that it would be impossible simply to consign Mutt's words to the flames without glancing at one or two of them. As if to postpone this treachery she picked up an envelope and held it under the light of the anglepoise lamp. 'Mrs Vivian Crosby' . . . She selected another one and then another; they were all addressed to the same person.

One of the open letters was dated 30 June 1947 and headed simply 'Paradise'. Her eyes fled across the words, skipping whole sentences, frightened of what they might discover, yet unbearably curious.

Vivi, darling

I write these letters in the evenings when the children are in bed . . . It comforts me to write to you like this . . .

To be absolutely honest with you, Vivi, it's the least bit terrifying. The real problem is that, once you start down a road like this, things get away with you and carry you along with them . . .

. . . Oh, Vivi, this is the exhausting part. I have to be so vigilant. And the real danger comes not from him but from Hubert's cousin Mousie . . .

Puzzled, Joss glanced swiftly through the rest of the letter, hoping to pick up some clue to this fear, and then reached for another.

Darling Vivi,

This is the last letter I shall write to you, exactly one year since I first arrived at Paradise. After all, this had to be part of the acceptance, didn't it? . . . I suppose if I am to fully commit I must finish with Madeleine Grosjean. After all, she disappeared out there in India . . .

Impatiently she seized another. It was quite short, describing a blackberrying outing and a picnic with Bruno and Emma, but it was the last page that caught Joss's attention.

Anyway, a good day here in Paradise. I wonder if ever I will show it to you. Oh, what joy to imagine you here, if only I could see you face to face, Vivi, and explain it all properly. You would understand, I know you would.

God bless you, darling.

All my love, Madeleine

Holding the page in her hand, Joss stared ahead, brow furrowed. Madeleine. Her grandmother's names were Honor Elizabeth yet these letters were certainly in her handwriting. And surely she'd already mentioned Madeleine Grosjean . . . Confused, oddly frightened, Joss began to sort the letters, checking the dates and stacking them into some kind of chronological order, resisting the temptation to pick one out at random. Once she'd achieved this object she went upstairs and into the Porch Room. Mutt was sleeping deeply, her face peaceful, and Joss was loath to disturb her. She went back down to the hall, listened for a moment at the bottom of the stairs, and then crossed into the kitchen. As she waited for the kettle to boil she paced to and fro, debating with herself, fighting the temptation.

Presently she carried her mug of tea back to the study. Here in this quiet room, where Mutt's presence and influence were most to be found, Joss opened the first letter and began to read. Her face intent, elbows resting on the desk, shock slowly merged with fascinated disbelief as her grandmother's story began to unfold.

PART TWO

Paradise

St Meriadoc

Cornwall

8th June 1947

Vivi, darling,

Yes, this is where I am. In Paradise. Will you ever believe the things that have happened to me? To be honest, I don't know where to start my story – or at least *how* to start. In one way it seems very adventurous, romantic, the stuff films are made of, and then again, it could look shabby and underhand. Now that I need to write it down, the adventurous feeling is fading and the *wrongness* – and the danger! – of what I have done presents itself more forcefully. I am masquerading as another woman, you see. I am no longer Madeleine Uttworth – or Madeleine Grosjean, that was – I am Honor Trevannion. And Lottie is no longer Charlotte Uttworth but Emma Trevannion.

They died, you see – first Hubert, then Emma, then Honor – in Karachi on the way to catch the boat. Hubert hadn't yet been discharged and he was coming back to Multan but he was determined to get Honor and the children away. They were to spend a week in Karachi so that Honor could do some shopping, spend their last few days on holiday together, but then Hubert fell ill. I think it was botulism, probably from some tinned food. It was certainly quick enough. Honor managed to get a telephone call to the hospital in Multan asking me to come to them, to help her with the children. I packed my few portable treasures and caught the first train out. Oh God! I shall never forget that journey, the crush of people, the noise and the heat, Lottie bored, cross, thirsty – I thought it would never end. I can still recall certain images as we passed through the Sind: the brown dry scrub on the dunes, a sand-coloured camel, the sense of absolute stillness. There were little mud villages, flat-roofed, quiet – and then an unexpected splash of colour – a bright, singing red as a woman appeared between the huts. When the train stopped to replenish the water, and we got off to stretch our legs, the heat seemed to deaden voices, weighing down upon us, killing the desire to speak. On again and, at the edge of a flood of water like brown stew, a man, dressed all in black, sitting on his horse: man and horse both immobile, indifferent, watching the train pass on its journey to Karachi.

And by the time we got there, Hubert and Emma were dead and Honor was ill. There was a young Indian doctor with her, rather out of his depth and very relieved to see me. He promised to return in the morning but by then Honor was dead. He made out the certificate and hurried away again, leaving me to deal with everything else.

It was Honor who told me to use the tickets to get us back to England. I'd been in such a dither wondering what to do (I'd written to you by now, of course, but I just had this feeling, though your letter was very practical and charitable, Vivi, that you couldn't quite see me and Lottie fitting in with your new life in America) and, as you know, things are bad in India: riots, killings, and Multan in particular is a trouble spot. In March, after some particularly ghastly murders, the Army was brought in and introduced a twenty-four-hour curfew. Honor begged me to get Bruno back to Cornwall.

'It is what Hubert would have wanted,' she said again. 'He'd want you all to be safe.'

He'd been so unhappy about Lottie and me staying on. 'If you haven't sorted something out with your sister in America by the time I go home then you're coming with me,' he'd said. He was such a super person, Vivi. So alive, so confident, and so generous. You know, I couldn't believe that Hubert would die . . .

Poor Bruno, poor little boy. He'd lost all his family in a matter of days and we were all that he had left. Lottie and me. And I'd lost my two dearest friends and little baby Em. I tried not to allow my own grief to show because of the need to comfort poor Bruno but I was frightened about what would happen to the three of us – and then, quite suddenly, the way seemed so clear. There, in that hotel room where Hubert first became ill, were all their papers: the tickets, the Trevannion family passports. I don't think that Honor had been thinking things through clearly, she was too ill, but she'd been insistent that I should get us all on the boat somehow. My idea was that we should actually become that family, the three of us together. I thanked God that they'd called me Mutt. M. Uttworth, do you see? Muttworth. Mutt. It was Hubert who'd started it and Bruno thought it was terrific fun – even Lottie chanted Mutt, Mutt, rather than Mum, Mum. Honor never quite got used to it and continued to call me Madeleine – but Honor was dead.

I explained to Bruno that someone might take him away from us if they didn't believe I was his mother – oh, I wasn't deliberately trying to frighten him, Vivi, I really thought we might be separated, that I wouldn't be able to use their tickets, and I wanted to get us out. What else was I to do? Take them back up-country to the hospital and try to go on working, with two babies to look after and the British about to be thrown out at any moment? Send Bruno, not yet five, home on his own? It was a kind of revelation, standing in that hot, sticky hotel room, with Lottie wailing and Bruno, silent and afraid, curled up on the bed beside her, watching me. The means to escape was right there under my hands with Hubert's and Honor's blessing. Paradise or Karachi? Which would you have chosen, Vivi?

Perhaps there was another way. Perhaps I should have gone to the Commissioner and explained or talked to the purser on the ship, but I didn't. The ship was due to sail, packed to the last square inch with people trying to get out, and I wanted to be on it, not sitting in that stuffy, fly-ridden room, helplessly tied up with red tape. And we *were* on it: Mrs Honor Trevannion and her two children. Almost at once I saw the danger. Some of the women wanted to talk to Bruno and I knew that he was frightened of saying something he shouldn't. Oh, the poor darling! I kept thinking: Let's just get home and then I'll try to think more sensibly about all this, but meanwhile, those kind women, mainly army, accepted that Bruno and I were just too shocked and grief-stricken to be able to communicate properly. At that point I could still barely take it in that I'd lost the two people dearest to me: my closest friends. In the end the other passengers left us to ourselves and this gave us a little breathing space to adjust.

Somewhere in the Indian Ocean Lottie became Emma. Remembering to call her Emma wasn't too difficult for Bruno – she was so like his own little sister that he'd often muddled their names – but it was very hard for me. I felt that I'd killed her. But when I saw Paradise, Vivi, I knew I'd made the right decision and Bruno is back where he belongs. I shall look after him, never fear. I loved Honor as if she'd been my sister, and I shall love Bruno as if he were my own son.

How I wish I could see you, again, and meet your American husband. Will it ever happen, do you think? God bless you, darling.

Your loving sister,

Madeleine

Paradise
17th June 1947

Vivi, darling,

I'm wondering whether to keep the first letter until I've written a bit more and then send it all on to you. When I read the letter through I realized I hadn't told you about the actual homecoming and I dithered, wondering whether to post it just as it was or to add some more. Anyway, I decided to wait a bit so that you can get a fuller picture of what happened and see how I finally finished up here at Paradise. You must believe that I fully intended to give myself a day or two, once we got to Liverpool, to reconsider the whole situation. After all, it wasn't too late and I wanted to be absolutely certain that it was right for all three of us. I prayed about it, Vivi. Do you remember Sister Julian at the convent? Oh, how we loved her. During those long weeks of the sea voyage I found myself thinking about her, remembering things she said to us when we were children, but does God hear us, do you think, if we're deliberately deceiving people?

What I didn't expect was to be met at the dock. There we were, struggling with cases, ~~Lottie~~ Emma screaming her head off, and suddenly this man appeared. He was so kind, so quick. He dealt with the porters and swept us through Customs and into a taxi. Simon Dalloway.

'Hubert asked me to get you sorted out this end,' he said. 'I've only just heard the sad news. I am so terribly sorry . . .'

Something like that. I can't remember his exact words, I was too shocked. Fortunately, so was he. Apparently the purser had explained the whole situation about Hubert's sudden death to him and he completely took over: sent a telegram to Cornwall, hurried us away. It was all taken out of my hands. That's when it first began, you see. I'd told that first untruth to get us on the ship, I'd said I was Honor, that Lottie was Emma, and now it was impossible to admit the truth. And what about Bruno? I felt responsible for him – more than that: I'd promised Honor that I'd look after him and I love Bruno as if he were my own child.

Simon was kind, so kind. So sweet to Bruno and Emma, very gentle with us all, putting my confusion down to grief. I went along with it, let him shepherd us all on to the train bound for Bristol. He'd got the tickets, organized a hamper, and I suddenly realized that Honor would have known that this had all been planned for her and the children. Following Hubert's instructions Simon had booked us into the Royal Hotel for the night before the final leg of the journey to Cornwall the next day. At dinner, with the children in bed, he talked about St Meriadoc – and the pitfalls began to open at my feet – but, even then, I felt I could manage. It was when he began to talk about Hubert, how they'd been at school and gone on to train together, that I began to see that, although I knew Hubert very well, I didn't know him in the same way as a wife would know him. The thought of Hubert – thinking of what I'd lost – reduced me to tears and, like the army wives on the ship, Simon backed off sharply at the sight of them. I was still so shocked by grief, oh, the horror of waking to it new each morning; and the realization that I'd never see Honor or Hubert or baby Em again was terrible.

Bruno had had a strained, wary look while Simon was with us, and I was afraid that the deception might be too much for him, but I also wondered what might be waiting for him in Cornwall. I decided that it was only right to escort him home and see what awaited him there. There was still time to tell the truth. I even found myself wondering if they might take me on as a nanny.

I can imagine your face, Vivi, the shaking of your head. It was always you, wasn't it, that stopped me plunging into trouble, making a fool of myself. I thought of writing to you the first time Johnny disappeared but something stopped me writing then; admitting to you that Johnny had let us down. I felt ashamed and couldn't bring myself to write the words. I could imagine your old, critical way of looking at me that was rather like Mother's judgemental, assessing glance at our father when he'd been overgenerous with presents for us or had drunk a little too much wine. Sensible, steady people don't seem to realize that when you've been a fool you don't need anyone to rub it in: you feel quite inadequate enough without that. When I received your answer to my letter, back there in Multan, I sensed your anxiety; that you didn't really want your destitute sister and her child rocking the boat of your shiny new life. I didn't blame you for that. Despite writing to each other and exchanging photographs over the last eight years, we'd drifted a bit, hadn't we? Me, with my missionary zeal, rushing away to be a nurse in India and you enrolling in a secretarial course and then joining the WAAF when war broke out. Neither you nor Mother approved of my going to India, did you? You thought there was something histrionic, not quite suitable about the whole thing. Honor said that her people felt exactly the same. She was an only child and her parents were killed in the Blitz. When you wrote to tell me that Mother had died of that ghastly cancer Honor was such a brick. She and Hubert saw me through so many things. What would she think of me now, I wonder. I'm sure she'd see that I'm thinking of Bruno, trying to do what Hubert wanted.

Do you remember *Goblin Market*, Vivi? You were Lizzie, weren't you, 'Full of wise upbraidings'? And I was Laura, tempted by forbidden fruit. I still have the copy you gave me for my fifteenth birthday. I've always kept it with me and it was one of the very few things I brought from Multan in that hastily packed bag. Remember that Easter holiday, Vivi, just before the war broke out? I was torn between becoming a missionary or eloping with Robert Talbot and you would wait up for me each evening with those 'wise upbraidings'.

Dear, you should not stay so late,
Twilight is not good for maidens;

129

Should not loiter in the glen
In the haunts of goblin men.

It always makes me think of you letting me in through the garden door, both of us weeping with silent laughter as we crept upstairs, quiet as mice so as not to wake Mother. But you were right about Robert. Because of him I lost my longing for God and fell between all the stools in the end. What a fool I was, Vivi . . .

I miss you so much.

My love, darling.

Madeleine

Paradise
30th June 1947

Vivi, darling,

I write these letters in the evenings when the children are in bed and Hubert's father is in the drawing-room reading the newspaper or listening to the wireless. I haven't posted the other two letters yet. Silly, isn't it? It comforts me to write to you, like this, but I'm still drawn to the idea of building up the picture as a whole. I've decided to bring you right up to date and then send them all off together.

To be absolutely honest with you, Vivi, it's the least bit terrifying. The real problem is that, once you start down a road like this, things get away with you and carry you along with them. Arriving here with Simon, it seemed suddenly impossible to explain the situation. Hubert's father, James, was so pleased to see us all and so overcome by the sight of the children. Over and over again he'd touch Emma's hair or tip Bruno's chin so as to look at him. 'Just like Hubert at that age,' he'd say. And you could see that he was struggling to keep back the tears.

He is a darling old boy, often with his head in a book and rather frail, but you could see that the children were like a breath of new life to him. There was never quite the right moment to explain to him at the beginning and, as each day passes, it becomes more and more impossible. It seems as though I might destroy some of the comfort he's getting from it. And he loves Emma. She makes him laugh; she is so natural and takes everything in her stride. I really feel that it would be almost cruel to take her away and leave him and Bruno by themselves.

We don't talk too much about Hubert: James is typical of the stiff-upper-lip generation – remember Mother after Papa left us? Nothing is to be talked about which might be classed as emotional – but he loves to hear about Hubert's work. That's easy for me, of course, because I worked with him for six years but I still have to watch what I say and this is the exhausting part. I have to be so vigilant. And the real danger comes not from him but from Hubert's cousin Mousie. I had no idea that there would be other people apart from Hubert's immediate family – and I knew that he was an only child and that his mother had died – so you can imagine the shock to find an aunt and two cousins living ten minutes away! The aunt is a kindly soul and Rafe is a fairly standard fourteen-year-old boy, still at school, but his older sister is a different proposition.

Oh, Vivi, can you imagine anyone more observant, more judgemental, than a seventeen-year-old girl? Mousie loved her cousin Hubert and she is critical of his widow – and there are so many tiny traps, zigzagging across my path like the sticky strands of a spider's web. I get caught in them and then I have to twist and turn and struggle to extricate myself. She watches me, as if puzzled, and I am frightened of her.

'You!' I hear you cry. 'You've never been frightened in your life.' Oh, but that was before I had my baby, Vivi. Once you have a baby you have a hostage to fortune and nothing is ever the same again. But now I have found Paradise and I can tell you that it is worth the struggle. I want to describe it so that you can picture us here. Paradise is part of a small estate, you see, hidden in a sheltered valley. It's approached from a long deep lane which plunges down and down, with glimpses through farm gates of the sea and of high, wild cliffs. Down you go, between two grassy banks, high and straight as a wall with a wild thorny hedge on top, until you run into the little cove. It's U-shaped, like a narrow horseshoe, as if the sea has crept up secretly one night and taken a bite from the land. First, on the seaward side, there's a boatyard that is no longer used and next to it a row of four cottages, called – imaginatively – The Row. Each has its wash-house, like a rather large porch, extending into the small yard in front, and running along behind them, just one big step from the door, is the sea-wall. This is the north coast, Vivi, and the houses turn their backs to the wild Atlantic. Across the road from the cottages there is an old quarry and this secret magical valley widens and runs inland. High up in this valley is St Meriadoc's Well: a tiny, bubbling spring, half hidden beneath a few granite slabs, moss-grown and half buried in tall, feathery grasses. A thousand years ago the saint's disciple built a cell beside the well and this is all that is left of it. Mallow still grows here, eight feet high with big rosy-purple flowers, and I like to think the disciple used it as a medicine. Its sap can be used as a soothing ointment and its leaves to draw out wasp-stings. There's comfrey nearby too, and Aaron's rod. On a hot June afternoon it is possible to imagine him here at the door of his cell, watching the kestrel that hangs motionless in the dazzling blue air above him and listening to the lark, as he prepares his simple meal or sweeps the bare floor of his cell with a twiggy broom made from the branches of the tamarisk trees which cling along the valley's sides.

The spring grows into a little stream that runs down towards the sea and beneath a little bridge, so narrow that you can only just drive a car across it, and which divides this cove with its row of cottages and the boatyard from Paradise and The Lookout, a Victorian folly built halfway up the cliff, rather like a miniature lighthouse. It's a funny old place, perched high on the rocks as if defying the gales and the tides, but empty at present. Beyond the bridge, the path splits into two: one branch goes up to The Lookout, and then on across the cliffs, and the other takes you along the lane and through the big gateway into the driveway to Paradise. At last, we are here, Vivi, on 'The Walk to the Paradise Gardens'. Hubert loved that music, you know. There was an Englishness about Delius, he said, that transported him back to all he missed most and he had a record of *A Village Romeo and Juliet* and 'On hearing the first cuckoo in spring'. I grew to love it too. Anyway, here is Paradise, Vivi, which is now my home.

Imagine, then, a tiny Queen Anne house, grey stone washed white, slate-roofed. It has a demure look, like a very smart doll's house and it is set amongst a great climbing tangle of rhododendrons, although across the gravel from the front door is a little lawn, green as an emerald, but plush and soft underfoot. I was in time to see the rhododendrons in flower, Vivi, creamy white, crimson, and a yellow one with the most heavenly scent that I can smell from my bedroom window. The rooms are cool and elegant: drawing-room and dining-room on either side of the long hall and behind them the kitchen – square, roomy, looking north – and a charming little parlour behind the drawing-room which James uses as an office.

He lets me sit here at this lovely old desk to write my letters but I should like to have all this clutter out and make it such a pretty little room. I call him James, Vivi. He asked if I would like to call him 'Father' but how could I? I thought at once of our father and knew that it would be impossible. The word stuck in my throat. I feared that he might think 'James' too informal but, luckily, he rather likes it. I think it makes him feel young again, and rather dashing. I tease him a little, very gently, deferring to him over certain things – my hat for church, a frock for afternoon tea with some neighbour – and his back is a little straighter, his eye brighter, because of it. He's a darling.

He's calling for me, Vivi. I'd no idea it was so late. More next time but, for now,

All love, darling,

Madeleine

She puts down the pen and looks about the room, folding the letter hastily and tucking it into the writing case. She is beginning to grow used to the fact that she owns very little – she brought so few belongings with her from Multan – but it seems strange and a little frightening to have nothing familiar to connect her to her life with Johnny and India. She has Honor's things, of course: that little bag with its label 'Wanted on Voyage' contains objects that constantly remind her of Honor. This writing case is amongst these, along with her pretty gold fountain pen. Mutt screws on its lid just as James appears, pushing open the door, smiling half enquiringly, half apologetically.

'Not interrupting anything?'

'Heavens, no.'

Her smile is warm with affection and he beams back at her gratefully; she is quick to love, this girl of Hubert's, and her presence is already easing his loneliness. His son's death has been far more of a blow than he will ever show but the arrival of his family is a blessing.

Mutt slips a hand within his arm – Dear old boy, she thinks – and wishes that she were not deceiving him.

'I think we need our nightcap,' she says, drawing him into the room. 'Just a tiny one for me, of course, but it helps me sleep.'

'Well, of course it does.'

He likes to feel her fingers on his arm, strong and comforting, and he straightens his back a little as he makes for the cupboard. This last drink ritual was a solitary affair when

Margaret was alive; she'd go upstairs, leaving him beside his little fire to brood over the events of the day whilst she prepared herself for bed. He misses her dreadfully, of course he does, but he admits to himself that this is rather fun: Honor perching on the corner of the desk and watching him whilst he measures out a finger of the precious whisky. He begins to tell an amusing wartime anecdote relating to rationing and she chuckles appreciatively.

Inside herself, Mutt is marvelling at the little scene: can it be true that she is sitting here with Hubert's father? She imagines how his face would change if she were suddenly to interrupt his story with her own. 'Listen,' she might say. 'I'm not really Hubert's widow. It's all a terrible mistake . . .'

Instead she nods encouragingly, laughing with him, and the odd thing is that she is comforted by a sense of rightness, of being where she truly belongs. It seems so much like home, this lovely valley, and already she has a strong affinity with this dear old man. He is very like Hubert, although the thick black hair is now white. His thin, clever face is still lively and the brown eyes have a twinkle: just so will Bruno look in the distant future. She smiles, filled suddenly with tenderness, and it is as if he instinctively knows that this special smile has nothing to do with his story but is an acknowledgement of some passing connection with his son and his grandson. He smiles back at her, raising his glass as if in a salute to her thought, and she swallows some whisky quickly.

It has always been so, she thinks; love sweeping over her, lifting her on its warm sparkling wave, engulfing her senses and her reason. And this love is not only to do with attractive young men but embraces the elderly and children too: those Indians in Multan, in their poverty and need, and her own friends. The flood of emotion always carries her along with it, and she is buoyed up with her longing to help, but occasionally the current is too strong for her. Often someone is at hand to hold her head above the water – Vivi, perhaps, and later on, Honor and Hubert – but sometimes she is left, out of her depth, struggling against the undertow.

James finishes his story without showing that he senses a quenching of her spirits. He thinks he understands it, knowing how a joyful memory has its twin face of grief and loss. Just so has he felt about Margaret – looking with delight upon the first open flower of the camellia; remembering that she will never share it with him again – and his compassion stretches out to this girl who still smiles bravely though her eyes are shadowed with fear. He cannot speak any words of comfort, however; that is not his way. He gets to his feet with a remark about the lateness of the hour, but he touches her shoulder as he passes on his way to the hall.

'Good girl. Good girl,' he mutters, as though she might be a favourite horse or a well-loved dog. 'Sleep well, my dear.'

She watches him go and then carries the glasses into the kitchen.

12th July

I'm feeling very low tonight, Vivi. James has gone out to dinner with some friends, and I'm alone for the first time at Paradise. You'd think, wouldn't you, that I'd be glad to be alone? No pressure, no need to think before I speak; nobody to put on an act for; but the truth is, actually, I feel unbearably lonely. The children are in bed and I've had a couple of whiskies and, just suddenly, I felt the need to talk to someone who really knows me, so that I don't have to pretend. Do you remember how we'd try on each other's clothes and experiment with make-up and laugh and laugh about such silly things? Remember when you chopped off my hair with nail scissors? How wonderful it was to be free of all that weight of hair but Mother almost screamed with shock, hand over her mouth, eyes popping, which set us off even worse. Thank God, Honor was dark and had brown eyes. Mine, as you know, are hazel but the Customs man only glanced at the passport photograph and I'd pulled on a silly hat, tilted over my eyes, and carried Lottie in my arms as a kind of shield. She hates to be carried and I knew that she'd struggle and scream and distract the attention away from me. In the end everyone was glad to push us through as quickly as possible. I mustn't call her Lottie. I only do it when I'm tired – or when I've drunk too much whisky.

Vivi, I feel so guilty. What am I doing here? Why ever did I think I could pull this off? Some wretched woman turned up here this morning, her husband was one of Hubert's chums, thought I'd like to go over for lunch and so on. I was terrified that I might slip up. She began to talk to Bruno, saying how like his daddy he was, asking how old his little sister was and I can't forget the expression on his face. I sometimes kid myself that Bruno thinks Lottie *is* his sister, that he's forgotten Emma. Oh God! I have to remember that Lottie *is* Emma, don't I? What is he thinking, Vivi?

Anyway, I burst in with some nonsense and distracted her but I can't get over it. If I can't bring myself to call James 'Father', how can I expect so much from this poor little boy? How he must resent me for trying to take his mother's place, yet I know that he loves me and I think he would miss me if I were to go. In an odd kind of way, James protects me. He's so courteous, so old-fashioned, that he wouldn't dream of asking me personal questions. It would never occur to him that a lady could do the things I'm doing and so, you see, he's made it safe for me. He's the angel standing at the gate of Paradise with his flaming sword, turning this way and that, except that I'm still inside even though I've eaten of the tree of knowledge. Or is it the fruit of Goblin Market?

I think I've drunk too much whisky and I'd better get to bed before James comes home and finds me like this. More later. Goodnight, darling.

*   *   *

Joss put the letter aside and then picked it up again, folding it mechanically. There was too much here to understand all at once: Mutt wasn't Honor Trevannion. Yet Joss was distracted from the sheer shock of this by other impressions that were affecting her so powerfully. Mutt's dilemma, her warm personality and humanness, struck Joss forcibly. Almost she'd been able to forget that she was reading about her grand-mother and had identified with this young woman who'd taken such a chance, torn by doubt and fear, yet driven by some deep-down conviction that what she was doing was right.

Mutt's granddaughter caught her breath: how had Mutt dared to risk so much? Glancing back at the pages Joss was touched by the description of the flight from Karachi. She tried to picture the atmosphere of terror in India in those hot, unstable days, and the scene in the hospital room: she envisaged the long voyage home and tried to imagine how Mutt had lived with a permanent fear of discovery.

Somewhere in the Indian Ocean Lottie became Emma.

What must it have felt like, giving your daughter a different name and a new persona? And this child, Joss was obliged to remind herself, was her own mother – who wasn't Emma Trevannion at all but Lottie Uttworth. Mutt had counted the risk worth it to give her daughter security.

Once you have a baby you have a hostage to fortune and nothing is ever the same again.

And what about Vivi, to whom Mutt wrote with such intimacy and affection? Joss was touched by Mutt's need to communicate with her childhood companion, reminding her sister of their shared past, seeking approval. Was Vivi still alive, out in America, imagining her sister and daughter long dead? Clearly the letters had never been posted . . .

Unable to grasp it all, Joss postponed the necessity to come to some serious judgement and reached eagerly for the next letter.

Thursday morning

Much better today, Vivi. I simply mustn't allow myself to get morbid, and this morning I feel confident again that I am doing the right thing. Bruno gave me such a hug after breakfast and I held him very tightly and just whispered, 'I know how much you must miss Mummie and Emma, darling. I'm just trying to look after you.' And he looked at me, Vivi, so solemn and kind, and he said, 'It's all right, Mutt. I'm glad you're here.' Oh, I felt such a flood of relief and gratitude, as if he'd given me absolution. And I love him as if he were my own son. I am his godmother, you know. And Simon is his godfather, although it was all done by proxy, of course. Simon reminded me of that and I was able to look intelligent about it. He sent a beautiful, little engraved mug, and I could remember Honor showing it to me.

It is so odd being called Honor. I hoped that the children's nickname for me might be taken up by everyone but no-one seems able to be quite so intimate. Even Mousie can't quite bring herself to use it. I am afraid of Mousie, Vivi. She watches us as if some instinct warns her that something is wrong but she doesn't know what it is. I become nervous when she is with me and I retreat into silence. Aunt Julia, who reminds me of a very dignified peahen – a bosom like a jelly-bag and a long, long neck with a tiny head perched on top – puts my shortcomings down to grief and encourages Mousie to be kind and patient. And poor Mousie is trying very hard to deny all her instincts and to be sweet to me. I realize now that I'd never have brought this off if Hubert's mother were still alive. Men are uncomplicated and direct and much easier to deceive than women. They say exactly what they mean and assume that we are doing the same thing. Apart from this, both James and Simon are affected by a show of grief or of fear and act accordingly: with a rather anxious kindness and an immediate change of subject. Women see through all that kind of thing immediately and though some of them might be polite about it they are not so easily taken in. You can't deflect women with those tricks.

Mousie must have loved Hubert so much; she knows everything about him, his passions and his dislikes, his tricks of speech and his habits. Yet she can't have been more than a child when she last saw him. He wrote to her from time to time – you might imagine how that tiny piece of information made me feel! – but, with the war and the distance between them, communication was very patchy. Luckily there aren't too many photographs: they have the wedding group – remember the one I sent to you? – and also a family one with Bruno as a baby. This is more worrying because Honor isn't wearing a hat but fortunately she is gazing down at the baby so you don't get a full-face shot.

I said at once: 'Gosh, I looked so much younger then, didn't I? But of course it's nearly five years old.'

I felt so ashamed of myself, Vivi. Thank God Bruno wasn't there. Mousie has several snapshots of Hubert before he went to India and one or two little keepsakes – an old wristwatch, broken, that belonged to him, and a book of poetry, Browning, with Hubert's name on the flyleaf – which she treasures. She's actually rather a sweetie but she has a knack of keeping me on my toes. I have no idea which was Hubert's favourite walk, or about the pony he had, and oh, countless tiny things which I should have known after six years of marriage. That's why I say I'd never have fooled his mother. It became clear fairly early on that he'd never mentioned me by my nickname, which is a terrific relief, nor by proper name as far as I know.

Mousie is puzzled but because of Bruno she doesn't come near the truth of it. I feel horrid, holding her at arm's length like this, but what am I to do? I just pray that I cease to be a nine days' wonder and we settle down more naturally. There's so much to describe to you, Vivi, so much to tell. I haven't really explained about Johnny, have I? I don't know how to go about it, I suppose. Looking back, I think he reminded me of our father: he was such fun, so happy-go-lucky, and very good-looking. He wasn't French, though, he was very English, and I was so proud to be seen around with him. Hubert and Honor were a bit cautious about him and I know you would have been too. You would have said that he wasn't 'sound'. As you know, he did something in tea – he had an office in Lahore – and had all sorts of connections but there was something elusive about him and I think that they felt he should have joined up once the war was really under way instead of disappearing on business for weeks at a time. He didn't want children straight off and I continued with my nursing but once Emma was born he simply vanished more often and for longer periods.

At one point we wondered if he'd been killed but after a while we heard some rather unpleasant rumours about him setting up with another woman. Well, I'd had to face the fact that there were other women, Vivi, but it was all quite horrid. I'd begun to suspect that he was a gambler as well as a few other undesirable things, and then I began to have dunning letters from people I'd never heard of and discovered that the rent hadn't been paid for months. I believe, now, that he was the black sheep of someone's family, sent out to India before the war to a friend or relative. He was always a bit cagey about what he did and where he went but he did it with such an air and with enormous charm. I must admit that it was beginning to wear a bit thin, though, and the rent was the last straw. Hubert and Honor bailed me out, as usual. They were such good people, which sounds a bit stuffy, doesn't it? But they were. Hubert was so clever with people. He'd get straight on to their wavelength and he was such a comfort. Honor was very motherly, warm but sensible. I often think about her and then I feel hot under the collar, imagining her looking at me from the shadows, as I walk in the Paradise gardens with her child. She was so straight, so sweet – but she'd have wanted Bruno to be properly looked after, not by an old aunt or his grandfather, but by someone who knew him from a baby and shares his history. He simply loves it when I talk to James about Hubert's work.

I can hear the children's voices; they've been with Aunt Julia and Mousie down at The Row.

God Bless, darling.

Madeleine

She stands for a moment, watching from the kitchen doorway. The little group have walked up from The Row over the cliff path, Emma being wheeled in the little collapsible pushchair that hasn't been used since Rafe was a small boy, and they are all rather hot and tired. Mousie kneels before Emma, smoothing the child's fair, tangled blonde hair and dabbing with a handkerchief at some smears upon her cheek.

Mutt is touched by the tenderness in Mousie's gestures and filled with anxious love at the sight of her daughter. She is shouting with excitement – 'Baa, baa black sheep' – and her face is bright with anticipation. Aunt Julia's capacious bag contains some tea-time treats and Emma is greedy for sweet things.

'Stand still,' implores Mousie – but she is laughing too, and she gives Emma a quick kiss on her rosy cheek before standing up with a gesture of helpless resignation.

'Your sister,' she says to Bruno, 'is a little monkey.'

Just for a second his expression freezes into a kind of still watchfulness and then he looks at Emma – still chanting the one line of the nursery rhyme – and he smiles with an extraordinary adult affection.

'She can't help it,' he tells Mousie with a rueful tolerance. 'Daddy used to say . . .' He hesitates awkwardly, stumbling over his words, and Mutt comes swiftly to his aid.

'Have you had a lovely time?' she cries, as if she has only at that moment appeared. 'Do be quiet for a moment, Emma, darling, we've all heard your rhyme. Poor Mousie.' She smiles sympathetically at the younger girl. 'Are you exhausted yet?'

She sits on one of the kitchen chairs and puts an arm about Bruno, giving him a quick hug, her heart beating fast. These are the moments she dreads, fearing that Bruno might be caught unawares. She is filled with guilt each time she sees the expression on his small face change from innocence to uncertainty, hating this need to be continually on guard, but she manages a smile as she watches Aunt Julia unpack her bag. She knows better than to suggest that this formidable woman might find the children wearying; their noise makes as much impression on her as the waves have upon the rocks in the cove. Tall and stately, as she stands at the table, her presence is both formidable and reassuring. Emma climbs onto a chair, hoping that there will be a pot of jam in the bag and looking eagerly for the little cakes that Aunt Julia brings out with a small flourish. Mousie steadies Emma as she screams with delight and the chair rocks unsteadily beneath her.

'She screamed all the way home,' says Bruno, almost admiringly – and indeed he is impressed by Emma's cheerful determination to have her own way. He finds her ignorance of what has happened in India restful. The horrid memories that trouble his dreams coupled with his terror that Mutt might be taken away from him are like shadows waiting at the edges of his waking hours. In Emma's company, he too is free of these fears; her passionate love of life carries him along with all the natural force of some great element: water or wind. She and Mutt have always been part of his world and he is prepared to go to any lengths to keep them with him. 'She doesn't like riding in the pushchair unless she's tired,' he explains to Mousie and Aunt Julia, wondering if they can understand that terrible frustration of being pinned down when you need to run and jump and climb. Emma has no words yet to explain this, but he knows exactly how she feels. 'She likes to be in charge.'

'She insisted on pushing the chair herself and I was afraid that she might topple over the cliff with it,' admits Mousie. 'The walk back was a bit of a tussle but she agreed to ride the last bit. I brought something to show you.'

Mutt watches with apprehension as Mousie opens the satchel bag she wears over her shoulder on a long strap and brings out an envelope. The photograph shows Hubert on the deck of a large ship in a group of other young men: he half frowns, half smiles at the camera, his hands stuck in the pockets of his trousers.

Mutt pretends to study the photograph, her cheek pressed against Bruno's head as if for comfort – although whether it is to console him or herself she cannot tell.

'Hubert sent it from India,' says Mousie. 'It was taken on voyage.'

She waits for a moment but there is no response from Honor, who appears to be engrossed in the photograph yet unwilling to comment on it. Mousie experiences a now-familiar sense of confusion. Hubert's widow sends out conflicting signals – now friendly warmth, now cold rebuff – and she is puzzled. Anything to do with the past seems to be out of bounds and Mousie longs to talk about Hubert, whom she loved so much. Even Bruno seems reluctant to talk about his father. She hopes that the photograph might ease the path to reminiscence and that she might learn something more about him; it seems terrible that he might be forgotten, his name never spoken again.

When Mousie mentions this privately to her mother she is not encouraged to dwell on it.

'Give her time,' her mother says. 'Remember how we were when Daddy died . . .' and, though she could argue that the memory of her own father is not shrouded in silence, Mousie allows the subject to drop. Nevertheless, her instincts warn her that there is a mystery here that she cannot fathom. She studies Honor secretly, envying her easy graceful way with

Uncle James and observing the genuine affection with which she charms Jessie and old Dot. Mousie longs for that kind of mature sophistication although, at present, she feels more comfortable with the children than with the older members of her family. She likes young men, though she is rather shy with them, but she cannot help comparing them unfavourably with all that she can remember of Hubert. Her early bitter reactions to the news of his marriage have faded but she is fascinated by Honor. Mousie sees, from the few photographs Hubert sent, that Honor has changed; the long bell of hair has been cut short and curls very prettily; the face looks thinner and the eyes deeper set.

'It's the grieving,' says her mother. 'The poor child has lost weight, you can see that by the way her clothes hang on her.'

Mousie feels guilty; ashamed at her readiness to be critical of the woman Hubert loved and who must miss him so terribly. She misses him too, hoarding up her few mementoes and remembering her cousin with a longing adoration. He would have been disappointed in her reaction she tells herself now, bracing herself against her own grief and smiling at Honor whose arm cradles Bruno so tenderly.

'I thought you'd like to see it,' she says casually, though still confused by the silence. 'Later on, Bruno might want it.' Gently she retrieves the photograph, replaces it in the envelope and puts it away.

'Tea-time,' says Aunt Julia firmly – and Mutt breathes a huge silent sigh of relief and her hold on Bruno relaxes.

3rd August

Vivi darling,

We've been having rather a busy time here in Paradise. First of all, guess what. Simon came down to stay for a long weekend. He comes at intervals to see everyone, which I think is rather sweet of him, and James is so fond of him that it's quite touching really. They talk about Hubert and the things he and

Simon used to get up to, cricket matches and sailing and goodness knows what, and dear old James relives it all over again. Simon and Rafe took us out sailing – they keep a boat in the old boatyard – and we took it in turns with the two of them: Mousie with Bruno and then me with Emma, who was utterly silent with joy and amazement. She sat so still next to me on the thwart – or whatever the seat is called! – as we skimmed across the silky silvery water, out past the sharp black rocks, the gulls swooping and screaming round the cliffs towering above us. It is so odd, Vivi, to look back at the shore from the sea. Odd and terribly exciting. I felt a wild, piercing sense of freedom, as if some umbilical cord had been cut, and I was able to soar, untrammelled by earthly cares. The triangular white sail was like a bird's wing, stretched taut over the crumpled surface of the sea, while the clean, fresh wind fled past me, tingling on my skin. Oh, how I loved it.

Simon said, 'I expect you didn't get much chance to sail in India' and I was able to reply confidently, 'No, none at all.' He said: 'Hubert would have missed that,' and I just nodded but Rafe could see how thrilled I was by it all and he smiled so sweetly at me and said rather shyly, 'Now that we've broken up for the holidays I'd be very happy to take you out any time you like.' 'I'd simply adore it,' I replied at once – and then prayed quickly that there was no record anywhere of Honor suffering from seasickness!

On Sunday afternoon we went picnicking up the valley to the Saint's Well. Fuchsias grow wild here, tall bushes of delicately arching stems with red, bell-shaped flowers – and there are butterflies everywhere. We laid the rug down where we imagined the door of the cell might have been and Simon rolled up his sleeves and built a little fire on a flat stone beside the stream to boil the kettle. Bruno was beside himself with delight and made a dam while Emma paddled, being very splashy and noisy and refusing to hold Mousie's hand.

I wondered if Mousie might be attracted to Simon but she

made no sign of it, no silly shyness, or sidelong little glances; no showing off or flirting. She's training to be a nurse at Truro but – although she's direct and practical and wonderful with the children – she seems much younger than her age and I am fearful that she might find herself trapped here with her mother and uncle. You might think it odd that I use that word 'trapped' when it's clear that St Meriadoc is such a spectacularly beautiful place but I know that when we were seventeen, Vivi, we'd have wanted a bit more from life than this group of older people – however sweet they are – and a younger brother, even in a paradise like this one. If someone like Simon had shown up when we were her age we'd have fought over him like cats.

He's awfully attractive. Quite tall, very tough-looking, nice hands, and I think his legs would be good; straight and strong. He shows no interest – not that kind, anyway! – in Mousie. It's as if we're the two adults, he and I, and the others are all children. Perhaps it's because he's known her for ever. I'd like to take her in hand a bit. Her hair is thick and a quite pretty colour, light brown with gold and reddish lights in it, but she bundles it into a plait without much care. Eyes a lovely, dark slatey blue and a clear, creamy skin, but no touch of make-up, not even a little slick of lipstick. The trouble is, I'm afraid to get too close; she sees too much.

She was aware of Simon and me lounging on the rug with our cigarettes whilst Rafe helped Bruno with his dam and Emma paddled. It was so good, there in the hot sun, with the cold clear water bubbling out of the well and a lark so high that we couldn't see him but could only hear his golden voice, the notes falling, tumbling down to us through the blue air. I was reminded of Meredith's poem and recited a few lines to Simon:

> 'Tis love of earth that he instils,
> And ever winging up and up,

Our valley is his golden cup,
And he the wine which overflows,
To lift us with him as he goes.

It fitted so perfectly with this glorious valley and the lark's song, and I could see that Simon thought so too.

'There he is,' he cried suddenly, and he leaned, pointing upwards, so that his bare arm brushed my cheek.

Oh God, Vivi. That warm touch of his skin against mine, I can feel it now. I actually jumped, my heartbeat was all over the place, and he looked at me, just one look, and then got to his feet, very calm, very natural, and strolled over to the dam.

'Pretty good,' he said. 'You'll make an engineer yet, young Bruno.'

I couldn't have moved, my legs wouldn't have supported me, I simply lay back in the sunshine, shielding my eyes with my hands – which trembled slightly.

But that's quite natural, isn't it, Vivi? After all, I've been married and I miss having a man to lie with and hold me. My body missed Johnny terribly after he'd left, it still does, even though I know with my brain that I wouldn't want him back. I'm only twenty-seven and it's not wicked, is it, to be attracted to a man? Of course, I can quite see that everyone here, including Simon, would see it as disloyalty to Hubert's memory – after all, he's only been dead for a few months – but the truth of the matter is that I've been alone for nearly a year and I do get so lonely. It's not just the physical side, though I *do* miss it, it's the company and the jokes that I miss; knowing he's your person, whatever his faults and failings. It's sharing his cigarette and driving in the rain with him, dancing to 'Whispering' all close and romantic, and waking in the night and watching him sleeping.

I was grateful when Emma stamped up out of the stream and simply threw herself on top of me, all damp and warm and shrieking with delight. It broke the tension and I was able to pack up the tea things and pull myself together.

We're all having supper together this evening, a real family party, though goodness knows what dear old Dot and Aunt Julia are concocting. The rationing is really bleak and if it weren't for Home Farm and the herring from Port Isaac I'm not sure how we'd manage to feed ourselves. Dot looks after James – well, all of us, now – and she's an old sweetie. Her husband worked most of his life at the boatyard and died at the beginning of the war. On the other side of Aunt Julia is Jessie Poltrue. Like Julia she's a war widow, although her children are grown and gone, one son working the fishing fleet at Port Isaac and the other at Padstow. Dear James is a kindly old pasha to all us women but I think he's delighted to see Simon and have some adult male company for a change.

And so, dear Vivi, am I. Simon speaks my language, that's the point. He's young and witty and attractive and he shows me what I'm missing. But I'm not going to complain or start regretting things. I'm so lucky to be here, in one piece, with kind people and my baby safe. Sitting there beside the little stream, pretending not to be looking at Simon, I remembered *Goblin Market* and poor Laura longing once more to hear the goblin cry and to taste the fruit again. And Lizzie says to her:

> 'You should not loiter longer at this brook:
> Come with me home.
> Let us get home before the night grows dark:
> For clouds may gather
> Tho' this is summer weather,
> Put out the lights and drench us thro'
> Then if we lost our way what should we do?'

I've left a bit out in the middle but you know what I mean, Vivi. It was just as if you were warning me. I miss you so

much. And Honor and Hubert too. I feel that I've lost you all
at one stroke.

I love you, darling.

Madeleine

The supper is a great success: each person sitting round the
dining-room table is aware of an undercurrent of excitement
though only Mousie, sitting between Bruno and Emma, can
accurately guess at its source. Beyond Bruno is Rafe and then
Honor who sits beside James at the head of the table. Julia is
on the other side of Emma next to Simon on James's left
hand. Jessie's older son has bagged a brace of rabbits and Dot
has concocted a delicious pie.

Julia, helping Emma to a minute portion of pie, is convinced that the conviviality is the result of the cocktails Simon
produced earlier. He usually brings a bottle or two with him
to Paradise, much to James's delight, and this evening everyone apart from the children has a drink. Julia enjoys her
measure, it reminds her of naval parties and Ladies' Nights,
and she feels young again and rather frivolous. It is she who
persuades Honor to allow the children to join the party,
arguing that it is unfair that they should miss the pie and that
such treats in these times of rationing are few and far between.
Smiling at Honor's look of surprise – Julia knows that she is
looked upon as a strict disciplinarian – she adds that, after all,
Simon is Bruno's godfather, which adds to the occasion.

Nevertheless, she restrains Emma securely in her highchair
and provides her with the glass snow scene, a charming object
with which she is allowed to play on only very special
occasions. Julia, keeping her occupied with the snow scene
and mouthfuls of rabbit pie in turn, is too busy to notice
Simon at her right side. She cannot see, as Mousie can, how
often his eyes rest on Honor or his strange restlessness as if he
is subduing some need deep within himself.

Honor, on the other hand, is devoting her attention to James, although she exchanges remarks with Rafe from time to time when he is not explaining to Bruno the art of sailing. Mousie sees that Rafe is taking a great deal of trouble with Bruno and her heart warms to her brother. He is a keen sailor and it is clear that Bruno has enjoyed his first experience on the water; Rafe is describing in vivid word pictures how Hubert taught him to sail in the *Kittiwake* when he, Rafe, was no older than Bruno is now. The little boy's eyes are alight with interest and pleasure and Mousie smiles with approval upon her young brother and looks again at Simon.

He is good-looking, she is prepared to acknowledge that much, and he has very good manners, yet her loyalty will not allow him to be Hubert's equal. The girls she is training with are not in the least inhibited when it comes to describing their boyfriends and she can see that Simon has sex appeal but, although she cannot quite put it into words, she feels there is something missing at a deeper level. He hasn't Hubert's *attractiveness*; that quality that drew old and young to him is missing in Simon, despite his glamour and sophisticated good looks. She can easily imagine Simon working in the big city hospital or being fascinated by research but he would never be satisfied, as Hubert had been, to work with the poor and the inarticulate. He would be too restless for the patience required in a country practice where stopping to pass the time of day, to discuss the weather and the crops, are all part of the duties.

Mousie swallows a piece of rabbit with difficulty, remembering how she'd dreamed that Hubert would come back to St Meriadoc and work here amongst his own people. When she started her training, she'd hoped that one day they might even work together. With an effort she turns her attention back to Simon. He has finished his helping of rabbit pie and is leaning forward now, talking seriously, whilst Honor and Uncle James listen intently: Honor's gaze is fixed on Simon's face whilst

Uncle James, chin dropped, eyes hooded, turns his glass round and round. It is interesting, notes Mousie, that Honor has that same quality of attracting everyone to her: no wonder Hubert loved her.

Simon is thinking exactly the same thing: no wonder Hubert fell in love with her. Even as he talks he is aware of Honor's interest in him; a special form of concentration that somehow invests him with an ability to be rather witty and clever. He has no doubt that she makes dear old James feel exactly the same and that it has absolutely nothing to do with the cocktails. She has a magic, this girl, that reaches deep down inside and brings out things you didn't know you had in you: you want to shine for her. He saw it with young Rafe too, earlier, when they were having a drink in the drawing-room; she was encouraging him to talk about sailing – not merely flattering him but leading him to describe not only the skill involved but also his feelings about it. Rafe glowed in the magic beam of her interest and that too had nothing to do with the drink he was enjoying at the same time. It might be old Jessie with her bunions or Bruno with a broken toy – to each was given that special exclusive attention: no wonder Hubert fell for her like a ton of bricks.

Simon sips some wine: poor old Hubert, what damned rotten luck. Though they hadn't stayed closely in touch through the war – both of them were busy and neither was a natural letter writer – yet they'd remained good friends right through school and their training together and he'd been deeply touched when Hubert had asked him to stand god-father to his son. Now, as Honor describes the working conditions in the hospital in Multan, he tries to recall what, exactly, Hubert had written about this wife of his. Of course there was the usual stuff about how lucky he was and what a lovely girl she was but nothing had quite prepared him for Honor. He likes the children's name for her: Mutt. Oh, dear old Julia might huff and puff about it being unsuitable but there is something rather charming about the nickname and it suits her. There is a slight austerity about the name 'Honor' and, though she can be wary, he has seen behind that façade she uses to protect herself. The nickname makes her more accessible.

'It was Hubert's fault,' she'd told him. 'You know how he uses nicknames.'

Well, he does know – and he doesn't intend to tell her that Hubert's rude nickname for him had been Vlad the Impaler because of Simon's innumerable conquests at the nurses' home whilst he and Hubert were training at Barts. Remembering, he hides a smile with his napkin, pretending to wipe his lips and catches Mousie's gaze. There is another of Hubert's victims. He wonders if anyone remembers that her name is Mary and, as he smiles at her, he also wonders if he might have had a little fling with her had Honor not suddenly appeared upon the scene. Something in Mousie's clear, slate-blue gaze makes him feel that he probably wouldn't have risked it: anyway she is almost like a sister to him.

He doesn't feel like that about Mutt. By sending that telegram Hubert practically passed her into his care and he feels that it is quite fair to chance his arm once the mourning period is over. Not that he intends to use his Vlad the Impaler technique here: goodness, no. Old James would have him out on his ear double quick and, anyway, that's not the way he's feeling; he wants more than that. She's got under his skin, this Mutt, with her sweetness and her sudden flashes of wit. They speak the same language and he knows that she feels the way he does; he's sure of it even though it's early days and she's behaving very properly . . . But, good God, that moment up by the well when she'd been lying beside him on the rug and laughing at the children! He'd lit her cigarette and they'd listened to the lark, oh, way up above them, and she'd recited some poetry to him; well, that didn't mean much, he'd never been one for poetry, not like dear old Hubert, but it was rather nice – something about the valley being the golden cup and the lark's song the wine pouring into it – and then he'd seen the lark.

'There he is,' he'd cried, and his arm had brushed her cheek as he'd pointed, and he could feel the contact as though his flesh was on fire from her touch, though her cheek was cool and soft . . .

Julia is murmuring to Simon, offering him a second helping, and Honor turns to speak to Rafe and to Bruno so that James is left to himself for a moment. He looks down the table, savouring the atmosphere, wishing that his dear Meg could have been in her place to smile back at him with that little secret look of contentment she wore when all was proceeding happily. Julia misses her sister too; he knows that. Not that she talks about it – goodness, no, neither of them would feel quite comfortable about that – but they understand each other and have their own ways of conveying sympathy. He looks with affection at his sister-in-law as she helps Simon to pie before turning back to administer to Emma. It is clear that Julia approves of Hubert's little family and is doing her best to make them feel at home.

His heart constricts a little as he looks at Bruno's absorbed bright little face: he might be Hubert sitting there, years ago when Margaret was a pretty girl of a wife and he, himself, just back from the war and glad of the peace of this quiet valley. How she would have loved the boy – and Emma too. She'd longed for a daughter but they'd been blessed with only the one child – who, when he was grown, had this calling to work abroad. Neither of them had attempted to dissuade him though they'd both hoped that he'd come back to them before too long. It had broken Margaret's heart – never very strong – to think of her grandchildren so far away and separated further by war. How she'd missed Hubert. They rarely talked of it, that wasn't their way, but the house wasn't the same once he'd gone and they'd both been ready to welcome Julia and the children in their own moment of tragedy. Margaret had been glad to have her sister nearby: they'd always been close friends.

James sighs and smiles rather sadly at Honor, who is watching him with that particular brand of empathy that so characterizes her.

'Do you have a sister, my dear?' he asks. 'Or brothers?'

Her stricken expression recalls him at once to the present. He remembers that her parents were killed in an air raid, and she has no siblings, and curses his tactlessness. Before she can answer, he apologizes.

'I remember now,' he says remorsefully. 'I am so sorry. I was thinking about my wife and how close she and Julia were.'

He rambles on, trying to hide his clumsiness, aware that the atmosphere is not quite so sparkling, and then Dot comes in with some confection she's made specially, and the cries of admiration and delight get the whole show back on the road again. James heaves a sigh of relief and reaches for his glass. Damned good wine Simon's picked up somewhere; better not to question him too closely.

'Good boy,' he murmurs approvingly – and is pleased to see that Simon has attracted Honor's attention, something to do with Emma and the pudding, and is making her laugh. He smiles upon his family, raises his glass to Julia, who smiles back at him. All is well.

15th August 1947

Today is Independence Day in India, Vivi, and I've felt so strange all day. Honor and Hubert would have understood these mixed emotions. We worked so hard in that little hospital and had such a strangely intricate relationship with those dear, infuriating people. We – the British – relied heavily on the loyalty of the Indians yet always, underneath, was the profound fear of treachery. In Multan – always a bit of a trouble spot – it certainly brought the three of us, me and Honor and Hubert, very close.

Have you wondered, Vivi, how I am managing for money? Well, there was some for the journey that I have eked out very carefully, but James has realized the embarrassment and is coming to my rescue. He won't hear of my working – he insists that the children need me here – but he has opened a bank account for me and gives me a small allowance and, this was a shock, has begun enquiries into Hubert's pension. I had a jolt of terror when he talked about that.

'Do you have Hubert's death certificate?' he asks.

Well, yes. I have all three death certificates. Honor's and Emma's are taped carefully between the backboard and the paper cover of *Goblin Market* along with my own papers. I sent a telegram back to Multan saying that Dr Hubert Trevannion and Mrs Madeleine Uttworth and her daughter had died of botulism and that his wife and children were on their way home to England.

I had to think quickly but I've always been good at that, haven't I? You were the sensible, practical one, but in a real crisis I was the one to have all the bright ideas. Do you remember how Mother used to say, 'To be a successful liar you need a long memory'? Well, it's true. Once I was married to Johnny I needed to be able to get us out of scrapes quite often – and without warning – and I learned to think on my feet. It's not just a question of remembering what you've said but also being able to look ahead so as to see the pitfalls. He had this ability, Vivi, to invest rather questionable acts with a kind of glamour; to make the upright, moral types seem flat-footed and dull. Yet underneath I had a tiny nagging sense that it was all a bit grubby. To begin with it didn't matter. I loved him, you see. I utterly adored him and he could get round me with no trouble at all. Once Lottie was born things changed. I didn't want muddle and cheating for her, can you understand that?

I used to envy Honor and Hubert. They'd achieved what I'd

wanted when I decided to go out to India with the IMS rather than going through the army route. I wanted to be amongst the Indians, to work where it really mattered, but somehow Johnny pulled me off course. I worked hard, make no mistake, but there was a wholeheartedness about Hubert and Honor which was lacking in me and, when Johnny came along, his love and approval was more important than all the rest. It was like Robert Talbot all over again, distracting me from my wondering about being a missionary.

Honor and Hubert managed to balance their lives and I envied them so much. Sometimes I feel that I've become a part of their lives now and that some of their goodness and wisdom is rubbing off on me. I admired Honor so much. I don't mean physically. She had no s.a., if you know what I mean – and she was inclined to put on weight, especially after the children – but she had a serenity that nothing could shake. She was compassionate without going off the deep end and bursting into tears of sympathy like I did sometimes. Oh, Vivi, the poverty and the cruelty we saw! And she was so wise and practical without getting personally involved and taking on too much. I used to do that, try to be all things to all men, and then be unable to do my work properly.

Honor and Hubert loved me, though. That always surprised me.

'Look after the children if anything happens to me,' she'd say. We'd promise each other that we'd do that – it was terribly important out in India in those times to know that we had each other.

'Mutt's the right name for you,' Hubert would say after some disaster. 'What a woman!'

But, at the end, I was the one Honor wanted. I was the one she sent for and she knew I'd get there like I'd always promised I would.

I'm even wearing her clothes. I brought with me what I was standing up in but not much more and rationing is so strict that

I have to wear Honor's things. I've explained to everyone that I lost weight after Hubert's death and I'm using his mother's Singer sewing machine to take in seams and I've had to let down the hems.

'Have you got taller too?' Mousie asked – and all I could think of to say was that I felt it was a bit of a change from short skirts. Goodness, I feel so frightened at times.

Are you living like a queen in America, Vivi? I hope so, darling.

All love,
Madeleine

30th August

I wakened early this morning, Vivi. How I wish I could show you Paradise. Leaning from my bedroom window, looking out beyond the gardens, I can see tall, fragile trees – all spindle-limbs and feathery arms – drawn in a smudgy charcoal against soft, dense mist which rolls up the valley from the sea. A woolly bundle moves in the meadow below, ambling down the slope as it follows in a rabbit's track; a dark narrow path marked in the silvery dewy grass. Other sheep appear and a crow alights, walking stiff-legged and jaunty, glossy head on one side as it peers sharp-eyed for a tasty breakfast snack. And now the scene is washed in gold, as the sun edges up over the rim of the world, and dazzling light floods along 'the golden cup' – our valley – and into the shadowy corners of the garden.

When Margaret – Hubert's mother – died, James moved permanently into his dressing-room at the back of the house. He says he likes to hear the sea on wild nights, and all his things are there, but I feel rather guilty having this wonderful room as my own. We had a touching little ceremony yesterday (Honor's birthday – I can't tell you how odd and unreal it all was) when he offered me Margaret's jewels and one or two precious items. She owned some good pieces: a lovely double string of pearls with matching ear-rings, a pretty garnet necklace set in silver, a few rings – one diamond, a ruby and a charming sapphire engagement ring.

'I know she'd have been so happy for you to wear them,' he said, rather gruffly – it was all got over very quick because I could see that he was deeply affected by the little scene – and I kissed him and said I would be very touched to have them.

You can imagine, Vivi, how I felt! I tell myself that it will all be passed on to Bruno and so, in the end, it will be as it should be – but then I wonder how Emma will feel when that day comes and nothing is for her. I'm trying not to think about that at the moment.

I can hear her upstairs singing to herself in her cot. She's a happy child, warm and loving, and she and Bruno adore each other. I'm beginning to believe that Bruno is trying to forget about India. He no longer wants to talk about those small things that formed his life and I think it's because he's afraid of being confused and letting something out of the bag. I know how he feels! His father's work is apart from this – he likes to hear about that, but more and more he gently and politely discourages conversations about Sushila and old *mali* and I wonder if it's because it reminds him of Honor and other happier times.

Emma is getting noisier, I must go and fetch her.

In his own room, listening to Emma's imperious shouts, Bruno brings the story he is telling himself to a good stopping place and wonders if there will be time for a walk to The Lookout before tea. He loves the strange old house on the cliff and it features in many of the stories he makes up in his head. Jessie has told him about wreckers and smugglers, and he weaves these tales together with the things he remembers about India so that the frightening parts are somehow dis-armed, their terror made bearable. Sometimes, if it is a really good story, he acts it out as a game that can last for several days. The grown-ups often have roles, although they don't know it, but Emma is too young to play – and, even if she weren't, he has a feeling that she wouldn't quite understand the seriousness of his make-believe. This feeling, which comes from the same place inside him as the ideas for his stories, tells him that, young though she is, she is already rooted very firmly in the real world. Her small feet are planted squarely on the earth and her needs are the needs of the body: food and warmth and company. If he is busy working out a story, or letting words make shapes in his head, he will forget every-thing else but she is never utterly entranced, as he is, by music or by the magical twilight hush; only wild elemental things – the sea pounding the cliffs or a wild westerly gale – excite in her that particular deep-down delight. He knows that when she screams like a steam train or roars like a lion she is trying to express that joy.

He can hear her now, singing loudly as she tramps up and down in her cot. He hears, too, Mutt coming upstairs and he thinks about the little scene yesterday, when Grandfather gave her Grandmother's jewels. He is getting used to these moments when Mutt gets flustered. 'Flustered' is an Aunt Julia word and it means exactly how Mutt behaves when the India story crashes into the Paradise story. He can quite understand why Mutt has her own pretend game and he is very happy to play it with her. Much though he loves Aunt Julia and Mousie and Rafe, he couldn't bear to be without Mutt and Emma. Even when he deliberately reminds himself that Mummie and Daddy and baby Em are gone for ever, the knowledge that Mutt and Emma are here with him makes it not quite true. It's as if they have all become mixed together and though he feels badly – as if he doesn't care enough about Daddy and Mummie and baby Em – something tells him that he has to allow this acceptance to happen.

'Do exactly as Mutt tells you,' Mummie said to him in that terrible place of heat and terror, and he'd felt her relief that he would be going to safety with Mutt.

Sometimes, now, Mummie and Mutt seem to be one and the same person, just as Emma – who was once called Lottie – now seems to be baby Em too. He is glad, though, that Daddy is just Daddy and can be talked about with Mousie or Grandfather, even though he has to be careful that it doesn't lead on to other things. This is why the stories are good – because he can make the terrible sadness into something exciting or brave and then he feels better. He wonders how Mutt manages and sometimes hugs her consolingly to show that he understands how frightened she must be. She has that look, then; an odd look of someone who is grateful and ashamed at the same time. Flustered.

Bruno climbs off his bed and goes into the nursery where Mutt is lifting Emma from her cot, and Emma is crowing with satisfaction, and he feels safe and happy.

Downstairs, James folds his newspaper and rouses himself. Although he is often glad to slip away to the peace and quiet of his study, he likes the sound of the family bringing life back to this old house. Listening to the footsteps overhead, Emma's shouts and Bruno's childish treble, he smiles to himself with satisfaction as he relives the gift ceremony.

It was Julia who nudged him into awareness.

'It would be a nice touch,' she said. 'Hubert's wife should have Margaret's jewels and it would be a very generous gesture. Welcoming her here, James, d'you see? A little formality in showing her that she belongs. Margaret would have wanted it.'

He was distressed that he hadn't thought of it for himself but hastened to gather together the few pieces Margaret had treasured. Not that she'd set much store by it, his dear Meg, being more concerned with the garden and her tapestry work than with personal adornment. Julia was right, though. He'd never been very good at flowery speeches but this time he'd made a pretty good fist of it, all things considered, and Honor was moved by the gesture.

As he sits listening to the noises above him, James thinks about how she gazed at the trinkets with a kind of humility, as if reluctant to accept them. He had to be quite firm, saying that Margaret would have wanted her to have them, and then he was knocked sideways again by the thought that his dear old Meg would never know this lovely girl or Hubert's children and he came over choky and gruff. Honor saw his distress and thanked him very sweetly, overcoming her own emotions and ignoring the fact that he damned near broke down, just giving him a quick kiss and saying that she'd love to have the gewgaws. Nothing more: no gushing or anything of that kind. He was grateful for that: couldn't be doing with all that fuss and nonsense.

He puts the newspaper aside and goes out to greet them as they come downstairs.

'Rafe telephoned,' he says. 'Wonders if you'd like to go sailing?'

Later

Rafe took us sailing today. I am at my happiest on the water, Vivi, free of the land and all the responsibilities it holds. We row out past the rocks – I'm getting strong and can manage quite well although Rafe and I usually take an oar each – and then, once we're past the headlands, we raise the sails. The boat was built here in the boatyard before the war. It's odd to think of a boat as beautiful, I suppose, but the *Kittiwake* is. She has such lovely lines. Rafe is so proud of her, and he is teaching Bruno to sail. He allows him to take the tiller and shows him how to watch for a breeze, the cat's-paws dimpling across the water. Emma is simply ecstatic, laughing with delight, rapt with the wonder of it all.

One day I shall take the *Kittiwake* out alone – oh, what freedom that will mean to me; to feel her responding to my touch, to see the sails filling with wind. One day – but not yet. I have a great deal to learn. I know now that the sea is strong –

not cruel but simply indifferent – and I understand that it has to be respected. Rafe knows so much that I am completely in awe of him but he loves to share his skill and is thrilled when we make progress.

The children are rosy with sun and sea air, falling asleep over their tea, whilst James sits by and smiles benignly upon us. His flannels fall sharply from his thin, crossed knees and his faded shirt is as soft as butter. I lay my hand upon his shoulder as I stand up to fetch something and he smiles at me, heart-breakingly like Hubert.

'I loved Hubert so much,' I say to him – just suddenly. And it's true, Vivi, I *did* love Hubert, though not in that way. Is it wrong to deceive James so badly? We comfort him, I'm sure of it. He looks so kindly at me and says, 'So did I, my dear.' Bruno is watching us, across the table, and I feel that familiar sensation of guilt. I can't explain it to him, yet, you see; he's too young. Suppose he grows up hating me for making him a liar?

No, no, don't think of that. Think of the sea, the exhilarating sensation of the soft warm air pouring over my skin, the chuckling sound of the water beneath the keel. Hubert would love to see Bruno sailing the *Kittiwake* – perhaps he does see him. I have this deep-down conviction that, despite everything, God still watches over me.

Lots of love, darling,
Madeleine

15th September

Such fun, Vivi. Simon is here for a few days. We're all so pleased to see him. Did I tell you that he's a GP – he has a practice in Exeter – and spends one day a week at the Royal Devon and Exeter Hospital? It's nice because it means that I can talk intelligently to him about his work. It is clear that he takes his duties as godfather to Bruno very seriously, and asked me all about schools and so on. Well, you can guess my reaction as these new pitfalls opened up before me. Apart from the fact that I had no idea where Hubert had been at school, I also began to see how tricky this whole area of education might be. Imagine taking Bruno along on his first day and saying, 'I'm Bruno's mother.' How shall I deal with that? How will *he*?

James stepped in with, 'Well, of course he'll go to Truro just as Hubert did,' which gave me a clue – and then they were off, discussing schooldays, and giving me a chance to pull myself together. Thank God that Bruno's not five until December, which gives us another year to prepare for that first ordeal. On the other hand Emma has her second birthday while Simon is with us. Can you imagine how odd it is, Vivi, to celebrate your child's birthday on the wrong date? Lottie was born on 13th October, and now will spend the rest of her life exactly one month older than she really is. I tried not to think about it and, despite the rationing and the difficulties of buying anything really good, she had a splendid time. Dear old Dot had saved up everyone's fat and sugar ration and made a wonderful cake – with two candles on the top – and Aunt Julia had knitted her the most delightful dolly stuffed with old stockings for which Emma immediately conceived an enormous passion. I was so pleased to see Aunt Julia's face – utterly gratified but trying not to show it. Rafe, bless him, had made a wooden cradle for the dolly and Mousie and Jessie between them had sewn tiny sheets and pillows and crocheted a coloured blanket.

I can't tell you how emotional I felt seeing this combined effort: a true family present. I had to slip away into the kitchen, on the pretence of putting the kettle on the range, and wept briefly but violently into the dishcloth. Do you remember our birthdays, Vivi, and our father always thinking up the most wonderful surprises? Do you remember Flopsy, the angora rabbit, and your fairy bicycle? Oh, how I envied you that bicycle; I was speechless with desire for it.

Well, I had made Emma a party frock from an evening gown that I'd seen Honor wear only twice: a pretty blue-coloured taffeta and not at all my kind of thing. I was able to detach a length of trimming which, with careful removing of the old stitching and then washing and pressing, Bruno was able to give her as a hair ribbon to match the frock. He'd also done some negotiation over his sweet ration with the baker in Polzeath and had obtained a pink sugar mouse. What riches! James was rather baffled by the whole event, his idea of a decent present being a book, but rather charmingly picked a posy of flowers from the garden and put them in a tiny vase by her breakfast plate.

To be honest, she hadn't really any idea as to what was happening but enjoyed herself enormously. We sang to her at tea-time as she stood on her chair in her party frock, her eyes blazing as blue as the taffeta and the dolly clutched to her chest, and when the cake was brought in with the candles alight she positively screamed with excitement. Bruno helped to blow out the candles and then Simon produced his present. Two tortoiseshell kittens, Vivi, the prettiest you've ever seen. It was so sweet and clever of him to bring two because, the moment he saw them, Bruno's eyes simply shone with joy.

'One each,' Simon said firmly. 'I expect you to take care of them, Bruno, until Emma's a little older.'

Emma was fascinated by them, but – to my relief – her affection was not transferred from the dolly, which might have hurt Aunt Julia. Oh, it was good to see Bruno going off with Simon to find a box for the kittens to sleep in and an old blanket. He suddenly looked taller and older – Bruno not Simon – and I wished that I'd thought of it earlier. It's exactly the thing to distract Bruno from his terrible loss and give him responsibility. Thank God we eat so much fish here!

When I looked in on Emma later that evening she was fast asleep – still in the frock from which she'd refused to be parted – with Dolly clutched to her stained and crumpled chest and a blissful smile on her face.

Once Bruno was in bed Simon took me out to dinner at one
of the hotels in Polzeath and we danced.

She puts down the pen and rests her elbows on the desk,
wondering how to continue. Simon will be leaving very soon,
to drive back to Exeter, and yet she needs this small respite
from him; from all of them. The letter is an excuse – 'Long
overdue,' she says ruefully. 'Must catch the evening post' –
and she slips away, hoping that if she tries to put down the
events on paper it might help her to be more rational. It calms
her to write like this to Vivi; in analysing her feelings to her
sister she is able to see things more clearly. She pushes
her hair away from her face, closing her eyes: what with
Emma's birthday party and the dance, it has been a very
emotional weekend.

The light knock makes her jump and as Mousie puts her
head round the door Mutt hurriedly shuffles the paper away,
turning quickly with a smile.

'I wondered if you'd like me to take your letter to the post?'
Mousie smiles back at her. 'I've got my bicycle with me so it
won't take me long and I'm off home now.'

'That's very sweet of you.' She makes a face of comical
despair. 'You know, I still haven't finished it. Utterly hopeless
but I'm simply not in the mood. Thanks anyway.'

Mousie nods and leaves her sitting there but she frowns to
herself as she slips on her cardigan and goes through the
kitchen and out into the dusk. She reflects on Honor's
reaction; how she instinctively made as if to hide the letter
just as a schoolchild might shield her work from a neighbour
she suspects of cheating. The invisible barrier is always there
between them and Mousie feels partly saddened and partly
irritated by Honor's behaviour.

In attempting to analyse it she wonders if perhaps Hubert
and Honor were not happy together and whether Honor has
to make an effort to hide the fact that the marriage wasn't all

that Hubert's family assume that it was. Deep down she suspects that this is a rather horrid kind of wishful thinking, all a part of her jealousy, but she cannot account for Honor's reluctance to talk about Hubert and her own instinctive feeling that something is wrong.

As Mousie hoists herself into the saddle, freewheeling down the drive and into the lane, she wishes that they could be friends. Intermittently she catches glimpses of a different Honor, light-hearted, warm, funny, and she believes that they could become much closer if only the barrier could be dissolved. She guesses that Simon sees this other Honor too, and is very much attracted to her. Today there has been an odd restraint between them as if they are afraid of showing too much of their true feelings to each other and to the family.

Mousie wonders if anyone else has noticed but has no intention of bringing it to her mother's attention. She has been accused too often of an overactive imagination, and her mother is very protective of Honor's widowed state. Nevertheless, as she sweeps over the little bridge towards The Row, Mousie can't help remembering Honor's reaction and she wonders to whom she is writing.

In the drawing-room at Paradise Simon is wondering too. He is rather put out when Mutt murmurs something about a letter and slips away. Good manners dictate that he should smile and nod at her as she goes, whilst continuing to listen politely to James, who is holding forth on Denis Compton's fine batting form this season, but he has been hoping for a few minutes alone with her and he feels frustrated. Soon Mousie says that she must go home; she has been helping to bath the children and put them to bed and now she says that she'll be late for supper if she doesn't get a move on. After she's been gone for a decent interval, Simon begins to indicate that he too must be on his way. James glances at the clock, apologizes for monopolizing the conversation and begins to get to his feet.

'No hurry,' says Simon quickly. 'I've got to get my bags down. I'll look in when I'm ready to go.'

James nods, settles back in his chair and picks up his newspaper. Simon goes out into the hall and stands for a moment, listening. He hears a noise on the landing and, glancing up, he sees Bruno staring down at him.

'Hello, old chap,' he says quietly. 'Got a problem?'

Bruno comes slowly down the stairs, one step at a time. His hair is peaked and his eyes are wide and confused. Simon goes swiftly up to him and sits down on a stair near the top.

'Bad dream?' he asks sympathetically – and when Bruno nods, he slips an arm about him protectively and gives him a hug. 'Want to tell me about it?'

Bruno shakes his head but sits beside Simon, leaning against him. As they sit together Simon looks down into the hall, holding the child gently but mentally planning ahead. It's a nice little house, a charming gentleman's residence, and the valley is a delight, but he can't imagine settling here. He is interested in cardiovascular research, which might mean studying abroad in America or Australia. He wonders how Bruno would react to another move after such an upheaval and whether he would resent being taken from his father's home to a far-off country. Emma is too young to remember her father, and he has no doubts that she will adapt very readily, but Bruno is a different proposition. He is an imaginative and sensitive child and it might be difficult for Mutt to explain her new allegiance . . .

Simon grimaces to himself. He's jumping the gun a bit, taking a lot for granted, but he could tell when he was dancing with her that she wasn't indifferent to him. Oh, they behaved very properly, stuck to all the social conventions, but underneath all that he felt her response to him. He mustn't rush her, he reminds himself – that could be fatal – but she is too warm, too much in love with life to spend the rest of it as a widow here in this backwater, no matter how beautiful it is;

and she's intelligent, that's so important, and can talk about his work.

He smiles reminiscently as he sits there waiting for Bruno's nightmare to fade. When he took her out she'd looked so beautiful in her strange-coloured frock, apparently unaware of the other men's admiring glances, but the really good thing was that they had a wonderful time together. It was such a relief to be away from the family, to be able to relax, though just at first they were tongue-tied with a kind of shyness. But once they'd had a drink they loosened up; they laughed at the same things and he loved the naughty twinkle in her eye that mocked the rather stuffy couples, so proper and upright as they danced.

'This has been such fun,' she said – but then she got that stricken look, probably remembering poor old Hubert and feeling guilty, and he had to remind her that she was still a young woman and was allowed to be happy now and again. He was very restrained and he could see that this was winning him points. She was so grateful that he'd found the kittens and brought them along for the kids and they got a lot of amusement out of thinking up silly names for them.

'Bruno wants to call them Pipsqueak and Wilfred,' she told him.

Remembering, Simon looks down at Bruno, who leans against him, relaxed now and half asleep.

'OK now, old chap?' he asks.

Bruno nods and Simon takes him back to his room, tucks him in and goes to fetch his bag.

In James's study, Mutt stares at the sheet of paper, re-reading the last sentence but quite unable to continue with the letter. Now it is Simon's turn to knock, telling her that he must be on his way back to Exeter, and she folds the sheets into the writing case and comes out to him, shutting the door behind her.

Later

It's over a week since I wrote that last sentence, Vivi. You'd have guessed at once, wouldn't you, if you'd read it? Guessed that it wasn't a bit as casual and straightforward as it sounded just written down like that in one easy sentence. I simply didn't know what to write after it, you see.

Oh, the heaven of dressing up in something pretty – another of Honor's frocks but this one made of a dark prune-coloured silk and only needing a little effort to make it fit properly. Thank goodness that Mother made us work hard at our dressmaking. I can't wear Honor's shoes, though. Her feet were bigger than mine and I've been able to say – with some truth – that since we mainly wore sandals in India I shall have to get some sensible shoes before winter. I've hidden quite a lot of her stuff in a trunk in an old lumber room and one day I must destroy it. Meanwhile I had to do my best with an old pair of strappy sandals although I did find her very pretty black velvet beaded bag that added a little glamour.

He looked so handsome in his dinner jacket. Simon is not quite as tall as either Johnny or Hubert, but he has very dark hair and disturbing brown eyes. So different from Johnny, who was blond and ruddy-looking. We took each other by surprise, once we were dressed up, and suddenly we both felt shy. There was an absolute silence in the car – until he suddenly announced that he'd been saving up his petrol ration for weeks for this visit – and it wasn't until we'd had a drink or two that we began to relax. I pulled myself together and began to ask about his work, which I find fascinating, and it wasn't until we got up to dance that I lost my self-control.

It was a typical seaside hotel, with a tiny orchestra playing behind the potted palms and the guests rather staid and polite, so that quite suddenly I felt a terrible desire to giggle and behave badly. I knew that Simon felt the same and he kept catching my eye and daring me to laugh. It made me feel young again – do you remember how we used to get a fit of the giggles in the most unsuitable places? – and I felt a huge affection for him. I told him how clever he'd been over the kittens, and how Bruno wanted to call them Pipsqueak and Wilfred. Pip, Squeak and Wilfred are characters in a comic strip and Bruno loves them. Then we began to think of names and we got sillier and sillier.

The thing was that just for a short time we'd both forgotten that I was the grief-stricken Honor Trevannion and I could just be me, Madeleine. Oh, the glorious relief of it. He'd begun to call me Mutt, catching it from the children, and it was wonderful to be there, just firmly in the present, enjoying ourselves.

And then we got up to dance. A week later and still I sit here not knowing what to write. I don't know how to describe the sensations I had when he put his arms round me. He's one of those dancers that hold you very close but not in any way suggestively. He stooped slightly above me so that his cheek was almost touching my hair and I could hear him humming just below his breath. Beside those other terribly formal men – chins held high, eyes on the far distance, hands planted firmly in the middle of their partners' shoulder-blades – he had a very sophisticated kind of shuffle, which was both intimate and relaxing, and it was impossible to put a foot wrong. I felt terribly feminine and sexy and I wanted the music to go on for ever. It was 'The Way You Look Tonight' and just out of the blue I remembered dancing to it with Johnny at a party in Lahore.

When we sat down I was very quiet and he looked a bit anxious and asked if I was OK. I said lightly, 'Oh, just memories,' and his expression changed as if he'd suddenly recalled that I was Honor Trevannion, a grieving widow of just a few months. But that wasn't what I wanted and I didn't know how to recreate the atmosphere we'd shared without seeming like some hard-faced bitch. After all, Hubert was his friend. I wondered what he was thinking about me, I couldn't bear to think he was suddenly despising me, and I just blurted out, 'I can't tell you what it means simply to enjoy myself again.'

Of course, the minute I'd said the words I realized that they could have been misunderstood but, bless him, he didn't react like that at all.

'You've had a terrible time,' he said, 'and there's no harm in trying to forget it for an hour or two.'

I was so grateful that I wanted to burst into tears. Crazy, isn't it? I think it's the strain beginning to tell.

'This has been such fun,' I told him. 'It's heaven here in Cornwall, and it's such a relief to feel safe again after the riots and the killing, but there's so much I miss.'

I stopped then, Vivi, because I'd been going to say that I missed my work, and that particular camaraderie I'd had with Honor and Hubert, and I could see myself getting into difficulties. I miss all sorts of things about India: the Hindu spring festival of Holi, when people threw coloured dyes over each other in celebration of love and fertility, and Diwali, their October festival of lights; and the Muslims' great feast, id ul-fitr, after the fasting of Ramadan. So much, Vivi, I try to deny because remembering is dangerous – and painful. Johnny and I used to travel to Kashmir when we went on leave; a long train journey from Lahore to Rawalpindi, to begin with, and then on by taxi to Srinagar. We'd hire a shikara – a huge house-boat complete with servants – on the Nagin Bagh. It was so beautiful, Vivi; the gardens full of tangled roses, the lake fringed with willows and the water reflecting the pink and white of the orchards of plum and cherry and almond trees: we saw bulbuls and kingfishers and hoopoes and, breathtaking in the distance, the Himalayas with their highest peaks covered in snow. We had such fun.

Looking at Simon across the table I knew that there was so little I could tell him – or anyone, apart from you – about those years. He put my hesitation down to a different kind of confusion.

'You must remember that you've had a terrible shock in very frightening circumstances,' he said, 'but you're still a young woman and you must think of that too. Give yourself the chance to be happy now and again.'

'Oh, I am happy,' I reassured him – and then could have bit my tongue out again. 'As happy as I can be, anyway, in the circumstances,' I added quickly. 'Everyone's so kind to me.'

He smiled at me, then – oh, such a smile, Vivi – and said, 'I'm sure they are.'

I felt myself blushing, right up into the roots of my hair, and he stood up and held out his hand to me and I followed him back onto the dance floor without another word. They were playing 'Ev'ry Time We Say Goodbye' and dancing with him was different this time; he held me just the same as before but there was an electrifying sense of awareness and I was convinced that he could hear my heart hammering away. If he did then he gave no sign of it, and when we went back to our table because the food had arrived – we had fish again, it's always fish! – he began to talk about some research he's working on and to describe an elderly patient who's allowing himself to be used as a bit of a guinea-pig. It restored us both to normality – well, nearly – and I blessed his social sense.

Afterwards, I wondered how Honor would have behaved. She was great fun, very warm-hearted, but there was something left out; a lightness of touch. I've put that badly, haven't I? By saying that something was 'left out' I'm implying that she lacked something good or important. Actually, it's quite the reverse. Even before we were married, when we were training together, men were always very respectful towards her; they never went too far with her. She had a deep-down goodness, which held them naturally at arm's length. My trouble is that I've always loved men, loved to be in their company.

Anyway, I tried to think of how Honor would have reacted to Simon and exactly how much Hubert had told his old friend about her. Somehow, I simply couldn't imagine the Hubert I knew sitting down for long enough to write lengthy letters to anyone – though I have to remember that he did do just that occasionally for Mousie – and if Honor ever wrote to his family then no-one has told me about it so far and she certainly didn't mention it to me.

This is the problem, Vivi; this waiting for the unexpected to jump out at you. That brief time with Simon, when both of us forgot everything except our two selves, was the most wonderful relief. The trouble is, I daren't forget that I'm *not* myself. I'm not Madeleine Grosjean, not even Madeleine Uttworth: I'm Honor Trevannion.

We said goodnight sensibly – he just lightly touched my cheek with his lips – and we had a nightcap with James, all very friendly. And that's that.

Love, darling,

Madeleine

Joss got up from the desk. She felt stiff and tired and she was aware of an inclination to weep. She'd given up all attempts to assess the rights and wrongs of Mutt's actions and had given herself wholly to the narrative of the letters. The little scene by the stream, described with such tenderness, had touched Joss deeply. How often she'd longed for that very kind of intimacy with George that Mutt described: '. . . the company and the jokes . . . knowing he's your person . . . dancing all close and romantic . . . watching him sleeping.' Oh, how often she'd imagined the luxury of such a relationship with George, knowing that it must be denied whilst every instinct cried out that it was right. How well she could imagine that light brushing of Simon's warm bare skin against Mutt's cheek and the mad, wild heartbeat; and how comforting to be able to hold the damp, wriggling body of your small child in your arms so as to give yourself a chance to recover.

Poor Mutt had lost her husband and her closest friends yet something was giving her the courage to hold on despite her terrors.

Faith is the conviction of things unseen.

Even though she'd hidden the roots of her faith it had continued to uphold her.

Joss took a deep, shaky breath and went out, through the hall and into the kitchen. Filling the kettle, she relived the birthday party scene: her own mother, Lottie-Emma, standing on her chair whilst the family sang to her. Joss smiled tenderly: it wasn't difficult to imagine the small Emma in such a state of excitement. Her mother was still just as capable of joyful celebration and delight in a party frock – even if she no longer insisted on wearing it to bed.

Joss made some coffee, thinking now of the young Mutt upstairs dressing for the dance: turning before the looking-glass, assessing herself in Honor's made-over frock. She imagined Mutt, filled with apprehension, humming to herself as she picked up the black velvet bag whilst Simon waited downstairs in the drawing-room, tall and handsome in his dinner jacket. She could identify with that breathless excitement, forbidden yet irresistible; the delicious shyness breaking out into giggling and wild, foolish happiness.

And then we got up to dance . . .

Joss shivered, hugging herself. 'George,' she muttered with wistful despair. 'Oh, George. I do love you.'

The kettle was boiling. She made some coffee and carried it back to the parlour.

2nd October

How you would have laughed, Vivi, if you could have seen us today. It would have taken you back to our childhood: Indian summer days in the hot, dusty Wiltshire lanes, picking black-berries for Mother. Out we went with baskets, Emma and Dolly riding in an antiquated push-chair that once was Hubert's, with Aunt Julia in command. The juicy fruit, each one like a cluster of shiny black pin-heads, was picked with care; even Emma was allowed to help, although she invariably squashed the fruit between her small fingers and her mouth was stained purple by the time we'd finished. Honeysuckle is still flowering in the hedges and I picked a crown, delicate and pale, and threaded it through the buttonhole of my shirt. Bruno pressed on faithfully with Aunt Julia but Emma soon wearied of gleaning and began to wrench the last few blooms of summer from the dry ditches, running to and fro until she was exhausted and glad to climb back into the push-chair with Dolly and her booty.

Aunt Julia would have made a splendid general: no spray was too high, she simply hooked the poor things down with a walking stick, and no effort was too great. Bruno was not allowed to miss a single berry; each one was pointed out to him, spotted by her eagle eye. He has a great fondness for her and they worked together very companionably whilst I brought up the rear, encouraging Emma onwards and pushing the little chair. Julia's very sweet to me – after all, she too lost her husband during the war – but she has James's horror of any display of emotion. They both have ways of showing their sympathy – a brisk pat on the arm, a murmured 'well done' of approval – but I can't tell you, Vivi, how much I sometimes long for a hug. Hubert was good at hugs. 'Daft old thing,' he'd say, 'You *are* a Mutt,' and Honor would smile, but they were both affectionate, loving people. Having our babies brought me and Honor particularly close and I miss that closeness with people of my own age. That's why it was so good with Simon.

We were allowed a little treat for our labours: a picnic by the Saint's Well. Aunt Julia had managed some little fairy cakes, milk for Bruno and Emma, and a Thermos of tea. I think that she and Jessie and Dot save all their fat and sugar rations to make these things for the children, who loved the little party, although Emma had to be forcibly restrained from paddling in her shoes and socks.

We left Aunt Julia at The Row and crossed the little bridge to Paradise. Bruno always likes to visit The Lookout. It's more like a lighthouse with its great bowed window curving out over the sea. The boatyard manager lived in it before the war and it's quite sound, though rather damp. For some reason it fires Bruno's vivid imagination and he uses it as a kind of playhouse. I must admit that it's a wonderful setting for make-believe games. We didn't have the key with us so he had to content himself with running up the rocky path to peer in at the kitchen window while we waited in the lane.

Coming home across the meadow, clouds of tiny white moths fluttered up from the long damp grass: Emma reached for them, trying to catch them, chuckling with delight. I sometimes have ideas of getting a pony for the children – Hubert had one when he was a small boy – but I don't know how expensive it might be to feed.

I've had a letter from Simon. It was simply to thank me for the weekend, saying how lovely it was for him to spend some time away from his work in a family atmosphere. Right at the end he suggested that I might accompany him to the wedding of a friend of his: he makes it very clear that he'll be staying with this friend – Simon's to be the best man – and points out that, whilst I might not like the idea of being left to my own devices whilst he's doing his duty, the rest of the time could be rather fun. He says he'd book a hotel for me, organize the travelling, and wonders – this is in a PS – if we might go to the theatre.

It's rather sweet of him to think of me, isn't it?

Anyway, a good day here in Paradise. I wonder if I will ever show it to you. Oh, what joy to imagine you here, if only I could see you face to face, Vivi, and explain it all properly. You would understand. I know you would.

God bless you, darling.

All my love, Madeleine.

23rd October

Knowing how clear-eyed and practical you are, Vivi, it will surprise you to read that I actually spent several days considering Simon's invitation. You would have said at once, 'You can't possibly go,' having seen the complications immediately. I think I knew too, deep down out of sight, but I wouldn't acknowledge it; I wanted to go so much, Vivi. I could imagine it all so clearly: the opportunity to dress up a little, the fun, the company of people of my own age. I'd had that moment with him, you see; that moment of stepping apart and being simply us – Simon and Madeleine – with none of the responsibilities we all carry with us. For that moment I wasn't anyone's mother or wife or widow, I wasn't pretending to be another woman, I was just me – and it was wonderfully releasing. I've tasted the goblin fruit, Vivi, and I want more of it. Do you remember?

'I ate and ate my fill,
Yet my mouth waters still;
Tomorrow night I will
Buy more:'

Except that I didn't eat my fill, it was just a little taste, and Simon's invitation offered more. I did actually believe that I could go to London. I went into my bedroom to look at a tussore silk costume – Honor's, of course – which might be pressed and tweaked into respectability, and wondered if I might have enough clothing coupons for a pretty hat or a new blouse to freshen it up a little. I think that the suit must have been a little tight for her because it's practically unworn and I won't need to alter it, except that the skirt is a tiny bit short. I was trying it on, humming 'Ev'ry Time We Say Goodbye', when Bruno suddenly came through the doorway behind me.

I didn't turn round. We simply stared at each other through the glass and I could see that he was looking at the suit. Do you know, Vivi, I was simply unable to speak: I couldn't think what to say to him. I felt so cheap, planning my little outing in his dead mother's clothes, and I could think of no words to explain the situation to a small boy of not quite five years old.

He disappeared as silently and quickly as he'd arrived and I sat down on the edge of the bed, still in the costume, and faced the fact that I wouldn't be going anywhere. As I sat there, the horror of what I'd been contemplating made me shiver: after all, Simon's friend is a doctor too, and it's possible that there might have been someone at his wedding we'd trained with who might still remember me or Honor. It occurred to me that, outside Paradise, I am very vulnerable and in that bleak moment I felt the bars closing round me.

I changed out of the suit and went straight downstairs to reply to Simon's letter. I wrote things like, 'It's rather too soon to trust myself on such an emotional occasion' and, 'I think I might feel a little out of my depth amongst so many strangers' and then I went to look for Bruno.

I could hear Dot in the kitchen talking to Emma who loves to 'help' her cook; this means licking spoons and running her tiny fingers round the mixing bowls to catch any remains of the delicious cake-mix. There was no sound of Bruno's voice and, not wanting to disturb them, I passed through the hall and out into the porch. It was a quiet, still afternoon, after a week of wild gales from the west, and the garden had that peaceful, waiting atmosphere of late autumn. It's such a different kind of waiting from the breathless expectancy of spring; that is a yearning, restless time when you can feel the tremendous energy that is about to be released. There's a pulsating violence about the early spring, isn't there, Vivi? Shoots – delicate but tough – force their way upwards through the cold, heavy earth, whilst tender new buds are breaking open their armour casing so that they can burst into leaf. Birds, which have spent the winter months peaceably together in flocks, will fight their erstwhile companions over a mate. Then, a wild urgency possesses the countryside so that the waiting seems almost intolerable.

Now, with the last showers of gold still waiting to fall from the beeches at the bottom of the drive, and smoky-blue drifts of Michaelmas daisies in the border under the wall, this autumnal waiting is a growing, contented detachment from things achieved: a serene acceptance of the much-needed fallow time ahead.

I saw Bruno at once. He was riding Hubert's old tricycle down the drive: elbows akimbo, feet pedalling furiously, he was really pushing it along. At the gate he turned the handle-bars sharply, so that the gravel flew beneath the rubber tyres, and then he stopped: head on one side, legs straddling, he held a long, earnest conversation with nobody I could see. Presently he took hold of the handlebars again and came back up the drive. His head was down and he was muttering furiously but, halfway along, he paused again to shout to his invisible companion and I caught the word 'Badmash'. With a great sigh – as if at someone's incompetence – he slid from the saddle, opened the little hatch at the back of the tricycle, brought out a small catapult and loosed off a pebble into the shrubbery. Leaping back onto the tricycle, he came on at great speed and I quickly stepped out of view, reappearing as he reached the house as if I had only just arrived in the porch.

One glance at his flushed, eager little face told me that he was in the grip of some exciting game of his own invention, a world away from me and Honor's silk costume, and I felt quite weak with relief. I saw a moment's confusion in his eyes, as the two worlds collided, and I smiled at him.

'I think there might be Cornish splits for tea,' I said to him, 'with blackberry jelly and clotted cream. I hope Pipsqueak and Wilfred haven't got at the cream. Shall we go and see?'

He slipped from the saddle, watching me, and I went down on one knee and held out my arms to him.

'I love you,' I told him – oh, how I hugged him – 'and I want you to be happy.'

'I am happy, Mutt,' he said, quite seriously as if to reassure me. 'I love it here with you and Emma and all the family.'

And he took my hand, Vivi, and we went into the house together.

As he dips toast fingers into his egg, Bruno is thinking about how he felt when he went into Mutt's bedroom and – for one heart-stopping moment – saw Mummie standing with her back to him. The costume, the smell of the silk, triggered off so many tiny memories that he'd been knocked off balance: the Paradise world colliding with the Indian world with a terrific shock. Then he'd seen Mutt's face in the mirror and he'd felt relieved but confused and he'd run away again quickly. He'd known that if he'd allowed it he might have burst into tears, because the memories were making him remember all the people and things that he'd lost, but another part of him was already making up a story that distracted from the hurt. He'd let himself go along with the story, finding his tricycle and dashing off on it, acting out the story while it unwound itself in his head. It was a good story and when Mutt had appeared he'd almost forgotten what had happened earlier. He could see that she hadn't, though. She had her flustered expression – caught between feeling sorry that they had to play this game of pretend but not knowing what else to do. She'd hugged him.

'I love you,' she said, 'and I want you to be happy.'

He knows that this is quite true and he tried to comfort her, explaining that he is happy here with all the family round him.

Now, eating his egg and watching Pipsqueak and Wilfred playing on the floor, he knows that he wouldn't want anything to change.

Emma's face is smeared with jam that has somehow got into her hair and Mutt is laughing at her. She looks at him, making a face that says, 'Isn't she hopeless?' and he makes it back at her. He likes the way she makes him feel grown up.

'We might go down to The Lookout after tea,' he says casually. This is cheating because he knows that when Mutt's had a flustered moment it is easier to get his own way over certain things. 'Just for a minute,' he adds quickly.

The thing is that he gets his best ideas in that strange house, standing in the great window staring out to sea; stories and odd words and memories of things people have read to him all swill in and out of his head, just as the sea floods in over the rocks.

'We'll see,' says Mutt. 'Perhaps just for a minute' – and they smile at each other with complete understanding.

December

It's nearly Christmas, Vivi, and more than six weeks have passed since I wrote that last letter: a month of storms and rain and a beastly influenza which knocked Jessie and Dot and Julia down like ninepins in a row – or The Row – and then proceeded to attack James and the children. Mousie, Rafe and I escaped it and, between us, we nursed the old and the young back to health. Poor Bruno's birthday passed almost unnoticed and we intend to make it up to him at Christmas. Goodness, I am exhausted and I've lost some weight, rushing between The Row and Paradise, but it was good to be useful and to try my nursing skills once more. Mousie will make a very good nurse, that's certain, and Rafe is such a blessing.

I don't have to tell you, dear Vivi, that I've always got on better with the male of the species. They are less complicated than we are – 'And,' I can hear you saying rather tartly, 'much more susceptible.' Well, yes, I can't deny that. I think Rafe has a little bit of a crush on me at present – violent blushing if I brush his arm, slight stammering if we are alone – it's very touching. Mousie is contemptuous and, embarrassed for him and defensive of his self-respect, she blames me for it and is furious with him. Fifteen is such an uncomfortable age for a boy, although Rafe is very independent and mature for his age. With no father he has had to grow up quickly and Julia sees to it that he shoulders the family responsibilities in his father's stead. She is very tough, very much like the army wives I knew in India, and I suspect that she considers me rather easygoing and emotional with the children.

There's something missing in me, Vivi. I never acquired that maturity which implies superior wisdom simply because – between one day and the next – I happened to become an adult, or a married woman, or a mother. When does this magical transition take place? Perhaps it's a conspiracy and everyone feels as I do but they simply don't admit it. Actually, Honor had that adult quality, a kind of gravitas that made you feel safe with her, yet she could be fun too. Sometimes, when I wear particular items of her clothing, a little of that gravitas rubs off on me like fairy dust. In her tweeds I feel a little more sober, more ready to deal with emergencies and – you'll laugh at this, Vivi – on certain days that I know are going to prove difficult I deliberately choose those garments. In her grey flannel coat and skirt, along with sensible brogues, I *am* Honor Trevannion; going off to Polzeath to buy stamps at the post office and collect the children's orange juice from the surgery.

Well, I am Honor Trevannion now. I have her name, her clothes, her home and her son, and it's only fair to try to do as she would have done with them all.

I discovered something else, Vivi, once I'd made the decision about Simon's invitation. I can't send you these letters, can I? Perhaps I knew that too, but couldn't face it. Writing to you is my lifeline to the truth, to what I really am, and I'm afraid to cast it off in case I forget the truth and lose myself utterly. I think we all long to have one person in our lives who truly knows us and, despite everything, loves us unconditionally. How can I send the letters? Will you feel you must tell your husband and, if you do, what then? One more person who knows the secret – and it's not just my secret, Vivi. At night, alone, I rack my brains and try to see a way out. I pray for a miracle: I long to go to Mass this Christmas. If I were to make my confession how could I go on afterwards, still living a lie? What I really want is to be let off; to be given a blessing on what I am doing here at Paradise.

Have you guessed that it's one of those rare evenings when I am alone and I've had one too many glasses of James's whisky? I miss him when he's not here. He protects me from myself.

I think about you, dear Vivi, and wonder what you're doing this Christmas.

It is true that Rafe has a crush on Honor. Something about her vulnerability and courage awakens his chivalry and he does what he can to make life easier for her. He helps in the garden, splits logs, takes letters to the post box up on the Polzeath road. His mother expects him to do these things for her as a matter of course – he is the man of the house now his father is dead – but Honor reacts differently when he helps her. 'You *are* a blessing,' she might say – or 'I don't know what I'd do without you.' He is warmed by her gratitude, although he tries not to show his pleasure.

Mousie sees through him, though. His sister thinks that he's making a bit of a fool of himself and, when she over-hears Honor's grateful endearments, she shoots those sisterly glances at him – which are an odd mixture of amusement, indignation and embarrassment – and he feels foolish. He knows it's because she can't bear to see him behaving without dignity but he doesn't see it like that. Ever since his father died his mother has expected great things of him, and Mousie helps her to keep him on his toes, so that he always feels slightly stretched. He can relax with Honor; she has an odd knack of treating him as an equal and yet that sense of expectation he feels with his mother and sister is missing with her. He especially loves taking her out in the boat, teaching her to sail it, encouraging her to be confident in handling the *Kittiwake*. He senses the freedom she experiences when she's at sea and it gives him enormous pleasure to help her towards being independent.

One evening after an afternoon on the water, with James out with friends and the children in bed, she makes him some supper: just the two of them. She talks so naturally to him, not asking him what he'll do when he leaves school or treating him like a child but really talking to him. They exchange thoughts and ideas, and presently she pours drinks for them both. He watches, rather shocked, as she tips a finger of whisky into a glass and then pours some water on top. He drinks it, though; he's too shy to say that his mother wouldn't like to see him drinking and rather proud that Honor looks upon him as one of her grown-up friends; like Simon, for instance.

'It's been such fun,' she says when he gets up to go home – and she kisses him lightly on the cheek, one hand resting on his shoulder.

At those moments he can feel himself blushing and guesses that he looks what Mousie would describe as 'a prize idiot', and he is filled with a whole confusing mix of emotions. He goes home by the cliff path, so as to give the fresh wind from the sea the chance to cool his cheeks, and when he gets in he gulps back cups of cold water from the tap in the hope that his mother won't smell the whisky on his breath.

15th January 1948

I've just reread that final paragraph, Vivi, and, despite its rather dreary note, we had a delightful Christmas. It was a replay of Emma's birthday, but with a tree and charming home-made presents for everyone – and Simon brought a goose. Did I say that he was coming for Christmas? James invited him and I have to admit that he added considerably to the fun. He's so good with the children and had found lots of tiny treats that we hadn't managed to rustle up in Polzeath or Wadebridge. It was good to be home for a traditional Christmas and Bruno was enchanted. I wish you could have seen him carefully examining the tree decorations, the same ones with which Hubert had decorated the tree when he was the same age as Bruno is now: delicate, frosted glass balls in different shapes – an owl, a clock, a mouse – and Victorian papier mâché bells, hand-painted red and green, and with tiny clappers. There were tiny carved wooden musical instruments and little birds, and each branch held its own candle. When they were lit on Christmas Eve, and we brought the children into the darkened drawing-room to see the finished tree, the gleaming, magical look of it quite took my breath away. Simon and James stood one on each side, beaming proudly, and I have to say, Vivi, that I was glad of the shadowy darkness. Looking at the children's awed faces – one of those rare occasions when Emma is silenced by events too great for her – I thought of Honor and Hubert, and I wept.

Fortunately, Emma's silence, never very long-lived, was broken by the sight of the angel at the top of the tree and her demanding to be lifted up to look at it. I could see Simon watching me across the room but, surprisingly, it was Mousie who slipped an arm about my shoulders and gave me a hug.

'It must be a bit strange after India,' she said – and I nodded gratefully, although it was much more complicated than that.

'It's wonderful,' I answered honestly, wiping away my tears.

'You've made us feel so much at home. I don't know how to thank you all.'

'You don't have to thank us,' she answered in her direct way. 'This is your home. You're our family now.'

It was one of those moments in life where you can go deeper in with someone, move the relationship on to a different plane and allow it to grow, and I can't tell you how I longed to do it. She's closest to me in age, she's following my own profession, she adores the children: yet as we looked at each other I felt fear. Of all the family, Mousie is the only one whose intuitiveness tells her that something is not quite right. It would be impossible to come really close to her and be able to hold anything back: when she gives her friendship it will be all or nothing, uncompromising and total, and she will expect the same in return. It was a valuable gift she was offering me and I was unable to receive it from her.

I couldn't risk it.

I returned her hug and made some remark about the children – but we both knew. She smiled at me and went to Bruno, leaving me alone. For a moment I didn't know what to do, where to go: I was outside the magic circle, cold and alone. Then Simon was beside me, offering me a glass of sherry, murmuring something nonsensical but bringing me to life again. His words, just for me, were as warming as the sherry, and I felt close to him because he is an outsider too. Simon, bless him, doesn't suspect anything is wrong but he hopes that I can imagine him taking Hubert's place, once a decent interval has elapsed, and, man-like, he's going to seize his opportunities when they come. His intuition – different from Mousie's – tells him that I am not indifferent to him and that in due course I shall reward his patience. In his own way he's just as clear-sighted as Mousie but, though his demands are different ones, it would be just as impossible, in the long term, to deceive him either.

Simon would have given me true companionship –

emotional, mental, physical – and more babies. It's clear that he wants his own children and he would have been wonderful with Bruno and Emma; it would have meant friendship with other people of our own age and simple ordinary fun.

I sometimes wondered, once my passion for Johnny was spent and I saw him for what he was, whether I was in love with Hubert. I certainly loved him but as if he were my brother – or so I told myself. Later I wondered if it had been more than that, but now I know it wasn't. I'm in love with Simon, Vivi.

A Happy New Year, my darling.

She's in love with him, thinks Mousie, watching them from across the room. Perhaps, after all, this is Honor's secret. Did she fall in love with him when he met the boat? Perhaps she's been afraid that the family will find out and be shocked. After all, Hubert had been dead only a few weeks when they arrived at Liverpool.

Mousie feels the usual mix of irritation and sadness. Just for a moment, when she saw the tears in Honor's eyes, her own petty emotions were washed away in a genuine surge of affection. It might have simply been a result of the magic of the tree, the children's awed expressions, the pride on Uncle James's face, but she experienced something bigger than her own jealousy of this older, sophisticated woman; a feeling that overcame her annoyance with Rafe's obvious adoration for Honor and her own suspicions of Hubert's widow. The naked loss on Honor's face showed Mousie that judging other people might lead to terrible injustice, and she'd instinctively put an arm about the older woman.

'This is your home,' she said. 'You're our family now.'

Just for a moment they looked at each other, unhampered by preconceived ideas and emotions, and then Honor withdrew herself. She returned the hug, made a joking observation about the children, but the moment in which they might have gone forward in closer friendship passed and they are no further on.

Or is that true? Watching Honor, standing alone for a moment in the shadows, Mousie knows that something deep inside herself has changed. She is hurt by Honor's withdrawal and feels the foolishness that accompanies rejection but, as Simon moves to Honor's side and they begin to talk in that peculiarly intimate way together, Mousie also feels a great compassion for Honor. She sees that Honor's need for Simon is as all-consuming as Emma's passion for the angel on the Christmas tree that she is now clamouring to hold. Simply being held up to look at the angel isn't enough: she needs to possess it. There is a similar expression on Honor's face: as if she has seen something magical but forbidden.

Poor Honor, thinks Mousie. Whatever the truth of her life with Hubert, she is in a very difficult situation now.

Watching Emma's storm of tears, which is a result of the denial of the angel, Bruno is glad of Aunt Julia's rock-like presence. Her unchangeability soothes him. It doesn't occur to her to give in to Emma's passionate wails but simply stops her mouth with some small edible treat. Emma's cries turn to a pathetic, intermittent wailing but her cheek bulges satisfactorily and her pudgy hands grasp willingly at one of the smaller wooden toys that she is allowed to hold. He doesn't know the word 'hedonist' but he does know that Emma likes life to be a succession of small treats: tiny islands of pleasure placed at regular intervals in the humdrum sea of day-to-day. Such is her generous delight in sharing these treats that most people are glad to grant them for the pleasure they derive from her overwhelming joy.

'Enjoying yourself?' His grandfather is smiling at him and, from behind that lined, worn face, Bruno can see his own father like some young, vigorous ghost smiling out at him.

189

He nods, suddenly unable to speak, and his grandfather pats his arm understandingly.

'Good boy. Good boy,' he says rather gruffly and turns away to talk to Rafe.

'Look,' says Mousie, showing him the tiny carved toy, whilst Emma beams at him.

'Birdie,' she says rather thickly, her mouth still full of toffee, wanting Bruno to share in her pleasure of the tiny bird. Aunt Julia gives him a toffee and pats him on the head in passing and Bruno knows that this gesture is the equivalent of Grandfather's muttered 'Good boy,' and is indicating her approval because he doesn't shout to get his own way. He sees dimly that Emma's passion somehow results in undeserved rewards for himself and he feels a glow of gratitude towards her.

'Good little chap,' James says to his sister-in-law. 'Very like Hubert, don't you think?'

'Very.' Julia permits herself a smile as she looks at the little group. 'Hubert would be proud of him. He's a brave little fellow. Of course, Emma is too young to understand what's happened but she's a dear little soul.'

'We're not doing too badly either, Julia.' He allows himself to share a moment of uncharacteristic self-congratulation with her. 'Those two of yours are a credit to you.'

For a moment they think of past Christmases: Julia thinks of Hugh, home on leave, playing with Mousie and Rafe in those years before the war. James thinks of Margaret and the quiet, happy times together; and he thinks of his son. They exchange a long look, each silently acknowledging the other's pain, and then the mantle of stoicism descends on them once more. They straighten their shoulders, lift their chins and look about them cheerfully. The party is a great success.

19th February

I'd forgotten how melancholy the English spring can be, Vivi. I sit in the drawing-room looking out into the twilight, a wood fire crackling behind me, watching the sky change colour: patches of gun-metal grey, robin's-egg blue, salmon pink. The lawn is frosted with a light scattering of snow, icing the snowdrops and crocus that are flowering in the grass, and I can hear a thrush singing amongst the camellias. A blackbird flies swift and low over the silent garden, alighting with its stuttering, warning cry on a bleak, bare branch, and there are lambs crying in the fields below the house. Quite suddenly the crimson sunset colour drains out of the sky and I see the thin beaten-silver disc of the moon tangling amongst the black twigs of a thorn tree.

This is Paradise, Vivi, and the serpent is a worming, gnawing creature called Discontent: the sting of the wasp, the smarting of the nettle, the piercing of the thorn, all belong to him. Do you think that God punishes us? I don't. We punish ourselves by making Him small; cramming Him into man-sized boxes, making Him in our own image, and actually imagining that He thinks like we do. On evenings like this I catch a glimpse, just a glimpse, of what He is offering us. It's odd, isn't it, that Satan offers to Christ — and to us — those things that we believe are Godlike: empires, angels protecting us, freedom from starvation and want? He tricks us into believing that these things will make us safe and great and happy, whispering in our ears, creating a restlessness. God remains silent, continually offering a poverty of spirit, promising nothing but love.

Sorry, Vivi. I find that, more and more, I have to talk things through with myself so as to try to understand my feelings. It's best when I sit and write to you like this, sharing everything just as we did all those years ago before the war. I hear your voice and imagine what you would be saying to me.

I love Simon.

191

'Remember Robert Talbot and Geoffrey Stack,' I hear you cry. 'Remember the young PP, for whose spiritual top marks we vied and fought like cats, and the young man who taught us art for one whole, blissful term.'

I do think of them – and all the others too, including Johnny – but Simon is different. I can hear your snort of contempt and I long, oh how I long, to see your face. Did ever other girls love like we did, Vivi? It seems that from the age of twelve we were in a continual state of longing, whether the object of our passion dwelt between the pages of a book or ran the local riding school. I fell in love with Geoffrey simply for his long legs in jodhpurs and riding boots. Yet how innocent we were. Oh, the heart-stopping joy of those deliciously chaste kisses; the thrill at the unexpected – yet longed-for – touch of a hand. But I've eaten the fruit of Goblin Market and I want more, much more than that now.

We took Bruno to the pantomime at Bodmin for his belated birthday treat; he'd never seen anything like it and he was speechless with delight. His eyes never left the stage, Vivi, and nor did mine. He sat between me and Simon – Mousie and Rafe and Aunt Julia further along the row – and Simon laid his arm along the back of Bruno's seat, oh, so casually and naturally, so that his fingers were just resting on my shoulder. It was all I could think about; the touch of his fingers burning through the thin material of my frock. Honor's frock. It was this, oddly, which exerted control over me, the memory of her wearing it preventing me from covering his hand with mine, and I was able to pretend that I hadn't noticed.

As I stared sightlessly ahead, unmoved by Aladdin's plight, I thought about Honor and how she would have reacted. It was a pointless exercise: Honor would never have allowed herself to be in such a position. Yet the sight of the fine, blue wool stretched over my knee, the glimpse of its well-cut sleeve, held me steady. I clapped in all the right places, hands held high, smiling brightly, and bent solicitously to Bruno to share in his pleasure and explain the plot to him from time to time.

I knew that Simon was watching me, admiring me in my motherly role, approving my love and tenderness for my son. Honor's son. Bruno's rapt excitement, the way he clutched me when the genie shot up through the trapdoor, also held me steady. I love him too, Vivi, which makes it all so terribly complicated.

I imagine that I hear your voice telling me that it was already complicated, that, once I'd taken that decision in the hotel room in Karachi, my life could never be simple again. I make up little scenarios for myself; fairy stories in which everything comes right in the end and we live happily ever after. The serpent whispers in my ear and tells me that I can have it all, that I need only to stretch out my hand to take it, and his restless whispering drowns out the silence where God lives.

In returning and rest you shall be saved: in quietness and trust shall be your strength.

It's surprising how much I must have taken in unconsciously during those convent years, and now comes back to comfort me.

It's evening now. The moon is sailing free of the thorn tree, its cold light silvering the frosty grass, and the trees cast sharp black shadows across the drive. I can hear James coming out of his office, ready for a drink.

Today would have been my birthday, Vivi, and I would have been twenty-eight.

Love you, darling.

Simon can barely keep his eyes from her. She looks so beautiful but tonight there is a remoteness about her that both attacks his confidence and fuels his determination. The presence of the family is frustrating and he senses that she is holding him at arm's length because – apart from James and Emma (who is being looked after by Jessie) – they are all here

together, belatedly celebrating Bruno's birthday. Simon grimaces ruefully to himself: 'arm's length' is exactly the right
phrase. He is unable to resist stretching his arm along the
back of Bruno's seat so that his fingers just touch Mutt's
shoulder. Oh, he's done it very casually so that it looks like
one natural movement combined with leaning back to make
himself more comfortable. His height and length of limb have
secured him the seat at the end of the row and his posture is
very relaxed.

Bruno is far too preoccupied with the pantomime to notice
what his godfather is doing but Mutt is aware of him: Simon
knows that. She isn't responding this evening as she has done
in the past, though. She's particularly maternal this evening,
her whole concentration bent on ensuring that Bruno is
enjoying himself. Simon is surprised that, despite his approval
of her behaviour towards her son, he feels unusually jealous
and becomes even more determined to get a reaction from
her, however slight.

There's something different, though: a new coolness has
quenched the warmth of her personality. He finds himself
studying her covertly across Bruno's head. Is it something to
do with her hair or her clothes? She watches the stage,
apparently totally absorbed, unconscious of his stare, and he
moves his fingers so that they touch the thin material of
her frock and the warm shoulder beneath it. Suddenly he is
aware of Mousie, further along the row, watching him. He
smiles quickly and shifts in his seat, folding his arms across his
chest.

Although he laughs and applauds in all the right places, he
is thinking hard, planning ahead: somehow he must find the
opportunity to be alone with her again.

Later

I never told you what James gave me for Christmas, did I?
He's not a man for gifts – and in these strict days of rationing

it's a problem anyway – but he presented me with his wife's tapestry frame. I rather prefer this kind of gift, something special that has been used for years within the family, and I was absolutely thrilled with it. He was rather anxious that I might be offended that a half-done tapestry was still stretched over the big, tilting frame, but I was very moved to think that I should be taking up where Margaret left off. She was obviously very clever with her needle: dark red flowers of the japonica, held stiffly on a thick branch with bright green leaves, against a cream background. There's also a small round frame and a workbox full of silks and wool.

I used to get top marks for needlework, do you remember, Vivi? You found it tiresome, fiddly work but it was one of the very few areas in which I could hope to please Mother. I see the evidence of Margaret's work all over the house: an impressive set of chair covers in the dining-room, a big medieval-type tapestry on the landing, and smaller charming flower studies in lovely, plain frames.

James was so pleased at my reaction. I've taken the big frame and set it up in the dining-room. I should like to have it in James's office – two big windows facing north and east, oh, I do envy him his privacy – but this does splendidly. He is so good to us; it can't be easy having two small children suddenly wished upon you, yet he manages very well. He has a detached quality that enables him to drift above the day-to-day, absorbed in a book or in his office . . .

He told me yesterday that, after his death, the two farms would have to be sold to pay the death duties. You can imagine my shock at this subject so casually introduced into the conversation. I said I didn't want to talk about his dying and he smiled, such a sweet, Hubert-like smile, and said that he didn't actually have it in his diary but that we needed to discuss certain things.

'Everything goes to you and the children,' he said. 'No change there. Of course, if you were to marry again . . .'

He hesitated and I knew that he was thinking about Simon. I felt my face grow hot and my stomach churned about.

'I shan't marry again,' I answered.

I said it so quickly, with such certainty, and immediately afterwards I felt a great peace begin to fill me.

'You're very young to make that decision,' James said. He looked so kind, so understanding. 'You don't have to rule it out but if you were to do so then I would make a new will. The estate would revert to Hubert's children to be held in trust until they come of age.'

I saw then that he wouldn't want Paradise and St Meriadoc being passed on to any children I might have by Simon and this whole, wretched deception came clearly into my mind. He wouldn't want Emma or me to have any of it either, if he knew the truth of it, and my brief moment of peace was shattered.

'It was simple for me and Margaret,' he was saying, 'having only one child. My dear, forgive me for speaking about it but I want to leave you safe if I can, and not in the hands of Bruno's wife or Emma's husband, so it will all come to you and I shall trust you to leave it to Hubert's children. I've arranged a trust for their school fees but, beyond that, you'll be hard pressed, I'm afraid. There are the rents from The Row, of course . . .'

'I have my pension,' I said quickly. 'We shall be fine. Please don't worry.'

'The place is in good heart,' he said, 'I've seen to that, but things have changed since the war. Very well, we won't talk about it any more at present. How about a drink?'

So Paradise is to be mine, Vivi, but not just yet. I had a letter from Simon this morning. He's beginning to press me a little, suggesting a visit to Exeter. He shares a flat with a fellow medico, and his proposals are all very proper, but I have the feeling that he thinks the mourning period should be coming to a close. He's coming down for Easter.

What shall I do?

Just as with Margaret's jewels, it is Julia who prods James into action over his will.

'You should let Honor know how she stands,' she tells him. 'We're not getting any younger and she needs to understand how things are.'

'I can't see a problem,' he mutters, feeling that it might be embarrassing. 'I changed my will when Hubert had a son. Everything goes to his widow, or if she's died, then to Hubert's children. It's quite straightforward.'

'But Honor doesn't have second sight,' Julia insists. 'She might assume that when you die she'll have to move out, d'you see?'

'Nonsense,' he says irritably – but he acknowledges the possibility of it and forces himself to discuss it with her.

First, he makes a little ceremony of giving her Margaret's large tapestry frame. Honor frequently admires her needle-work and it gives him pleasure to think that Margaret's legacy will be put to good use. Honor is delighted and it is easier then to introduce the subject of the will. It is clear that she is just as uncomfortable as he is and tries to brush the subject aside. He is obliged to mention the subject of her marrying again – Julia has touched on this too – but she answers very promptly.

'I shan't marry again,' she says – and he suddenly feels a deep compassion for her, left so young with such small children. Watching her laughing with Simon he has wondered whether the two of them are falling in love and, though he wouldn't blame her in the least, he is determined that St Meriadoc must be held secure for Hubert's children. Of course, if she marries again after his own death there will be nothing he can do about it and he wonders if he should make a new will leaving the estate in trust to the children. Yet she is so sure.

'I shan't marry again.'

Well, he'll leave it a while and see what happens. He wants her to be safe as she grows older, not dependent on the whim of any future in-laws she might acquire, and she is happy here at Paradise. It is what Hubert would have wanted.

He is pleased to see that she's already started work on the big half-finished tapestry and for some reason this gives him confidence that he's made the correct decision and that he is right to trust her.

23rd March

We've been down to The Lookout today, by the cliff-path. The day starts with thick mist drifting smoke-like from the sea, blotting out the waxy faces of the magnolia, misting the windows. Quite suddenly a breeze ripples through the garden, tearing the cloudy vapour apart and revealing a patch of tender blue sky. An unexpectedly violent downpour, and then the wind begins to rise and the clouds are whirled away. We set out at last in brilliant sunshine and vibrant colours: the icy green of the wild sea, the gold of the forsythia and the pinky-red of the ribes – all is vivid where, an hour before, all was grey and dim. After the sheltered garden, the cliff-path is high and exposed: the wind tears past us, whipping our hair into our mouths and stinging our eyes, our clothes are whirled about our legs, and we have to shout to one another to make ourselves heard above its screaming. I pick Emma up, since she can make no headway on her short legs, and, with Bruno clinging to my free hand, we stare down through the flying creamy foam to the heaving, billowing mass of water which seethes around the cliffs and smashes into the rocks below.

We are quite grateful to reach the relative peace of The Lookout, to watch the magnificent drama of sea and sky from the great bowed window, although the gale seems to shake even this solid rock-built fortress.

'I love it here,' says Bruno, staring out, arms resting on the broad, low sill. 'I shall live in The Lookout when I grow up, with Pipsqueak and Wilfred. You and Emma can be at Paradise and I shall come here.'

'That's a good idea,' I answer lightly.

I never go too deeply into the future with Bruno, unlike Aunt Julia who is always asking him if he is going to be a doctor – like his father – or a sailor, like his uncle. It would thrill her if he were to join the Navy, keeping up her family's tradition, but I never burden him with these things; time enough . . .

So, 'That's a good idea,' I say, 'and Emma and I will come to visit you.'

'We'll have tea at the table here,' he says, his face lighting up at the prospect, pointing at the big deal table which faces out towards the sea, 'and then we'll sit by the fire and tell stories. Are we going to light the fire today?'

This is a big treat. James has given us permission to light the fire in this enormous room: it helps to air the house, he agrees, as long as we make sure it's properly out by the time we leave. Bruno and I set to with twigs and matches and some paper spills and soon we have a jolly little blaze going. Emma droons about, singing to herself, wrapping herself in the dust-sheets which cover the few pieces of furniture. Presently the inevitable picnic will take place, after The Lookout has been thoroughly explored, the upstairs windows opened and the minimal amount of housework accomplished.

'You could live here too,' says Bruno out of the blue later, fearful perhaps that I have been hurt. 'Only who would live at Paradise?'

'Well, of course, Grandfather will be there,' I tell him cautiously.

'But not for ever,' he answers anxiously. 'Grandfather is old and sometimes he isn't very well. You'll be there too, won't you, Mutt?'

And out of nowhere, Vivi, I hear Honor's voice saying, 'You'll look after the children if anything happens to me and Hubert, won't you, Mutt? You know I'll have Lottie.'

We always promised each other and we meant it. We were

like sisters and I used to think of Goblin Market then – and of you:

> Afterwards, when both were wives
> With children of their own;
> Their mother-hearts beset with fears,
> Their lives bound up in tender lives;
> Laura would call the little ones
> And tell them of her early prime,
> Those pleasant days long gone
> Of not-returning time:

Except that I can't talk to anyone but you of those pleasant days long gone.

'Of course I shall be there,' I answer Bruno. 'I promise.'

Emma who, with the aid of a chair, has managed to climb up onto the table, somehow tumbles off and sets up a great wailing. We both rush to rescue her and the moment passes in a necessity to get out the picnic in order to distract her. The sight of the tiny sandwiches filled with grated chocolate – it helps to spin out the ration – dries her tears at once; she sits on the table, her fat legs swinging, eating with great appreciation. The amazing blue-green light from the sea and sky reflects in her wide eyes and, watching her, I am seized with the familiar terror that every mother knows.

How would it work for Emma if I were to marry Simon and have other children? Would he love her as if she were his own? I try to imagine him living with us at Paradise and somehow I can't: he won't fit into the picture. He is passionate about certain areas of research, has already talked about working abroad, and I try to imagine explaining all this to Bruno: why I am marrying Simon and why we are moving on again instead of staying at Paradise. Would Bruno understand? Would he think I was cheating? Have I the right to take him from his home and how could I leave him but take Emma without everything being told? How could I leave him, anyway? I love him. He has returned to the window with his sandwich and is staring out with delight: his small, immobile figure seems to be part of the scene. He belongs here, Vivi, and I have promised him . . .

I wonder if you have children too. I'm sure you have: perhaps a son who is a small edition of your husband, Don, or a little girl who looks like you used to once. Everything changes once you have a child.

Apart from all that, Vivi, how could I risk marrying Simon? Imagine how easy it would be to make a mistake once the barriers were down and my guard relaxed. How natural to say something like, 'Oh, I remember how Honor and Hubert used to . . .' And think of the more personal questions Simon might ask once we were married. Of course, in one way it would solve the dilemma of who I am, wouldn't it? I'd simply become Mrs Simon Dalloway. No more questions asked once those awful formalities – marriage certificates, death certificates, etc. – were out of the way, but the risks are simply too great. If I can't trust his love enough to tell him the truth now, then I certainly daren't take the chance of him discovering it later when there would be even more complications.

I hope he'll believe me when I tell him that I don't love him.

This time Joss was not quite able to hold back her tears. Some level of her consciousness continued to assess with dismay the threat these letters posed to her own security yet she still held the true realization at bay, enthralled by the predicament of her grandmother's journey. Joss was impressed at the development of Mutt's self-knowledge, her brave – if utterly human – way of dealing with her hopes and fears, and her unshakeable faith.

She didn't need to read any further to know that Mutt's and Simon's love had had no future: Mutt had made her bed and must lie in it alone. With the true compassion of fellow feeling, Joss picked up the dwindling sheets and began to read the last remaining letters.

29th March

It's done. He went back to Exeter this afternoon and now, although it's late, I simply had to write about all this. I'm in such an odd state, Vivi: exalted and trembly and foolish because he told me he loved me. He took me by surprise, you see. Mousie had taken the children down to The Row after lunch on Saturday so that I could paint and hide the Easter eggs. We'd hard-boiled them earlier so that they were quite cold and I'd found an old paintbox with small squares of good bright colours, though the paint was hard and cracked.

Well, the children went off quite happily and I wrapped myself in an old apron and settled at the kitchen table. James had gone down at Home Farm, and Simon was expected in time for dinner. I was listening to the wireless, some cheerful dance music on the Light Programme, and quite suddenly the door opened and there he was.

Oh, Vivi, it was disastrous. I forgot my plan; forgot about being distant and sensible; forgot that I was Honor Trevannion. I simply sat there, my paintbrush held aloft, beaming at him with delight. I just said 'Hello' or something silly, still smiling at him, with my heart all over the place and thinking how dear he was. It was quite the stupidest thing I've ever done. He responded in the most natural way. He closed the door behind him, came round the table and kissed me.

Fool that I am, Vivi, I responded to that too. It was the shock, you see. I'd planned it all out in my head how it would be. I saw myself coming down for supper, the children tucked up and dear old Dot having left the dinner under way, and greeting him rather coolly but quite friendly, in a very Honor-ish way, so that the evening got off on the right note.

Then, I'd planned to slip away to bed whilst he and James were having a nightcap so that the first evening was dealt with and I'd feel in control.

Sunday had already raised problems. Aunt Julia had suggested that she and I should go to St Endellion to Holy Communion together early on Easter morning (usually the whole family goes to Matins, or Evensong in the summer). How can I tell her that I can't receive? It was bad enough at Christmas not going to Midnight Mass, but now, on Easter morning, I cannot receive. Anyway, I saw her have the idea that I hadn't been confirmed and, after a moment of considering this and digesting it, she let the suggestion drop at once. I feel a traitor because I know very well that the family already suspect that I am almost an atheist, although none of them goes to the early service except on special occasions. Do you remember the Stations of The Cross each Good Friday with Sister Julian and how we'd all shout 'He is risen' on Easter morning? I feel as if I am denying Him just like St Peter. Even if I'd tried to bluff it out that Honor was a Roman Catholic (something Hubert would have almost certainly mentioned) I still can't go to Mass again until I've been to Confession. And then what? What would a priest say to me, I wonder.

Anyway, my plan was to remain cool, in control, and in company. Sunday was to be a family day, with the Easter egg hunt after lunch followed by a special tea, and I'd suggested that Aunt Julia, Mousie and Rafe should all come up for dinner in the evening. I'd been so sensible, so clever in thinking it all out so that Simon and I should have no opportunity to be alone until the last moment when it would be too late. I was going to be distant and calm and then, at the last possible moment, make it clear that I'd been thinking things over and seen that I'd given him quite the wrong impression. I was very fond of him, I'd been planning to say, but I didn't have any intention of marrying again.

Instead here he was, in the kitchen, kissing me. I was still sitting down, an egg in one hand and the paintbrush in the other, and kissing him back like any love-struck girl. No, that's not true. I kissed him in the way any woman who's had a lover kisses a man she wants – and no man can mistake that. Simon didn't. He pulled me to my feet, paused briefly to relieve me of my egg and paintbrush and then continued where we'd left off. I remembered my plan far too late but eventually controlled myself enough to draw away from him. He pulled himself together too, and there was a moment of horrid embarrassment on both sides.

It needn't have been like that. It could have been so nice if I hadn't made up my mind that I couldn't go through with it. It would have been so easy to smile at him and show him that it was quite all right; to make it clear that he wasn't taking liberties but only responding naturally to the signals I'd given him over the last six months. In those brief moments I saw so clearly how wonderful it might be with him: love as well as passion and our minds tuned to the same pitch. It seemed to me, at the time, that it would be criminal to kill something so good.

No gold stars then, Vivi, if you'd guessed that I didn't do it properly. I did the cowardly thing of telling him that I wasn't ready to fall in love again whilst giving the impression that if he hung around long enough I might change my mind. I apologized for leading him on – naturally he said at once that it was his fault – and muttered something about being lonely and finding him very attractive. Dot arrived at the garden door just as he'd begun to say that he'd wait for as long as it took and I was saying that I had no plans to marry again. Fortunately we heard her in enough time to compose ourselves, I was back at my egg-painting before she actually appeared, and Simon was saying loudly that he'd take his bag up, was he in the usual room and so on, and suddenly it was all over.

If Dot suspected anything she didn't show it. She got on with various preparations for dinner whilst I sat painting eggs as if my life depended on it, and letting her chatter away as she always does. It cast a different light over the weekend, though, as if we were both tingling with electricity that sparked between us. Neither of us could forget that kiss and, although I followed my plan and didn't see him alone again, it was almost as if we'd started something rather than finished it.

I wonder if your marriage is working out for you, Vivi? You look so happy in your wedding photograph and he looks really nice in a tough, strong-jawed way. And I shall never know, shall I? How easy it is, once you have irrevocably lost something, to imagine that the one thing you can no longer have is the only thing you ever truly wanted. At this moment I long for the relationship we once shared, you and I: that odd, close – and often painful – comradeship that is peculiar to siblings. I long for my religion that was once as natural as breathing and so much a part of the fabric of my life. And I long for Simon.

I've lost everything that was important to me – but I have gained Paradise.

The Easter egg hunt is great fun although Emma cannot quite get the hang of it. Once Bruno has found the first egg – balanced carefully in the lower branches of the wisteria – she expects them to be anywhere she chooses to look and there are wails of disappointment punctuated by shrieks of delight. Rafe is there to help them, to guide them towards the painted eggs whilst pretending to be as amazed as they are each time one is discovered. Rafe is enjoying himself. Often he finds Mutt at his elbow, reminding him where she has hidden the eggs, and they laugh together at the sight of Emma staggering purposefully in Bruno's wake, screaming encouragement. She is just as happy if he finds one, possessiveness having been entirely left out of her character, and anyway he shares them scrupulously between the two of them.

'Because she is too small,' he says seriously to Rafe, 'to find them on her own.'

Rafe puts the egg into the basket with the others and grins at Mutt.

'I hope Emma likes hard-boiled eggs,' he says. 'There must be a week's ration here.'

Mutt makes a face. 'Thank goodness for Home Farm,' she says, 'and Emma will eat anything. But I've been thinking, Rafe. Why shouldn't we have our own chickens? There's plenty of room out in the kitchen garden.'

For a moment they are drawn together in their mutual enjoyment of the garden. Mutt is beginning to love working in the Paradise gardens almost as much as she loves sailing, and Rafe is ready to encourage and assist. James is always ready to describe the glories of the past, and has gladly given his permission, and they have quite a few plans for the grounds, which have deteriorated since the war began. With no able-bodied man to help, and Margaret falling ill, large areas have been neglected, and Mutt and Rafe would like to see it all restored to its former beauty.

Emma sits down suddenly in a patch of long wet grass and begins to howl and Mutt runs to pick her up. Their discussion is abruptly brought to an end but Rafe feels that warm glow of sharing with her; the joy of all that lies ahead fills him with contentment.

Bruno, too, is happy. His sharing of the painted eggs with Emma is not totally altruistic: his natural generosity is assisted by the knowledge of the present that Simon has brought with him from Exeter. He has found a baker who has made two chocolate eggs on which the children's names have been written in icing. There is a little silence when he opens the cardboard boxes to show them – such luxury has not been seen for years – and then everyone cries out at once. Bruno sniffs the special, delicious smell of the chocolate. All through church and lunch he thinks about the eggs; a lovely secret thought.

There's something else too: something just for him. He puts his hand into the pocket of his shorts and feels the shape of the little red bus.

'After all,' says Simon, 'you *are* my godson, old chap. We men have to stick together.'

Bruno doesn't mind sharing his godfather with Emma – he can see that it would be unfair if she'd been left out of the kittens and the chocolate eggs – but it's good to have something just to himself.

He can see that Simon is happy too, which is good, but it is to Rafe he instinctively turns now. With Rafe he feels the same sense of security he has in the company of Aunt Julia and with Mousie.

'That sister of yours,' says Rafe feelingly – and Bruno laughs too, shrugging and rolling his eyes just as he's seen the grown-ups react to her escapades.

Watching Mutt swinging Emma into the air to distract her from her wet knickers he feels a deep sense of belonging.

'Time for tea,' Mutt is calling – and they all set off together towards the house.

9th April

I had a letter from Simon a few days ago. It was beside my breakfast plate and James watched me as I opened it, though he pretended to be absorbed in his own letters. It occurs to me that the chemistry I described, zinging between me and Simon during that weekend, might have been obvious to other people too, and I feel anxious and guilty. I wonder what James thinks of me, having told him I wouldn't marry again, and I fear that he might misunderstand and disapprove in some way. In an effort to appear calm and unaffected I helped Emma with a few mouthfuls of her porridge and cut the top from Bruno's egg before I opened the envelope.

We eat breakfast in the dining-room, and sometimes the sun streams in, circling Emma's head with a fuzzy golden halo and smoothing the gleaming rosewood of the oval table to a deep richness. It glints on the dark blue and gold-leaf patterns of the eggshell-thin china teapot and strokes its way over the silky stitches of Margaret's big tapestry hanging on the wall. Its warmth blesses and cheers us, making us eager for the day ahead and nourishing our plans and ideas.

The morning of Simon's letter it was raining. The dirty grey sky leaked with an unrelenting drizzle and the room felt chill and bleak. We'd had a warm spell – the spring comes and goes here, tantalizingly showing us her glories and then retreating behind a sharp shower of hail or a wild gale from the west – and this sudden reversion to winter was depressing. Emma was grizzling – as irritatingly persistent as the rain outside – and Bruno was asking if we could walk over the cliff to The Lookout after breakfast. James smiled gently at nobody whilst managing to convey sympathy for me and tolerance towards the children.

'We'll see,' I said to Bruno. 'If it clears up, perhaps,' and opened Simon's letter.

To my horror I saw that my hands were trembling, just a little, and I quickly laid the sheets on the table beside my plate, pretending that I wanted to spread my slice of toast with some of Julia's bramble jelly. I bent my head over the plate, my eyes scanning the lines of small, cramped writing. It was a sweet letter, Vivi, apologizing for taking advantage of my 'vulnerable state' and telling me that he'd fallen in love with me. He wrote: 'I shouldn't be so surprised that I feel the way I do. After all the things Hubert told me about you, I was half in love with you before I'd even met you . . .'

He went on to assure me, if somewhat clumsily, that Hubert would be pleased to think that we might be gaining comfort from each other, but a cold dread had already fallen across my mind.

All the things Hubert told me about you.

What things, Vivi, had Hubert told his oldest friend about

his wife? My first reaction was one of overwhelming relief that I hadn't already somehow given myself away to him. I looked up and saw that James was watching me. There was such far-seeing wisdom and affection in his eyes that fear clutched at my stomach. I knew then that I couldn't bear to see disillusionment and disgust in those eyes and that I had no choice but to follow my chosen path.

I smiled at him. 'A bread-and-butter from Simon,' I said lightly, 'thanking us all for such a lovely weekend.' Oddly I found it difficult to speak: my chest felt tight and the words came out rather breathlessly. Folding the sheets and carelessly stuffing them back into the envelope I wiped Bruno's fingers and danced Dolly upon the table to distract Emma. 'Perhaps Bruno's right. We should visit The Lookout and give it an airing. But we'll go round by the lane, I think. Too wet for the cliff. What sort of morning have you got, James?'

'Oh, an office morning for me, I'm afraid.' He drank up the last of his tea and pushed back his chair. 'Humdrum, boring old paperwork.'

He slipped away and I smiled at the children. These two were now my life, my work, my whole future, just as I had seen it in that hotel room in Karachi, and nothing must distract me from it. No goblin cries, no delicious fruit, no more kisses . . .

After lunch I wrote back to Simon while the children were resting upstairs and James was nodding over the newspaper in the office. I sat at the dining-room table and wrote to him that there was no future for us, that my mind was quite made up, and that, having experienced true love and companionship, I knew that I didn't love him in that same way. I asked him not to pursue it but to be kind about it, although I added that I was very fond of him and hoped that we would always be friends.

By writing to me he let me off the hook, because it is always so much easier to do this kind of thing at a distance, but I couldn't have gone to Exeter to see Simon so I decided that it was quite in order to write to him. Don't think it was easy, though, Vivi. I hated it. All that morning whilst I was winding the children into scarves and pushing their warm little feet into gumboots I was mentally writing that letter. Phrases and sentences jostled about in my head as we went down the drive, Emma jumping with passionate glee into every puddle, and I rehearsed it a thousand times as we lit our little fire and Bruno chatted non-stop to me and to the variously imagined friends with which he peoples his life.

Aunt Julia came up to Paradise after tea, as she sometimes does, to help to bath the children and put them to bed. I left her reading a story to them and slipped away up the lane to post the letter at the box up on the Polzeath road. I was afraid I might lose my nerve if I didn't send it straight away.

It was a cold, sweet evening with a new moon already setting away in the west. Honesty was flowering in the lane, sheltering with ragged robin and campion beneath the bare thorny hedges, and the rough wild cliff-top land was criss-crossed with great banks of yellow-flowered gorse and the foamy-white blossom of the blackthorn. Oh, the peace of it all. The sea leaned gently against the sheer, steep cliffs and the hoarse croaking of a raven drifted up from the valley near the Saint's Well.

I stood beside the post box for a good five minutes holding the letter in my pocket. I prayed then, Vivi. I prayed for guidance and wisdom so as to do the right thing for all of us, and all the time I was held by a kind of peacefulness. The walk and the silence and the beauty had made me calm and just then I wanted nothing more than to stay here, safe from the torment of passion and the agonies of love. That sense of peace remained with me all the way home.

Aunt Julia finishes Bruno's story, hears his prayers and then tucks him firmly into bed.

'Goodnight, dear boy,' she says. 'Sweet dreams,' and hurries downstairs.

James is reading peacefully in the drawing-room but he looks up as she comes in and sets his book aside: her expression indicates that all is not well. Julia closes the door firmly but quietly and sits down on the sofa.

'I'm worried about Honor.' She comes straight to the point. 'She seems rather *distrait* and ever since Easter I can't help wondering whether she's fallen in love with Simon. What do you think?'

This is very straight talking, even for Julia, and James crosses his legs whilst he decides how to answer her. It is quite true that during the Easter weekend he began to notice that Honor and Simon were sharply aware of one another, and when his letter arrived earlier in the week James was unable to ignore her reaction to it.

'A bread-and-butter from Simon,' she'd said lightly – but he'd seen how her hands trembled and noticed her distraction with the children.

He feels such compassion for her, imagining how wretched she must feel to be torn between several loyalties. James suspects that Honor believes that Hubert's children should grow up here at St Meriadoc and he wonders how Simon would approach the tricky situation of assimilating himself into this place where he'd been a guest and, even more difficult, taking over his old friend's family. It would be a daunting prospect even for someone as confident as Simon.

He stirs, aware of Julia's eyes fixed upon him.

'I think it is a possibility,' he begins cautiously. 'But even if she has I don't see what we can do about it. I think we should trust her.'

'It would be quite wrong for Bruno to be uprooted again,' Julia says strongly. 'He is just beginning to recover from his father's death and I think it would be disastrous for him to adapt all over again to a new father and away from his family.

Emma's too young to be a real problem, but even she is settling so happily here.'

'But what can I do about it?' asks James helplessly. 'I can't forbid them to fall in love.'

Julia puts up her chin – he is reminded of Margaret – and stares him squarely in the eye.

'It might be necessary to tell her that you can't afford any muddle when it comes to the children's inheritance.'

He looks at her, dismayed. 'I've already explained to her that, should she marry again, the estate will be held in trust for Bruno and Emma. She said that she had no intention of marrying again and I believed her. I told you about it.'

'So you did.' Julia frowns. 'Even so, watching them over Easter I would have said that there was something between them that went beyond friendship. She's been preoccupied and jumpy all week, and this evening she's been in another world entirely. Don't think I'm criticizing her, James. Simon is a charming, attractive man and she's young – don't imagine I don't sympathize! – but she needs to see the whole situation clearly. She's such a warm-hearted girl and I don't want her swept off her feet.'

'You think that this might be a reaction to Hubert's death?'

Julia is silent for a moment. 'It might be,' she says at last. 'I remember how I felt when Hugh was killed. It would have been heaven, occasionally, to put the burden onto a strong man's shoulders and leave it all to him. Luckily for me, I had you and Margaret to turn to before I could do anything foolish. Honor is younger than I was and, I suspect, much more susceptible. I don't want her to make a mistake.'

James looks at her curiously. 'Don't you like Simon?'

'Oh, he's a nice enough fellow. She could go further and fare worse but I don't want her rushed into anything. Simon is behaving very well, very properly, but you just look at that jaw of his! He's a man who gets what he wants and, at this moment, he wants Honor.'

'You sound very certain.'

'I was fairly certain that Simon was in love with her but now I think that Honor is beginning to feel that way towards him too. To begin with I thought that it was too soon, and that her love for Hubert would protect her, but I wonder if there's an element of falling in love on the rebound here. Responding to Simon takes her mind off her grief. It gives her something exciting to think about. Totally understandable, in my opinion.'

'Yet you still feel it would be wrong for her.'

'It *might* be wrong for her,' Julia corrects him. 'She needs time and I have this feeling that once Simon sees his advantage he'll push it.'

'Perhaps *you* could speak to her,' James ventures. 'Surely this sort of thing is better from another woman?'

She shakes her head. 'We're not on those terms. And Mousie is too young. Despite her natural friendliness Honor still keeps herself a little distant from us. Fair enough, I'm not a one for messy emotions all over the place either. That's why you should approach it from the point of view of the will.'

'I don't know how I should start,' says James wretchedly. 'Good grief, Julia! What could I say? I'm not her father.'

'You are the children's grandfather,' she says – but she can see his dilemma. 'We need something which will make her review the situation carefully. She needs something with which to protect herself if Simon pushes too hard.'

Julia pauses, raising her hand warningly, and presently Honor comes in through the hall. She smiles at them almost dreamily as if possessed of a great inner contentment.

'Whoever called this place "Paradise" is right,' she says. 'It's the most beautiful place in the world. I can't get over how lucky I am to be here.' Her smile becomes more practical and she looks with great affection upon the older pair. 'I'm going to get the supper.'

They remain silent, until they can hear movement in the

kitchen, and then James raises an eyebrow questioningly and Julia shrugs.

'Perhaps,' he suggests gently, 'she has something with which to protect herself after all.'

12th April

He came to Paradise yesterday whilst the family was at church. I met him at the top of our valley by the Saint's Well. He telephoned, Vivi. I had a feeling that he wouldn't just accept the letter and after a day or two I began to feel edgy. The sense of peace wore off and I felt tense and expectant. It would have been simpler if he weren't attached so firmly to the family by other relationships but as it is he can't simply fade out of all our lives. I began to wonder how he would handle it and from there it was a short step to a kind of expectation: imagining how it would be when I saw him next. My peace was shattered and my nerves were stretched. Each time the telephone rang I jumped and trembled – and then, at last, it was Simon.

'I'm coming down,' he said at once. 'I'd like to see you on your own, Mutt. Don't argue about it, please. Just give me this one chance. I have an idea . . .'

His idea was that I should miss Matins, giving a headache as an excuse, and meet him high up in the valley. He could leave the car up on the Polzeath road and walk down the track.

'I'll see you by the well just after eleven,' he said, and simply hung up.

I see now that it would have been wiser simply to explain to James that Simon had proposed and I had refused but I complicated matters further by going along with Simon's plan. As soon as they'd set out for church I slipped away. All the way along the valley I was thinking about that picnic where it had first started, this thing between us, with Mousie playing with Emma in the stream whilst Rafe and Bruno were building the dam. I remembered the hot sun and the lark singing, high up above in the still air . . .

And ever winging up and up,
Our valley is his golden cup . . .

He was waiting for me. It was a chill, dank morning, no larks singing, and he stood with his hands thrust down into the pockets of his British Warm. He was nervous, of course, defensive, but his posture was aggressive and that helped me. Acknowledging my own weaknesses I'd put on Honor's tweed coat and skirt and sensible walking shoes and, as usual, some essence of her rubbed off on me. It enabled me to keep my shoulders back and my chin up. This time I wasn't listening to sentimental dance music and painting eggs: this time I was prepared.

I knew just how Honor would have behaved, in the unlikely event that she would ever have got herself into such a situation in the first place. She would have been firm and kind and rather sweet; not that brutal, straight-from-the-shoulder treatment which you used to deal out to your poor swains, Vivi, but just as effective. From the beginning there was an unreality about the whole meeting and I suddenly saw that he'd been wrong in insisting on it. Somehow his instinct had utterly failed him. He would have been much wiser to allow a little time to elapse and then turn up again for one of those jolly weekends, bringing little presents for the children and reminiscing with James over a glass of whisky. A kind of rapport would have gently established itself between us. We might have gone sailing or taken a walk, and then the old magic would have crept in and undermined me again.

There was no magic by the Saint's Well that morning: only the clear, cold sound of the water and the sharp, strong scent of the ramsons. He watched me walking up our valley, his head lowered slightly, his face expressionless. I didn't change the rhythm of my pace when I saw him but I made my expression friendly, even affectionate. I think he'd counted on my previous reaction and when he didn't get it my coolness

215

unnerved him even more and I saw his shoulders hunch beneath the camel coat.

I felt quite strong and in control of myself although I was praying 'Help me! Help me!' beneath my breath, whether to the saint or to God I still don't know. The help I was already getting from Simon's unwelcoming stance was reinforced by the way he began by calling me Honor. Nothing could have recalled me more firmly to what I was trying to achieve. It reminded me of the children and my responsibility towards them, of dear old James and the family, and even of Honor and Hubert themselves. Again his instinct failed him: the familiar, friendly nickname 'Mutt', which he'd used until now, would have softened me: called my true, weaker self into being. Her name, which he repeated almost nervously at regular intervals, was like a shield thrust into my hands and, as my courage grew, a verse from one of the psalms repeated itself in my head.

'He shall defend thee under His wings, and thou shalt be safe under His feathers: His faithfulness and truth shall be thy shield and buckler.'

The sense of unreality continued, rather as if we were actors in a play, and all the passion that had flamed between us in the kitchen at Easter was now quenched into a cool exchange. Something about me, perhaps to do with Honor's clothes and the way I had slipped into her persona, had a paralysing effect on him. It made him believe the phrases I'd written in the letter and I saw his confidence waver and fade. He behaved as if a chasm lay at our feet and he spoke to me across it. He talked about the future he'd planned for us: he has been offered a research post at the Baker Medical Research Institute in Australia and he described a new life for us all, free from sad memories of the past. The more he spoke the deeper and wider the chasm grew until, confused and angry, he accepted defeat.

At the end the only thing I feared was physical contact – his kisses might slip beneath my guard – but yet again his instinct failed him and he merely turned away with a brief gesture of frustrated farewell and strode off towards the Polzeath road.

I can hardly remember getting back to Paradise but quite suddenly I felt weak, no longer upheld by that inner strength I'd had at the well, and I lay down upon my bed. The children found me there, bringing me flowers picked in the lane, and Emma scrambled up beside me and patted my face with her soft, pudgy hands, crooning a little song. Bruno stood stiffly beside the bed, his face taut with anxiety.

'Are you really ill, Mutt?' he asked.

I roused myself, wondering if he were remembering that tiresome influenza, and managed to smile at him reassuringly.

'Just this wretched head,' I said. 'I've been reading too much again. Don't worry, darling.'

And then Aunt Julia came in, bringing me a hot-water bottle and an aspirin, and shushing the children, and after that there was silence. It was then, with my shield lowered and my defences weak, I realized that I would never hear that goblin cry again, nor taste the sweet, delicious fruit, and I thought of poor Laura trudging home, creeping to bed and laying silent until Lizzie slept:

> Then sat up in a passionate yearning,
> And gnashed her teeth for baulked desire, and wept
> As if her heart would break.

I wept too, Vivi, cradling the hot, comforting bottle in my arms, with the sheet over my head so that nobody would hear me. I wept not only for myself and Simon but also for Hubert and Honor and Bruno and all that we'd lost. It wasn't until later that I wondered if Bruno hadn't been thinking about the influenza but of the hot, airless hotel room in Karachi and remembering how quickly he'd lost his parents and his sister. Perhaps he feared that I too might die. It was this thought that roused me out of my storm of self-pity.

I got up, washed my face, put on some make-up, brushed my hair and tied a scarf over it. It was a bright yellow and blue cotton and I found a navy-blue high-necked jersey that had once been Hubert's and pulled it on with a grey flannel skirt.

When I opened the drawing-room door, Julia, James and Bruno were seated at the gate-leg table in the window playing Monopoly. They turned and their expressions – cheerful, welcoming, relieved – warmed my heart and gave me courage. Bruno scrambled down and came to me.

'Are you better?' he asked eagerly.

'Quite better,' I answered. 'And when you've finished your game we'll go for a walk over the cliffs to The Lookout to blow the last cobwebs away.'

I sat down on the sofa where Emma was curled, fast asleep, her smooth perfect limbs carelessly disposed, her tiny flushed face peaceful. Sitting there, watching her sleep, listening to the murmuring voices from the table, I made my commitment. The decision had been taken for good or ill, back there in India, and now I must live with it: no more goblin fruit – 'honey to the throat but poison in the blood' – but an acceptance of that decision once and for all. Can I stick to it?

All the morning, whilst he is in church and on the walk home, Bruno is worried about Mutt. She says that she has a headache but he senses something more, much worse, and he feels anxious. When they get back to Paradise and find her in bed he is filled with fear: the memories press in on him and he can recall how Father fell ill first, then baby Em, and then Mummie; lying amongst the damp, crumpled sheets too weak to comfort him. His throat seems to close up with tears and he knows that he simply couldn't bear it if anything were to happen to Mutt. He stands beside the bed, stiff with fright, his bunch of flowers wilting in his clenched hand.

'Are you really ill?' he asks her, and though she tells him again that it is just a headache he doesn't believe her.

Aunt Julia hurries him and Emma out of the bedroom, telling him that Mother needs to rest and he realizes that now he has almost accepted that Mutt *is* his mother and it is impossible to imagine life without her. He can barely swallow any lunch and afterwards Aunt Julia and Uncle James play Monopoly with him whilst Emma falls asleep on the sofa. Rafe has gone sailing and Mousie is on duty at the hospital but Bruno is quite content with these two old people, who talk quietly as they play, giving him the chance to think about Mutt.

And then suddenly she is there, opening the door and smiling at them, and his relief is so overwhelming that he can hardly speak.

'Are you better?' he cries, and she says that she is quite better and that when the game is over and Emma wakes up they'll go over the cliffs to The Lookout.

He goes back to the game, reassured and quite cheerful now, and it is he who suddenly mentions Simon, asking when he will be visiting again. He is aware of Aunt Julia's hand on his shoulder, gripping tightly whilst he makes his move, but he doesn't think too much about it: all is well.

Julia watches Honor as she sits down beside the sleeping Emma. Her older, wiser eyes see the result of bitter weeping that the make-up and the gay headscarf cannot quite disguise and there is something in Honor's down-turned face, as she looks at her sleeping child, that rends Julia's heart. She tries to analyse the expression – renunciation? resolve? – and when Bruno asks his question so innocently she is filled with dread. Honor glances up quickly.

'Do you know I quite forgot to tell you,' she says lightly. 'He's been offered a research post in Australia. Very exciting for him but very sad for us. You won't be seeing much of your godfather from now on, Bruno, but I'm sure he'll write to you. We shall miss him, won't we?'

Neither James nor Julia asks Honor how she has suddenly acquired this information; instead they study the board with great concentration, answering Bruno's questions about Australia, and, presently, when Emma wakes up, the three of them set off to The Lookout.

At last James and Julia look at each other.

'I think we underestimated her,' says Julia after a long moment.

James resists the desire to point out that he has never been in doubt; he simply nods in agreement and begins to put away the board.

'She's a good girl,' he murmurs.

His instincts have not played him false: Paradise will be safe in her hands.

8th June 1948

Darling Vivi,

This is the last letter I shall write to you, exactly one year since I first arrived at Paradise. After all, this had to be part of that acceptance, didn't it? The goblin fruit includes pretending that I am communicating with you properly, that one day you will receive these letters and reply to them. Yet I can't bring myself to destroy them. These letters to you contain the last record of who and what I truly am, and the truth of what happened, but if I am to fully commit I must also finish with Madeleine Grosjean. After all, she disappeared out there in India.

A man arrived at the door the other day – just a stranger who had lost his way whilst out walking the cliffs – but I was filled with a sudden unreasoning terror. Supposing Johnny were to try to track me down, through Honor and Hubert, or suppose you and Don made some enquiries? I imagine that the news that Lottie and I died in Karachi with Hubert has filtered back and that nobody will bother to question it. Nevertheless, it made me see that I am still vulnerable and I was frightened.

Trevannion is an uncommon name and I have yet to brave the moment when the children go out into the world and face the new dangers that could arise with the making of friends who just might recognize the name.

I must become Honor Trevannion. I must allow her firm kindness, her decisiveness, her strict way of loving gradually to sink into my character. I've managed quite well so far but I cannot afford any distractions.

So no letters, Vivi. I must do without the comfort of sharing with you. Do you remember how we used to chant those last lines of *Goblin Market*, laughing at them whilst deep down believing in them?

> For there is no friend like a sister
> In calm and stormy weather;
> To cheer one on the tedious way,
> To fetch one if one goes astray,
> To lift one if one totters down,
> To strengthen whilst one stands.

I shall miss you, Vivi. When I lie awake at night wondering how I shall answer Bruno when he's old enough to see the flaw, to ask the real question 'Why did you pretend to be my mother?' then I shall wish that I had you to help me through. I hope he'll understand the panic and the way those decisions were taken and how the smallest deception can entrap so quickly.

I think he will understand, though. There's something wise about Bruno, some grace which is far beyond his years, which even now casts its healing over me. When he smiles at me, hugs me – knowing the truth as he does – I feel as if I have been granted the absolution I can no longer receive from Confession.

And there's something else, Vivi, I cling to when I feel myself, Madeleine, being slowly but inexorably rubbed out. I remember words that Sister Julian read to us.

Do not fear, for I have redeemed you,
I have called you by name; you are mine.
When you pass through the waters, I will be with you;
And when you pass through the rivers,
They shall not overwhelm you . . .
Do not fear, for I am with you.

If *He* knows me by my name then nothing else really matters, does it? This is my antidote to the goblin fruit.

There will be so much I shall want to tell you: all those small but significant events that shape the pattern of our lives as our children grow up. I shall be thinking of you, Vivi, and wondering if you will be telling your own children about the way we were and the fun we had. Perhaps I am already an aunt, and Emma has a cousin she will never know and I shall never see.

I love you, darling. *That* will never change.

Your sister,

Madeleine

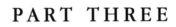

PART THREE

CHAPTER SIXTEEN

Bruno couldn't sleep. Emma had gone yawning upstairs hours ago and still he paced the big room, lights switched out and curtains open to the clear night, whilst Nellie watched him from the sofa. As he walked to and fro, or paused to stare out into the darkness, he wrestled with the problem that now confronted him. How was he to juggle the complications of the inheritance with the need to protect Emma?

In all his conversations with Mutt down the years, she'd pleaded with him that Emma should never know the truth: that somehow, after her death, the deception should be maintained.

'You belong, Bruno,' she'd said. 'This is your home and these are your family. I know that what I did would seem unforgivable to most people but you've always understood why I did it, haven't you, darling? What will Emma feel once she knows that she doesn't belong here? Or that you aren't her brother?'

Her very real distress had never failed to move him. Despite the terrible loss of his own family he'd always been able to understand her dilemma and why she'd acted so impulsively fifty years before during those last terrible days in Karachi.

Even now he could feel the prickle of terror on his skin, the despair deep in his gut: he could still remember his over-whelming relief when she'd appeared in their hotel room with Emma jabbering cheerfully in her arms. The thought of being without Mutt, that vital living link between the unknown future and the shocking past, was not to be borne.

Only he, watching her down the years, had sensed the struggle. Some instinct showed him that her guilt would never let her rest: that she took nothing for granted. She looked after them all and the valley had become not only her sanctuary but also her true home. Her creative spirit expressed itself in the Paradise gardens where she and Rafe had worked so tirelessly, and in her tapestry work that now adorned the local churches. He knew, too, that sailing was her greatest joy: that as the gap between the boat and the shore widened so this same joyful spirit, passionate and carefree, shook off the shackles of capable widow and mother who held the cares of family and estate in her hands.

It was odd, thought Bruno, that he should be the one who knew her best and loved her most. Because of her he'd been obliged all his life to lie, to be on his guard, to watch his tongue. He'd had to deny the memory of his own mother and sister, to accept and live the deception into which she'd plunged them. Yet from the earliest days he'd been aware of her courage – the more so because he suspected that it was hard won and that to be assured and sensible did not come naturally to her. Those odd quirks of memory, fifty years old, showed him his father putting an affectionate arm around her and saying teasingly, 'You *are* a Mutt. What a woman!' He'd felt a kind of empathy with her even then, hearing in that tone of voice the implication that Mutt, though grown up, was still capable of foolish things that seemed to make her an ally with him. She was down there with the children, laughing, loving, ready for fun, whilst the grown-ups watched indulgently from their higher plane.

As Emma grew up he'd seen the same qualities in her that he still glimpsed in Mutt. She too was passionate, given to laughter, generous, which made it not only sad that Mutt could never let the barrier slip with her daughter but almost tragic that Emma was more fiercely Trevannion than any of them. She loved Paradise, adored Bruno and Rafe and Mousie, and told everyone who was remotely interested about her father's work as a doctor in India. After she was married she'd come racing down to Cornwall at every opportunity, insisting that St Meriadoc was her real home and where she most belonged.

They'd almost quarrelled over Raymond Fox, Bruno and Mutt. This was the first time his sympathy for Mutt had given way before a genuine sense of anxiety for Emma. He'd already had a shouting match with Em, each of them deriding the other's lack of taste when it came to choosing a marriage partner, and later he'd gone up to Paradise to have it out with Mutt. Now, listening to the sea's rhythmic shush-shush against the rocks below the window, he saw the scene in his mind's eye as clearly as if it were being enacted on the black glass in front of him.

'She loves him,' says Mutt, not looking at him, opening the drawers of her desk and closing them again with a bang.

'Emma loves everyone,' he answers impatiently. 'She's always falling in love. Ever since she was about twelve she's imagined herself in love. I've never known a girl like her for needing to love someone and to be loved in return.'

She turns then, staring at him almost fearfully across the back of the chair as if some new idea has occurred to her. 'But she's always known how much we've loved her, hasn't she?' she asks anxiously. 'Oh, Bruno, do you think that she's missed having a father? More than we realized?'

He guesses that she is feeling inadequate, worrying that she hasn't managed to fulfil all Emma's needs, and he is seized with a mixture of irritation and compunction.

'I've no idea,' he answers restlessly, not in the mood for soul-searching. 'She's never given me that impression. The point is whether this wretched Fox loves her, and in my opinion he doesn't. He's a cold, calculating type. She won't be happy with him, Mutt.'

He sees her expression change from worried introspection to thoughtful consideration of his words.

'He's steady,' she says at last. 'He won't do anything foolish or make a fool of her with another woman.'

His laugh is short and explosive. 'You're dead right about that,' he answers crudely. 'He wouldn't know what passion was if it struck him in the face.'

'You're young,' she says quietly. 'You can't imagine what it's like to be abandoned or to have no security. I don't want that for Emma.'

He studies her, realizing that he knows very little about Mutt's own past except in relation to his own family. Some tacit agreement from those early years has cast a cloak of silence over the years in India and, until now, he had the impression that her husband had died in an accident. Now he wonders if it had been more complicated.

His irritation subsides a little but he has no intention of giving way yet.

'Emma will never be abandoned while I'm alive,' he says, 'but even the fear that she might be doesn't mean she has to marry a man like Raymond Fox. There are other decent men who will love her in return. Don't imagine I'm doing a "no-one is good enough for my sister" act. I simply want her to have a reasonable chance of happiness.'

Mutt rises from her chair and begins to wander about the room, tidying some books, picking up a newspaper; her fingers trail idly across a tapestry that lies on the oval, inlaid table.

'You're not looking at Raymond as a woman would,' she says at last.

'Clearly,' he says crisply.

'When it comes to marriage, Emma might want more than charm and fun . . .'

She sits down abruptly at the desk again and he wants to ask her if those were the qualities she looked for in marriage and whether they failed her. He sees her fumbling with some papers, clearly distressed but not wanting him to see, and he sighs with frustration.

'He's wrong for her,' he insists stubbornly.

'That's what she says about Zoë. That you married her for all the wrong reasons. I did question it myself, if you remember, but you answered – quite fairly – that you had the right to do what you liked with your own life. Emma feels exactly the same.'

The tiny core of him that always stands apart – watching his own life as an onlooker might, taking notes – observes her restless fingers folding and refolding an old envelope, records that the easy intimacy between them born of shared secrets has slipped behind the cooler, controlling persona that Mutt uses when she needs to take charge of a situation. It is a defence mechanism to be employed when she feels vulnerable and unsure of herself but he is too young, too inexperienced, to wrench it down and to insist that they discuss this matter as equals.

Nevertheless, because it is Emma's happiness at stake here, he tries again, pushing against that barrier in an attempt to extend the boundaries of the trust between them.

'So you have actually discussed it with her?' he asks lightly. 'That you think that she might be marrying for the wrong reasons?'

He watches her averted face, sees her bite her lip, and has an odd impulse to go to her and put his arm about her.

'Come off it,' he might say. 'You are a Mutt, aren't you? Can't we talk about this properly?'

He might say it, if he were ten years older or more

confident, but his own insecurities hold him back. The silence between them is stretched, tense.

'We've talked about it,' she answers evasively at last. 'Of course we have. She's in love with him and he loves her.' Her chin goes up a little higher, her back is a little straighter, and his heart sinks as the gulf is widened and her confidence grows. 'Oh, yes he does. After his fashion Raymond has given his heart to Emma. She'll be looked after and he'll be a loyal husband and a responsible father.'

'Sounds like fun,' he says, his voice brittle with defeat. 'You don't think that a bit of passion might be nice or even some kind of meeting of minds?'

The silence this time is of a different quality. Something else has joined them in the parlour: a gentle remembrance of times past that relaxes Mutt's shoulders and softens her expression. When she speaks her question takes him completely by surprise.

'Have you heard from Simon recently?' she asks. 'It seems a long time since you had any news of him.'

'Yes,' he says, confused. 'Well, I had a letter a month or two back. He sent a photograph of the twins with Tessa on the beach at Bondi. I meant to show it to you.'

She turns to look at him. 'Don't be too harsh on me,' she says gently. 'Passionate people need a framework of stability. Emma loves the good things of life and she likes to share them. Raymond is in love with her and he will want to make her happy, according to his lights. She will be able to entertain, give parties, dress well. He'll see to that because it will be good for business but there will be times when Raymond's stolidity and lack of imagination will be invaluable to Emma. She'll use them – and him – as a defence against her own mistaken passions. Friends and enemies will blame him and she'll be free to be loved for herself.'

'It doesn't sound a particularly honest way of going on,' Bruno says after a moment.

Mutt chuckles. 'We have to do the best with what we've got. Your father used to say, "Never let the best be the enemy of the good," and it's worth remembering at times, especially when it comes to relationships.'

He smiles back at her. 'That sounds particularly cynical to me.'

'To me too,' she admits.

She gets up, light and quick as a girl, and comes to him with arms outstretched.

'It's so hard to get it right for other people,' she says almost desperately. 'Especially when you love them so much. You and Emma. Should I have stopped you from marrying Zoë?'

He puts his arms about her, knowing that his unchanging love brings her some kind of comfort.

'You didn't have a hope,' he says. 'You're quite right, Mutt. Why do we think we can get it right for other people when we get so much wrong for ourselves? If Emma's made up her mind there's no more to be said about it.'

They look at each other, unity restored – but both still suppress private fears.

A door opened upstairs and Bruno tensed, listening: the lavatory was flushed, water gurgled in the cistern, and he heard footsteps overhead. Presently the bedroom door closed again and there was silence. All at once he made up his mind. Taking Nellie through to her bed in the kitchen, shrugging into his coat, all the while he was listening for any further sound from Emma.

'Stay,' he told Nellie, ignoring her beseeching expression. 'Good girl, then. Stay.'

Shutting the door gently behind him, pausing to glance towards The Row, where all was dark and quiet, he set off up the cliff-path that led towards Paradise.

CHAPTER SEVENTEEN

It was impossible to get back to sleep. Emma turned on to her left side, tucking the pillow into her neck, and tried to relax.

Breathe deeply, she instructed herself. In and out . . . in and out . . . Think of a garden. Which garden? Any garden with a path winding through it, like the path between the rhododendrons that led from the meadow to Paradise. 'The Walk to the Paradise Gardens' was one of Mutt's favourite pieces of music . . . Would Joss find the garden at Paradise too much with all her work to do? Well, Rafe would be there as he'd always been: how he loved the gardens and how hard he'd worked in them. He and Mutt had done so much to restore them to the great glory of the pre-war Paradise. Bruno, of course, was useless. Grubbing up perfectly good plants, trampling on new seeds, because his mind was always on some plot or other. Poor Bruno. He'd been having one of his downers, she'd seen that as soon as she'd opened the door. How shocking that business with Zoë and the baby had been, and yet he still stood up for her, lending her money . . . Lending! That was rich. She'd never paid him back once. Funny how she'd never liked Zoë, not from that very first minute. Could never understand what he saw in her. Well, yes, plenty of sex appeal if you like the undernourished, sly look. She, Emma, hadn't been impressed.

'Don't be confused by sex,' she'd told him – but he hadn't listened. And then he'd had the nerve to criticize Raymond. At least Raymond, for all his faults and failings, had never let her down. Mutt had been right about that. He'd been steady as a rock. OK, yes he was tight-fisted, but she and Joss had always been his first concern and even if friends joked a bit about his always being last to the bar, or winked knowingly at his readiness to drone on about his latest financial wheeling and dealing, well, fair enough. To be honest, she'd often slipped things on to his shoulders; used him as an excuse.

'Oh, Caroline, *The Ring Cycle*? I should have loved to, but you know old Ray. The opera simply isn't his thing, he'd be dead with boredom before the end of Act One . . .'

'A villa in Tuscany for a month? Six adults and nine children? Sounds utter heaven, but, darling, can you imagine old Ray . . .?'

'What a brilliant idea, Rowena. A little shop in the High Street selling hand-painted pottery and some old furniture . . . A partner? Me? Oh, sweetie, it sounds so exciting but can you see dear old Ray coughing up? No chance, I'm afraid. I'll come and fleece the punters for you any time you like, but a partner? I should have loved it but it's got to be No, I'm afraid.'

'Jenny? That plan you had for a joint eighteenth party for Joss and Sarah. Dear old Ray simply won't wear it. He wants his girl to have the great moment all to herself . . . I know. I know, but you've got two more coming up, remember. She's his only chick and he doesn't want her to share the honours. You know what fathers are like . . . Yes, I thought he'd be glad to halve the cost too, but there you are. Aren't men simply extraordinary? You never know where you are . . .'

Oh, he'd got her off the hook time and time again because

she knew herself: she'd have given in. She hated to see people disappointed or hurt; longed to help out, make them laugh, bring comfort. Right over the top. 'You are a twit,' people would say to her, but lovingly as if they didn't mind her being a twit, and that was nice because it was always such a surprise to find that people loved her. As if it were some kind of special present that needed to be treasured. The trouble was that she'd got into such states about it all until she'd found that dear old Ray, quite unwittingly, could protect her from herself. But she'd made it up to him; she'd pulled her weight. All those dinners for clients or influential people, everything perfect, just as he liked it, nothing too good for them. She'd smiled, listened, flirted, whilst often she was simply screaming with the boredom of it all, but nobody ever guessed. Even dear old Ray didn't realize how excruciatingly dull she found his associates – but then he wasn't sensitive to other people or their needs. Bruno had been right about that. He was too heavy-handed, ready with a patronizing little pat, kindly in many ways, but never seeing a real need. Though there had been a time when his obtuseness had stood her in good stead. He'd never guessed about Tony: he'd never noticed a thing. Oh, how she'd loved him: secret meetings, breathless telephone calls, little notes. She'd felt alive, her muscles loosened with desire, free and wild with happiness. Only the thought of darling, innocent Joss had held her steady – and dear Bruno. She'd sat in the rocking-chair in that great room downstairs, hair down, feet up, talking, talking. And he'd given her tumblers of whisky and mugs of coffee and let her pour out her feelings. God, she'd really loved Tony. But after all, it hadn't lasted. All that passion – and it had died just as quickly as it had flared up, and she'd been very glad, then, to have Ray and all his security at her back. Glad that she hadn't succumbed to Tony's crazy pleadings, given in to his suggestions that she should leave it all and go away with him. What a disaster it would have been: Tony would have abandoned her just like all his other women. Not that she'd stayed with Ray just for security – of course not. She loved him . . .

Emma turned restlessly on to her back. The trouble was that deep breathing and imagining the garden hadn't worked at all and here she was at – what was the time? – nearly two o'clock and still wide awake. She'd lie quietly and offer a little prayer for Mutt. What was it that Mutt had always said at bedtime when she and Bruno were children? 'The Lord grant us a quiet night and a perfect end.'

That was a good prayer for Mutt at this particular time. Take a deep breath and offer it up for Mutt. The Lord grant her a quiet night and a perfect end – and watch over her, dear Lord, and over darling Joss too, up at Paradise tonight looking after her . . . It was funny how she'd felt that Joss should be left with her grandmother this evening. It was one of those strong feelings she sometimes got, a premonition, that had made her feel rather odd and a bit weepy. Of course, Mutt and Joss had always had that special closeness. Joss would come home from weekends at Paradise with stories of terrific fun with all her friends and old Mutt being a great hostess, never embarrassing, and everyone adoring her. People said that about grandparents – that they were often more relaxed with their grandchildren than with their own – but she'd known exactly what Joss meant. Mutt was great fun, always ready for a little jolly and especially good with young people, so it was odd that she was kind of buttoned up when it came to family things. Of course, losing Daddy out there in India must have been utter hell but Mutt could never quite understand how important it had been that she, Emma, wanted to know every little thing about him and all that had happened out there. Things like where they'd met and how they'd felt and what it was like when he proposed . . . Of course it must be painful, she could see that, but it meant so much. Yet every time she broached the subject Mutt would come over a bit odd, although she was more ready to talk about the hospital and the work. Even Bruno never wanted to talk about India.

'It's my past too,' she'd say, rather plaintively, but neither of them would ever really sit down and have a good talk about it all, and there were very few photographs to fill in the gaps, though the ones they did have showed that Daddy had been a very attractive man. Well, Bruno was just like him and so that helped her to imagine him. She thought she could remember certain things, just little flashes here and there, but she could never be certain whether it was real or something she'd liked to have happened. All she could really remember was her life here at St Meriadoc.

How happy they'd been, she and Bruno, growing up here. So safe and happy with darling Mousie and Rafe down in The Row. Sailing in the *Kittiwake* and picnics up the valley by the well. Then later, with Bruno bringing his naval friends home and giving lovely parties in The Lookout. Mutt had been wonderful then; letting them do their own thing, never interfering, encouraging their freedom. Yet there was that little feeling, a sense that Mutt was always wanting her to be worthy of Paradise . . . No, that wasn't fair. It was more that the little estate – or the bit that she, Emma, would inherit – was not just a right but also something that must be deserved. It mustn't be taken for granted.

She and Bruno had always joked about it all. 'I'll have Paradise and you have The Lookout,' she'd said. The rest of the estate had never come into it until Ray turned up. He'd immediately seen the possibilities of development, never ceased to hint about it after every trip to St Meriadoc, and it would be utterly exhausting if she ever had to fight off his juggernaut tendencies in regard to the cove . . .

Emma sat up, crossly punched her pillow into shape, and lay back against it. She was supposed to be praying for Mutt, not carving up her estate. Perhaps if she were to do that thing of stretching and relaxing every single muscle. Starting with her toes . . .

And, anyway, Bruno would sort it all out. When it came down to it, even Ray wouldn't seriously consider ruining The Row after all these years. Especially with poor, darling Pamela so used to the peace all around her. It would be unthinkable – and now there were problems with George . . . Feet next. Stretch and relax. Ah, that was good.

Joss wouldn't be drawn about George but she didn't need Joss to tell her that Penny and George had never been right. She'd had her suspicions right from the beginning, never mind how everyone had said what a darling Penny was. There'd been a withholding of something, a reserve that made it very difficult to really know her or really love her . . . Now stretch out each leg. Ye-es. Now the other one. Very good. What was she thinking about? George. What a duck he was; a lovely man. Such a dear little boy he'd always been. He and Joss had been such chums, always off on their bikes or out in that little dinghy. What a pity children had to grow up . . . Ooh, how good to stretch the arms right out . . . And again. Mmm. Who had she thinking about . . . Joss? . . . George?

She slept at last, arms flung wide, breathing peacefully.

CHAPTER EIGHTEEN

There was a light shining from beneath the parlour door. Bruno stood for a moment in the hall, considering. Some instinct had brought him over the cliff to Paradise but now he waited, uncertain of the next move. This unexpected sense of confusion, caused by his instinct abruptly switching off, was similar to the dislocation he experienced when the two worlds of imagination and reality collided. Thinking about Mutt, remembering the past, he'd forgotten about Joss. Even as he thought about her, the parlour door opened and she came out into the hall. At her gasp of surprise and alarm he raised his arms, as if in a gesture of reassurance, but she continued to stare at him as if she were seeing him for the first time or adjusting to some new situation.

'Sorry,' he said. 'I wasn't thinking. I had a feeling about Mutt and just came on up. I haven't got used to you being here yet, I suppose. Sorry to frighten you.'

She came towards him, out of the shadows, and he saw that she was struggling with some strong emotion. Bruno reached out and took her by the shoulders.

'What is it? Is it Mutt?'

Joss shook her head and then nodded. 'Yes, I suppose it is in a way.' Her eyes, blurred by tears and shock, slid away from his and then anxiously fixed themselves on his face again as if seeking reassurance. Some familiar quality of compassion in his look seemed to give her confidence and he felt her shoulders sag a little as she relaxed in his grip.

Without speaking he led her into the drawing-room and pushed her gently into the corner of the sofa. Carefully he piled charred logs and embers together, then, picking up the bellows, puffed life into the fire with gentle, rhythmic movements. Grey ash glowed bright, a tiny flame pulsing and trembling whilst blackly scorched wood scintillated with a hundred flickering sparks. Huddled in the chair, her hands pressed between her knees, she watched him silently whilst her tired brain rocked with the effort of assimilating this new knowledge: Mutt, for all these years, had been living a lie yet Joss's heart went out to her and tears rose once more to her eyes as she recalled the words and phrases her grandmother had written so long ago.

Bruno laid down the bellows and looked at her.

'Want to tell me?' he asked.

That detached part of him saw the imperceptible withdrawal, the tremor that tensed her knees and shoulders; noted that some indefinable fear made it impossible for her to meet his eyes. He hesitated, still crouching before the fire, realizing that her dilemma was one that related directly to him. Somehow, he intuited, the trustful ease with which she'd always approached him was damaged: his reliability was in question. Still crouched, he swore silently and then rose to his feet in one quick movement, thrusting his hands into his pockets.

'Perhaps you found something,' he hazarded, rather as if they were playing some kind of guessing game. 'Some document that's puzzled you.' A quick glance at her troubled face gave him no assistance. Suddenly he remembered Emma's remark about the American. 'Or maybe it was a photograph.'

She swallowed, biting her lips, but still avoiding his eyes and he sensed something else besides this new lack of confidence in him. His hands clenched into fists as frustration rose inside him. 'Come on, Joss,' he wanted to say. 'Help me to help you,' but her white, unhappy face and restless eyes restrained him. There was an uneasiness about her that suggested guilt and suddenly he had an idea.

'I suppose you haven't by any chance come across a copy of Mutt's will?' he asked lightly. 'I must admit it would simplify things if you have.'

She stared at him then. 'Would it? I can't imagine how.'

Her voice was almost childishly defiant and she shrank back into the cushions as he came to kneel beside the arm of her chair.

'Come on, love,' he said. 'Don't play games. Tell me what you've found.'

'Letters,' she said, eyes wide and dark. 'I wasn't going to read them and then I found I simply couldn't resist. Mutt asked me to find them . . .'

Her voice trailed away into silence and he frowned.

'Letters? What kind of letters?'

'She wrote to her sister but never posted them. There must be more than a dozen of them. They explain it all. How she came here and who she really is.'

Bruno closed his eyes for a second. 'Christ!' he muttered. 'I don't believe it. *Letters!*'

They stared at each other. His shocked expression restored her as nothing else could have done and she drew her legs up into the chair, leaning closer to him, as if she saw that he might need some kind of consolation too.

'I can't take it in,' she told him. 'Nothing is what I thought it was. I just couldn't grasp it to begin with but, after a while, how it affected me – all of us – didn't matter so much as what I felt about Mutt.'

She hesitated as if hoping for some response, perhaps

encouragement, but Bruno remained silent. There was something else in his face besides horrified disbelief, and after a moment she identified it: he was angry.

'Letters!' He swung himself to his feet and went across to the fire. Picking up the poker he stabbed it furiously against the logs. 'All these years of secrecy, of promising to protect Emma from the truth and remembering to think twice before I speak, and meanwhile she writes it all down in *bloody* letters and leaves them lying about. My God! I simply can't believe it.'

Huddled in her chair, Joss watched him anxiously. Despite her own shock during those first moments when she'd looked at Bruno and thought, But he isn't my uncle and nothing is what it seems, she'd felt an overwhelming compassion for her grandmother: a strong identification with the young woman who'd written those letters, full of self-doubt and guilt but – having set her hand to the plough – trying not to look back.

'They weren't lying about,' was all she could think of to say in defence of Mutt. 'They were underneath lots of things in a drawer' – but she knew that it was a feeble protest.

'In a drawer,' he repeated contemptuously. 'Oh, well, that's perfectly all right then. No-one is going to be looking for anything in a drawer, are they?'

She got up and went to him, taking his arm. 'You need to read them,' she said. 'They aren't just casual letters dashed off for fun. It was Mutt's way of retaining her identity and trying to assuage her guilt. I can understand that. I expect she simply couldn't bring herself to destroy them and then, as the time passed, they sort of faded and she forgot them.' She shook her head impatiently. 'I'm not getting this right.'

Bruno was watching her unsympathetically. 'What about *my* identity?' he asked. 'All my life I've denied my mother and my sister. I've lied and prevaricated and thought it worth it for certain reasons. And now it's blown wide open, all gone for nothing, because Mutt has an urge to commit her qualms to paper. Why letters, for God's sake? And if you write letters, why not post the bloody things? Perhaps she *has* posted some and other people know the truth.'

Joss dropped his arm. 'It's not like that. You must read them, Bruno. Remember that she simply asked me to find them and if I hadn't read them nobody would be the wiser. Please. Just keep an open mind until you've read them. After all, they won't be telling you anything you don't know except for the way Mutt felt right at the beginning.'

There was a silence. It was clear that Bruno was making an immense effort to take hold of his temper: a muscle jumped in his jaw and his eyelids drooped, giving him an un-characteristically brooding look. Joss felt a twitch of fear. He seemed like a stranger and her sense of disorientation returned: they were not related, nearly everything that she had been told about her family was untrue, but even as she looked at Bruno she suddenly had an inkling of what it must have been like for him. Any guilt she was experiencing was quenched by her instinct that this was the right course to take.

'Read them,' she pleaded. 'Don't judge her until you've done that.'

He took a deep, barely resigned breath and nodded. 'OK. Where are they?'

'I'll get them,' she said quickly. 'They need to be read in order. Build up the fire and I'll make some coffee.'

He looked impatient, as if he felt he was being manipulated and wheedled into a receptive frame of mind, and she accepted the fact that her behaviour must seem almost patronizing. How could she, knowing the truth for a brief few hours, presume to advise Bruno, who had lived with it for fifty years? Before she could apologize or explain her feelings he had turned away and was piling logs into the grate. She hesitated for a second or two and then hurried out, down the hall and into the parlour. As she sorted and piled the letters her hands shook and she paused at one point, listening, wondering if she'd heard Mutt's bell. There was only silence.

Bruno was sitting beside the fire, leaning forward, hands clasped loosely between his knees. Joss dragged forward the small round table and placed the letters beside him. He glanced at them and then at her; his eyes crinkled a little.

'Sorry, love.' His voice was gentler. 'It's been one hell of a shock for you too, I imagine.'

She nodded, biting her lip, and he shrugged and shook his head as if in despair at the situation.

'I'll get that coffee,' she said – and left him to it.

In the kitchen she was seized with a sudden fit of shivering: her hands trembled and her teeth chattered.

Shock, she told herself. The spoon clattered against the mug and she spilled the milk as she poured it into the jug. Part of her was with Bruno reading the letters, willing him to empathize, other thoughts jostled to the forefront of her mind as she waited for the kettle to boil. Her mother: what would she say if she knew? Well, she must never know. The secret must be kept. Joss stared round the kitchen, hugging her arms across her breasts, trying to come to terms with the fact that she had no right here: that she and her mother and Mutt were interlopers. It was impossible to take it in.

Suddenly she needed to see Mutt. Her grandmother had still been deeply asleep when she'd looked in again earlier, halfway through the letter reading, and she'd felt oddly cheated – as if something significant might have been ex-changed between them. Perhaps now, Mutt might be awake again and she, Joss, could somehow indicate that she knew the truth and that everything was all right: that, whatever had happened in the past or might happen in the future, Joss's love for her was unchanged.

She made the coffee and took it into the drawing-room. Bruno didn't look up; his face was set and absorbed. Joss slipped out again and up the stairs. She hesitated at the door, her heart banging in her side, and then gently turned the handle and went into her grandmother's bedroom.

Mutt wasn't there. Joss could tell at once that the room was empty even before she saw the lifeless figure on the bed. Mutt was gone and it was too late, now, for the truth.

CHAPTER NINETEEN

It was nearly two hours later when Bruno set the last letter aside, sitting for some moments in silence before glancing at Joss, curled in the corner of the opposite sofa. He'd been hardly aware of her presence – the unobtrusive making up of the fire and a fresh mug of coffee at his elbow as the night wore on – but now he saw how pale she was and stirred himself to deal with the results of her discovery. He'd been moved by the letters but not surprised by the revelations of Mutt's dilemma. She'd turned to him too often down the years for him to be unaware of her need for his 'absolution', as she called it. Now, he could only be grateful that he'd given it unstintingly and continued to reassure her. He'd known the real Mutt who'd hidden behind the cool, sensible façade of widowhood; known the light-hearted, compassionate woman who fought with her own devils of guilt and insecurity.

The real surprise to Bruno was that touching record of the brief flowering of love between her and his godfather. Of course, it had been finished and Simon had emigrated whilst he, Bruno, was still a small child, yet he felt almost hurt that she'd never spoken of it. Because of their shared duplicity he'd assumed not only that he was Mutt's only confidant, but also that his comfort and support would have been sufficient for her. Now, with humility, he saw how lonely she must have been. He felt a great need to see her.

'You were quite right to insist that I read them,' he said to Joss. 'And you've been sitting there all this time, poor love, trying to come to terms with all this. Look, we'll talk, I promise, but first I need to see Mutt. Can you manage—'

'She's dead,' she said. Tears suddenly ran from her eyes and streamed down her cheeks. 'Mutt's dead, Bruno.'

'But when?' he cried, leaping to his feet as if even now he might not be too late. 'You said she was asleep.'

'She was,' she said, gazing up at him. 'I went up when you began to read the letters and she'd gone. You must go up and see her. She looks so calm that I'm sure she must have died in her sleep. Mousie will be up soon – she promised to be here very early – and she'll know what to do.'

Her eyes were red and swollen and he guessed that she'd been crying in the kitchen alone, miserable and confused. He hesitated, seized by both the sense of his own loss and by compassion for Joss, and then kneeled down and put his arms about her. He could do nothing more for Mutt now, and Joss was suffering. She began to weep, her mouth square with sobs, turning her face into his shoulder. He held her gently, his mind working on several different levels: controlling his own grief, remembering certain extracts from the letters still fresh in his mind, wondering how on earth they would go forward as a family. Part of him could understand Mutt's need to record her feelings – could even grasp her reason for being unable to destroy them – another part was still furious with her for leaving him with this terrible dilemma. Why had she not asked *him* to find the letters? Why on earth entrust the task to Joss and risk so much?

'What are we to do?' he murmured aloud, his arms tightening about Joss, who still sobbed against his shoulder.

She released herself, accepted his handkerchief gratefully and blew her nose.

'I just can't believe it. It's been such a shock,' she muttered. 'And now with Mutt gone . . .' She hid her face in the handkerchief briefly and then scrubbed her cheeks. 'I was thinking about it in the kitchen,' she told him, 'while you were reading the letters. I can't take it in that we don't really belong here. Me and Mum and Mutt are impostors, if you see what I mean.'

Bruno stood up and went back to the sofa near the fire. He looked calm but his mind leaped desperately to find words that were both true and comforting.

'You are exactly who you've always been,' he said. 'You are Mutt's granddaughter and Emma's daughter. Nothing has changed there. As for your relationship to me – well, all I can say is I've always thought of Emma as my sister. We were all so close, you know. The letters show that, don't they? Mutt and my parents were a threesome, though I can hardly remember your grandfather. Your mother and my sister were much the same age and, given that I had to lose my mother and my sister so tragically, imagine the comfort of having Mutt and Emma, who were already family to me anyway.'

She sat quite still as she watched him; only her hands, pleating and folding the handkerchief, indicated her inner turmoil.

'But you were angry,' she reminded him. 'When I told you about the letters, you were angry.'

'Of course I was angry.' His own banked-down emotions flared briefly. 'We had an agreement, Mutt and I, that no-one would ever know, and though I've told you the truth about how I felt – and still feel – about Mutt and Emma, there were times when it was damned uncomfortable. Of *course* I'm angry. I'm gutted about Mutt too. To be honest, I can't quite think straight. How are we going to deal with it now that you know? It's no good my saying that as far as I'm concerned nothing has changed, is it?'

Joss frowned, trying to wrestle with the problem, her heart heavy. 'It's difficult,' she began haltingly, 'because part of me wants to say that Mum simply mustn't know. It's bad enough for *me* but it would simply finish *her* to know that she's not a Trevannion and that this isn't her home at all.'

'Of course it's her home,' said Bruno impatiently. 'She came here when she wasn't two years old. We are her family. Where else would be her home?'

'Yes, but you know what I mean.' Joss leaned forward in her chair. 'You're right to say that I'm what I've always believed myself to be. Mutt, my parents, my home – all those things remain the same, but Mum won't feel like that. She's been lied to all along the line. Hubert wasn't her father, you aren't her brother, this isn't her inheritance. And it all means so much to her. She's . . . she's *defined* by it because it's all so much a part of her. I want to say that she simply mustn't know the truth but that means that I'm implicitly encouraging something wrong. Paradise and St Meriadoc belong to your family, Bruno, not mine. Mousie and Rafe have more right to it than we do, so how do we get round that?'

He was impressed by her intelligent grasp of the situation, her self-control, and felt a sense of relief that he could share this terrible responsibility with her.

'It was quite wrong of Mutt to ask you to deal with the letters.' He decided to start at the beginning of this new turn of events. 'She might have guessed that you'd read some part of them, even if only by mistake. A line or a phrase would be bound to catch the eye. After all, they weren't all in envelopes. Why risk it?'

'Perhaps she thought I'd be too honourable to look at them.' Joss bit her lips. She'd been trying to deal with that one alone in the kitchen: telling herself that out of unprincipled curiosity she'd opened Pandora's box and, because of her weakness of character, others would suffer even more than she was already suffering.

'Balls!' said Bruno impatiently. 'For God's sake, don't let's do that kind of hair-shirt stuff. The only thing that makes sense to me is that, even if she were not aware of it, Mutt decided it was time that you knew the truth. I can't think of any other reason for it.'

Joss was comforted by Bruno's stark, almost brutal, response but unable to go along with his reasoning.

'No.' She shook her head. 'Mutt was very anxious that they should be found. Probably the American's visit frightened her and she suddenly remembered the letters and wanted them to be destroyed. She wanted it just to be between me and her. She trusted me.'

'But did she actually tell you not to read them?' Bruno ignored the tremor in her voice, determined to lead her away from the negative bog-land of self-pity and guilt, towards the positive ground of rationality even though he was by no means convinced by his own argument. 'I'm sorry, love, but the more I think about it the more I feel that deep down she wanted you to know the truth about her. After all, I saw Mutt every day. Nothing easier for her than to tell me about the letters and ask me to get rid of them. I know you and she were very close but she must have seen the risk. That's not a criticism, Joss. After all, what a thing to ask anyone to do. Look . . .' He paused then, and when he spoke again his voice was softer; creating a scene, evoking an atmosphere. 'Some-one we love is at the end of her life – but here is a package of letters, a diary, doesn't matter what; something they've handled, and in which some thought or memory is recorded.' He glanced at her. 'There's something about the written word, isn't there? Something that's much more important even than a well-worn garment or an object that the beloved has treasured. Here in your hand is some essence of that person you've known and loved, something you want and need because of all that it might reveal. Something more of them; something, even, which might relate to yourself. How can you possibly give it up or consign it to the flames?'

'I did feel exactly like that.' Joss's lips trembled and she covered her mouth with her hand. 'And you're right about catching a glimpse of some words. Even so . . .'

'Even nothing,' said Bruno firmly. 'Mutt knew all about the weaknesses and temptations of human nature. Old and ill as she was, I think some subconscious desire was driving her, whatever her surface thoughts and words might have been.'

'It might be so.' Joss was willing herself to believe it although deep down she felt certain that it was much simpler than that: Mutt had rightly realized that Bruno would be furious once he knew about the letters and so she'd trusted her, Joss, to find them. 'But what now? Do we carry on as if nothing has happened? The trouble is . . . how has Mutt left things in her will?'

He shook his head. 'I don't know.'

'She should have left everything to you but I can see that would arouse suspicion. Do you think that she might have left Paradise and The Lookout to you? That would be good, wouldn't it? After all, if only The Row was left to Mum, nothing need change. Mousie and Rafe would be quite safe and I can buy my little cottage from the estate. No, no, not buy. Nothing should change hands. I'll rent it just as Mousie and Rafe do theirs. That would be OK, wouldn't it?'

He smiled a little at her eagerness to maintain the status quo without benefiting, wondering how to phrase his own fears.

'Of course, your father always wanted to develop the boat-yard,' he said. 'Knock down the old shed and build a hotel.'

'That's crazy,' she answered at once. 'It's not possible. Oh.' He saw her catch his meaning. 'You mean he might try to persuade Mum . . . Oh, no.' She shook her head, horror in her eyes. 'He couldn't. It would ruin the cove, and what about The Row? Anyway it wouldn't be his to develop.'

'If the boatyard and The Row should be left to Emma,' Bruno said gently, 'we must consider every eventuality. If something happened to her it might then belong to your father under the terms of *her* will. Of course, she might now make a new will leaving it all to you.'

'But that would be all wrong,' she protested. 'And what about Mousie and Rafe?'

'*What* about Mousie and Rafe?'

Mousie's voice echoed in from the hall, cheerful and rather amused, and they heard the front door close behind her. It was nearly five o'clock.

CHAPTER TWENTY

Whilst Joss remained in her chair, momentarily paralysed by shock and fear, Bruno swept the letters into a pile beneath the cushioned seat of the sofa. He rose quickly to his feet and went out into the hall.

'Mousie,' Joss heard him say. 'Oh, love, it's bad news, I'm afraid. Dear old Mutt is gone. Peacefully in her sleep, but poor Joss found her and we've been having a moment to recover. We were just deciding how to let you know.'

A brief silence.

'Well, I can't say I'm terribly surprised.' Mousie's voice was barely audible. 'Poor Joss. We're never prepared for it, somehow. Perhaps I should have stayed after all, but I had a feeling that Mutt wanted to be alone with Joss tonight. Did Joss telephone you?'

'Come and see her.' Bruno avoided the question. 'She's still suffering from shock, I think.'

Joss took a deep breath. Her limbs were stiff, her head ached, and she found that she was shivering again. She stood up carefully and tried to smile at Mousie as she came into the room.

'Poor darling.' Mousie put her arms about her and rocked her as if she were a child. 'Poor Joss. Goodness, how cold you are. Come over to the fire.'

'I'm OK really.' Joss crushed down a sudden desire to bawl like a child. 'It was all so gentle and quiet. One minute she was sleeping and then, the next time I went in . . .' She swallowed piteously. 'I don't think there was anything I could have done.'

'Nothing at all,' Mousie told her firmly. 'The doctor warned us that this might happen and we must be glad that there was no pain. Sit down there and get warm. I'll go and see her.'

She glanced warningly at Bruno, who obediently piled more logs onto the embers and reached for the bellows, smiled reassuringly at Joss and disappeared.

'This is terrible,' whispered Joss rapidly as soon as she'd gone. 'I've lost my bearings. It's like a nightmare where things look the same but everything's different. Just then, with Mousie, I had the same reaction as when I saw you earlier. I thought, Oh, it's Bruno, and then: but, hang on, he's not who I thought he was – yet actually you're just the same. It's I who am different. How can I go on like this now that I know the truth?' She leaned forward. 'How on earth have you managed all these years?'

He sat back on his heels, watching the flames, his face bleak. 'Try to remember that it was rather a *fait accompli* as far as I was concerned. You don't have much control at four years old, you know. And anyway, it was what my mother wanted. No, no,' he saw her expression, 'not that Mutt should impersonate her but that she should bring me back here. Before she died she made me promise to do everything Mutt said. You've read the letters so you can have an inkling of what it was like. Mutt and Emma became my family. My one terror was that Mutt might die too. She and Emma helped me to bear the misery and fear. How could I expose them even if I'd wanted to? And at what point? When I went to school? My

253

twenty-first birthday party? When I got married?' He gave a little mirthless chuckle. 'Mutt offered me this house when I got married but I didn't want it. The Lookout was all I ever needed. Had I accepted it, it might have made things simpler now. I could have passed it over to you without any questions asked. After all, that's Emma's dream. Mutt's too. Those were almost her last words to me. "I want Joss to have Paradise".'

'But how could I have Paradise now?' she asked him almost angrily. 'It would be quite wrong . . .'

She fell silent as Mousie came hurrying down the stairs and into the drawing-room.

'A good, peaceful slipping-away in her sleep.' She smiled at them both as if to reassure them. 'Nothing could have been done for her.'

'"The Lord grant us a quiet night and a perfect end",' murmured Joss – and then flushed as she realized that these were the words Mutt had said to her at bedtime when she was a small girl, staying at Paradise.

Mousie glanced at her curiously. 'Bed for you,' she said firmly. 'It's the Bodmin practice today, isn't it? Not an early start then. Hot-water bottle, a couple of paracetamol and a few hours' sleep. I'll wake you in time, don't worry. Go on up while I do the hottie.'

They went out together. Bruno waited for a moment and then slipped upstairs and went quietly into the Porch Room. He too was aware of the absence of spirit as he stood looking down at the figure in the bed, at the peaceful, care-smoothed face.

'You knew I'd be angry, didn't you?' he murmured. 'And I was. Letters! Good grief! But see what you've done now! You *are* a Mutt, aren't you?' He took her hand, touched it with his lips and kissed her brow gently. 'I'm glad I read them, though.'

He stood for a moment still holding her hand, his gaze inward as he remembered certain passages from her letters, until he heard Mousie going into Joss's bedroom. Tucking Mutt's hand beneath the cover, he gave her one last kiss and left the room. He hadn't reached the hall before Mousie was behind him, following him downstairs.

'No point in dragging the doctor out this early,' she said. 'I'll make some tea, I think. Would you like some or should you be going back in case Emma wakes?' She looked at him, a professional assessment, gauging his weariness and strain. 'It's always a shock, even when you're half expecting it, isn't it? You didn't tell me earlier. Did Joss telephone you? Was she worried about Mutt?'

He shook his head. 'I couldn't sleep and suddenly I had a very strong feeling that I should be here. I was too late to see Mutt but at least Joss had some company after the shock of finding her.'

'I'm glad,' said Mousie. 'Perhaps I should have stayed but I had one of those feelings too. It seemed to me that Joss and Mutt should be here together. Odd, isn't it?'

'I think you were absolutely right. From what I can gather something very special happened between them earlier on.'

'Oh, that's good,' she answered with impulsive warmth. 'They were so close, those two, and Joss brought her a great deal of comfort. Thank God that Emma was here too. Mutt was quite relaxed when I left her last evening, though she'd had something on her mind these last few days. Strange . . .'

He watched the puzzlement in the intelligent, slate-blue eyes and felt a tiny twinge of fear in his gut.

'Strange?' He spoke lightly, eyebrows raised, and she seemed to recall herself and shook her head.

'Nothing important,' she said. 'Or anyway, not at the moment. You look exhausted. Go home and try to get some sleep before Emma wakes. There will be an awful lot to do later. Go on, Bruno, there's nothing more you can do here.'

There was no alternative but to let himself out into the grey morning. A damp breeze touched his face and a soft mist wreathed and curled through the branches of the rhododendrons. Hands thrust into the pockets of his jacket he walked quickly down the drive, anticipating Emma's reaction, persuading himself that Mousie would not find the letters. He wished now that he'd seized his chance when Mousie had gone to deal with Joss's hot-water bottle, but he'd had no plan as to where to hide them and feared to be caught red-handed. As soon as he could he would remove them to safety but some deep instinct warned him that it would be foolish to destroy them: perhaps, all too soon, they might be needed. Now that Joss knew the truth there would be further problems and he wondered how she would deal with this new knowledge. His guess was that Raymond Fox would travel at once to St Meriadoc, so as to be on the spot at the reading of the will, and Bruno could well imagine the dilemma in which Joss would soon find herself.

He tried to empty his tired mind, to think about Mutt: immediately grief closed up his throat, making it difficult to swallow, and suddenly he saw how very much he would miss her. Despite his anger, the letters had touched him deeply and, remembering that younger, vulnerable Mutt, his heart was weighted with sadness and loss.

He let Nellie out, filled the kettle and went to revive the fire, all the while bracing himself to the task of telling Emma that her mother was dead.

Joss was already asleep. She'd obediently swallowed two tablets with some water, gratefully clutching the hot-water bottle.

'Sleep.' Mousie had spoken the word as if it were part incantation, part order. 'You've done wonderfully, my darling. Now rest. I'll bring you a cup of tea at nine o'clock.'

Alone at last, her head beating painfully as a result of weeping and strain, Joss had slid beneath her quilt and closed her eyes. Phrases from the letters, fragments of conversation, images conjured from the past, jostled in her weary brain. If only Bruno were right and she could believe that Mutt had wanted to share her secret, then she might be able to forgive herself; it was unbearable to accept that she'd betrayed Mutt's trust. Yet she suspected that both of them knew that he'd been making a generous attempt to exonerate and comfort her. As she willed herself to relax she tried to relive the shock the letters had first had upon her: to re-create that disbelief at the realization that Mutt was an impostor. At some deep level she understood that if she could only concentrate on Mutt's deception then her own behaviour might seem a little less disgraceful, which made her feel even more ashamed.

As she'd stirred restlessly, turning her aching head on the pillow, it slowly dawned upon her that Mutt would be the last person to judge her. The writer of those letters would not condemn her but would, rather, be full of compassion at the knowledge of the burden of secrecy that she, Joss, must now bear in her turn. Just as, earlier, Bruno had tried to take the weight of guilt from her so now it seemed that Mutt, in her turn, was easing that burden.

Joss had stretched, her cramped muscles relaxing, her heart a little lighter, and composed herself to sleep. For the first time in hours she'd thought about George: George, who was not after all her second cousin, who was no relation at all. She'd reviewed this information, from this angle and that, and saw that it made no difference: that the relationship that had been forged over their lives remained unchanged. The awareness of him, only half a mile away, had filled her with a warm peacefulness. Tomorrow she would see him.

Turning on to her side, clasping the comforting bottle, Joss slept.

CHAPTER TWENTY-ONE

George woke early, pulled on the long tartan dressing-gown that hung behind the door, and went downstairs. Rafe was already up, making coffee, drawing back the curtains.

'Weather's changed,' he said. 'Pity. I was enjoying the nip in the air and the sunshine. Did you manage to sleep?'

'On and off.' George took his mug of coffee gratefully. 'The trouble is that this problem gets between me and everything else. I worry at it like a terrier at a rat-hole.'

'That sounds reasonable under the circumstances.'

An uneasy silence fell between them. Rafe swiped at the draining-board with a cloth, screwed the top on to the jar of coffee, aware of his helplessness. Pamela, he felt, would have had the key word, the right phrase, to help George through to some kind of conclusion or at least convey sympathy and encouragement. He, who had spent his life teaching and enabling, felt at a loss to help his own son.

George sensed his father's frustration and felt equally impotent. He swallowed some coffee and went to look out of the window, racking his brains for some light-hearted remark that would ease the tension. The sea slopped untidily at the cliffs; grey and unfriendly as dish-water, it heaved itself up against the land and slithered back from it again as if finding the effort too great. Presently it turned its back on the unyielding coast and began to slip gently away.

'I was wondering if I might get a sail in while I was here.' George said the first thing that offered itself. 'Sailing helps to clear the mind somehow.'

Rafe came to stand beside him at the window, as if considering the possibility.

'Not much wind.'

'No, and anyway I ought to be getting back.' Rafe was silent. 'It's just, you know . . . not much point in hanging round here . . .' George stopped. 'I don't mean that. It's always great to see you both. But I think I'll go back and tell Penny that the deed is done. She'll be wondering how you are . . .'

'My dear fellow, you must do exactly what's right for you.' Rafe slipped an arm along his son's broad shoulders, gave him a brief hug. 'You know you are always welcome here. Just stay in touch.'

'Of course I will.' George finished his coffee. 'Will Ma be OK?'

'Your mother will be fine. She wants what is right for you, that's all.'

'If only we knew what that is it would be a start. Relationships are so complicated.' He shook his head as if baffled. 'I keep wondering why, you see. She seemed quite happy in London with all her friends. She'd settled in so well, had a good job. Perhaps I should never have asked her to give it all up.'

'But you'd hardly have seen each other,' Rafe pointed out. 'And she seemed very ready to marry you and move down here.'

George nodded, shrugged. 'Well, that's how it seemed to me. She got on very well with some of the other wives too, although very often when we were at sea she'd go back to

London to see her friends. Of course, having Tasha made that more difficult, but then she decided she wanted to be out of the city and I thought that having the cottage would settle her, you see. Her heart was so set on it.'

'Perhaps,' said Rafe carefully, 'she was trying to distract herself. Perhaps it was her way of trying to make things work; to take her mind off . . . whatever his name is.'

Some odd kind of delicacy made him unwilling to name Penny's lover but George had no difficulty with this.

'Brett,' he said, supplying the name without any particular emotion. 'You could be right. I was angry because it seemed that the minute he appeared on the scene she gave in at once. Now I'm beginning to believe that he's been around for longer than I realized.'

'Is that likely?' Rafe remembered the theory he'd put forward to Pam last night. 'You wouldn't have suspected something?'

George shrugged. 'Why should I? You don't naturally assume that your wife's having an affair with a former lover, do you? Especially when you think he's thousands of miles away.'

Rafe studied him. There was no sign in his son's face of any real jealousy: no bitterness. He was reminded again of the rugby match tickets and Jeremy MacCann: George, once more, was suffering from a sense of being hard done by at Penny's hands whilst at the same time feeling sympathy for her.

'What do you *really* want, George?' he asked involuntarily. 'Given a free choice?'

George chuckled. 'How do you spell it, Pa?' he asked. 'First things first. I want to make certain Penny and I have done everything we can before we chuck it in.'

'And then what?' asked Pamela from behind him.

'I'll take that step when it comes.' He bent to kiss her. 'Good morning. I'm going to dash off, Ma. I want to tell Penny that you've been told, as she asked me, and that you are very sad but not angry. The last thing I want is for her and Brett to feel they're star-crossed lovers, defying the world. They need to see that it's all quite depressingly ordinary and nothing special.'

'You're clearing the decks,' she said thoughtfully.

'If you like.' He looked amused at the expression. 'Will you tell Joss I'm sorry not to have seen her?'

'Joss?' she asked quickly.

There was a brief silence.

'And Mousie,' he said evenly, 'and Bruno and Emma. And Mutt, of course. I just have this feeling that I mustn't allow any time to be wasted. I've got a few days' leave, that's all.'

'You must do whatever you have to,' she said, putting her arms around him. 'Just stay in touch, my darling. Give our love to Penny and Tasha, and remember that we're here if you need us.'

'I know that.' He held her tightly for a moment. 'Thanks, Ma. I'll phone when I get home.'

He disappeared upstairs whilst Pamela stood quite still, her head bent thoughtfully.

'I was just bringing you some coffee.' Rafe spoke normally, an ear cocked towards the stairs. The bathroom door closed. 'What did you mean,' he lowered his voice, 'about clearing the decks?'

'Just a feeling I have.' She held out her hand and he put the mug into it. 'He never did like muddle, did he? He always wanted things cut and dried, and hated anything that wasn't above board. Well and truly off with the old before on with the new.'

'Any more clichés?' Rafe asked drily. 'You sound surprisingly cheerful about it this morning.'

'Oh, Rafe, I think I am,' she answered. 'I think . . . oh, dear, I can feel another cliché coming on. I think I can see a light at the end of the tunnel.'

'Or a cloud with a silver lining?' he suggested cheerfully. 'Well, thank God. When he's gone you can tell me what it is because I'm damned if I can see it.'

At The Lookout, Emma was staring miserably at the fire, her arm round Nellie, who sat beside her on the sofa.

'So suddenly,' she murmured. 'I can't believe it. And poor darling Joss there all alone with her.'

Bruno didn't correct this impression. He, too, had been making coffee but Emma's stood untasted on the table.

'It could have been much worse,' he said, hearing the conventional uselessness of the words but too tired to think of anything original. 'And wonderful for Mutt to slip away like that without pain.'

Tears streamed down Emma's cheeks and she wiped at them with the back of her hands.

'I wish you'd woken me up,' she said. 'When you went.'

'It wouldn't have mattered,' he told her. 'I didn't see her alive either.'

'I must go and see Joss.' She made as if to move but sank back again, as if defeated by the heaviness of grief.

'I told you that she's asleep,' he reminded her. 'Mousie will get her off to work but she needs to rest.'

'Surely she doesn't have to go to work,' protested Emma. She laid her cheek against Nellie's head. 'They'll understand, won't they? Poor Joss . . .'

'She'll want to go.' Bruno had never been able to convince Emma of the work ethic. 'And quite right too. Work is the best thing for her. It'll take her mind off things. Why don't you go up to Paradise and see how Mousie is coping, and then you'll be able to have a word with Joss when she wakes up?'

'I'll do that.' Emma pulled herself together. 'Mousie will have telephoned the doctor and I suppose one of us will have to contact the undertaker . . .'

'There's a lot to be organized,' he agreed. 'I need a shower and a shave and then I'll follow you up after I've told Rafe and Pamela.'

She glanced at him, grateful for his presence. 'You look exhausted,' she told him anxiously. 'Could you snatch an hour's sleep? Why don't you try?'

'I might,' he said. 'I'll see how I feel after I've showered. As long as you're OK?'

She nodded, although her lips trembled a little. 'It's just so hard to believe she isn't there any more.'

'You're allowed to cry,' he told her gently. 'You don't have to be brave with me.'

'I know that,' she said. 'But you're right about being busy. It distracts. I'll go and get dressed and then get up to Paradise. It's not right to leave it all to Mousie and, anyway, I want to say goodbye properly to Mutt. Oh God! I can't believe it.'

He watched her go out, mopping her eyes, and then drank his coffee in one gulp. Bending to stroke the recumbent Nellie, he wondered if Joss might think about the letters; whether she'd have the opportunity to move them to a safer place. Taking the mugs into the kitchen, letting Nellie out, all the while he was thinking of how and when he might transport the letters away from Paradise.

CHAPTER TWENTY-TWO

Joss woke suddenly. She heard the front door close and voices, muffled, in the hall. Awareness of loss and anxiety squeezed at her heart and she huddled beneath the bedclothes, dredging up the courage to face the day. So much had changed, despite Bruno's reassurances that she was still exactly the same person she'd always believed herself to be. Emma was her mother, Mutt her grandmother, true enough: but there was no link now to Bruno, or to Mousie and Rafe, and she'd already had a taste of how difficult it would be to pretend otherwise. It was not in her character to mislead or conceal, and the few moments that she'd had with Mousie had shown her how different these relationships would be from now on. Yet with Bruno himself, after that first adjustment, she'd found herself confiding and talking as if there were no difference. The love and trust between them, nurtured over the years, had paid off and their friendship had proved to be above family ties; stronger than blood. Yet there *was* a difference.

Joss rolled onto her back, pushing the tepid bottle to one side. The difference was that Bruno shared the secret with her. If anything, this knowledge would be bound to strengthen those ties: with the other members of the family she must always, now, be on her guard. How, she wondered, had Bruno survived all these years of secrecy? Would she be able to do the same? Fear stiffened her muscles as she thought about her mother and the complications that lay ahead regarding the will. How could she, Joss, now accept anything from the estate and how could she approve her mother inheriting above Rafe and Mousie, especially if her father were to interfere? She knew his ways: if her mother were to inherit the boatyard then he would try to convince Emma that the development of the cove would be in everyone's best interests: that Mousie, as well as Rafe and Pamela and all their family, would share in the profits.

Joss stirred, gritting her teeth with anxiety, already seeing his campaign: patient, relentless, good-humoured. The trouble was that it could split the family. Rafe and Pamela would be devastated at the idea but their two eldest children would almost certainly be in favour of such a lucrative project. Olivia and Joe would instantly grasp at an opportunity that, with their growing families, was likely to increase income and would be impatient with the suggestion that their parents would hate to be uprooted from the cove or made miserable were they to stay. Joss could well imagine how difficult it would be for Pamela to resist once she was shown how the development would bring such financial help to her children.

Olivia and Joe had never had the passion for the valley of St Meriadoc that she, Joss, and George shared. Neither of them could wait to get away; both were ambitious and their visits rapidly dwindled as they became more successful, although this was blamed on growing pressure of work and the complications of travelling with ever-increasing broods of small children. They would be indifferent to the loss of peace and natural beauty: unmoved by the fact that The Lookout's prospect would become a noisy holiday centre. It would be bad enough for Rafe and Pamela, and Mousie – yet of all of them it would be Bruno, the true inheritor and only legitimate beneficiary, who would actually suffer most. The tranquillity and privacy that he valued so much would be destroyed and, even if it were his cousins who benefited financially, it was quite wrong that this destruction should be instigated by someone who had no rights at all over the estate that belonged to Bruno's family. How, Joss asked herself, would she be able to remain silent if all this were to happen? Perhaps, after all, a time might come when it would be necessary for the truth to be told and the letters shown. They must be kept in a safe place, just in case.

The thought of the letters brought her upright and on to the edge of the bed. She wondered if Bruno had managed to conceal them whilst she and Mousie were out of the drawing-room. With luck he would have carried them away to The Lookout and hidden them in his study, which was generally considered out of bounds. As she brooded on their whereabouts the door opened and Mousie came in, carrying a mug of tea. She set it down on the table beside the bed and touched Joss lightly on the head. It was a gentle caress, at once affectionate and encouraging, and Joss smiled at her. Staring up into those warmly familiar slate-blue eyes, just like Rafe's and George's, confusion welled inside her and she crushed her hands between her knees in an attempt to stiffen her resolve and summon up courage.

'Did you sleep?' asked Mousie. 'Good. Emma's here, just in time to see you before you go off to Bodmin. I've made some porridge.'

Joss nodded, not quite trusting herself to speak, and Mousie went out quietly. She picked up the mug and drank the hot, reviving tea. It seemed impossible that, only a few hours ago, she'd believed that her new knowledge would not affect the relationship between her and George. It could not change the past, this was true, but how would she manage now? Sometime today she would see him. Joy mixed with fear churned in her gut. Perhaps this was how it would be from now onwards: nothing would be straightforward ever again. She was not a stranger to complexities. From childhood she'd attempted to balance her father's cramping meannesses and humiliating contempt for weakness against his great capability to care materially for his family: to square her mother's overflowing generosity and loving warmth with her inability to cope with unpleasantness and anger. Attempting to understand them, trying to decide which of their traits was a force for good and acting accordingly, had shaped her own character. Now she must take on a different kind of compromise.

Joss finished her tea and went to have a shower.

Downstairs, Mousie was comforting Emma, explaining that Mutt had died peacefully in her sleep.

'But she seemed so much better,' said Emma tearfully. 'She was quite bright yesterday. I really thought she was improving.'

'That can often happen.' Mousie stirred the porridge. 'A lucid spell just before the end. Be glad that she didn't suffer any more.'

'I am. Of course I am. But if I'd known I would have stayed here last night.' Emma's tears spilled over again. 'I feel I was so heartless going off to The Lookout.'

'But you couldn't have known. None of us could. She might have got better and then had another fall. And what then? At what point would it have been reasonable for you to start thinking, Mutt might die today, and what would you have done about it? Would you have moved down here to be with her, just in case?'

'She'd have hated that.' Emma blotted her cheeks with a tissue. 'She was very independent.'

'Quite. And she had Bruno, who saw her every day, and the rest of us nearby. And don't forget that she's had Joss with her for the last few months, which has been such a joy for her.'

'Yes, I do realize that.' Emma tried to smile. 'Sorry, Mousie. I'm being pathetic. It's just . . . getting used to the idea, I suppose.'

'It's always a shock.' Mousie touched her shoulder and put a mug of coffee beside her. 'Even when you're expecting it, you never get used to the finality of it. Coming to terms with the fact that your chance to make amends, have one more joke, share a hug – whatever it is – is gone for ever.'

Mousie turned away to hide her own emotion and Emma's eyes filled with tears again.

'Sorry,' she said again. 'I think I'll go up and say goodbye to her, Mousie. Shall I?'

She hesitated and Mousie smiled at her encouragingly.

'I think you should,' she said. 'Joss'll be down in a minute . . .'

Emma stood up, bracing herself so that she should not break down in front of her daughter, preparing herself for what might lie ahead. They met in the hall. Shocked by the look of suffering on her child's face, Emma forgot her own loss and hugged her tightly.

'You did so well, darling,' she told her warmly. 'How wonderful that you've been with Mutt these last weeks. You gave her so much happiness.'

Joss smiled rather wanly but gratefully. 'Are you going to see her? Would you like me to come with you?'

Resisting the urge to cry 'Yes! Yes, please!' Emma shook her head. It looked as if Joss had been through quite enough.

'I'd rather be alone,' she lied. 'You understand? Just this last time.'

'Of course.' Joss couldn't quite hide her relief and, feeling an odd sense of satisfaction, Emma went upstairs.

Joss watched her out of sight, listened to the sounds of busyness from the kitchen, and went swiftly into the drawing-

room. The curtains had been drawn back and the fire built up
– clearly Mousie had decided that today the comfort of a log
fire and a warm room was necessary – but Bruno's used mug
still stood on the small table and a newspaper lay where Joss
had left it yesterday. She went quickly to the sofa, lifted the
padded seat and gave a sigh of thanksgiving: the letters were
gone.

George had already set out and Joss was on her way to
Bodmin by the time Bruno arrived in The Row to tell them the
sad news.

'Oh, Bruno, I am so sorry.' Pamela stretched out a hand
towards him and he took it between his own. 'Rafe and I had
tea with her in her bedroom a few days ago and I have to say
that she sounded very weak.'

'She'd made a bit of a comeback.' He gave her hand another
squeeze and let it go. 'Yesterday she was quite bright,
mentally, but very tired. I think it was all too much for her to
recover from: the fall and then that infection. I'm sorry to have
missed George.'

There was a small, uncomfortable silence; then they spoke
together.

Rafe: 'Things are a bit tricky for him at present . . .'

Pamela: 'I don't see why Bruno shouldn't know . . .'

'No need to say anything,' said Bruno quickly – too quickly.
'None of my business. I just wondered if he'd gone back
to sea or whether he might be here for the funeral, that's
all.'

'He's got some leave,' said Rafe awkwardly, 'just a few day
but I'm sure he'll be down. He was very fond of Mutt.'

'We all were,' said Pamela sadly. 'She was a darling and
we've had such fun together. And we're very grateful to her.
There's no way Rafe and I could have afforded to live in a
place like this if she hadn't been so generous about the rent.
Nor could Mousie. We've been terrifically lucky.'

Another silence. Bruno, unable to reassure them that nothing would change, said nothing.

'Poor Joss,' said Pamela, sensing some embarrassment and seeking a change of subject. 'Such a shock for her. Well, for all of us, of course . . .'

'Absolutely,' agreed Rafe quickly. 'What a pity George dashed off before we could tell him.'

'Never mind,' said Bruno. 'After all, there's nothing he could do. But I'd better get up to Paradise. Sorry to have to be the bearer of bad tidings . . .'

He almost added, 'when you've got enough on your plate already,' but remembered again, just in time, that Joss had told him in confidence about George and Penny. He hesitated, raised a hand in farewell and went out feeling frustrated. He could only hope that Rafe and Pamela would put his odd behaviour down to grief: he'd been too quick with his reply and shown no surprise – or concern – that George might be having problems.

With Nellie at his heels, he crossed the narrow bridge and walked swiftly up the lane. The donkeys were at the gate and he paused to speak to them, rubbing them between the ears whilst they snuffled through the lower bars at Nellie. Their grey coats were furred with the mist that curled in gently from the sea, drifting smoke-like across the meadow and hanging in the black, bare branches of the beech trees, and he shivered, turning his collar up against the chill, and giving their soft noses a final pat before turning away.

He let himself in through the garden door and paused in the hall, listening to the low murmuring of voices from the bedroom above, before passing into the drawing-room. He went quickly to the sofa, lifted the padded seat and gave a sigh of relief: the letters were gone.

CHAPTER TWENTY-THREE

Rafe and Pamela remained silent for a few moments after he'd left them.

'I'm glad we saw her – last Friday, wasn't it?' said Rafe at last. 'It would have been horrid if we hadn't been to visit her, wouldn't it? The valley won't be the same without Mutt. She's so much a part of it all.' He sighed, his heart heavy. 'Poor old Bruno.'

'There was something wrong with him,' said Pamela. 'Did you notice?'

'Well, after all his mother has just died,' he pointed out reasonably. 'What would you expect, poor fellow?'

'It wasn't that.' Pamela frowned, trying to define her reactions to the encounter. 'Not that kind of thing. Of *course* he was upset, that's not the point, but he was too quick when we talked about George. It wasn't the obvious response. Bruno has a sympathetic streak, hasn't he, even when he's wrapped up in a book? If you've got a problem he notices. Today, when we hinted about George, he kind of blanked us and that's not like him. He wasn't even surprised. I felt that he already knew something was wrong and didn't want to distress us by making us think we had to tell him about it.'

Rafe shook his head. 'Too complicated,' he said. 'I think he was just not himself.'

'And did you notice that after we'd talked about living here – how we couldn't have afforded it if Mutt hadn't been so generous – there was a very odd silence?'

'Well, what answer could he have made?' replied Rafe prosaically. 'It's only the truth, after all.'

Pamela sighed with frustration. 'There was something wrong,' she insisted. 'I didn't say it in the hope of any particular response, it just happened to be how I felt. Having said it, though, I think he might have responded with . . . oh, I don't know. Something, anyway.'

Rafe stared at her, baffled. 'What sort of something?'

'Well, something like, "Don't worry, nothing will change." Or, "Well, you're part of the family." I don't know exactly what but *something*. There was just a very awkward silence.' She got up and moved towards him, her hand outstretched, feeling for him. 'Have you ever thought what might happen to us once Mutt was no longer the head of the family, Rafe?'

'No.' He took her hand and held it, drawing her close and putting his arm about her. 'I can't say I have. Bruno and Emma will inherit and I can't see them turning us out, can you?'

'No.' She rested her head against his shoulder. 'But there was something.' She shivered. 'Oh, Rafe, I feel upset. First George, and then hearing about dear old Mutt, and now Bruno behaving oddly.'

'I think you're overreacting,' he told her firmly. He glanced out of the window, seeking a distraction for her – and for himself. He was going to miss Mutt very badly. 'It's a rather dreary morning but would a little walk do us good? Shall we go and talk to the donkeys?'

She brightened. 'Let's take them some carrots,' she said.

'But I don't want to be too long, Rafe. I want to be here when George telephones to say that he's home safely.'

'We've got plenty of time,' he assured her. 'He can't possibly be there yet and I want to hear your theory about George; this light at the end of the tunnel. After this sad news I can do with some light. Get your coat and I'll fetch the carrots.'

George had travelled fast through the quiet lanes to the dual carriageway and was already turning off the A30 at Launceston on to the road to Tavistock. As he travelled his mind was busy on several different layers and he barely noticed the familiar landmarks. As he passed over the Tamar he glanced briefly downstream where the mist smoked along the river and wreathed itself between the tall trees that clung to the steep, high banks. Driving up out of the deep valley, he thought about his mother and smiled to himself.

'You're clearing the decks,' she'd said – and she'd been right. He hated to hide the truth from them, it was not in his nature, but it was difficult when the secret was not simply his own. Joss felt the same, he knew she did. It was in her character: she too had a dislike of subterfuge. Even as a child she hadn't been like other girls – whining to their mothers, sulking if they didn't get their own way.

'I'm not playing any more,' they'd say, flouncing off; or changing the rules of the game to suit themselves if they weren't winning.

Joss had always played fair and square, not grimly like Olivia, who would kill rather than lose, but with a sweet seriousness of purpose and a cheerfulness in defeat. Only he knew how difficult she'd found her father's patronizing attitude to her friends and his predilection for giving homilies on watching the pennies. The phrase 'I didn't get where I am today . . .' might have been coined especially for Raymond Fox. Joss had grown increasingly reticent, afraid to expose her friends to his heavy witticisms at their expense, and especially cautious with young men of whom she was fond. She'd escaped to St Meriadoc whenever she could and, once she was qualified, she'd moved back to Cornwall.

Driving carefully through Milton Abbot, picking up speed again as he left the village, George saw Joss's face in his mind's eye: dark winged brows above hazel eyes, the straight little nose and wide curling mouth. If only they hadn't lost touch during that crucial growing-up time they might not be in this terrible situation now.

Clearing the decks.

He hadn't been able to explain to his mother that it was necessary to believe that he'd done everything possible to make his marriage work as much for Joss's sake as for anyone else involved. Neither he nor she would want muddle or doubt: it must be all or nothing. It was Penny who had brought them to this point of telling his parents and, at the back of his mind, he wondered whether she might regret it. Perhaps, now it was out in the open, it might make her think carefully about what she was doing. The idea of leaving him was one thing but once that idea was defined, given shape and purpose by words, it grew into a daunting reality that might frighten her into reconsideration – and this must remain an option for her.

As he drove through the outskirts of Tavistock towards Yelverton, the anxiety and depression that had dogged him for the last few weeks – ever since Penny had announced her intention to leave him – closed down on him. She was fond of his parents and their reaction might carry some weight with her.

'Give them our love,' his mother had said – and he intended to do just that. He had no intention of making Penny feel guilty or ashamed. She must be given the chance, if she wanted it, to remain with him in a loving relationship. He would do nothing that would drive her into her lover's arms for comfort; but he'd done with anger and shouting and with pleading. Perhaps it was too late, anyway, but he felt he must give it his best shot now for as long as it took.

Taking the back lane out of Yelverton, approaching the little cottage, he saw that Penny's hatchback was in the single parking space beside the house. Just past the gate the lane was wider, and he pulled in tight under the thorn hedge, reached for his grip and climbed out. He felt sick with apprehension and confusion, trying for some calm, friendly opening that would start them off on a level base: no recriminations, no attempt at emotional blackmail.

He let himself in, calling out to her: 'It's only me.'

The front door led immediately into the sitting-room, which was empty. He glanced through to the long narrow kitchen, and then shouted up the stairs.

'Hello. I'm back.'

Even as he climbed the short steep staircase he knew that she'd gone. He couldn't have immediately said what was missing but subconsciously he knew that this atmosphere of emptiness was not simply a case of Penny being out shopping or with friends. As he looked into the two bedrooms and checked the bathroom the certainty grew. The rooms were too tidy: there was none of the usual clutter that seemed to spawn and spread in so small a house, and he was becoming increasingly aware of a sweet, almost sickly smell which, as he returned to the sitting-room, was quite suddenly intolerable.

As he opened the window, breathing in cold, fresh air, he saw the pot of hyacinths. Penny had bought the bulbs in Tavistock market just before Christmas and put them on the window-sill so that they would catch the sunlight. Now, the blue, bell-shaped flowers, weighing down the thick pale-green stems, were fading but their scent was still strong in the airless cottage. He carried them through to the kitchen to give them some water and saw the letter, pinned down on the kitchen table beneath the green, hand-painted coffee jar. It was one of a pottery set that Penny had bought in Wade-bridge; there was another jar to hold sugar and a third for tea. He'd made a little shelf for them and she'd set the three of them in a row, delighted with them. He stood the jar back on the shelf and opened the letter. It was written with the spontaneity that was a part of her character:

I am just so sorry, George, but this is the only way I can do it. It seems underhand – and it is, of course – but there's no point in it dragging on any longer. Brett was staying in Yelverton and came to get me and Tasha as soon as you'd gone yesterday. By the time you read this we'll be on a flight home to New Zealand.

It was wrong of me to marry you, George, knowing that deep down I still had feelings for Brett. I actually did believe that making the commitment of marriage would finally exorcize any love I had for him. It didn't work like that and, anyway, a year later he came to find me. I shouldn't have deceived you then but I was so mixed up because part of me *did* love you and I wasn't prepared to give in to Brett too quickly because of what he'd done before.

The fact is we should never have split up, he and I know that now, and I'm really sorry you've been hurt by our mistakes. But there's no point in going on com-pounding the wrong. Also I've missed my home and family terribly, not because of anything to do with you, but just because it's where I belong.

The other thing I have to tell you is that Natasha is Brett's child. You probably won't believe this, you'll think I'm trying to get away with keeping her, but it's true. I went to London just after you'd gone back to sea a year ago and that's when I met up with Brett again. I'm afraid we got carried away but by then I'd had my period and that's how I know she's his. Even then I didn't admit it because I still wasn't sure I could trust him. You don't have to believe me, there are other ways of testing it, but I hope you will and let us go peacefully.

Sorry, George, and thanks for all the good times. I've left the name of my lawyer but obviously I'm the one responsible for the break-up and I'm not asking for anything except that you don't despise me too much.

She'd scribbled something that had been crossed through several times, and then written her name and he guessed that she hadn't quite known how to finish it. As he stood with the letter in his hand, trying to take it all in, the telephone rang. He remembered his promise to let his mother know he was home safely and took up the receiver, trying to compose himself. It was a woman from a shop in Tavistock trying to contact Penny to say that something she'd ordered had arrived. George dealt with it calmly, saying that he would ask his wife to get in touch, and replaced the receiver. After a moment, he lifted it again and dialled his parents' number.

'Hi, Ma,' he said when his mother answered. 'I'm here but Penny isn't. She's done a runner with Brett, taking Tasha with her and leaving a letter saying that it's all over. They've gone back to New Zealand.'

'Gone?' She was clearly shocked. 'Oh, George, my dear boy . . .'

'Bit of a conversation stopper,' he agreed. 'Sorry if I sound callous, Ma, but I don't quite know what the form is for this.'

'Of course not,' she said quickly. 'It was good of you to phone when you must be quite shattered. I simply don't know what to say to you and you probably need time to adjust. I have to tell you, though, that Mutt died last night. Poor Joss found her. You can imagine what a shock it was for her. She telephoned from the practice in Bodmin and I thought she seemed rather disappointed to have missed you . . .'

She talked on for a moment, trying to get them both

through this difficult moment, but George suddenly felt as if he'd been thrown a lifeline.

'Look, there's nothing I can do here,' he told her. 'If it's OK with you I think I'll come straight back. Maybe I can be useful.'

'Oh, do,' she agreed warmly. 'It would be wonderful to have you here. Only, drive carefully. You're probably in shock.'

Once he'd hung up he stared round the kitchen, feeling some kind of responsibility for this little cottage, which once had been their home and was now silent and unwelcoming. It would have to be sold, he told himself, and he wondered what would happen to the objects they'd chosen together – the pottery set and the other things that Penny had been unable to take with her.

He saw now that the hyacinth flowers were not just fading but beginning to decay, their petal edges brown; the strong scent seemed weighted with an odour of failure and deceit, and he was filled with a terrible sadness. He took the pot out and put it in a sheltered place in the back porch: later the bulbs could be planted under the hedge in the garden and next spring they would flower again.

CHAPTER TWENTY-FOUR

By the time Bruno got back to The Lookout he was feeling the effects of twenty-four hours with no sleep. The day had been busy, emotional, and he'd been grateful for Mousie's calm professionalism. She'd got them through it all: Mutt's body taken away by the undertakers, plans made for the funeral, Emma held steady by a hundred and one tasks.

'I shall stay here with Joss until the funeral,' she'd told Bruno when the rector had gone and the tea things were washed up and put away. 'Ray will be down tomorrow so Mousie and I are going to Polzeath to do some shopping and then we'll make up beds. Why don't you go home and try to catch up on some sleep? You look exhausted.'

He'd been glad to take her advice. Collecting Nellie from the kitchen he'd walked back over the cliff, although the dense vapour-like mist made it impossible to see very far. It was thicker now, covering his coat in tiny, shining droplets, flattening the sea that lay almost motionless against the cliffs. He felt it press damply upon him – obscuring familiar landmarks, deadening sound – chill and cheerless.

Once inside, he went to light the fire in an attempt to lift his own spirits and saw the red light of the answerphone blinking. Joss's voice was expressionless, her message brief, as if she'd realized that Emma might well be with Bruno when he listened to it.

'Glad you found those letters. Is it OK if I drop in on my way home about five? See you later.'

Bruno pressed several buttons and replayed it: no mistake. Mechanically he went about the task of reviving the fire, piling the charred logs together on their bed of hot ash, working the bellows until the heart glowed red. Nellie nudged at him, pushing her nose beneath his arm as he sat on the leather pouffe beside the flat granite hearth, sitting close to him as he put an arm about her neck.

'In a minute,' he told her, piling on new logs. 'I know you're hungry. Let me get this going.' She licked his ear encouragingly, watching the sizzling tongues of flame with bright, eager eyes, and he felt an odd comfort at her presence. Once the wood was well alight, he went out into the kitchen with Nellie prancing at his heels and, all the while he prepared her supper, he was thinking about Joss's cryptic message.

Glad you found those letters.

There was no question in his mind which letters – though he could have easily bluffed it with Emma, had she heard it too – but did she imagine that he had them? He glanced at his watch: nearly twenty minutes to five. The telephone rang and he snatched up the receiver before the answerphone could click into play.

'Hi,' said Rafe. 'Sorry to trouble you, we can guess what a dreadful day it's been for you, but we wanted to say that George is back and ready to be of any use. You can never tell at times like these, can you, but he's here if needed.'

'Thanks, Rafe.' For a moment Bruno couldn't remember where George had been and why he was back. His brain simply refused to function properly. 'That's kind.'

'Pamela is asking if you'd like to come over to supper.'

Bruno hesitated. 'I don't think I will. I'm going to try for an early night. Emma's staying up at Paradise with Joss. I have to say that Mousie has been fantastic, Rafe. I'm not sure what we'd have done without her.'

'Well, she's had plenty of experience.' He took the praise of his sister lightly. 'Don't forget we're here if you need us, any time.'

He rang off and Bruno stood for a while in thought. Perhaps Joss had snatched the letters and dropped them off at The Lookout on her way to Bodmin while he'd been with Rafe and Pamela. He racked his memory: had her car been gone from the quarry? Impossible to remember. He went out to the kitchen, checked the sitting-room, searched his study, but there was no sign of Mutt's letters. Despite the earliness of the hour he poured himself a stiff whisky and went to sit beside the fire, waiting, with Nellie curled beside him on the sofa.

Joss arrived just before twenty past five.

'Beastly weather,' she said, coming across to warm her hands at the fire. 'It was horrid driving through the lanes. I see that George is back.'

Bruno got up, realizing that she was trying very hard to behave normally, and pushed her gently down onto the sofa.

'George is back,' he agreed, sitting opposite on the pouffe, 'although I don't know where he's been, and what's all this about the letters?'

She stared at him. 'George went back to Meavy,' she said slowly, taking one thing at a time, 'and it's a bit odd that he's come back so soon.' She frowned. 'You must have realized what I meant about the letters. They weren't there so I imagine that you were able to get them last night when Mousie and I were upstairs.'

'No.' He shook his head. 'I'm afraid that's not so. Do you mean that you haven't got them?'

'Of course I haven't. I told you: when I got downstairs this morning they'd gone.'

They looked at each other, puzzled.

'But that's impossible,' said Bruno. 'Wait a minute.' He closed his eyes, as if calling up the scene. 'When Mousie arrived I put them under the seat . . .'

'Maybe Mum found them. Oh, my God . . . !'

'I've been with Emma all day,' said Bruno impatiently, 'and she hasn't given the least impression that she'd found a cache of letters under the seat of the sofa. Good grief! Why should she even bother to look?'

'Then where are they?' cried Joss.

'I don't know. Give me a minute to think . . . Hang on! Mutt's cleaner turned up but she didn't stay long. Mousie told her to do a quick clean round downstairs and leave it at that. I wonder if she saw them and put them somewhere safe and then forgot to mention it. It's possible, I suppose, given the sort of day it was.'

'And there's something else,' Joss told him, her hazel eyes wide with fear. 'I thought about it when I got to work. What happened to *Goblin Market*?'

He stared at her blankly. 'To what?'

'Mutt's book,' she prompted him impatiently. 'The one she treasured so much and quoted to her sister. She said that the death certificates and things were hidden in the back of it.'

'Christ,' murmured Bruno softly. 'I hadn't given it a thought. I wonder what drawer she left *that* in. You'll have to find it, Joss. It's something Emma might easily come across. Damn and hell, what was Mutt thinking about?'

'She probably wasn't thinking at all.' Joss defended her grandmother, though she looked drawn and anxious. 'It was all so long ago. As the years passed, the book and the letters would have become less important. It was only right at the end, when the American came, that she suddenly remembered them. Where can they be, Bruno?'

'Let's not panic.' He saw that it was time to be reassuring. 'Go on up to Paradise and have a look around but don't make Emma suspicious. Shall you go over to see George?'

'George?' For a brief moment it seemed that she had forgotten George. 'Oh, Bruno, I don't know what I shall do about George. For a mad moment last night I thought that all this needn't matter and then, when I woke up this morning, I couldn't see how I could behave as if nothing has changed. Mutt and Mum and I are impostors. How can I pretend that everything's just as he's always assumed it is? I simply don't know how to handle it.'

'But you don't think the time has come for the truth to be told?'

'Oh, no!' She shook her head, staring at him in horror. 'What about Mum? How could we?'

The telephone rang and he took up the receiver.

'I was wondering if Joss is with you?' Emma's voice was anxious. 'She said she'd be home by five and the fog is really thick now.'

'She's right here, Em.' Bruno made his voice light, cheerful even. 'She's on her way up to you now.' He replaced the receiver and looked encouragingly at Joss, eyebrows raised.

'OK,' she said, as if obeying instructions. 'Maybe it'll be in the same desk. And I'll look round and see if the cleaner's left the letters somewhere.'

'Try not to worry,' he told her, 'and telephone if you need me.'

When she'd gone he sat down again by the fire, waiting. He heard Mousie come in through the kitchen and into the sitting-room. She dropped her bag down beside him on the sofa, but remained standing, and presently he looked up at her.

'So where do we go from here?' he asked.

CHAPTER TWENTY-FIVE

'So where do we go from here?' Rafe was asking Pamela. George had arrived back at St Meriadoc just before four o'clock and now, nearly two hours later, had gone upstairs to have a bath. 'Do you think the bath is symbolic? Washing away the past and all that kind of thing?'

'How does he look?' asked Pamela urgently, as if George might reappear at any moment.

'Peaceful,' answered Rafe after a moment or two, 'but subdued. As if he can relax at last . . . no, not quite that. Hang on while I think about it.'

They sat opposite each other at the table and Pamela felt about for his hand that he stretched out to her across the newspapers and other odds and ends, pushing aside his coffee mug.

'He sounded rather flat,' she suggested anxiously, as if this might help his assessment.

Releasing his hand, she felt about for the objects that lived on the table. A pretty, hand-painted spice jar that held pencils; a square pink and white china dish into which Rafe put special chocolates or sweets; a covey of small, carved birds. She picked one up, smoothing the grainy wood with one finger, feeling the sharp beak and clawed feet.

'He *does* look peaceful.' Rafe was clearly sticking to his original impression. 'But it's rather as if he's arrived at where he wants to be through good luck rather than good judgement and he's feeling deeply relieved and very thankful. Rather as if he's been let off the hook, if you see what I mean.'

Pamela arranged the four birds into a line, beak to tail, and imagined them marching across the table while she considered Rafe's diagnosis.

'Well, that would be about right, wouldn't it?' she asked.

'You mean if your theory is correct?' Rafe turned two of the birds round so now two pairs faced each other, beak to beak. 'Well, I admit it looks very likely.'

'He realized that he was in love with Joss at about the same time that Brett came back into Penny's life and, though George was prepared to stick with his marriage, Penny wasn't. I think that one part of him was hurt and angry that, unlike him, she wasn't even prepared to try whilst another part of him longed to be free. Now she's let him right off the hook and although he's got what he wants he's probably feeling a bit ashamed. Penny's taken all the blame and he'll feel embarrassed about that.'

'And what about Tasha?' The birds were now balancing on their toes, beaks resting on the table as if digging for worms. 'Do you believe she's not George's baby?'

Pamela was silent for a long moment.

'I think we must let it go,' she said at last, 'and I suspect that George feels the same. If Tasha had been older or he'd been able to spend more time with her it would be a different story. Penny's right to say that at that age she needs her mother and a stable relationship. Penny adores Tasha and I think she knows that she'll get everything she needs in New Zealand. I think it would be wrong to fight it and especially now that there's a doubt over who her father is.'

'And, after all, if Brett *is* her father it shows that Penny did actually try for a year before she gave up on her marriage.'

'He'd let her down before. Perhaps she was making certain that this time he was serious. A young man doesn't take on a child unless he's committed to the relationship and he's had every chance during the last twelve months to disappear again. We must believe that Penny and George mistook their hearts and that now they both have the chance to start again with the right people.'

The birds paired off, two and two, were now roosting in the branches of a heavy glass candlestick that stood in the middle of the table. Pamela settled them more securely with gentle fingers and heaved a great sigh of relief.

'It's a pity that it's all come together,' said Rafe. 'Penny going off and poor old Mutt . . .'

'Oh, no,' answered Pamela quickly. 'It will get George and Joss over any awkwardness. They won't have too much time to think about themselves and the guilt and all the other emotions. Life will just make them get on with it. Much better.'

'If you say so.'

'I do say so. Although I did feel for Joss this morning when she telephoned. She simply couldn't hide her disappointment that George had gone. I expect it was coming on top of Mutt. They were very close.'

'Poor Joss. I can't believe I never guessed. She's a good girl, Pammie.'

'She's a darling,' agreed Pamela warmly, 'and I can't wait to tell her how thrilled we are about her and George.'

'You won't say anything.' He sounded shocked. 'I mean, not before George has . . . Dammit, we don't even know we're right, do we?'

'Of course we're right,' she answered serenely. 'And of course I shan't say anything until it's official. What do you take me for?'

Rafe let out a great breath of relief and got up from the table.

'I don't care where the sun or the yardarm is,' he said. 'I need a drink.'

'Perhaps George will go up to Paradise and see her and Emma later on,' mused Pamela. 'I wonder how they're managing.'

From the moment Joss had arrived, Emma hadn't stopped talking. Words streamed from her mouth as earlier the tears had streamed from her eyes: the undertakers . . . so friendly and kind . . . Mousie, such a tower of strength . . . how odd it had been, making out a shopping list when poor, darling old Mutt . . . the rector had been so sweet . . . made them laugh about things that had happened in the past . . . her own wedding . . . Joss's baptism . . . then, after he'd gone, trying to get ready for Ray . . .

Talking eased her grief, shaping it into something manageable, holding misery at bay.

'And I've been looking everywhere for Mutt's address book,' she said. 'Of course we'll put a notice in the *Western Morning News* but there are one or two people I ought to contact. I've searched high and low—'

'Searched?' The word pierced the numbness that occluded Joss's brain. 'Did you . . . find anything?'

'Not a thing.' Emma sounded exasperated. 'Every time I got started there was some kind of interruption. The undertakers arriving or a telephone call or Mousie needing something.'

'I think I know where it might be.' Joss tried to sound casual. 'Can you manage supper? I'll have a look while you're getting it ready.'

'That would be kind, darling, but you look exhausted.'

'So do you.' Joss smiled at her mother, willing up her own strength. 'But I'm starving. If you can cope with the supper it would be great.'

'Of course I can.' Emma got up, only too ready to be distracted. 'I bought some lovely fish for your father to-morrow but I thought we might have something quick and simple. I bought some lamb chops . . .'

'Fine,' said Joss quickly, wondering how she'd manage to eat anything at all. 'If you're sure there's nothing I can do?'

'Nothing at all,' Emma reassured her. 'Why don't you just sit and rest?'

After she'd gone, Joss tried to collect her thoughts. She was struggling with a sense of dual identity: it had been strange to come back to Paradise, knowing that life could never be the same again whilst having to behave as if nothing had changed except, of course, that Mutt was gone. How, she wondered, had Bruno lived with his secret for so long? The thought of Bruno brought her to her feet. She looked around the room, even lifting the chair seat once again, and went quietly through the hall into the parlour. There was no sign of anything that might contain the letters and she crossed to the bookshelf, glancing quickly at the titles, knowing in her heart that Mutt would never have put *Goblin Market* in such an obvious place.

Of course, she might have removed the papers and certificates at a later date and put them somewhere else . . .

Emma came in behind her, making her jump. 'I wondered if you'd like a drink?' she offered. 'I thought it might do us good. There's some Rioja in the larder, probably Bruno's choice. What do you think?'

'Great,' said Joss. 'Good idea.' She smiled brightly. 'Just looking for that address book. I could have sworn I'd seen it in here somewhere.'

'I was looking in the desk,' said Emma, coming further into the room, as if she might help in the search, 'but then Mousie came in about something.'

'Don't worry,' said Joss quickly. 'A drink sounds brilliant. It'll unwind us a bit. I feel on edge.'

'That's what I thought.' Emma was pleased to have her offer accepted so readily. 'I'll go and get it organized.'

She pattered away and Joss drew a great gasp of relief. Perhaps it would be better to keep Emma company, thereby limiting her exploration, and look for the letters and the book when she was safely asleep. Hastily she pulled out the drawers of the desk, checking each one: no letters, no *Goblin Market*. The address book was lying on the table, beneath a piece of tapestry. With a little cry of relief Joss seized it up; with luck this would deter Emma from further searching for the time being.

The telephone rang and she heard Emma hurry out into the hall to answer it. Quickly Joss took up Mutt's big work-bag and riffled through it.

'We're fine,' she heard her mother say. 'Good idea . . . We'll see you in the morning then . . . Yes, I'll tell her that. God bless.'

Joss came out of the parlour, holding the book, just as Emma replaced the receiver.

'Bruno,' she said. 'Just checking we're OK. He's going to have an early night. Oh, and he said to tell you that he found those letters he was telling you about.' She raised her eyebrows at Joss's blank expression. 'Mean anything to you?'

'Yes,' said Joss quickly. 'Of course, I remember now. They were something to do with his book. Some correspondence he needed. I'm glad he's got them. And look what I found.'

She held up the address book and Emma gave an exclamation of relief.

'Good,' she said. 'I'll get our drinks and we'll check through it together.'

Joss sat down by the fire, dazed. Bruno had found the letters – but where? Before she could puzzle it out Emma arrived with the drinks and there was no chance for further thought.

CHAPTER TWENTY-SIX

'Sorry for the interruption, Mousie,' Bruno said. He sat down again in the corner of the sofa. 'It would have been cruel to leave Joss worrying. So you've read the letters . . .' He leaned forward, forearms resting along his thighs, his hands loosely clasped, needing to create an atmosphere of intimacy. 'Let's start right at the beginning. You heard us talking as you let yourself in . . .'

Mousie was sitting on the pouffe with her fingers laced round her knees, her expression guarded and watchful, but she began quite readily.

'As I opened the front door I could hear your voice. You were talking about the boatyard and The Row, and I caught Emma's name and something about her making a new will. Joss said words to the effect of, "Oh, no. That would be wrong. What about Mousie and Rafe?" At this point I guessed you hadn't heard me come in and I thought it would be less embarrassing all round if I made my presence known. I called out to you and there was one of those pregnant silences and, as I glanced through the half-open door, I saw you gather up a heap of papers and sweep them under the cushion. I was a bit surprised and I wondered if you'd actually realized that it was me – it could have been Rafe, he's got a key – and then you came out and told me about Honor . . .'

She paused, hesitating over the name, and Bruno at last recognized the emotion she was trying to conceal; an emotion he'd experienced himself earlier: Mousie was angry. Whilst he waited, watching her sympathetically, a small part of his brain registered this fact, considered it, and put it by.

'Everything happened in a bit of a rush after that.' She took up her story again. 'Getting Joss to bed – and other things – and it wasn't until after you'd gone that I made myself some coffee and went into the drawing-room. In your hurry to conceal the papers one of them had caught on the chair and was hanging down below the cushion and then I remembered that odd scene when I'd first arrived.' She hesitated. 'I assumed that you'd simply forgotten it with all the drama going on but, given that this was something you clearly wanted kept private, I felt it was sensible to gather up whatever it was and put it all safely out of sight. The trouble was that when I lifted the seat the sheets of paper were all over the place and I had to collect them almost individually. It was impossible not to catch a glimpse of some of the writing.' A pause. 'I recognized it,' she said at last, 'but what really caught my attention was the name at the bottom of the letters. Madeleine.' She looked at him directly. 'It was a name that had been on my mind this last few days. The American, Dan Crosby, had written it in his letter. Madeleine Grosjean was his great-aunt and he was trying to find her.' She shook her head sadly. 'And to think that all the time we talked, he and I, she was lying upstairs. Mutt knew it, of course, when I read the letter to her. "It's too late," she said. Imagine what she must have been feeling. Vivian's grandson looking for her and not being able to acknowledge him . . . And then there was the photograph.'

'Photograph?' Bruno frowned, trying to remember. 'Emma talked about a photograph.'

Mousie's gaze slid beyond him as if she were looking at something long past: her expression was a mixture of frustration and sadness.

'I think it started with the photograph,' she said, 'all those years ago when Hubert got married. I loved him, you see, in that romantic, intense way that little girls fall in love with older men. I was twelve or thirteen and he embodied everything I admired. I adored him. I used to dream that when he came back from the war I'd be grown-up and he would fall in love with me. And then we had the letter saying that he was married and enclosed with it was the photograph.' Her little chuckle contained no mirth. 'I know it sounds utterly foolish but it was such a shock. It was just before we came back to Cornwall. Your grandfather let us have the cottage – well, you know all that. Anyway, I was fascinated by this picture of the girl Hubert had married. I was jealous of her, in her silly little hat, and looking so pretty and happy. I studied her very closely and I hated her.'

There was a longer silence and, after a while, she looked at him again.

'I'm sorry, Bruno,' she said sadly. 'I'm talking about your mother, your real mother . . .'

'Go on,' he said gently. 'It's OK.'

'Well, the years passed.' Mousie took a deep breath, remembering. 'And then we heard that you were coming home, Honor and the children, with Hubert following on later. You can imagine how we all felt when we heard that he had died.' She bit her lips and shook her head. 'And then you arrived, the three of you. Uncle James, Mother, even Dot and old Jessie were overwhelmed with sympathy and grief. They took you all in with open arms, but I . . . all I could feel was that something was wrong. Well,' she shrugged, 'you've read the letters. I reacted exactly as she recorded it and I wonder if my intuition was based on the photograph. It was years since I'd looked at it and when I saw it again a few days ago, or the copy of it that the American boy sent, I realized what it was that had troubled me. The girl who came home with you and Emma wasn't the girl who was standing with Hubert in the photograph. It was a double wedding, you see. Honor and Hubert with Madeleine and Johnny Uttworth. I tested it out on Emma and she said at once, "Doesn't Joss look just like her grandmother?" And so she does. Take away the silly hat and Joss looks very much like Madeleine did then. But even Emma didn't pick it up at once, that the brides were with the wrong grooms. Then she said something like, "But isn't it odd?" Before she could finish we were interrupted by something, perhaps the telephone rang, I can't remember what, and the moment passed.'

'And you think that your suspicions were founded on that?'

Mousie nodded. 'Yes, I do. And they were compounded by Honor's behaviour. She guessed that I sensed something was wrong and her own guilt made her nervous. But she was right in writing that it was you who prevented me from coming near the truth. Whilst you treated her as if she were your mother it would never have occurred to me that it could be otherwise.'

'And that's what's making you angry?'

Her look was swift, surprised, and then she laughed. This time there was genuine mirth in the sound and Bruno relaxed a little.

'Yes, I was angry. I've felt so guilty all these years because I could never totally accept her. There was always something withheld between us and I put it down to the old jealousy, because I loved Hubert so much, and I couldn't quite forgive myself for it. And now I see that actually my instincts were right and I'd been duped. Nobody likes to be fooled, do they?'

'I'm sorry, Mousie . . .'

'Oh, my dear boy, it's not your fault,' she said at once. 'I can understand the position you were in and the burden you've carried all these years, Bruno. How you've managed, I can't imagine.'

'Mutt described it very well, I thought,' he answered. 'The trouble is that generally we never quite remember the way things actually were at the time. We all crucify ourselves by imagining that we could have done just that bit more; we could have been kinder, stronger, more forgiving, more generous, because we've forgotten that, at that particular moment, we simply had nothing left to give. There have been times when I wondered why I went along with it but, luckily for me, I *can* remember what it was like in India then: the twenty-four-hour curfew in Multan, the atmosphere of violence and the overwhelming sense of terror. I desperately wanted to come home. Father was always talking about St Meriadoc and Paradise and the peace and beauty of the valley. To me he was so strong and comforting, so . . . *indestructible*, and when he died it was my most terrifying nightmare come true. I can still feel the stifling heat and the fear and then Mother falling ill. When Mutt walked into that hotel room with Emma in her arms she was like an angel straight from heaven. I often wonder what would have happened to me if she hadn't turned up. She and Emma got me through the terrible misery of losing all my own family.'

'I am so sorry,' Mousie said gently in her turn. 'I was very fond of her, you know, and she was very good to me. And to Rafe.'

'She used to try to convince herself that nothing was different, no-one was suffering, because she was here. She offered me Paradise when I got married but I never wanted it and you and Rafe seemed perfectly content. At the end she wanted Joss to have Paradise.'

'So what will happen now?'

Bruno shrugged. 'It's more difficult,' he admitted, 'now that Joss knows. It will be hard for her to accept anything from the estate but Emma would soon smell a rat if Joss holds out.'

Mousie looked puzzled. 'But surely you don't intend to continue to keep this a secret?'

Bruno stared at her. 'Emma would be shattered if she knew,' he said. 'Joss thinks she'd never get over it. You know how she loves it here and how proud she is of her family.'

'She can still be proud of her family,' answered Mousie sharply. 'She only has to read the letters to see that her mother was brave and warm-hearted and strong. And Joss is just like her. What more could a woman want?'

'But she'd feel she doesn't belong here, that the whole thing's been a charade.'

'I think you underestimate her,' said Mousie strongly. 'Great grief, Bruno! Once she gets over the shock Emma won't question her belonging here. She'll accept that she is a part of us all; how could it be otherwise after what has happened over the last fifty years? You can't possibly go on now as if nothing has changed. The edifice that was built up to hide this deception has been pulled down. It would be madness to attempt to rebuild it. Worse than madness: it would be dangerous. You don't know Joss very well if you think she could live a lie and remain as whole and happy as you have been. Up until now nobody but you has suffered from the deception and you have counted it worth the pain. Joss will never be able to be natural with any of us from this time forward.'

'But it's Joss who is insisting on it,' he told her almost angrily.

Mousie shook her head. 'Madness,' she repeated.

'But what am I to do?' he asked wretchedly. 'Joss is adamant that Emma shouldn't know, and as for the will . . .'

He paused and Mousie looked at him shrewdly.

'Do you know how your grandfather left the estate?' she asked.

Bruno shrugged wearily, indifferently, and then reconsidered.

'He would have left it all to Mutt, I suppose,' he said.

Mousie shook her head.

'Wrong,' she said. 'Uncle James would have left it to Hubert's wife. She wrote as much in the letters, remember? To Hubert, then to Honor and to her children. That's you, Bruno. Do you really intend to pay Inheritance Tax all over again?'

'What do you mean?' he asked blankly.

'The estate should have come to you fifty years ago, not to Honor. The tax was paid then, you shouldn't have to pay all over again. Think about it.'

'I can't think about it,' he said at last. 'I got no sleep last night and my brain won't work.'

Her assessing look was totally professional.

'You need to sleep,' she agreed. 'But you should find the will and that book with the death certificates hidden in it, Bruno. Raymond arrives tomorrow and then your problems will really begin.'

CHAPTER TWENTY-SEVEN

George walked up to Paradise as soon as he'd finished breakfast. A light south-westerly breeze was lifting and shredding the mist so that the sun gleamed fitfully between trailing skeins of candy-floss cloud, warming the black bare twigs of the thorn hedge to a ruddier hue and touching with a brighter gold the yellow daffodils blowing in the wet ditch below. He could hear a soft, piping note somewhere near at hand and presently saw a flash of coral and white as the bullfinch flew up into a holly tree.

He paused at the field gate. The donkeys were across the other side of the meadow, grazing quietly, and he stood for a moment watching them, deeply and gratefully aware of this new sensation of freedom but fighting a sense of guilt at having been presented with it so easily. Soon he would see Joss, able at last to tell her his true feelings, and – as nervousness and excitement twisted in his gut – he stretched suddenly, arms wide, as if this movement might expel the tension inside him.

Leaving the donkeys, he went on up the lane to Paradise, passing between the granite pillars on to the drive. Small clumps of snowdrops, heads drooped, glimmered moony-pale amongst the rhododendrons, and a tide of purple crocus flooded the small lawn with their darkly vivid colour. A blackbird flew out from the sturdy branches of the wisteria, piercing the silence with his stuttering, warning call, alighting for a moment on the top of the high stone wall before dropping out of sight.

Feeling that under the circumstances a certain formality was in order, George avoided his usual entry through the garden room and knocked instead at the front door. Emma answered it, opening it wide when she saw who it was, beaming at him affectionately.

'How nice to see you, George,' she said. 'How are you?'

He kissed her lightly. 'I'm so sorry about Mutt,' he said. 'I came to see if there was anything that I could do.'

'That's very sweet of you.' A sudden flash of speculation quenched the sadness in her eyes and he instinctively braced himself so as to deal with her curiosity. 'Is Penny with you?' she asked brightly. 'How is she? And Tasha?'

Joss had come out of the kitchen and was standing by the door in the shadows at the back of the hall, watching him. George met her eyes above Emma's head and was shocked by the expression of anxiety on her face. Just for a moment they exchanged a long look, each probing and guessing at the other's thoughts and emotions. With an effort, George turned his attention to Emma.

'They aren't with me,' he answered shortly. The unexpected brevity of his reply resulted in a surprised silence and he raised his hands, as if making a reluctant decision. 'You might as well know that Penny has taken Tasha back to New Zealand. She's decided that they will be happier there.'

Joss had already turned aside, probably to hide her expression of relief, but Emma's eyes were round with shock.

'But, George,' she gasped. 'Gone back to New Zealand? My goodness, I can't believe it.'

'I'm sorry,' he said. 'Coming on top of Mutt it's a bit much, isn't it? The trouble is, there's no other way to break this kind of news.'

He glanced rather helplessly towards Joss, who came forward to put an arm about her mother. She smiled at him and he saw more clearly the pallor of her face and the faint wariness of her expression. He guessed that she didn't want her mother to know that his news was not too much of a shock to her and smiled back at her with a tiny nod of complicity.

'Come into the kitchen,' Joss said. 'We've only just finished breakfast – somehow we simply couldn't get started this morning – but there's some coffee in the pot.'

'It's Joss's day off,' said Emma, allowing herself to be led back into the kitchen, 'and I was trying to persuade her to have the morning in bed. Oh dear, what a time we're all having.'

'I couldn't rest somehow,' said Joss quickly. 'You know how it is? I'm too tensed up, I suppose, and I didn't sleep very well.'

'Perhaps a walk would do you good,' George suggested, anxious to get her to himself, longing to explain the happenings of the last twenty-four hours. 'We could take the donkeys. You know how they love a stroll.'

For one brief moment Joss's face lighted with pleasure; from a child one of her greatest pleasures was taking the donkeys for a walk round the lanes and up the valley. It wasn't so much of a walk but more a very slow amble, holding the end of their leading reins and waiting beside them patiently as they munched the wayside grass. As he watched her he saw the light die from her eyes and it occurred to him that she was taking her grandmother's death very badly. He felt ashamed that he'd put his own needs before her grief but before he could make amends she smiled at him.

'Perhaps later on,' she told him. 'That would be good.'

Emma, distracted but still curious, raised her eyebrows.

'Why not now?' she asked. 'It's so much brighter this morning and it would do you so much good. You don't have to worry about me, you know. I've got plenty to do, clearing out and tidying up. And your father will be arriving later.'

George took his coffee, noticing that Joss's hand trembled slightly. He looked at her, trying to catch her eye so as to exchange one of those private signals they'd shared since childhood, but she evaded him. It was as if the current of affection that flowed so naturally between them had been suddenly switched off and he felt a real sense of loneliness. It was clear that Mutt's death had deeply distressed her, and his own news coming on top of it had now completely knocked her off balance. He realized just how important her reaction had been to him; that, ever since he'd left the cottage at Meavy, he'd been needing to share the news with her, to talk it through so that it could assume its proper proportions. He was passing through a period of transition and he'd hoped that Joss would make the journey with him.

He saw, however, that it couldn't be quite as he'd imagined it and he quickly assessed this new situation.

'Later will be fine,' he agreed, as if Emma hadn't spoken. 'Meanwhile, there must be something I could do. How are you off for logs?'

Joss looked at him gratefully. 'There are plenty in the woodshed,' she said, 'but we've used up all the smaller ones. Rafe usually deals with it but if you could manage to split some of the big ones . . . ?'

'Not a problem.' Maybe she would find the opportunity to come and talk to him while he was working. 'I'll finish my coffee and then get to it.'

'I still can't get used to the fact that we won't hear her bell ring.' Emma's eyes filled with tears. 'It just seems so impossible . . .'

Before either of them could comfort her they heard the

sound of an engine, a car door slammed and the front door was tried by someone who clearly expected it to be unlocked. The knocking that followed was loud and impatient. Emma got up and hurried into the hall.

'Ray!' they heard her exclaim. 'My God, what time did you leave? I wasn't expecting you for another hour at least.'

George and Joss stood together in silence, listening.

'I didn't see much point in hanging around.' His voice, booming round the hall and echoing up the stairs, was as insensitive to grief and death as his knocking had been and George felt Joss wince. 'This damned fog held me up but it began to clear as I got nearer to the coast.'

'I'll crack on with the logs.' George spoke quietly. He caught Joss by the shoulders and held them for a moment as if to reassure her. 'You know where I am if you need me.'

He bent to kiss her cheek, reached for his jacket and slipped out through the garden door just as Emma and Raymond arrived in the kitchen.

Once he'd gone, Joss took hold of the back of one of the chairs as if for support. She hadn't been prepared for the difficulty of seeing George again, knowing as she did now that she wasn't the person she'd believed herself to be. It was as if, until this point, she and George had been all of a piece; not only because of similarities of mind and taste, and their love for this small valley hidden away on the north Cornish coast, but through blood and bone and family ties. Now, the truth divided them. Sympathetic though she felt towards her grandmother, still deeply moved by the thought of her letters, Joss was conscious that neither Mutt nor her descendants had any right here at Paradise and, the moment she'd seen George, she'd been struck by the utter impossibility of pre-tending otherwise. Even the news that Penny had gone didn't have the power to affect her as it would have done forty-eight hours earlier. Only her mother's grief and distress was preventing her from getting into her car and driving as far away from St Meriadoc as she could.

Yet she'd been so certain that the truth must not be told. Perhaps, after all, it *was* different for Bruno. Whatever the deception, he was at least a Trevannion and had every right to live here in the valley, in The Lookout: he belonged. As her parents came into the kitchen Joss braced herself anew to deal with the weight of her knowledge; with this requirement to look at every aspect of her life from a completely different point of view. She was hardly aware of her father's brief kiss, seeing only his familiar, assessing glance around as he sat down at the table.

All this will soon be mine, his look seemed to say. There was a faint but unmistakable air of anticipation in his expression that made Joss shudder a little. His acquisitiveness had always repelled her; now, with her new knowledge, it appalled her.

'When's the funeral?' he was asking. 'You said the undertakers had been, dear?'

Joss stared at him. She'd always hated the way he called them both 'dear'; there was a lack of intimacy about the word, as if he used it because he felt an endearment was appropriate to his wife and daughter without it really mattering what it was: she'd had bus conductors call her 'love' with more real affection.

'I'll make some fresh coffee.' Emma hurried to the percolator.

Joss could see that her mother was slightly ruffled by his arrival, no longer at ease. Already she was less the Emma of Paradise, Mutt's child, and more the compliant woman who was Raymond's wife; even her attitude to Joss was undergoing a change. Joss recognized it at once. Emma was on edge, prepared for a falling-out between her husband and daughter, and instinctively adopting a cheerfulness that might, with luck, placate the two of them.

Joss was seized with remorse. She wondered just how much

of her life her mother had spent being a kind of buffer and how different she was with Bruno and Mousie and those with whom she felt at peace. Joss bit her lips. Impossible, in that case, she told herself, to remove the comfort Emma received from these relationships.

'The rector thought Monday but he's going to telephone this morning.' Emma paused in her coffee-making and shook her head. 'I simply can't take it in,' she added miserably.

Raymond stretched out his large square hand and patted briefly the piece of Emma he could reach.

'She's had a good run for her money, dear,' he said, not unkindly. 'At least she hasn't suffered.'

'She suffered quite a bit in the last few weeks, actually,' Joss said. 'The break was quite a bad one.'

Her father smiled. 'I'm sure you were a great help,' he said, as if she were ten. 'All that expensive training must have come in very useful.'

'She was wonderful.' Emma was defensive. 'Mousie said so.'

'Ah.' His eyes became watchful. 'And how is Mousie?'

Emma looked so uncomfortable that Joss was puzzled.

'She's fine,' her mother answered briefly. 'So how long did the drive take you?'

The question was so clearly meant as a diversion that Raymond didn't bother to answer it: his fingers tapped out a rhythm and his eyes were speculative.

'Did you manage to get a look at the will?' he asked, following out his own train of thought.

'No.' Emma glanced uneasily at Joss. 'No, of course not. Won't it be with Mutt's lawyer?'

She managed to sound quite indifferent and Raymond frowned.

'It might be anywhere,' he answered irritably, 'but I'd like to see it all the same.'

'Why?' Joss couldn't contain herself. 'Do you think Mutt might have left you something?'

He looked at her consideringly, as if reminding himself that she was grieving for her grandmother, recognizing – but indifferent to – her contempt. Emma stood between them anxiously but neither of them looked at her.

'I have to look after your mother's interests,' he answered almost genially. 'Surely you must see that?'

Various retorts jostled at Joss's lips but now none of them was relevant. She let go of the chair-back and smiled at her mother.

'No more coffee for me,' she said. 'See you later,' and, taking up her plaid shawl, she let herself out quietly, closing the door behind her.

CHAPTER TWENTY-EIGHT

For a moment the only sound was the dull thud of George's axe. Emma pulled out a chair and sat down at the table. She began to pour coffee, her lips compressed, her eyes anxious.

'So you haven't seen the will?'

It was as if the exchange with Joss hadn't taken place and Emma stirred irritably.

'I've already told you I haven't. Why should I? Honestly, Ray, you're so . . . so tactless.'

He shrugged the criticism away, his face indicating that he was concentrating on the possible problems ahead.

'It's important to be prepared,' he told her, as if this were an excuse for his tactlessness. 'Surely you can see that? Anything might have happened in those last few weeks.'

Emma stared at him. 'What kind of thing?'

She was clearly hostile and knowing that he would need her assistance he made an effort to gain her understanding.

'Have you thought where the Inheritance Tax will come from this time?' he asked. His voice was softer now, almost meditative. 'When your grandfather died there were farms and land to sell but now there's nothing except Paradise itself. Or The Lookout and The Row. It'll be a tidy bit to pay.'

He saw that he had her attention; her face was shocked.

'But what are you saying?' she cried. 'How could we sell Paradise? Or any of it?'

He laid a thick white finger to his lips, knowing only too well how likely it was that a member of the family might walk in on them.

'It'll have to come from somewhere,' he murmured. 'We're probably talking at least a hundred thousand.'

'A hundred thousand *pounds*?'

He raised his eyebrows at her amazement. 'Why do you think I've been suggesting for years that Mutt should hand some of the estate over? If she'd given Bruno The Lookout and passed Paradise to you we'd have saved a fortune.'

'But Bruno's never said a word about tax.'

Raymond snorted with contempt. 'Bruno wouldn't have a clue,' he said. 'Stuck in some other world with his damned books. Well,' he shrugged, 'let's hope he's making enough money to get himself out of trouble.'

'But surely we won't have to sell Paradise?' She gazed at him fearfully. 'You know I've always wanted it for Joss.'

Raymond drew down the corners of his mouth. 'Well, it might have to go. It depends how the will is set out.' He wondered if she were frightened enough for him to play his development card and decided to scare her a little more. 'The whole estate might have to come under the hammer and then, when it's all sold up, you and Bruno would share out the remaining money.'

'But that would be dreadful.' Her eyes were huge with shock. 'I can't believe that could happen.'

'Oh, my dear,' his laugh was indulgent, 'you clearly haven't had any dealings with the Inland Revenue. They won't give a damn how they get their money, I promise you. Of course,' he pursed his lips thoughtfully, picking up his coffee cup, 'there might be another way, if only I could get a look at the damned will.'

She watched his leisurely gulps of coffee with fascinated revulsion, swallowing in unison with him, disliking his single-mindedness at such a time yet believing that if anyone could find an answer to a financial problem it would be Raymond Fox.

'How would it help?' she asked tremulously – and he saw that she was now on his side. 'Just looking at it can't alter the facts, can it?'

'It can't alter the facts,' he agreed, 'but we can be prepared. For instance, you know I've always seen that old boatyard as ready for development.'

'Oh, no.' She shied away from the idea. 'Bruno says you'd have to knock down The Row to make that work.'

'Not necessarily.' Raymond dismissed Bruno's fears with amused disdain. 'He has simply no idea about anything outside the pages of fiction. Nonsense.' He chuckled again, as if in amusement at Bruno's naïvety. 'Of course I can see his point. It would certainly spoil his view, although the architecture would be very carefully monitored, but at least he'd be able to stay in The Lookout. However, if that goes against the grain, we'd certainly get a good price for this place. It would make a first-class hotel . . .'

For a moment he was distracted by the idea of Paradise as a top-class retreat for the wealthy: saunas and a swimming-pool; a golf links right there beside the sea; a celebrity chef. He could hear people talking: 'You need a few days in Paradise, darling. It's utter heaven. Of course you have to book months in advance. . .' 'It's tiny but simply wonderful and very exclusive. Paul and I are going again this spring. The food is delicious . . .' Perhaps he could buy it himself from the estate – at a special rate, of course – and put in a manager . . .

'I don't know how you can even bear to think about it.'

Emma was staring at him with such disgust that he feared that he might have lost her reluctant co-operation.

'I'm only showing you the facts.' He tried to sound as if he were doing her some kind of favour. 'The next few days are going to be bad enough for you as it is, poor old girl, without the shock of this coming on top of the funeral. I just want to spare you as much as I can, can't you see that?'

She nodded unwillingly. 'I suppose so. It's just—'

'Look.' He leaned forward, almost conspiratorially, smiling at her. 'Why don't we see if we can find the will? You're entitled, as her only daughter, to read it, especially if it's been left here in the house. It's got to be located anyway. If it isn't here then you'll need to have a word with her lawyer about it but it has to be found.' His smile was kindly. 'These things are always difficult, dear, but it's got to be dealt with sooner or later. Better that you and I know the worst so that we can be prepared.'

She nodded again, albeit reluctantly, and he sat back in his chair with a silent gasp of relief.

'I suppose you've no idea where Mutt might have kept it?' He tried to keep his voice casual, though he was willing her to get on with it – God knows who might come wandering in – but he didn't want to undo the good work. 'In that old desk in her parlour is as good a place to start, I suppose.'

'I suppose,' she agreed wearily. 'I'll go and have a look.'

She got up and went out and he heard the parlour door close behind her. He stretched with relief and poured himself some more coffee, resigning himself to patience.

Joss could hear the thud of the axe as she slipped down the drive. Her one thought was to see Bruno; he was the only person with whom she could now feel entirely at ease. She told herself that she needed time to adjust and that a moment or two with Bruno would give her a breathing space. Also, she wanted to know where he'd found the letters. Last night, after

Emma had gone to bed, she'd continued her search for *Goblin Market* in the parlour but she'd been unable to bring herself to go into Mutt's empty bedroom. It seemed in some way unthinkable to go rooting about her grandmother's personal possessions so soon after her death but now she wondered if she should have ignored her finer instincts. Her father, she was certain, would not be so nice; he or her mother might now start to look for the will and come across *Goblin Market* quite by mistake.

Joss found that she was almost running, trying to keep pace with her fears. She slowed down, lest Mousie or Rafe might see her in such a hurry and imagine that something was wrong, and, walking more slowly now, turned up the steep path to The Lookout. She wondered briefly what George was thinking, whether he'd finished the logs and was puzzled by her disappearance, and gave a small groan of despair. He must have been surprised that she'd taken his news so coolly, merely offering him coffee and sending him out to split logs, when it had been the most important moment of their lives.

She saw that her knowledge would lie between them like a sword, cutting them off from each other, and more especially so if there should prove to be unfair provisions in the will. It would be intolerable now if she or her family were to benefit at Rafe's or Mousie's expense, and the arrival of her father had shown her even more clearly the difficulties that might lie ahead: his presence, determined and resilient as rubber, crystallized her fears into reality.

The sight of Bruno, standing in the great bow of the window and staring out to sea, filled her with an overwhelming relief. She waved to attract his attention and he raised a hand, turning back into the room as he came to meet her.

CHAPTER TWENTY-NINE

Bruno had been expecting her. Ever since his telephone call to say that the letters were found he'd known that she must have been on tenterhooks but – more than that – he'd guessed that she'd be finding the deception much more difficult than even she had first imagined. He'd had all night to think about Mousie's words: *Joss will never be able to be natural with any of us from this time forward* – and he wondered how she would react when he told her that Mousie knew the truth. Perhaps she had already guessed: once he'd had a moment to think about it he'd realized it could be the only solution although, for Joss's sake, he'd invented the theory about Mutt's cleaner finding them, not wanting to panic her until he knew the truth.

'I haven't found *Goblin Market*,' she told him as soon as she entered the kitchen. 'At least, it's not in the bookcase in the parlour or on the shelves on the landing. I couldn't bring myself to go into Mutt's room. And I was afraid I might wake Mum . . .'

She followed him into the sitting-room and sat down at the end of the table, wrapping her plaid more closely round her for comfort rather than warmth.

'I have a feeling that it'll be somewhere a little less obvious,' he said calmly. 'In the desk, perhaps, where the letters were?'

'I looked there,' she told him. 'Very quickly because Mum kept coming in and out and then, when you telephoned, I was able to have a better chance. And now Dad's arrived.' She paused. 'Where *were* the letters?' she asked. 'I couldn't believe it.'

He saw that she was in such a state of weariness and shock that her usual faculties had deserted her.

'Mousie found them,' he told her gently. 'It had to be her, didn't it, when you really think about it? Who else could have done it? She heard us talking about it when she came in and saw me bundle the stuff under the seat. Later on she remembered the scene and was afraid that the wrong person might discover whatever it was we were hiding.' He looked compassionately at Joss's scared face. 'When she took them out they scattered all over the place and, without meaning to, she saw enough to puzzle her.'

'Oh my God.' Joss pressed her fingers to her mouth.

Bruno nodded. 'Mousie was already . . . well, curious. You read in the letters that Mutt feared that Mousie knew something. The long and short of it is that she read the letters and now she knows the truth. And it doesn't matter a damn to her,' he added quickly. 'Why should it? Oh, she feels irritated that she's been taken in all for these years but, having read the letters, she understands Mutt's dilemma and, as far as you and Emma are concerned, nothing's changed at all.'

'But *everything*'s changed,' she cried almost angrily. 'It's crazy to say that.'

'Look.' He sat down at right angles to her. 'Remember that nobody has lost out financially because of what Mutt did. On the contrary, she looked after Mousie and Rafe and kept the estate going when my grandfather died. As for me, Emma has been as close as any sister could have been, and a very good friend. Mutt probably saved my life out in India, she got me home, and between her and Emma they made up for the tragic loss I'd had. Think how lonely I would have been without them. They represented continuity and security. And you, Joss, have been as dear to me as any daughter I might have had. If it had been I who had been Mutt's son would you feel differently about me now? Would you love me less or look upon me as a usurper? Do try not to see it purely in terms of blood and family ties.'

'I can't help it,' she said miserably. 'When Dad turned up this morning and started talking about the will before he'd been there two minutes I saw how different he is from all of you. I felt we were intruders, the three of us, sitting in the kitchen at Paradise as if it were already ours. And I thought about Mousie and Rafe . . . They're such kindly people, teaching and nursing, making a difference in the community; a completely opposite approach to my father's preoccupation with making money—'

'Hang on a minute,' he interrupted. 'Apart from the fact that the country needs people who generate wealth, let's just think about this. To begin with Mousie and Rafe aren't Trevannions. They descend from my grandmother's side of the family. OK. That might make us relations but it doesn't mean that because of some odd genetic quirk we're all saints. What about Olivia and Joe? From what I gather, their views on making money are rather the same as Brer Fox's, yet they're Rafe's children. You can't just lump whole families together under the headings of good and bad. Your contribution and Emma's – and certainly Mutt's – to the Trevannion family has been just as positive as Mousie's and Rafe's. Who would have looked after me and the estate after Grandfather died if Mutt had simply dumped me here and disappeared? Probably some very distant Trevannion relative who'd never have let the cottages at such low rents or worried about us all staying together. Mutt kept us a family and looked after everybody the best way she could. And don't forget that Olivia and Joe would be just as ready as Brer Fox to build a holiday complex down there in the cove if they thought it would make them some money; even if it meant dispossessing their own parents.'

'Dad's already thinking of it,' she said sombrely. 'I know he is. He was saying that he wanted to have a look at the will.'

She sounded calmer, however, and Bruno watched her thoughtfully, trying to assess her state of mind, gathering up his courage.

'Mousie thinks that Emma should know the truth,' he said.

She looked at him in distress, mutely shaking her head, but he sensed that she was too confused by this latest development to be quite so certain about it.

'Her view is that the burden will be too heavy for you,' he said, 'and I think she's right. She says that it's not fair to you and that we are underestimating Emma. Mousie believes that if we were to show her the letters she'd understand, just as we have, and be able to come to terms with it all.'

'I don't agree. I think she'll be gutted.'

Yet her voice was less confident and it was clear that she'd begun to doubt her own judgement. As she weighed up all the complications he watched the inward struggle reflected on her face and decided on a different approach.

'Seen George?' he asked, almost as if he were changing the subject.

'Oh.' It was a cry almost of pain. 'He came up to Paradise and told us that Penny and Tasha have gone back to New Zealand, and I simply couldn't think of anything to say to him. Not just because Mum was there but because it was all different between us. It was impossible to respond to him in the old way. In the end Mum gave him some coffee and then he went out to split logs.'

'"All different between us",' repeated Bruno thoughtfully. He raised his eyebrows. 'Yet you still don't think that the truth should be told?'

She stared at him almost fearfully. 'I don't know,' she said at last, 'but, anyway, not until after the funeral. It would be so awful for Mum, dealing with Mutt's not being here any more as well as the truth about who she is. Promise me that we'll wait until then at least.'

'OK.' Bruno sighed, frustrated. 'But it's going to become very awkward if Emma finds the will and Brer Fox starts laying down the law. We must get hold of it first. Of course it might be with Mutt's lawyer . . .'

The telephone rang and he got up impatiently to answer it.

'Hello, darling.' The gravelly voice, matured by years of Sobranies and Scotch was unmistakable. 'It's me. Zoë. You'll never guess where I am.'

Bruno instinctively put his hand across the mouthpiece, thinking furiously. When he spoke to her, his voice was curt.

'Wait a minute, will you? I've got someone with me. Hang on.'

He placed the receiver beside the telephone and went back to the sitting-room.

'It's Zoë,' he told Joss. 'Bloody awful timing but par for the course.'

'I've got to go back, anyway.' She got up at once. 'They'll all be wondering where I've gone and I have to see George.'

She looked so intimidated by the prospect that he gave her a brief hug.

'Courage,' he said – and she smiled at him.

'Thanks, Bruno,' she said. 'I wish you really were my uncle.'

'Look, love,' he said, 'it doesn't matter what the hell the labels are. Nothing has changed here.'

She nodded, pulling her plaid about her, and he went with her to the door.

'Shall I tell them you'll be up later?' she asked.

He hesitated. 'I'm not certain when,' he warned, 'but don't worry. I'll be there sometime this afternoon.'

She nodded again, and went away, and he returned to the kitchen.

'Do I hear a woman's voice?' Zoë sounded amused.

'Joss,' he answered briefly. 'So where are you?'

'I'm at Rock, darling.' She sounded almost as surprised as he was. 'Can you believe it? And at this time of the year too. I told you that Jilly and Tim bought a cottage here, remember? Apparently there were rumours of burst pipes during the cold spell so she's driven down to check it out, although it's quite warm here now. Anyway, London was dreary so I thought I'd go along for the ride. How about I come over for lunch?'

Bruno closed his eyes in despair. His two worlds, the real and the imagined, had not only collided they'd crashed together with such force that they were now flying apart and disintegrating around him.

'The timing isn't good,' he said with difficulty. 'Mutt died in the early hours of Tuesday morning and . . . well, you can imagine the rest.'

'Oh, darling, I'm sorry.' She sounded it too. 'Fancy old Mutt gone! I had a lot of time for her, actually.' A tiny pause. 'When is the funeral?'

'I don't know yet.' He felt edgy, suspicious. 'Probably early next week. Emma's down and Brer Fox has just arrived. There's an awful lot to sort out.'

'I'm not sure how long Jilly's staying,' her voice was thoughtful, 'but I'd really like to see you, darling. Especially now. Look, I can be with you in half an hour and I won't keep you long.' A pause – then her voice altered. 'Are you writing?'

He laughed mirthlessly. 'Are you kidding?'

She chuckled. 'Poor darling. Has reality kicked in? Never mind. We'll have a drink together, don't bother about the food. See you.'

The line went dead and he cursed long and hard. Nellie, roused from slumber, stared up at him intelligently and waved her tail gently.

'Don't *you* start,' he told her warningly. 'No walks and no lunch either, if you're not careful.'

She came to him with her tongue lolling out, as if she laughed at him, and reluctantly he began to laugh too.

'Everything's gone crazy,' he said, crouching down to stroke her, whilst she put a paw on his knee and licked his ear. 'Today has been cancelled through lack of support. Bloody women!'

She was unmoved by his expletive; continuing to butt her head gently against his shoulder until presently he relaxed and gave a great sigh.

'OK,' he said, standing up. 'Your lunch first and Zoë's afterwards. It'll have to be soup for her, not that she'll eat more than a teaspoonful. And what the hell does she want, anyway?'

But Nellie was only interested in her own pressing need for food and, once he'd filled her bowl and put it down for her, Bruno went to the larder to find a bottle of wine that might suit the taste of his ex-wife.

CHAPTER THIRTY

George wheeled the barrowful of logs round the side of the house and parked it beside Raymond's BMW. He stood for a moment, admiring this latest model, and then tried the front door; the latch was still down. Leaving the barrow, he went back to the garden and came into the kitchen just as Emma appeared at the other door leading from the hall.

'I can't find it in the parlour,' she was saying. 'Only this parcel with Bruno's name on it. Oh, hello, George. How are you getting on? George has been splitting logs for us,' she said to Raymond. 'Isn't that kind of him? Are you ready for some more coffee after all that hard work?'

She dropped the parcel on the table and went to wash up the mugs but George could see at once that Raymond was far more interested in the parcel than in the log-splitting, although he seemed hardly to glance at it. He murmured a greeting, smiled a brief acknowledgement of George's labours, but all his concentration seemed directed towards the package. It was clear too that Emma was feeling slightly uncomfortable, as if George's appearance was inconveniently timed. He wondered if he should make polite noises and disappear but something about Raymond's fixed expression puzzled him. With a slight shifting of his elbow, which rested on the table, he'd moved the parcel closer, edging it right way up so that he could see the writing on it: it was Mutt's writing. Even from where he was standing George could recognize it, although one of the words was in large capitals.

'For Bruno James Trevannion. Personal and Private.' And across the bottom was printed one word: 'CONFIDENTIAL'.

The unusual thing about it in George's view was that it was wrapped like an old-fashioned package ready for the post. The brown paper was folded carefully round the object inside and then tied firmly with string. Very slowly Raymond turned the parcel over, his thick forefinger idly probing the knots, although he still wore an almost indifferent expression on his broad, handsome face as if he were brooding on something else entirely and the parcel was simply an object to fiddle with whilst he concentrated on this other problem – as one might tap with a pencil or doodle on a pad.

Beside him, George felt Emma stiffen: waiting and watching, holding her breath. He realized with a little shock that she was actually prepared for Raymond to open the parcel and was bracing herself to prevent him from touching it. Instinctively, George went to fill the kettle. He smiled at Emma, glanced at Raymond, as if unaware of anything unusual.

'I think I need a shot of caffeine after all that effort,' he said – and thought he saw the faintest flicker of irritation pass across Raymond's face. 'Is Joss anywhere about? She might like some.'

'I don't know where she is.' Emma had relaxed a little but was still distracted. 'I'll give a shout up the stairs.'

'She went out.' Raymond was very certain. 'I heard the front door close, oh, half an hour ago, I should think. Perhaps she's with the donkeys.' He gave George a friendly glance. 'Emma can make the coffee if you want to go and find her.'

He was very easy, very relaxed, and George smiled back at him.

'She might be anywhere,' he answered, just as casually. 'I expect she'll be in soon.'

Raymond nodded and shrugged – an up-to-you-chum gesture – and sat back a little in his chair, stretching his shoulders.

George thought: I wouldn't want to play poker with you, mate.

He made the coffee, feeling Emma hovering beside him uncertainly, wondering if he were imagining the tension and that his suspicion was simply based on all the stories Joss had told him about her father's business acuity. After all, why on earth should Raymond want to open a parcel addressed so clearly to Bruno? It suddenly occurred to George that it was possible that neither Bruno nor Emma knew what was in Mutt's will and that Raymond, guessing that this was what the package contained, wanted to be ahead of the game. He felt a quickening of curiosity. It was more with a sense of mischievousness rather than any self-righteous intention that he sat down at the table and openly turned the parcel as if to read the writing for the first time, pulling it across the table.

'For Bruno, I see,' he said conversationally. 'Did Mutt leave it for you to give to him?'

Emma didn't see Raymond's swift upward look of warning.

'It was in her desk,' she said, puzzled. 'Odd really. It was actually right at the bottom of a folder containing Bruno's school reports.'

'Really?' George was beginning to enjoy himself. 'Why were you reading his school reports? Bit late in the day, isn't it?' He chuckled at his own feeble joke. 'I'll take it down to him, if you like.'

Raymond's large square hand reached for the parcel slowly, as if George had drawn it to his attention and he too were now reading the writing for the first time. As he turned it, he moved it almost unobtrusively back to his own side of the table.

'No need to bother,' he said. 'I expect he'll be here soon.'

'Oh, it's not a bother,' answered George cheerfully, preparing for a little light-hearted contest with Joss's father with a certain amount of pleasure. 'I shall be going right past his door.'

'You haven't had your coffee yet.' Raymond's hands, now clasped together and resting on the parcel, looked chunky. He leaned forward so that his weight rested on his arms, his broad shoulders hunched. 'There's no hurry, after all.'

George met his cold, blue-grey stare, sensed the weight and force of his personality, and was aware of an odd stirring of unease; the idea of a contest seemed suddenly foolish and he felt uncomfortable. He was glad to hear the kettle boil, to have an excuse to get up from the table to make the coffee, although Emma was already putting out the mugs and the milk.

'Have you brought any logs in?' she was asking him, obviously trying for a change of subject.

'Not yet.' He was feeling oddly humiliated, rather as he'd been as a small boy when Olivia and Joe outwitted him. He was convinced now that Raymond shouldn't have the opportunity to examine the contents of the parcel, yet he was powerless to prevent him. He saw exactly what Joss meant when she'd talked about her father's juggernaut tactics.

'He just goes straight on,' she'd said. 'Any moral issues, ordinary humanity or common decency are all thrust aside or gradually crushed beneath the wheels of his determination. He fixes his eyes on his goal and never wavers for a second. If you get in his path you simply go under with everything else. It's as if he feels that he has some divine right to take what he wants. It's scary. I used to get cross with Mum for giving in to him but as I grew up I realized that withstanding him is almost impossible. It's like trying to stand up to the Severn Bore or a hurricane.'

George was familiar with this feeling of helplessness; it reminded him of his childhood. Olivia and Joe had been bigger, stronger, more cunning: they had walked, talked, read their first words, ridden bicycles, whilst he was still in nappies. Nothing he learned to do could earn their admiration: they'd been there first. They'd sat on him, laughed at him – and were casually affectionate to him – but, for most of the time, their own fierce battles for supremacy excluded him and he'd been happy to grow up quietly outside the noisy, clashing circle of their endeavour.

Now, as he sat down again at the table and poured the coffee, he wondered what he would do when he'd be obliged to get up and go out to deal with the logs. He was certain that, on his return, the package would have disappeared and he would be in no position to question either Emma or Raymond about it. As he drank his coffee – very slowly – he prayed that Joss would return before that moment came. He would draw her attention to it, suggest that they walk down together to deliver it, so thwarting any plans Raymond might be making.

His gasp of relief was almost audible when the front door opened. Light footsteps hurried up the stairs and George watched Raymond's face grow thoughtful, listening, his eyes on the parcel.

'There's Joss.' Emma's voice was brighter, as if she too were relieved, and she sat more easily in her chair. 'I wonder where she's been.'

George kept his eyes on Raymond, expecting some sleight of hand when Joss appeared: he was convinced that in the moment of her arrival, whilst attention was fixed on her entrance, the package would somehow be spirited away. The door opened and Joss and Mousie came in together. Raymond rose swiftly to his feet and in one quick, smooth movement conveyed the parcel to the dresser behind his chair, pushing it beneath a newspaper so that it was half hidden, even as he was saying 'Mousie, my dear, how nice to see you,' and giving her a kiss. It was so adroit, so clever, that George was almost breathless with admiration.

He looked at Joss, longing to share this new discovery with her as he had shared so much in the past. She was flushed, her eyes bright with some kind of recent excitement, and he was filled with love and longing for her. She smiled at him across the kitchen yet he could still feel the barrier between them. With a tiny jolt of fear he wondered if he'd mistaken this new reticence in her: that it was nothing to do with Mutt's death but, rather, fear that he might demand too much of her now that he was free. After all, they'd never spoken openly of their feelings – he'd been too committed to his marriage for that to be possible – and nothing had been said that might now be acted upon. Perhaps Joss was not ready to see Penny's defection in the light of an opportunity for her own happiness – and his. It went against all his instincts to believe that this was true, yet there was a new kind of wariness that had never been present between them before.

With this sudden loss of confidence and his preoccupation about Joss, he forgot the little scene with the parcel. Mousie was explaining that she'd left a book in the drawing-room and had come up to collect it, meeting Joss on the way, and Emma was insisting that she should have some coffee.

'I'll get on with the logs,' George said.

Suddenly he felt flat, his spirits depressed, knowing that his new freedom was an empty gift without Joss to share it. He passed close to her, but politely as a stranger might, and she touched his arm.

'Sorry I dashed off,' she murmured. 'Things are a bit difficult. It's just . . . tricky. But it's not *you*. Honestly.'

'I'm glad about that.' He smiled, his heart lifting a little. 'No pressure. See you later.'

He went out, comforted by this little exchange, and began

to fill the log basket, carrying the wood in a plastic container between the wheelbarrow and the drawing-room. It wasn't until later that he remembered the package. He wheeled the empty barrow back to the shed and went in through the garden door to the kitchen. Raymond Fox was still sitting at the table, the women milling about him. Lunch was being prepared, and Mousie was being pressed to stay and join them, but there was no sign of the parcel.

George debated with himself and then spoke to Emma as she emerged from the larder.

'I'll be off now,' he said, 'or I'll be late for lunch. Shall I take that parcel for Bruno?'

'Oh, don't worry about that,' she said quickly but very firmly. She seemed preoccupied, edgy. 'Joss says that he'll be up later on.'

He nodded and turned to Joss.

'Let me know later on if you feel like a walk,' he told her. 'I shall be down at the field to take the donkeys out at around two o'clock.' Picking up his jacket from a chair, he went away without waiting for her reply.

CHAPTER THIRTY-ONE

Zoë slipped into the kitchen, quiet as a cat, dropped her overnight bag in the corner by Nellie's bed and hesitated by the inner door. Her black eyes took in the simple preparations for lunch – some rolls standing on a rack ready to be warmed in the oven and the soup in a saucepan by the stove – and she made a rueful little grimace. Well, she hadn't come for the food. As she listened for a moment, wondering if Bruno were alone, she shivered and wished she'd brought warmer clothes. She'd forgotten how cold it was on the north coast, and especially in this house perched halfway up its cliff.

No voices, no sound at all that she could hear; she took a few paces back, closed the door with a bang and called out: 'Hello, darling. It's me.' She passed through the kitchen and into the sitting-room just as Bruno emerged from his study and they stood for a second or two surveying each other. Zoë moved first.

'I'm sure I'm being a nuisance,' she said, putting up her face to be kissed, first one cheek and then the other, 'but there's no need to look *quite* so unwelcoming.'

'Am I?' He chuckled a little. 'Well, I warned you that your timing is bad.'

She shrugged ruefully. 'My timing is always bad. As far as I can see there's never a good time for anything and the older you grow the worse it gets. Honestly . . .'

She paused, checking herself. It was much too early to go along that path; she needed time to soften him up a little. Perhaps after a drink or two and some gossip . . .

'Honestly what?' he was asking, wary already. 'What brings you to North Cornwall in February, Zoë? I should have thought that the Maldives were more your scene.'

'And how right you are, darling. The trouble is nobody was offering. It was Cornwall or nothing.' She shivered again. 'I always forget how cold it is here. No wonder you keep that fire going right through winter.'

'Wait a minute.' He ran up the stairs and after a few minutes reappeared with a scarlet pashmina. 'Emma keeps it here for the same reason. She won't mind if you borrow it.'

Zoë raised her eyebrows disbelievingly. She suspected that Emma would mind very much but she merely wrapped the shawl about her thin frame and perched in the rocking-chair beside the fire, watching Bruno as he piled on more logs and fanned the wood into bright, leaping flames.

'Merlin,' she said suddenly. 'Do you remember how I called you that after I'd read the Mary Stewart trilogy? Calling up the fire. You've always been able to do that. Two bits of twig and a handful of ash and within minutes you'd have a blaze going.'

He shrugged. 'Keeping warm is important.'

'Too right, darling.' She spoke vehemently but, remembering her plan, immediately changed the subject. 'I am so sorry about Mutt. I liked her, you know.'

'So you said earlier.' Bruno put the bellows on the flat hearthstone and sat down on the sofa. 'She liked you too.'

She quirked an eyebrow. 'Don't say it like that, sweetie. Some people do. Odd, isn't it? Mutt didn't make judgements –

I think that was what I liked about her. She never made me feel raw and young.'

Bruno laughed out loud. 'You? Raw? Come off it.'

She laughed with him. 'I was born old,' she admitted, 'but it didn't do me much good, did it?'

She watched him, huddling the pashmina round her thin shoulders, out-staring his assessing look. It was strange that she didn't feel the usual requirement to straighten her back and lift her chin, in an attempt to hide the ageing process, but merely gave him back stare for stare. Perhaps it was because she knew him so well and knew also that, like Mutt, Bruno didn't judge his fellow men: that was why she was here today.

'You had a good career. Good grief, you were internationally famous.' He was answering her question – but carefully. 'Your problem was that, given the nature of it, it was bound to be a short-lived one.'

She made a gesture that disposed of the past. 'We've said all this before. It's history. How's life here at St Meriadoc?'

'Just as it usually is.' He stood up. 'Like a drink?' It was a rhetorical question. 'Well, actually *not* as it usually is for the obvious reasons. Emma's here, of course, and Brer Fox arrived earlier this morning.'

'They're up at the house?' She deliberately made the question light but was relieved by his answering nod. 'Brer Fox must be rubbing his hands with glee.' She took her glass and grinned up at him. 'You'll have to watch him, won't you?'

'Why?' Bruno sat down again on the sofa and then cursed as a sharp barking was heard. 'Hang on. That's Nellie back from her afternoon walk to the Paradise gardens.'

He went out and she heard the back door open. Nellie came gambolling in, tongue lolling, delighted to see a guest, and Zoë quickly put her glass out of harm's reach and stretched a hand to pat her.

'Careful,' Bruno said. 'Her feet are wet. Here, Nellie. *Here*, you wretched animal. On your rug.'

Nellie leaped gracefully onto the end of the sofa and curled onto her rug, one paw stretched out to Bruno's knee.

'She's such a nice, smiley person,' said Zoë, watching her. 'I wish I could have a dog but the flat's far too small. I sometimes long for a puppy. What fun it would be!'

'You'd hate having a puppy,' answered Bruno at once. 'The sheer relentlessness of it would kill you. It's a bit like having a child. . .'

He paused, picking up his glass, his face suddenly bleak.

Damn, thought Zoë. Damn, damn, damn. Just the wrong note to strike.

'Well, you're right, of course,' she said aloud; best to meet it head on, after all. 'I have this unfortunate character which always lets me down when it really matters most. No moral fibre or whatever they used to call it. So how is Emma taking it? Poor Emma. She'll be gutted but I bet old Brer Fox has got the valuers in already.'

Bruno grinned unwillingly. 'I haven't seen him yet,' he admitted, 'but you're probably not far out.'

In the silence that followed she noted his sudden abstraction, the way his eyes seemed to look inward, and sipped thoughtfully at her wine.

'I suppose it's share-out time,' she suggested casually. 'But you've always expected it, haven't you? You and Emma always knew how it would go. I can hear her now: "You have The Lookout and I'll have Paradise." The thing is,' she shifted in the chair, 'neither of you ever talked about the rest of it.'

Her keen black glance saw the small frown appear between his eyes although he continued to smooth Nellie's coat. She now lay half on her back, her head hanging over the seat of the chair, looking totally relaxed and quite absurd.

Zoë chuckled. 'That dog,' she said affectionately. 'Crazy animal. So what about the rest of it then, Bruno?' She decided to press him a little; he could warn her off if he wanted to. 'How has Mutt left it, do you know?'

He glanced at her almost measuringly, as if deciding what to tell her.

'I haven't seen the will,' he said slowly, 'but I'm hoping that the boatyard won't be left to Emma. That could be tricky.'

'Tricky?' She gazed at him in disbelief at such an understatement. '*Tricky*? Surely she'd have realized that Brer Fox would turn the cove into some kind of leisure complex before Rafe and Mousie can take off their black armbands. What would you do about it?'

Bruno shrugged. 'What *could* I do about it? Of course there's the Inheritance Tax to be paid.'

'And where does that come from?'

'Out of the estate.' He rubbed his fingers reflectively over his jaw. 'Something will have to go.'

'But what?' She settled back into the chair, tucking the pashmina more firmly around her knees. 'If Mutt has left the boatyard to Emma then that would give Brer Fox just the handle he needs. He always wanted to develop the boatyard and finding money to pay the Inheritance Tax would give him the perfect excuse.'

'Possibly. There are quite a few problems, though. It'll need planning permission, of course. Perhaps we'll have to sell Paradise. Anyway,' he seemed to pull himself together, abandoning the confidences, 'tell me how you are and how Jilly is. How about some lunch? Not too exciting, I'm afraid, but you didn't give me any warning. I'd offer you another drink but I suppose if you're driving it wouldn't be very sensible.'

'Well, that's just it.' She wriggled a little, looking rather forlorn. 'I've got a problem, darling.'

He looked amused. 'No change there, then. What is it this time?'

'I was hoping that I could stay for a day or two.' His expression changed so swiftly from amusement to surprise that she pretended dismay. 'Oh, don't look like that, darling. The truth of it is that Jilly rather used me as a cover so that dear old Tim didn't smell a rat and now I find that she's invited Greg Allen too. Three is definitely a crowd and I'm hoping that you might rescue me just for a few nights at least.'

He stood up, pushing his hands into his trouser pockets, and she felt a genuine pang of anxiety.

'I told you on the telephone, Zoë, that this is simply not a good time.'

'I know, darling,' she said quickly. 'Of course I see that. But I won't be in the way, really I won't. After all, Emma's up at the house. Please, Bruno. I wouldn't ask if it wasn't important, especially just now. I'll keep out of the way.'

'Oh, do me a favour, love,' he said crossly. 'I wasn't born yesterday. What is it really?'

She hesitated, curled back in the chair as she stared up at him, wondering how much to tell him.

'I've got a serious cash flow problem,' she said rapidly. 'They've switched off the power at the flat, the bastards, and it's freezing. When Jilly said she was thinking of coming down I offered to drive her if she paid for half the petrol. I thought I'd come on to you and ask if you'd help.'

'I'm flattered,' he said drily. 'You don't normally feel the need to drive all this way to ask for money. A telephone call usually does the trick. What's so different this time?'

She looked away from him. It had been worth a try but she might have guessed that he'd see through her.

'The truth is that I've got in a bit of a muddle.' She reached for the inevitable cigarette, caught his wry look and shrugged shamefacedly. 'I'm trying to give up, honestly.' She breathed in a lungful of nicotine and visibly relaxed, breathing out the smoke and settling herself more comfortably, folding her legs beneath her. 'The thing is,' she began again, 'I've had a bit of a difficult spell. I thought I had some work lined up, a really good commission with Sligo, and then it fell through. Anyway, I'd got deep in on the strength of it, maxed the credit cards and so on, fallen behind with the rent. Well,' she shrugged again. 'It's not the first time, is it? But then I had a bit of luck. I saw Sally Vine in Peter Jones and she was telling me about her mother. You remember Evelyn Bose, the artist? She's pretty ga-ga now, and poor old Sally's at her wits' end, but the plan is to let Evelyn's basement flat to someone who can keep her eye on her, spend some time with her, do a bit of shopping and so on. She's got someone to come in and do the cleaning and some cooking, but Evelyn gets lonely and Sally simply hasn't the time. So I said, "What about me?" and she jumped at it. I've always got on well with old Evie, and she likes me, so we struck a deal. A tiny rent in return for companionship.' She blew another cloud of smoke. 'So I get a comfortable flat for peanuts in exchange for listening to old Evie droning on about her lovers. I can handle that.'

'So what's the problem?'

'The fact is, I've had to get out of my flat but Evie's isn't available until the beginning of next week.' She pulled a face, not looking at him. 'If you must know, I've borrowed from all my chums and I can't bear the humiliation of hearing their voices when they know it's me on the phone. Jilly said she'd pay the petrol if I drove her down but Tim will be arriving on Saturday and they'll go back together. To be honest, darling, I haven't got anywhere else to go at the moment.'

CHAPTER THIRTY-TWO

Mousie leaned on the field gate, some withered apples in her pocket and Mutt's will tucked into the shabby leather bag slung over her shoulder. She'd managed to resist Emma's invitations to lunch, finishing her coffee and hurrying away as soon as could, and now she took a moment to catch her breath. It was only this morning after breakfast that she'd thought of the place where the will might be; a place where Mutt had put personal papers, letters and cards that she'd treasured. Oddly, this wasn't in the desk in her parlour but in a drawer in her dressing-table. During those early days after her fall, she'd asked Mousie to bring something – a letter from Emma, perhaps – from the drawer and it had been obvious that it was here she kept her special correspondence.

As soon as Mousie remembered it she decided that she would go up to Paradise and take a look. She saw Raymond's car sweep past, driving up to the house, and realized that she might need to have a plan: she'd say that she'd mislaid a book. After all, she'd spent a great deal of time in Mutt's bedroom and had more excuse than any of them – except for Joss – for gaining access to it.

Now, standing at the field gate with the will safe in her bag, she smiled to herself. As it had turned out, Joss had given her all the cover she'd needed, waiting on watch in the hall whilst she, Mousie, had run lightly upstairs and found what she was looking for almost immediately.

The donkeys came plodding to see her, heads nodding, blinking their extraordinary eyelashes. They jostled each other for prime position and she held out the apples and promised them a walk.

'Later,' she told them. 'Joss will be down, later.'

As she stroked their long ears she wondered how Joss would deal with this new and alarming discovery of her true identity. It was clear that, even whilst she was still attempting to assimilate the facts, Joss was more concerned for her mother than for herself. Mousie felt that this was a good sign; it indicated that Joss was strong enough in her sense of self to accept it. There would be moments, of course, when the sudden thought of it would knock her off balance – as if she were hearing it again for the first time – but these moments would grow fewer and, meanwhile, Joss would have the family and her work to support her through them. She'd had just such a moment when they'd met earlier at the bottom of the path to The Lookout.

'I've just been to see Bruno,' Joss had said. 'Are you coming up to Paradise?' – and then, quite unexpectedly, her face had been washed by a tide of vivid colour as if she'd just remembered who she was – and, even worse, that Mousie knew her secret. It was a purely instinctive response to put an arm around the girl and give her a quick, brief hug. She stood stiffly within the embrace, as if too dismayed by her knowledge to return it, and Mousie released her and stepped back a little.

'I can't tell you,' she said, 'what a relief it was to read those letters. But I have to apologize. I had no right, of course. It was pure curiosity. I hope you can forgive me?'

Joss flushed an even brighter red.

'I had no right, either,' she answered wretchedly. 'Mutt told me to find them, not to read them.'

'Oh, but what a responsibility.' Mousie shook her head sympathetically. 'I didn't have even that excuse. I saw her writing, you see, and then the signature. Madeleine.'

'That was it,' cried Joss eagerly, almost apologetically. 'That's what got me too. I simply couldn't help myself . . .'

As they set off together towards Paradise, Joss explaining why she'd read the letters, Mousie experienced a deeply intuitive fear that, if the whole truth were not told, Joss might spend the rest of her life in this way: apologizing because she felt that she had no right here, at St Meriadoc, any longer.

'But isn't it better,' she asked when there had been a lull in Joss's explanations, 'that we should know the truth?' She felt the girl's arm tense beneath her hand but continued quite calmly. 'I, for one, am truly glad to know. It's been a trouble to me ever since Mutt came back from India.'

'How do you mean?' Joss's voice was faint, anxious.

'Well, I knew that something was wrong, you see . . .'

Gently, quietly, she repeated what she'd told Bruno the previous evening, explaining her misgivings and telling how she'd regretted – but seemed unable to help – the with-holding of her trust. They reached the field gate and it was natural to stand there, watching the donkeys whilst they talked.

'I'd felt so guilty about it, you see,' she told Joss. 'Putting it down to the childhood jealousy and castigating myself for still being so weak and foolish. Then, once I'd read the letters, I was angry because I felt that I'd been right to be suspicious, after all, and that your grandmother had fooled me.'

Joss turned then, and looked at her, meeting her eyes bravely.

'And now?' she asked.

Mousie chuckled. 'Oh, my dear, now I just feel a fool for allowing it to come between us all our lives. Once I'd thought about the letters – even whilst I was reading them – I felt a huge sympathy for the position your grandmother was in. She was brave, resourceful and compassionate and I'm sure you must feel very proud of her. Who was it said: "It is in judging people that we most betray them"? I just wish that the shadow of suspicion on my side and the fear on hers hadn't been between us, stunting our friendship. I think Bruno had the right of it when he told me that Mutt and Emma saved his life. For the last fifty years she looked after us all and took nothing that might have belonged to anyone else.'

'And now?' Joss asked again.

'Ah.' Mousie looked thoughtful. 'Now, things could be rather different.'

'Bruno says you think we should tell Mum the truth.'

'I do. Lies cast long shadows. I think you'll find that out for yourself before too long.'

Joss turned away, looking out over the meadow, her face miserable. 'I don't think Mum will be able to deal with it,' she said.

'You underestimate her,' Mousie answered firmly. 'Just let her read those letters and judge for herself.'

'She'll feel we don't belong here any more.' Joss was only just able to control the trembling of her lips. She pressed them firmly together. 'I don't want her to feel that but, at the same time, it would be wrong for her – or me – to inherit anything.'

'You *do* belong here,' Mousie replied. 'We all love you. Nothing changes that. Try to see what your mother and you mean to Bruno. She couldn't be more a sister to him than his own would have been and you have been like his own daughter. You and Emma *are* his family, Joss, as much as I am or Rafe and his brood are.'

'But my father isn't.'

Mousie sighed. 'Raymond has never made any effort to be a member of the family,' she said truthfully. 'He has no wish to be. I agree that it would be quite wrong if he were to exert undue influence now over the estate. That's why I think the truth should be told. Do you know anything about Inheritance Tax, or death duties as it used to be called?'

When Joss stared at her, puzzled, she explained how Bruno might be called upon to pay it for the second time and the girl looked shaken.

'I think I know where the will might be,' Mousie told her, 'but it would be a good idea if Bruno could keep it until he's ready to let it be made public. Will you cover for me if I go up to Mutt's bedroom and look for it?'

Joss was only too ready to assist in the suppression of the will.

'Do you think *Goblin Market* might be there, too,' she asked eagerly but Mousie shook her head regretfully; the drawer was too shallow.

They had gone on together, entering Paradise like two conspirators, Joss punching the air in silent triumph when Mousie finally reappeared on the stairs brandishing the will in its long brown envelope. All the while she was drinking coffee, talking to Emma and Raymond, it had been as if the document were burning a hole in her shabby leather bag, and Mousie had been almost faint with relief when she'd managed at last to escape to the safety of the lane.

Now, still leaning on the gate, she allowed herself a quiet space to think about Mutt and to grieve for her. In her profession she was accustomed to death and too grateful to witness a peaceful, painless one to wish for anything different. Yet she acknowledged her loss, knowing that she'd miss Mutt who'd been a link to her own youth: to Jessie Poltrue and old Dot and, of course, to Uncle James and her own mother, Julia. How strange, and how moving, it had been to read about them in Mutt's letters: to see them through the eyes of this stranger come among them. Mousie was seized with a great sadness.

Often, back from the surgery in the late afternoon, she'd gone to Paradise to see Mutt and they'd shared a pot of tea. If the weather permitted she'd have been gardening or, during the dark winter days, she'd be sitting beneath the lamp in her parlour stitching away at her tapestry. If she'd ever been lonely or bored she'd never shown it.

'How lovely,' she'd say, putting away her work or washing her hands under the kitchen tap. 'Now that's what I call good timing. I was just about to put the kettle on. So what's the latest?'

They'd talk about the health of some of the local people – Mousie's macabre sense of humour never failed to set her off into fits of laughter – and they'd discuss the latest treatments. Mutt was always able to contribute intelligently and their work had been their most important point of contact. Quite suddenly Mousie realized how very much she would miss those sessions, chuckling together with the teapot between them; two women who had experienced the human spirit at its worst – and at its most courageous.

'Hubert would have been so proud of you,' Mutt had said impulsively on one occasion – and at once the shadow had fallen across them, tying their tongues.

Yet how could Mutt have told her the truth? Mousie saw herself, all those years ago, through Mutt's eyes – young, rather priggish, critical – and recalled that moment at the Christmas party when her offer of friendship had been rebuffed. Those feelings of humiliation and compassion had continued to colour her relationship with the older woman and she saw now that the withholding of the foolish nickname had been a way of keeping a measure of her own pride intact.

Silently she gave tribute to Mutt, grateful for all she had done for Bruno and for all of them in the valley, and, giving the donkeys a final pat, Mousie set off for The Lookout: the sooner Bruno took the will into his own keeping the happier she would feel. She climbed the steep path, let herself into his kitchen, and was calling out to him before she caught the murmur of voices.

Bruno met her as she came in, his broad shoulders blocking the other end of the big, light-filled room. His look was warning but his voice was natural and welcoming.

'Hello, Mousie,' he said. 'Look who's here.' He stood aside and she saw Zoë, sitting by the fire. 'You're just in time for a drink.'

CHAPTER THIRTY-THREE

Emma closed the front door behind Mousie and stood for a moment, giving herself time in which to think. She was still confused by what Raymond had tried to explain to her earlier about the Inheritance Tax, anxious now that with darling Mutt gone, things here at St Meriadoc would change. Misery seized her: how odd Paradise would feel without Mutt. Her heart was squeezed and wrung with grief and she gave a tiny sob, quickly putting her fingers to her lips as if to stifle the noise as Joss came out of the kitchen. Emma braced herself, forcing herself to smile, unwilling to allow her own un-happiness to weaken Joss, who was missing Mutt just as much and managing to be brave about it.

'I thought I'd catch up on some notes ready for tomorrow,' Joss said. 'Lunch is nearly ready but there's just something particularly important I'd like to deal with, if that's OK?'

There was something odd about her, Emma thought, some-thing almost secretive but tinged with a kind of low-key excitement. Immediately she dismissed the thought. The poor child was simply overwhelmed by events and Raymond wasn't actually helping by droning on about how the estate would be divided. If only he could have learned to be tactful with his daughter, been less proud of being the sort of man who called a spade a spade. When once – oh, years and years ago – she'd tried to defend Ray by saying that he always spoke his mind, Bruno had said, 'Yes, but what makes him think anyone wants to hear it?'

Emma saw that Joss had hesitated at the foot of the stairs, watching her, and she pulled herself together.

'Of course it is,' she answered. 'I can manage lunch. Work must come first, even at times like these. I'll give you a shout.'

On an impulse Joss crossed the hall and gave Emma a quick hug.

'It'll be OK, Mum,' she said seriously, rather as if she were making a promise, and Emma smiled back at her; grateful for that warm, unexpected gesture, filled with tremendous love for her pretty, clever daughter who was so like dear old Mutt.

'Of course it will,' she agreed bravely.

She watched Joss leap the stairs, two at a time and, taking a deep breath, went back into the kitchen. Raymond was standing at the dresser, moving and folding a pile of newspapers, his face set into frowning, angry lines.

'The damned thing's gone,' he said abruptly as soon as he saw her. 'It's simply disappeared. Did George take it, after all?'

She shook her head, looking puzzled, but her heart jumped anxiously. 'Do you mean the parcel? No, George didn't take it. He offered but I didn't think you'd be particularly pleased about it.'

'He suspected something.'

She could see that he was mentally reviewing the little scene with George, his broad pale lips compressed, his eyes speculative.

'I wouldn't be surprised.' She decided to allow herself a hint of censure. 'You were a bit odd about it, after all, weren't you?'

'Odd?' He looked at her narrowly. 'Do you think he could have guessed what it might be?'

She shrugged, collecting knives and forks together, beginning to set the table for lunch.

'Why should he guess? None of us knows what's in it. Why are you looking on the dresser? I thought you had it on the table.'

He looked slightly uncomfortable.

'When Mousie and Joss came in I thought it was best to put it out of sight. I turned round and put it on the dresser. Just here. Now it's gone.'

'Perhaps Mousie saw it and decided to deliver it.' She raised her eyebrows at his instinctive gesture of irritation at the suggestion. 'Well, why not? It was clearly addressed. And, anyway, what did you intend to do with it? You could have hardly opened it yourself.'

The silence went on for far too long. She stared at him, pretending disbelief, and he coloured a little.

'I've already explained how sensitive this could be.' He almost sounded defensive. 'I was merely going to check that the will hadn't been put in with other things, that's all. Don't forget you have just as much right to see Mutt's will as Bruno has. A quick glance would have forewarned us and nobody would have been the wiser.' He could sense her resistance. 'The sooner we decide how the tax is to be paid the better. At least, I imagine you don't relish the idea of selling Paradise to meet it, do you?'

Emma hid her twinge of fear, raising her chin as if in defiance at his threat.

'I've been thinking about that and I still don't quite see what could be done about it, even if we knew the contents of her will. It's horrid, talking like this when we should be mourning Mutt.'

Before he could answer her Joss came in and Emma braced herself again; an automatic reaction to the joint presence of

Raymond and Joss. Instinctively her voice lightened, her lips smiled and smiled, as if this air of determined cheerfulness might act as a restraint to their natural antagonism.

'Lunch,' she announced brightly, as a further distraction – but already Raymond was questioning Joss about the parcel.

'Did you see a package,' he was asking, 'wrapped up in brown paper and string? It was here on the dresser.'

'A package?' Joss shook her head indifferently. 'No. Was it going to the post?'

'No.' Raymond sat down again at the table. 'Your mother came across it when she was looking for something else. It contained something your grandmother had wrapped up long ago by the look of it. It was addressed to Bruno.'

Emma set the fish pie on a mat in the centre of the table and began to divide it up.

'To Bruno?'

Joss's voice was sharp and Emma hid a sigh. Now it would all come out and there would be an argument.

'Perhaps Mousie took it down to him,' she suggested quickly. 'Never mind about it now. Is that enough for you, Joss?'

'It was . . . oh,' Raymond was measuring the size of the parcel, squaring the air with his hands, 'about so big. You didn't see it, then? It's rather important that we know what's inside it.'

Joss shook her head. She looked shocked, almost frightened, and Emma snorted with silent indignation, in sympathy with her daughter. No doubt she'd already guessed that her father had intended to open it.

'But where did you find it?' Joss didn't seem interested in her lunch. 'What were you looking for?'

'Your mother was looking for Mutt's will,' answered Raymond smoothly. 'It has to be found, you know. Well, she came across this parcel and we wondered if the will might be inside it.' He was getting on well with his pie; nothing deflected Raymond from his food. 'Now it's disappeared.'

'But *where* was it?' Joss asked again.

'It was in Mutt's desk.' Emma answered the question. 'She kept our old school reports in one of the drawers and it was in a folder that had Bruno's stuff in it.'

She saw that Joss was staring at her in some kind of horror and she was obliged to remind herself that she had every right to sort out Mutt's things. Nevertheless, she felt a kind of creeping guilt in the face of Joss's reaction.

'We *do* have to find the will, darling,' she said gently. 'Apart from which, Bruno ought to have his parcel, whatever it is.'

'But where is it?'

Joss now seemed almost as anxious about its whereabouts as Ray was, and Emma breathed deeply, trying to contain a rising irritation.

'Shall we finish lunch?' she asked lightly. 'Then we can all have a look for it. Mousie might well have taken it away with her, thinking she was doing us a favour.'

'Yes, that's possible.'

Joss seemed to slump a little, relaxing in her chair, and Emma sighed with relief and cast about for a harmless topic of conversation. From experience she knew that – between her husband and daughter – there was no such thing. It was extraordinary how the least controversial topic could develop into a battle royal raging between them.

'It was so kind of George,' she began at random, 'to come up and help this morning. But what a shock about Penny taking Tasha and just going off like that. Mind you, I always had reservations about Penny.'

She saw, with relief, that Ray was not the least interested in George's domestic problems but was wrapped up in his own thoughts: no doubt parcelling out the estate to his satisfaction. Joss had picked up her fork and was eating her fish pie with a kind of studied concentration.

'I always thought,' continued Emma, 'that she was hiding something. Well, that sounds a bit dramatic but you know what I mean? There was a lack of real openness about her so that it was difficult to get close to her. Oh, she was very sweet, I grant you that, but it was all on the surface. I know she missed her family and her country – well, that's only to be expected and nobody would blame her for it – but I have a feeling that there's more to it than that.'

Although she was quite used to conducting these monologues at family mealtimes, in an attempt to keep the sparks from flying, she was surprised at Joss's complete lack of response. Ray might go off into his own world on these occasions but Joss usually made an heroic effort to keep the ball rolling between the two of them, partly because she always felt remorseful at allowing herself to be riled by her father.

Emma piled some more pie onto Raymond's plate and glanced invitingly at Joss, who shook her head with a little smile, and settled back in her place.

'*I* think we shall hear that there's someone in New Zealand. It wouldn't surprise me at all,' Emma prophesied, finishing her own lunch and debating whether she should have another small helping. It was a rather good pie, even if she thought so herself.

Joss shifted suddenly, as if she might speak, glanced anxiously at her father and instead took another forkful of pie. Emma frowned to herself. Clearly Joss didn't wish to have a discussion about George and Penny in front of Ray and she felt a little stab of curiosity. Of course, George and Joss had always been very close, so fond of one another . . . Emma put down her fork. She looked again at her daughter who had bent her head over her plate and was eating quickly and neatly, as if nothing mattered but to finish up her lunch. Emma saw that her cheeks were stained with colour and, as she watched the flush deepen, several things clicked smartly into place.

'Delicious, dear.' Ray had finished his second helping. 'Anything left? What was that you were saying about George?'

Emma scooped the last of the pie onto his plate and stood up.

'I was saying that he is a dear, good fellow and that he and Joss are taking the donkeys out for a walk this afternoon.' She nodded sharply at Joss, who was now staring at her in surprise, and began to fill the empty dish with hot water. 'Didn't I hear you fix a time with him, darling? It's nearly two o'clock and I don't suppose you'll want any pudding. Only fruit salad, I'm afraid, Ray, but there's cheese if you want it.'

Joss stood up, hovering indecisively by her chair, and Emma assumed her 'this is not a subject for negotiation' expression that she'd found useful when Joss had been a little girl.

'Off you go, then,' she said briskly. 'George will be waiting.'

They exchanged a look, encouraging on Emma's side, confused but grateful on Joss's, and she went out. Emma sighed with contentment, her spirits rising.

'I can't manage anything else at the moment, dear,' Raymond patted her arm. 'There's nothing to beat that local fish. Delicious.'

'Thank you, darling.' Emma beamed upon him. 'Now, why don't you go and relax in the sitting-room and I'll bring the coffee in to you? It will be nice to have a moment to ourselves. Here, take the newspaper . . .'

To her great relief he disappeared obediently; piling the plates on the draining-board, listening for noises from the drawing-room, Emma crossed swiftly to the dresser. She opened a drawer, checked that the parcel was well hidden and, taking a pile of dishcloths from another drawer, covered it more securely. She was determined that there should be no arguments, no fighting or bitter words, until after Mutt had been laid peacefully to rest; whatever the parcel might contain could wait a few more days. Satisfied that it was out of harm's way until after the funeral, she closed the drawer gently and went to make some coffee.

CHAPTER THIRTY-FOUR

George arrived at the field gate a few minutes after Joss had entered the meadow from the garden. Her relief at seeing him was so overwhelming that she was glad to be able to busy herself getting the donkeys into their head collars, smiling briefly at him, but feeling unnaturally shy.

'Which way shall we go?' It was clear that he was trying to pretend that nothing had changed between them. 'Up the lane and back down the valley? I'll take the Teaser.'

He took Rumpleteaser's halter and set off across the meadow, leaving her to follow with Mungojerrie. This was the usual form: the Teaser always liked to lead. Down the lane they clopped, over the narrow bridge and past The Row. The wind was stronger now, whipping up the choppy surface of the water into white spumy frills, whilst the seabirds swooped and drifted high above in strange, ever-changing patterns, crying mournfully. Golden shafts of sunlight struck down glancingly from behind the torn and harried clouds and all the while the sea roared as it advanced, pounding over the rocks and against the cliffs with ceaseless energy.

The tide and the wind combined made conversation

impossible and, as she led Mungo up the narrow lane, climbing and winding inland now, Joss was thinking about Mutt and the letters. She longed to read them again, remembering particularly the passages about Simon and trying to imagine what would have happened if Mutt had told him the truth. Would he have recoiled from her in horror as she'd feared, or would his love for her have given him the compassion to understand? As they passed between the high grassy banks, studded now with delicately pale primroses and shiny-bright celandines, Joss wondered whether Mutt had ever regretted that Sunday morning's work by the Saint's Well.

When George glanced back at her, checking their progress, she knew at once that the barrier was still between them. *Lies cast long shadows.* She could never be easy with him again until he knew the truth. Smiling back at him, nodding that all was well, she sighed heavily and deeply inside herself. In that moment when her father had entered the kitchen at Paradise she'd known that it would be impossible to continue to protect her mother from the truth. 'You underestimate her,' Mousie had said and Joss longed to believe that. Gradually the strong conviction that her mother should be kept in ignorance of the truth had been undermined – and her father's presence had contributed to this process – but it was impossible to imagine any scene in which she might be told. Remembering her own reaction as she'd read the letters, Joss shrank at recommending the same process. Yet perhaps she was indeed underestimating her mother's resilience and compassion; she might be more ready to accept that her own relationship with these people who loved her was under no threat than Joss gave her credit for.

Watching George's familiar stride, adapted to the Teaser's amble, Joss recalled how her own conversations with Bruno and Mousie had confirmed this assurance: how comforting they'd both been and how easy, with them, to feel that nothing terrible had happened after all. She was still herself,

Joss Fox; unchanged and still loved by those she valued most. If Bruno and Mousie felt like that about her after this startling revelation then why should George feel any different? She had to remind herself that Bruno had always known – and she shook her head in amazed admiration at his courage. Of course, it might be easy for people to condemn Mutt if they hadn't read the letters: the letters changed everything, showed Mutt as a young and vulnerable woman in extraordinary circumstances. Yet, even now it was almost impossible for Joss to believe that her mother was not Emma Trevannion, not Bruno's sister at all, but Lottie Uttworth . . .

She saw that George and the Teaser were patiently waiting at the point where the lane widened and she hastened to catch them up.

'They're going well, aren't they?' he asked cheerfully. 'Not so painfully slow as usual. Are you OK?'

They looked at one another and she was seized with compunction at his expression: there was no reproach, no self-pity, but even he couldn't quite hide the misery and confusion he felt at the unexplained obstacle that prevented the usual flow of affection between them.

'Oh, George,' she said, clutching Mungo's halter in both hands, 'no, I'm not OK. Neither of us is OK, we both know that, but I don't quite know how to deal with it.'

He looked relieved at once, glad that at least the acknowledgement of this obstacle was out in the open.

'Is it to do with Penny going so suddenly?' he asked. 'I thought I knew how you felt but then I wondered if you were knocked off balance by it.'

'No, it's not that. It's something quite different.' She was too concentrated on the problem of how to explain her difficulty to wonder how it might sound to him. 'It's nothing to do with you and Penny at all.'

'You said that earlier.' He frowned anxiously. 'But if it isn't to do with me or Penny, then what is it?'

'It's to do with me,' she said quickly. 'It's something you haven't known about me. Well, you'd never have guessed it. I'm not . . . what you think . . .'

Even as she shook her head in frustration at the inadequacy of her words an engine could be heard in the lane ahead.

'We can't talk here,' George said abruptly. 'Get Mungo over or he'll kick out. We'll go through the field at the top and down the valley. We can let them off there for a bit.'

The delivery van came round the bend, slowed at the sight of the donkeys, and the driver raised his hand as he drove on down the lane. As Joss and George crossed the wide field, bordered by hedges of furze and blackthorn, the wind tugged and buffeted at their hair and jackets so that they bent against it, hauling the donkeys forward to the shelter of the valley. They passed through the ramshackle gate and made their way down to the edge of the stream where they released the donkeys, which immediately began to graze.

It was so much quieter here; the wind roaring high above their heads and the trees, clinging along the valley's sides, bowing to its wild embrace. The last of the clouds were being bundled away to the east and the sun burst out suddenly with glorious warmth so that they looked at each other with relief. They could hear the tiny bubbling spring, half-hidden beneath the remaining granite slabs of the disciple's cell, and the hoarse croaking of a raven somewhere on the rocky ridge above them. Joss thought of that long-ago picnic, when Mutt had heard the lark's falling, tumbling song, and how, as Simon had pointed upwards to him, he'd brushed her cheek with his arm and she'd fallen in love with him.

George reached into his pocket and brought out a Bounty bar: one piece each, which was just as it had always been since the first time they'd been allowed to go off together without an older sibling or a parent to supervise. They'd always shared. Now, he held the piece of chocolate out to her, smiling his familiar smile, but there was a shadow in his eyes.

'I've been thinking about what you said back there,' he said. 'I realize I've been getting it wrong, haven't I? It was a bit arrogant to assume that you were prepared to be content with what I had to offer you, which was nothing at all, really. You're going to tell me that there's someone else, aren't you? I should have guessed it long ago, instead of taking it for granted that you'd feel like I do now that Penny's gone.'

He finished his chocolate and put his hands in his pockets, shoulders hunched. His head was lowered slightly, his face expressionless, and Joss stared at him.

There was no magic by the Saint's Well that morning: only the clear, cold sound of water and the sharp, strong scent of ramsons.

She thought: But I am not Mutt and George is not Simon.

'No,' she said quickly. 'No, you're quite wrong, but what I have to tell you is extraordinary and very complicated. Come and sit with me.'

Folding her plaid to make a cushion she drew him down beside her on the stone where once her grandmother had sat with Simon on a hot August afternoon fifty years before, and slowly, halting a little as she reminded herself of the details, she began to tell him her story.

Rafe watched the little procession go past The Row whilst Pamela listened to the clop of the donkeys' hoofs.

'How do they look?' she asked.

She waited patiently for his answer, her fingers trailing lightly over familiar objects: some remembered, others only imagined by feeling their shape and density. The four little birds were grouped together today, one at each corner of the pink and white bowl, and a pottery jar held a spray of catkins and pussy willow, the fluffy buds just bursting open on their stiff, tall stems. She touched the delicate tassels of the catkins, seeing them clearly in her mind's eye, knowing the hedge where Rafe would have cut them.

'They have a slightly muted look,' Rafe answered. 'Rather like they used to be on the last day of the holidays. It's silly, really, because I can't explain exactly why I say that. George is leading Rumpleteaser, and Joss is following with Mungojerrie as usual, but there's a dejected air about the party.'

Pamela frowned, turning towards his voice, picturing the scene.

'I don't think he's had a proper chance to speak to her yet, do you? I know he said at lunch that he'd told them this morning but it's one thing giving the bare facts to Emma and another explaining properly to Joss.'

'And Raymond was there, which couldn't have helped.' Rafe came away from the window and sat down beside her at the table. 'This news, coming on top of Mutt's death, will probably knock poor old Joss sideways.'

'She'll find it very hard,' agreed Pamela, 'to be truly happy for herself at this particular moment but I still think that having all this going on will make a good distraction for them. Neither of them would want to be the centre of attention. At the same time, I thought she would be pleased to hear the news.'

There was a little silence.

'I suppose,' said Rafe dubiously, 'that we could be wrong?' but Pamela was shaking her head.

'All my instincts tell me that this is right,' she said, 'but there are other aspects to it, Rafe. Have you ever thought what might happen once Mutt was gone? With the estate, I mean.'

'Well, I assume it will go on much as before. It will be left between Bruno and Emma, I imagine. I have wondered whether Mutt might have left the house to Joss. They've been so close, haven't they, and Emma won't want it for herself. Why, what were you thinking of, particularly?'

Pamela grimaced, as if undecided as to exactly what she had in mind.

'It might not be quite that straightforward,' she said at last. 'What about Inheritance Tax, for instance? Supposing something had to be sold off to pay it?'

Rafe rubbed his nose thoughtfully and then leaned both elbows on the table. 'If I thought about it at all, I would have expected Mutt to have already passed some of the property over years ago. After all, we always knew that Bruno would have The Lookout and Emma would get Paradise. I suppose The Row would be shared between them.'

'I wonder. Perhaps there's some difficulty which Joss knows about that might be a bit embarrassing for her just at present.'

'Difficulty?'

'Well, we've taken it a bit for granted, haven't we, that nothing would change for us, yet Raymond has made no secret about his idea of developing the boatyard.'

'He'd never get permission for it. Anyway, do you really think Emma or Bruno would sit by whilst we and Mousie had our lives ruined?'

'I hope not,' answered Pamela feelingly. 'I just wondered, that's all.'

She stretched a hand to him and he took it, holding it closely, whilst they sat together in silence.

CHAPTER THIRTY-FIVE

Walking down the steep path from The Lookout, Bruno was aware of the change in the weather. The bitter north-easterly wind had backed to the south-west, the ice in the muddy tracks had melted, and the turbulent air was soft and warm. He carried a parcel under his arm that he settled more firmly before glancing back briefly at The Lookout where Zoë stood in the window, staring out at the sea.

He crossed the narrow bridge and stopped at the first cottage in The Row, knocking at the door before opening it and passing inside, calling Mousie's name just as she appeared. From the tiny hall the stairs rose steeply to the floor above and he hung his jacket on one of the hooks beside the door before following her into the one big downstairs room. A counter with cupboards beneath it separated the kitchen from the living area: two dark green, wing-backed chairs, one on either side of the Victorian grate where a tiny coal fire burned, and an oak gate-legged table set in the window looking seawards.

These items of furniture – as well as some of the paintings and ornaments – had belonged to her mother and, as Bruno remembered the tall, stately Aunt Julia, he wondered how Mousie had reacted to Mutt's less flattering descriptions of her: '. . . like a very dignified peahen – a bosom like a jelly-bag and a long, long neck with a tiny head perched on top . . .'

It was rather a sad thought that very few people had known the fun-loving, scatty person who'd lived behind the more sober persona of Honor Trevannion.

'I'm sorry I couldn't talk earlier.' He put the bag containing Mutt's letters on the table. 'You saw the difficulty. I'm hoping you'll look after these for the time being. I'm not saying that Zoë is unprincipled but it's probably best to keep temptation out of her way.'

'Then I expect that you'll feel the same way about this.' Mousie held out the long brown envelope. 'It was in the dressing-table drawer.'

Bruno breathed a sigh of relief. 'I guessed that you'd found it when you said that there was something you needed to discuss with me. At least, I was hoping and praying it was. You had the look of someone who'd pulled off something clever. No sign of the book, I suppose?'

She shook her head regretfully, watching him draw the paper from its envelope.

'The drawer isn't deep enough for a book. I can't imagine where that can be. My real fear is that Emma will find it. You can imagine the shock if she should come across it and those death certificates are still where Honor,' – she shook her head irritably, reminding herself – 'sorry, where Mutt first hid them.'

'Mmm.' He was only partially listening to her, reading swiftly over the paper. 'This is better than I feared. She's left The Lookout and the boatyard to me and Paradise to Emma. It was witnessed by the vicar and his wife. I wonder why she didn't get Richard Prior to draw it up properly for her.'

'She missed old Michael Veryan terribly when he died,' said Mousie, 'and she never got on with either of the younger partners. Perhaps she was nervous; afraid that she might trip herself up if she went to see them.'

'It's clear that the question of Inheritance Tax never occurred to her. Or maybe she hoped that Brer Fox and I might pay it between us out of our own savings so that the estate shouldn't be sold up.'

Mousie snorted. 'Not even Honor would think Raymond could be that philanthropic. Can you imagine him putting his hand in his pocket whilst the boatyard remains undeveloped? He'll bring all his power to bear on you.' She gave a rather sad little shrug. 'I suppose, given one didn't know the truth, that development is the obvious way to go.'

'Not if I can help it.' Bruno folded the will and pushed it back into the envelope. 'I think we sit on this until after the funeral.'

Mousie looked at him. 'You agree, though, that Emma should be told then?'

He hesitated, putting the will into the bag with the letters, folding them together.

'Yes,' he said at last, almost reluctantly. 'For Joss's sake, if nothing else. I agree with you that she would never be able to be open and natural with the family again and I'm hoping that you're right and that we are underestimating Emma's reaction.'

'She must read the letters,' said Mousie firmly. 'The letters will do the trick.'

Bruno's eyes narrowed into a smile. 'Did they really have that much of an impact on you, Mousie?'

She nodded, smiling a little ruefully as she remembered her conflicting reactions. 'In the end, they did,' she admitted. 'They touched me deeply. I could remember so much of it, you know. She was so lovely and yet, with me, always slightly remote and holding me at arm's length. I could see the effect she had on Simon – and on Rafe, too – although I was angry with Rafe for succumbing to it, exactly as she wrote.' A little silence. 'Can you imagine what it must have cost to refuse Simon and to cut herself off from her sister with such finality? Thank goodness she had you, Bruno. How lonely she would have been, bearing it all alone.'

'I can't remember as much as you can. I remember the picnics and the blackberrying parties and Pipsqueak and Wilfrid. And I was reminded of Jessie Poltrue when I came in just now. I haven't thought of her for years.' Bruno sat down at the table in one of the Windsor chairs. 'What will happen now, Mousie?'

'If the truth can be proved I can't see why everything shouldn't turn out well.' She glanced at him sharply. 'What does Zoë want at this particular moment?'

'She wants shelter until she moves into a new flat next week . . . Why? What did you imagine she wants?'

Mousie shrugged. 'It's just rather neat timing, isn't it?'

'Oh, come on.' Bruno stared at her disbelievingly. 'You don't think she'd heard about Mutt? Good God! Where? How?'

'I've no idea. I'm just pointing out that her visit coincides neatly with the fact that by this time next week you'll be better off than you are now.'

'No.' Bruno shook his head. 'I really don't think that's why she's here. After all, why should she come all this way? I might be land-rich but she'll realize that there won't be much cash in it,' he grinned, 'especially after the way I described the problems to her earlier. Zoë knows that I shan't abandon her as long as she's reasonable. She's not really devious or grasping, you know. I'm sure her turning up now is just a coincidence.'

Mousie's expression indicated a doubtful acceptance. 'Fair enough. Forget Zoë and concentrate on Raymond. You've got to be prepared that he won't believe those letters. Or, at any rate, he'll try to contest their validity.'

'But how can he? I'm here to tell everyone it's the truth.'

Mousie laughed. 'It's clear that you're no detective writer,' she observed. 'Who stands to gain from the letters? You do. Of *course* you're going to endorse them. I've no idea whether they'd stand up in a court of law but you'll have a fight on your hands. You need those death certificates.'

'Damn,' he said softly. 'I hadn't thought about it like that. I'd come round to seeing that Emma must be told, and that the original will made by my grandfather must be re-proved or whatever the legal term is, but I'd assumed that the letters would be more than enough proof. Good grief, Mousie, is it likely that I'm going to sit down and write all those letters – apart from the fact that we all know Mutt's handwriting – in an attempt to gain the estate for myself?'

Mousie dropped a hand on his shoulder. 'Trust me,' she said grimly. 'Raymond simply won't give in that easily and it could get very messy and upsetting for Emma and Joss. This is the sort of thing that would come between us all and do much more damage than the truth, simply told. We must find the book and the certificates to back up the letters.'

'That's all very well,' he answered impatiently, 'but where do you suggest we start whilst Emma and Brer Fox are up at Paradise? You were damned lucky to lay your hand on the will so easily, Mousie. It could take days to go through the house in an attempt to find the book. What do we say that we're looking for and how do we discourage them from joining in the search?'

'I know. I know.' Mousie held up a placating hand. 'Of course, Joss will be keeping her eyes open for it.' She paused for a moment. 'If it all goes according to plan, what will you do with Paradise?'

'You mean will Joss live there?' He smiled at her association of ideas. 'Don't think I haven't thought about it. The real obstacle would probably be Joss herself. She'd find it difficult now to look upon it as her home when there's Rafe's brood with a more legitimate claim.'

'Unless, of course, she's living there with one of the brood?'

He looked at her quickly. 'Do you know about Joss and George?'

She chuckled. 'My dear fellow, I've known about Joss and George since they were children. It was a pity that he ever married Penny but now, so Rafe and Pamela tell me, it's all over and she's gone back to New Zealand. I don't think it will be too long before Joss and George do what they should have done five years ago. Why shouldn't they live at Paradise? If the old back drive were to be opened up, then her patients could drive out here without upsetting the peace of the valley. There's plenty of room, after all, to run her practice from Paradise.'

'But even if Joss agreed to it, how could I square it with Olivia and Joe? It would smack of favouritism even if nobody knew the truth. Of course, I could rent it to them . . .' He brooded on it for a moment. 'I've been thinking quite a lot, Mousie, this last day or two. What would happen to the estate if I were to die? I'm beginning to believe that I should make over your cottages to you and Rafe and leave all the rest to George and Joss. What do you think?'

'I agree that Joss and George are the natural inheritors,' she answered. 'They are the children you never had; you've always loved them most and it's exactly what Mutt would have wanted. Why not? If Rafe and Pamela then decide to leave their cottage to Olivia and Joe they might sell it on when they inherit it but at least they can't spoil the estate. Think it all through very carefully and don't do anything hastily. There's no reason why George and Joss shouldn't rent Paradise for the time being. That at least is the right solution, I'm certain of it.'

'As long as we can persuade Joss that she still belongs here.'

'I think George will do that for us,' promised Mousie. 'After all, if she marries him she'll be a part of the family, won't she?'

Bruno stood up and pushed the parcel towards her.

'Will you look after this for me?' he asked. 'Keep it safe until it's needed.'

For answer, she unlocked the big cupboard beneath the glass-fronted bookcase built into the recess beside the fireplace and put the package inside.

'Quite safe there,' she said, locking the door again. 'Now all we need is *Goblin Market* and the rest of the puzzle. I wonder where it can be.'

'I live in fear of Emma coming across it and rushing down to confront me,' admitted Bruno. 'Just at this moment it would be difficult to handle with Zoë around. I really don't think for a moment that she'd heard about Mutt, you know, but I knocked any possible pretensions on the head by hinting that I'd probably have to sell Paradise for Inheritance Tax and that Brer Fox was all set to develop the boatyard.'

'And how did she react to that?'

Bruno grinned. 'She was very sympathetic – for Zoë. But, to be honest, she's much more interested in her own problems than in mine.'

'You amaze me,' said Mousie drily. 'Does Emma know she's here?'

He nodded. 'I telephoned to say that I wouldn't be going up this afternoon. I needed some excuse, anyway. I don't want to see Brer Fox just yet if I can avoid it. He's dashing back to London tomorrow for a meeting, apparently, so I've said we'll meet up after he's gone. Emma was very happy about that – she can't stand confrontations at the best of times – but I have to admit that she wasn't very thrilled about Zoë being here.'

'She's always resented her,' said Mousie. 'And with some cause. Zoë hasn't done you many favours, has she?'

'We both needed different things,' he answered quickly, 'and I'm not the easiest person to live with, you know.'

'Don't worry.' Her smile was warm. 'I don't intend to

interfere at this late date, but you have to accept that some of us are not so tolerant as you are.'

He smiled back at her but his expression was abstracted. 'Emma will be all right, won't she, Mousie?'

She was suddenly reminded of the small boy who had so often come to her for reassurance.

'Emma will realize that none of us could love her more, even if she'd been Hubert's child. I feel quite certain of it. We've known Emma for fifty years and our feelings for her are not going to change now. Why should they? She belongs here as much as any of us and she will continue to come here as she's always done, staying with you or with Joss. Once she's read the letters I think that she'll accept the truth and even find it rather romantic. Trust me, Bruno. Emma will be fine.'

He nodded, accepting her wisdom. 'It's just . . . she's rather special to me,' he said.

'To me too,' said Mousie. 'She and Joss, and Mutt.'

'I'm afraid that she won't understand how I could have deceived her all these years, you see.' He was still anxious. 'Keeping such a secret from her when we've been so close.'

'You had no choice,' answered Mousie quickly. 'She'll see that's the case once she's read the letters. Her mother tied you into the secret and you could not have betrayed her. To begin with you were too young to understand and by the time you could grasp what had happened it was too late.' She made a sudden impatient gesture. 'Oh, how I wish that you and Joss would agree to tell Emma the truth now. I have a real fear that we shall be precipitated into it. Much better we choose our own time and the sooner the better.'

Bruno looked at her, perplexed by the unexpected burst of irritation. 'You think she's going to find *Goblin Market* and the documents?'

'I don't know. Something like that, I suppose.'

'I agreed with Joss that Mutt would be buried in peace but I'll talk to her again,' he promised. 'And thanks, Mousie.'

They exchanged affectionate embraces but, as Mousie let him out into the gathering twilight, both were preoccupied with the same question: where had Mutt hidden *Goblin Market*?

CHAPTER THIRTY-SIX

Raymond drove away early the next morning, shortly after Joss had left for her practice in Wadebridge. Emma waved the car down the drive and then pottered round the mossy pathways, pausing with delight before the camellias, which were already flowering in the shelter of the garden wall. Here grew pretty, pink Lady Clare and the darker red Adolphe Audusson whilst round their feet clustered white and purple crocus. The gale had blown itself out overnight and the day was still and cool; a soft grey canopy of cloud obscured the sun, wrapping the garden in a gentle silence disturbed only by birdsong. A robin accompanied her: he fluttered along the top of the high stone wall, his cheerful stave of song lifting her spirits.

Emma straightened her shoulders, enjoying a familiar relief now that Ray was gone. She pulled a strand of encroaching ivy away from the wall, smiling with pleasure at a patch of primulas almost hidden in the longer grass, her confidence growing, reassuring herself that it was quite right to keep the parcel hidden. She'd stuck with her theory that Mousie had seen it and carried it off to Bruno, and had managed to talk Ray round to her own point of view: that the parcel had been wrapped up too long ago to contain the will and that it was much more likely to be something that had belonged to their father, Hubert, which Mutt had decided should be passed on to his son after her death. Ray had very reluctantly accepted this reasoning but then had insisted on another search – including Mutt's own room, which had made Emma feel rather miserable – but which had produced nothing. Finding a card she'd sent recently to Mutt she'd suddenly been so overcome by grief that Ray had insisted she sit down by the fire while he'd made a pot of tea.

Emma crouched down, pulling away some of the longer grass so that the primulas should get more light, remembering how kind he'd been. He *could* be kind, dear old Ray, and that was what most people didn't understand about him: they simply didn't see the side of him that he showed only to her and occasionally to Joss. He *was* irritating: pompous and self-seeking. In the beginning, she'd hated it when he'd behaved like this in front of their family and friends. She'd been humiliated, identifying herself with his behaviour, trying to explain it away whilst excusing him and making light of it. Nevertheless, she'd learned to take aspects of it for her own use, which probably wasn't very admirable. Emma grimaced ruefully as she threw the long grass aside into a heap on the path and then wiped her damp hands on a piece of tissue. There had been many moments in their marriage when they'd been quietly happy together. Yesterday afternoon had been one of those. He'd brought her tea, made just how she liked it, and comforted her in his own kindly way as they'd sat there before the fire. And then Joss had returned.

Emma stepped back onto the path, her hands clasped in a kind of unconscious prayer of thanksgiving, remembering her child's face. Joss had come into the drawing-room, hesitating in the doorway, and her expression had been one of such joyous exultation that she, Emma, had automatically risen to her feet.

'Darling,' she'd cried. 'Here you are.'

She'd gone towards her, unable to think of anything else to say, almost dazzled by that look of happiness. Joss had looked from one to the other, as if not knowing quite where she was.

'Hello,' she'd said uncertainly.

Unaware of anything unusual, Ray had simply grunted a greeting and picked up his newspaper, but Emma had taken Joss by the arm and led her – as if she were a sleepwalker – into the kitchen where she'd pushed her down into a chair.

'Now,' she'd prompted her, refilling the kettle. 'You've had a lovely time with George and the donkeys . . .'

'Yes,' agreed Joss happily. 'Oh, Mum, I have.' She'd stared about her, as if she'd never seen the kitchen before. 'I love him. I've always loved him and now it's all right.'

Remembering those words, Emma began to understand how bad it must have been for someone of Joss's open, truthful temperament to be in love with a married man: how hard to keep her love hidden and under control whilst continuing to nourish the friendship that had been so important to them both since childhood. Now, it need be a secret no longer, she was free to show her love, and that new freedom had had a startling effect on her. Again and again, Emma's eyes had been drawn back to that glowing face, to share the joy that shone in her child's eyes. Then, quite suddenly, the light had been quenched.

'If only Mutt had known,' Emma had been saying. 'Oh, she'd have been so thrilled for you, darling. She loved George so much . . .' And she'd seen Joss's expression change, as if she'd remembered something, and the familiar, slightly wary look had come down like a mask.

As she stamped the mud from her shoes at the front door, Emma guessed that it had been the remembrance of grief that had been the cause of that change. For the rest of the evening, though, the happiness had shone out intermittently from behind the sadness, rather like a faulty electric connection or sun glimpsed between clouds.

In the hall, Emma paused. She'd planned to go down to The Lookout and had even considered taking Bruno his parcel, providing that he promised that – whatever it contained – he should not discuss it with Ray. As soon as she'd heard that Zoë was with him, however, she'd been seized with her usual irritation and now had no intention of allowing Bruno to open the package beneath Zoë's ironical black-eyed gaze. No, it could remain where it was, but she would go down and have coffee with them and be as polite as was possible. Suddenly she was seized again with the joyful thought of Joss's happiness that even the prospect of Zoë couldn't tarnish.

Smiling to herself, she went to get her coat.

Bruno observed their meeting with a sardonic watchfulness born of experience. He was not taken in by the bright smiles, the friendly cries of greeting, or the embrace that was carefully choreographed so that neither woman actually kissed the other.

'Zoë.' Emma assumed a look of caring concern. 'What a surprise! Is all well with you?'

She managed to imply that, from her quick assessment, Zoë wasn't looking at her best; she even patted her arm encouragingly. Instinctively, Zoë shrank from the gesture, wrapping her thin arms round herself as though she were feeling cold. She had retaliation at hand, however, in the form of Emma's pashmina. She reached for it, giving it a little flap – as though Emma were a bull and she a matador – before pulling it round her narrow shoulders.

'I'm fine, darling,' she said, stretching her lips in the brief imitation of a smile, 'except that I always forget how cold it is here. Bruno's given me this lovely shawl. Isn't that sweet of him?'

It didn't need the accusation in Emma's eyes nor the triumph in Zoë's to realize that he'd made a gaffe.

'Not given,' he said calmly. 'Merely lent. I can't think why you never wear enough clothes, Zoë.'

Emma seized upon this remark gleefully, though still seething inwardly at Bruno's insensitivity.

'Mutt used to say that once a woman got to a certain age the more that was left to the imagination the better,' she observed, allowing her glance to linger pointedly on Zoë's short skirt and naked neck.

'And you'd be absolutely right to take her advice, darling,' said Zoë, taking out a cigarette and leaning towards Bruno for a light. She caught his warning eye and pulled herself together: she couldn't afford to push her luck too far. 'Speaking of Mutt, though, I am so sorry.'

She sounded so genuine that Emma swallowed, torn between a desire for revenge and the opportunity to maintain an air of dignified grief. Bruno brought her some coffee and gave her a tiny wink, implying that he and Emma were on the same side whilst Zoë was merely an irritant that must be endured from time to time, and she relaxed, remembering her yoga classes, taking a few deep breaths. Bruno passed Zoë her coffee and wished that he hadn't given up smoking, wondering why she was always less abrasive, more vulnerable, when they were alone together and if any other people ever saw that side of her.

He'd discovered that there were a few financial difficulties regarding the new flat – some new furnishings and the matter of a deposit, though the usual three months' rent in advance had been waived – and he'd promised to help her out. Now, he saw that this subject might remind her to behave herself and he poured himself some coffee, feeling slightly relieved at this opportunity.

'Zoë's moving next week,' he told Emma, sitting down at the end of the long table. 'It sounds rather fun. She's going to be living in the same house as the artist Evelyn Bose. She's moving into her basement flat on Sunday.'

At the news that Zoë would be gone before the funeral Emma visibly brightened. She sat down at Bruno's right hand.

'What fun,' she said, deciding to be generous. 'Lots of parties, I expect.'

Zoë accepted the olive branch, perching on the chair opposite, blowing her smoke sideways.

'It's a bit of a break,' she admitted. 'You won't believe it but she still exhibits. Last year she had a show . . .'

Bruno sat back in his chair and sighed with relief. Whilst he listened to Zoë he was aware of Emma beside him, and remembered Mousie's warning, yet he simply could not see how the subject was to be broached: he reviewed and rejected every remotely possible opening with horror. He got up at one point, to let Nellie in from her morning potter in the valley, and spent some moments in the kitchen with her, soothed as usual by her undemanding affection. Suddenly, he was overcome by a keen desire to be working; to be in that other, far more satisfying world of the imagination, creating his own scenes and dramas.

'The fact is,' he told Nellie, 'I'm simply no bloody good at real life.'

She fawned upon him, tail wagging, tongue lolling happily, so that he laughed too, comforted as usual, and went back to the women.

CHAPTER THIRTY-SEVEN

Dan Crosby parked his car in the old quarry, reached for his small briefcase and climbed out. He glanced at the other three cars, trying to remember whether they were the same ones he'd seen last weekend and hoping that the girl might be around. He told himself that it was unlikely on a Thursday afternoon, that she'd almost certainly be at work, but he'd been unable to resist another trip to Paradise.

He smiled to himself: Paradise. As he walked away from the car, crossing the narrow bridge, he felt that the name was entirely appropriate. He hadn't looked directly at the row of cottages, in case it seemed as if he were prying in through their windows, but he did take a moment to stare across at the strange house perched on the cliff with its outflung window. It must be pretty wild up there with an Atlantic gale blowing – but impressive too.

He passed on up the lane and paused at the field gate; the donkeys watched him consideringly for a moment whilst he called softly to them, clicking his fingers encouragingly. They came towards him with their peculiar head-dipping amble and he pulled their long ears and rubbed their soft noses, remembering how the girl had talked to them and fed them and how he'd felt such a strong sense of empathy with her, even at such a distance.

'I haven't got anything for you,' he told them – but they stood patiently anyway, glad of the company.

Presently he left them, walking on up the lane and through the gateway, his heart jumping a little nervously now as he braced himself for another meeting with the small woman with the keen eyes and sweet smile. He'd prepared a little opening gambit – that his holiday was nearly over and that he couldn't go back without one more visit – and he held the small briefcase a little tighter under one arm as he knocked on the door, ready for another rejection.

He found himself confronting someone quite different: a pretty, friendly woman with fair hair tucked behind her ears, rather plump but nicely so, and an enquiring but not un-friendly look.

They spoke together and both of them laughed and sud-denly, and rather oddly, they were friends at once.

'I do hope I'm not disturbing you,' Dan said. 'I suppose you couldn't be . . . no.' He shook his head as if disgusted with himself. 'What a crazy idea. You're far too young. I was hoping to see Mrs Honor Trevannion. I know she's been ill . . .'

The woman's expression stopped him, her eyes were brimming with tears, and his spirits sank again.

'Mrs Trevannion died in the early hours of Tuesday morn-ing,' she told him sadly. 'She was my mother.'

'Oh, my God,' he said softly. 'I am just so sorry. I had no idea, please forgive me for troubling you.'

'No, no, it's quite all right.' She seemed to recover a little. 'Is there anything I can do?'

'I'd hate to trouble you at a time like this.' He hesitated and then gestured helplessly. 'Well, OK. I sent Mrs Trevannion a photograph of her wedding taken with my great-aunt. A double wedding. They worked together out in India, apparently, and then my great-aunt stopped writing. I hoped I might learn a little more about her. She seemed to disappear round about the time of India's Independence and, by that time, my grandmother – her sister – had married and moved out to the US. We found this photograph of a double wedding with their names on the back—'

'Oh, I've seen that,' the woman interrupted almost excitedly. 'Mousie showed it to me. I remember now her telling me that you'd sent it. Look, why don't you come in and have a cup of tea? I'm just making one.'

'Well, that's real kind.' He was a little confused by such a different reception but still felt awkward lest his enquiries were out of order at such a time. 'I have to go back to London at the weekend . . .'

She was welcoming him in, introducing herself: Emma Fox. They shook hands and he held up the briefcase, feeling foolishly shy.

'I have some more photographs here. Perhaps you'd like to see them? Were you born in India, Emma?'

'Yes, I was but I can't remember much about it, I'm afraid.' She was leading him across the hall. 'Do you mind if we go into the kitchen while I make us some tea?'

'Not at all.' He looked about him appreciatively. 'What a lovely house it is. Well, the whole place is so beautiful. It surely is Paradise.'

She beamed at him so warmly that he smiled back at her with real affection: he felt the oddest sensation that he'd known her always.

'Mousie showed me the photograph,' she was saying. 'And I said that those old photographs always made me feel rather sad. It was a nice one of Mutt, though, and she looked so much like Joss, even in her funny little hat.'

'Joss?' He sat down at the table and watched her prepare the tea. She took a cake tin from the larder and edged the Victoria sponge onto a pretty, flowered plate.

'Help yourself. Take a big piece.' She provided him with a plate and a fork. 'Joss is my daughter. She's an osteopath and she's been living here with her grandmother for the last few months. She's absolutely devastated by her death.'

'I think I've seen her.' He cut himself a piece of cake, beginning to enjoy himself. 'Not to speak to, though. A dark-haired girl, very pretty?'

'Well, *I* think she's rather special.'

Joss's mother spoke proudly and Dan's heart warmed to her.

'She's not here today?' he asked hopefully.

Emma shook her head. 'She's at her practice in Wadebridge today. She won't be home much before six o'clock.'

He could see her hesitating, wondering whether to suggest that he should stay on to meet Joss and if such a meeting would be appropriate at such a time.

'Would you like to see the photographs?' he asked tactfully, hoping to rescue her from her dilemma. 'I've only got the one wedding photograph, I'm afraid, but I suppose that there's a faint possibility that you might remember something. My Great-Aunt Madeleine had a daughter who would have been about your age. Her name was Lottie.'

She'd put the teapot on the table now, and was watching him open the briefcase.

'How odd,' she said slowly. 'Lottie. That name certainly rings a bell.' She sat down opposite him, looking puzzled. 'D'you know, Mutt spoke that name only a few days ago in her sleep. She called out several times. "Lottie. Lottie." She seemed distressed . . . Good heavens. Do you think she knew something about what might have happened to Lottie?'

They stared at each other across the table, the briefcase between them, a few photographs already lying there beside his plate.

'If my great-aunt and your mother were such close friends that they had a double wedding,' Dan observed thoughtfully, 'it wouldn't be surprising.'

'I know it was a terrible time in India just before we came home,' Emma told him. 'There were riots and killings. Where we were, in Multan, there was a twenty-four-hour curfew just before we came away. Perhaps something . . . well, something terrible happened to Lottie.'

'You mean she might have been killed in one of the riots?'

'I suppose your great-aunt and Lottie could have accidentally got caught up in a mob rising or something.' Emma was thinking it through. 'Bruno – he's my older brother – might remember, although I did ask him if he knew anyone called Lottie, after I heard Mutt calling the name in her sleep, and he said he didn't.'

'Maybe he wasn't thinking far enough back.' Dan was feeling excited. 'It's a long time ago. Perhaps if he thought real hard . . .'

Emma nodded, clearly as fascinated as he was. 'I'll ask him again.' She picked up the photograph. 'Now this is the photograph I saw, isn't it?'

'That's the wedding.' He gathered a few more together, ready to pass across the table to her. 'This is the original and there are the names on the back. That's how I managed to track you down. Trevannion is not a common name and Madeleine had written somewhere that you all came from Cornwall, England. My grandmother remembered that.'

She smiled at him. 'Is she still alive, your grandmother?'

A shadow touched his face. 'She died last year. She was a great old girl and I promised her I'd try to find out what happened to her sister. You know how it is? You get busy and preoccupied with your own life and then, when you grow old, your mind seems to go way back into the past. She got quite intense and upset about it. I remember she said once that, if she'd been a bit more generous, Madeleine and Lottie would have come to her after the war and perhaps then they'd have still been alive. She felt that they must be dead, you see, because the letters stopped coming.'

Her sympathy was evident and she reached across and touched his hand lightly.

'I am so sorry,' she said gently. 'It's awful, isn't it? To think that you've neglected some act of kindness when it's too late to repair the damage.'

He nodded. 'It's crazy,' he said slowly, 'but I just feel I'm trying to put it right for her, as far as I can.' He shrugged. 'I can't bring them back to life but I just want to try to lay a few ghosts.'

'I wish I could help you.' She took the photograph, holding it up. 'It's just so amazing to see the likeness. If you take away the hat,' she covered a part of the picture with her hand, 'that's Joss. There. Do you recognize her?'

He stared at the face, smiling out at him. He hadn't seen Joss smile but the likeness was certainly very strong.

'Yes,' he said slowly. 'I see a likeness to the girl who was here last Saturday. But this is very odd . . .'

He hesitated, frowning in consternation, and Emma turned the picture back so that she could look at it again.

'Now I remember why *I* said it was odd last time,' she exclaimed. 'How strange! Do you see? The brides are with the wrong grooms. Mutt isn't standing with Hubert. I wonder why not. Do you think it was for a joke?'

He was silent for such a time that she looked up at him enquiringly.

'It would seem a bit weird,' he said slowly, 'to do that for a wedding photograph you were planning to send back home to your own folk, wouldn't it? Unless you explained the joke, of course. Madeleine just wrote the words "Me and Johnny with Hubert and Honor Trevannion" on the back. See?' He took another breath. 'Could you just tell me again? Is this the lady you call Mutt?' He pointed. 'This is your mother?'

Emma nodded, still frowning. 'Yes, that's Mutt. How extraordinary. It *must* have been a joke, surely?'

'The thing is . . .' He bit his lip, his face worried. 'The thing

372

is,' he began again, 'that this lady you call Mutt is my great-aunt, Madeleine.'

They stared at each other, perplexed, tea and cake forgotten.

'But how can it be?' asked Emma reasonably enough. 'There's a muddle somewhere. Why do you think *she*'s your great-aunt and not the other woman? I still think it was taken as a silly joke and the wrong photograph got sent home to your family.'

'No, no.' He shook his head very positively. 'Look here. See this one.'

He held out another photograph to her across the table. The young woman was seated, staring straight at the camera, a baby cradled tenderly in her arms with its long gown trailing over her knee. Behind her a tall, fair man looked down on both of them with a proud smile.

'But that's Mutt.' Emma was clearly taken aback. 'Who is the man with her? And could that be Bruno?'

She turned the photograph to read the writing on the back: 'Me and Johnny with Lottie. Lahore 1945.' The writing was Mutt's.

Silently, feeling nervous now, Dan passed another snapshot to her. The two girls, clearly sisters, stood arm-in-arm, beaming at the unknown photographer; the younger girl's hair was cut short and the resemblance to Joss was even more marked. Slowly, Emma reversed the snapshot: the faded ink was slightly blurred but clear enough to read the words: 'Vivian and Madeleine in the garden. 1936.'

She looked at him, clearly frightened, and he stared back at her with distress; he hadn't been prepared for this.

'What does it mean?' she asked, her voice trembling a little. 'I don't understand it.'

'Neither do I.' He tried to keep his voice level. 'Do you have any photographs of your mother taken out there in India when she was young? Or when she was a child?'

Emma shook her head, her brow furrowed, shuffling the photographs as if they were cards and studying them.

'I don't understand it,' she said again. 'This is Mutt, you see. But who is the man, Johnny? And who is Lottie? Can she have been married before she met my father? Maybe she was a widow . . . No, that doesn't work.'

'Not with the wedding photograph as evidence,' he agreed. 'This man you see her standing with *is* Johnny, isn't it? It's the same man. Yet Hubert Trevannion is in the same photograph with them.'

Emma stared at it. 'Then who is this woman?' she asked.

There was a short silence; Dan heard the front door open and close again quietly and someone came into the kitchen behind him.

Emma gave a little cry of relief and Dan stood up quickly, recognizing the woman, feeling as guilty as if he were a thief, gaining access under false pretences.

'Mousie,' Emma was saying, her words tumbling out in a rush, 'something so strange is going on here.' She gestured with the photographs. 'We simply can't understand it.'

Dan knew that the woman called Mousie could hear the panic in her voice and he was relieved when she smiled quite calmly, giving him a little nod of recognition but concentrating on Emma.

'I can guess that it must be very confusing,' she said. 'I had a feeling something like this might be happening so I've brought some letters to show you. Will you come with me, Emma? They'll explain any confusion, I promise. We'll leave Mr Crosby to his tea and cake just for a moment,' she flashed him a quick reassuring smile, 'but this is rather private.'

Emma got up, looking puzzled and rather frightened, but she went readily enough. The door closed behind them and Dan sat down again at the table. He reached for his tea but his hand trembled so much that he set the cup back in its saucer and he continued to sit in silence, waiting.

CHAPTER THIRTY-EIGHT

'So what was that all about?' Pamela stood in the archway to
the kitchen, mug in one hand and cloth in the other, listening
as the front door banged shut behind Mousie. 'What's going
on?'

'I have no idea.' It sounded as if Rafe had moved to the
window. 'She's dashed in next door . . . Ah, here she is again.
She's got a parcel with her and she's crossing the bridge . . .
and going up to Paradise.' He turned back into the room. 'I
wonder who this young man can be to cause so much
consternation.'

'She said he was an American, didn't she?' Pamela put the
cloth and the mug on the table. 'I didn't quite catch what she
said. As soon as you said she was back from Polzeath I went to
put the kettle on.'

'Well, she came in and put our shopping on the chair, and
then she made some joke about the quarry becoming a
national car-park, or something. That's because of Zoë's car
being there, I suppose, and she asked who the visitor was. I
told her that I didn't recognize him but that I'd seen the car
there last weekend. I told her that it was a tall young man with

very dark hair and that he had a briefcase. I suppose I thought he might be someone to do with the funeral arrangements.'

'But she cried out, didn't she?' asked Pamela. 'That's when I came through. I wondered what had happened.'

Rafe frowned a little, trying to pin the memory down accurately.

'She cried, "Oh, my *God*, it's the American boy with the photograph." Something like that. And then she said, "And Emma's at Paradise alone." Her face turned quite pale and she had a look . . .'

'What kind of look?' she asked, after a moment.

'It's what we always used to describe as "Mousie being fey" when she was a girl. That's what Mother called it, anyway. There were one or two occasions when Mousie seemed to get ideas about things or people. Not seeing into the future or anything like that, just very strong intuitions. As she got older I think she kept them to herself but I still recognized it. Mother didn't encourage it, she thought it was fanciful, but I saw it as a rather useful gift. Anyway, that's what she looked like just now. As if she'd had a premonition about something and it was about to become fact.'

'Do you think she's guessed about Joss and George?' wondered Pamela, imagining Mousie in this new light.

'I expect so.' He gave a rueful chuckle. 'Probably you and I are the only ones who didn't. All this time, under our noses, we must have been blind . . . sorry, darling.'

She chuckled too. 'If I *weren't* blind I might have noticed something. The thing is that they've been in and out and under our feet all their lives so we've taken their relationship for granted. And so had they. It must have been such a shock.' She sighed with pleasure. 'He sounded so happy, Rafe, when he was telling us last evening.'

'He *looked* happy, so different from how he was when he went out to meet her, but sort of shocked, as well.'

She picked up quickly on this remark. 'I felt that, too, but I thought it could simply be relief that it was settled so quickly with Joss. She might easily have held him off until the divorce was through or in case Penny changed her mind; something like that. I imagined that he was still trying to come to terms with his good luck: one minute despair, the next joy.' She laughed. 'Or am I being crazy?'

'No,' answered Rafe slowly. 'Not crazy.'

'But you don't think it was that?'

He heard the anxiety in her voice and marshalled his ideas, recalling his reactions as he had learned to do since she had been unable to do it for herself.

'He looked very happy,' he reassured her; this was the most important thing, 'but he had the expression of someone who is trying to assimilate a new idea which has come as quite a shock. It was as if he were trying to think something through and come to terms with it.'

'But not the fact that Joss loves him?'

Rafe shook his head, remembered she couldn't see this response and said, 'No. I don't think that was a shock to him. I think it was a relief that it was established so quickly between them, and that they don't intend to make a secret of it any longer, but this was something else.' He laughed suddenly. 'Dammit, do you see what you've done to me? I've become a psychologist; reading body language and expressions like some old wise woman scrying runes in the tea-leaves.'

She laughed with him, sympathetically. 'But it's important,' she told him as if to comfort him. 'If you notice things then we can be prepared.' She reached a hand to him. 'So what could it be?'

'I don't know but I don't think it's directly to do with them, if that's any comfort. Or, if it had been, then they'd dealt with it as regards themselves and it's something else outside them now.'

Pamela groaned. 'How frustrating it all is. I just want them to be able to be happy after all this, although I shouldn't say that with poor old Mutt . . .'

'George is back.' Rafe was at the window. 'I think Joss will have to take her car up to Paradise tonight at this rate. Mousie's right: it's beginning to look like a car-park out there.'

'How does he look?' asked Pamela.

Rafe grinned. 'Like a man who's just had lunch with his sweetheart. Full of himself, beaming away like an idiot, two foot taller than when he went off to Wadebridge . . .'

They were both laughing when he came in and he laughed too, for sheer happiness.

'Whose is that car?' he asked. 'Got a visitor?'

'It's rather odd, actually,' Rafe answered. 'It was here last weekend. A young man with a briefcase got out and went up to Paradise and then Mousie came in and when I described him she threw a fit and went screaming up after him.'

'But why?' George went to stand beside his father, staring out at the car as if it might answer the puzzle. 'Emma's up there, isn't she?'

'Rafe thinks that Mousie had some kind of premonition that something was going to happen and when she heard about this young man she shot off,' Pamela explained jokingly to George. 'Make any sense to you?'

When he made no reply Pamela turned towards him, surprised, and Rafe said sharply, 'What's going on?'

Pamela cried, 'No Slips, George,' into the silence that followed and she heard him take a very deep breath like someone about to dive into fathomless water.

'Come on, George,' said Rafe. 'Let's be having it.'

'It's not my secret,' George said quickly, 'but Joss said that I could tell you, although we were going to wait until after the funeral. It's not about us, at least not in that way, although it rebounds on Joss. Really, it's about Mutt.'

'About *Mutt*?' Pamela groped for a chair and sat down in it.

'I'll tell you,' George said, as if coming to a very important decision, 'but you mustn't say a word to anyone until after the funeral.' He and Rafe sat down too. 'You won't believe it, I promise you. It starts when Mutt and the children came back from India. Can you remember that, Pa?'

'Well, of course I can.' Rafe settled more comfortably, elbows on the table. 'I was, what, thirteen? Fourteen? We were all so shocked at the news of Hubert's death. I remember when the telegram came from Liverpool and Uncle James came down here with it. "Why wait until now to tell us?" he kept repeating and Mother tried to calm him down. "The poor child must be devastated with grief," she said – something like that. "She's got the two children to cope with, and remember that she doesn't know any of us." Poor old Uncle James was gutted although he was very stoic. We'd lost Father during the war and Mother was very sympathetic towards Mutt in the way that generation was: rather brusque but kindly. I remember that Bruno was very quiet, living in a world of his own and playing games with imaginary friends, and I wonder now if that was his way of dealing with his grief. Emma was too young to know anything. She was an absolute sweetie and we all loved her. Mutt . . .' He paused, thinking back, giving a sad little sigh. 'She was very beautiful. I worshipped her in a young boy's romantic way with an older woman but I think that Mousie could never quite forgive her for marrying Hubert. Mousie adored Hubert and I think she was jealous of her. I taught her to sail, she took to the water as if it were her natural element, and she became very proficient, well, you know that . . .'

'But why do you ask?' Pamela couldn't control her impatience. 'Does it matter what Mutt was like all those years ago?'

'I just wondered what it must have been like for her.' George sounded as if he were trying to find a way to break the news as gently as possible. 'The fact is that she wasn't Honor Trevannion at all. Honor died with Hubert and their daughter

Emma in Karachi.' He grimaced into the shocked silence. 'It doesn't sound possible, does it? I'll try to tell you how it was just the way Joss told me but, remember, I can hardly believe it myself.'

He began to tell her story carefully and faithfully, trying to recall the words she'd used as they'd sat together beside the Saint's Well, whilst Pamela and Rafe listened in disbelieving silence.

CHAPTER THIRTY-NINE

Mousie telephoned Bruno just after Zoë had trailed away upstairs for her afternoon rest.

'I try to do it most days, darling,' she'd told him, yawning widely. 'Keeps me going. I can thoroughly recommend it, although one doesn't necessarily have to be alone.'

She'd raised an eyebrow suggestively and he'd grinned at the implied invitation: it wouldn't have been the first time but today he'd felt on edge and had shaken his head.

'Nice idea,' he'd said, 'but I'm not in the mood.'

She'd shrugged philosophically and drifted up the narrow, twisting staircase, disappearing out of sight just as the telephone rang.

'I'm at Paradise.' Mousie's voice was low and guarded. 'The young American Dan Crosby is here, and he and Emma have been looking at photographs.'

'Oh my God,' he said involuntarily.

'My reaction exactly,' she said drily. 'I hope you won't be angry but I've given her the letters to read. It was the only way, Bruno, believe me.'

'I believe you,' he said, after a moment. 'How is she?'

'I've put her in the parlour at Mutt's desk. It seemed the right place for her to read them, somehow, but I think you should be here. I've suggested that she reads them right through but she might suddenly need some support. When you get here I'll take Dan down to my cottage and tell him the truth about it all. I think that's only right now, but it's best he's not here when Emma comes out.'

'I quite agree,' he said quickly. 'I'll come straight up.'

He left Nellie sleeping peacefully and walked quickly up to Paradise; his gut was twisted with anxiety but there was relief too. He let himself in quietly and went into the kitchen. The young man got quickly to his feet; he looked deeply distressed, shaken by the drama he had unwittingly set in motion. Bruno held out his hand, smiling at him.

'I am just so sorry.' Dan gripped the hand gratefully. 'You have to believe that I had no idea about all this.'

'How could you know?' Bruno glanced at Mousie. 'Have you managed to tell him the whole story?'

She shook her head. 'Only the bare bones. I think he should come and have some tea and then I can explain it to him properly. He's as shocked as we are.'

'I certainly am. I feel terrible.' Dan looked it. His face was grey, as if with fatigue, his eyes blank. 'And at a moment like this too . . .'

'The time was right,' Bruno told him gently. 'Don't feel badly. Good will come of this now, I'm sure of it. It means a new start for us. For all of us. Go and have some tea and we'll meet later on.'

'You're very kind.'

He stumbled out after Mousie, the picture of misery, and Bruno stood alone, his mind focusing on Emma. He glanced at the photographs scattered on the table and, with a jolt to his heart, saw his mother and father smiling up at him. Picking up the wedding picture he scanned their faces carefully, trying to remember them like this: young, laughing, happy. Only tiny flashes from the past – his father swinging him high above his head, his mother's voice singing a nursery rhyme – rewarded his effort. His father's face was familiar – Bruno had a portrait photograph of him from about this time – but his mother's he barely recognized. He stared at her pretty face feeling some-how guilty, as if he had connived at the sudden dispatch to oblivion of her and his little sister's memory. He castigated himself as he recalled how quickly, after that appalling ending in Karachi, he had allowed the layers of his new life to wrap him about, concealing and protecting him from the pain of grief and loss. Those early months of his new life, hedged about with secrecy and full of numbing new experiences, had allowed only brief moments for mourning.

Bruno sat down at the table, folding his arms in front of him, willing up the memory of that hotel room: his father and sister dead and his mother lying in bed, her hair dark with sweat, too weak to comfort him. Her suffering had been like some sick animal chained in that stifling room with them: alive and anguished and uncontrollable. He'd been helpless in his longing to bring her relief, only able to crouch protectively beside her, holding her hand and wiping her face from time to time with the damp, crumpled cotton sheet. How strong and bright Mutt's sudden presence in contrast; how encouraging the feel of her arm about him as she'd kneeled with him beside his mother's bed. Her relief at the sight of Mutt had been palpable; tears had trickled down her cheeks and she'd held up her arms for Mutt's embrace.

'Do exactly as Mutt tells you,' she'd told him. 'Promise me, darling,' and he'd promised, the tears clotting in his throat, and all the while Mutt had held him steady.

Afterwards, on the voyage home and here at St Meriadoc, he'd learned to weave the memories of India into stories that he enacted as games, making it possible to deal with them but, in doing so, retreating further and further from the unbearable reality.

Bruno rested his chin on his arms, still staring at the photograph, and it was here Emma found him.

She'd finished the last letter with tears streaming down her face, piling the letters together and looking about the familiar room without quite knowing what she was doing. She sat at the desk, the words fresh in her mind, the image of the young and vulnerable woman still clearly before her.

'Mutt,' she murmured from time to time. 'Oh, Mutt,' and then wept again with despair and love.

She got up and wandered about the parlour, touching an unfinished tapestry, imagining her mother at the desk writing to the sister she would never see again, so that the tears continued to flow. Presently she felt the need to share her experience, to make it real by the confirmation of seeing the truth of it in someone else's face, and she went almost blindly out into the hall. Through the half-open kitchen door she saw Bruno's shoulder and bowed head and she went in to him.

'Oh, Bruno,' she cried. 'Poor, darling Mutt. Oh, how I wish I'd known this before she died.'

He got to his feet and put his arms about her, gaining solace from her embrace and allowing the shadows of the past to slip gently away. She looked up into his face and saw his compassion and affection for her.

'It was how she wanted it,' he comforted her. 'Don't cry, Emma.'

'What a shock.' She took his proffered handkerchief and wiped distractedly at her cheeks and eyes. 'I can hardly take it in. Yet while I was reading the letters she seemed so alive that when I'd finished I couldn't believe she wouldn't walk in. I had to start all over again convincing myself that she was dead. I wish I could tell her that I think she was brave and that I love her. All those years of secrecy.' She took a hold on her emotions and tried to control herself. 'And you, Bruno. However did you manage it? I know it wasn't right of her to put such a burden on you when you were so small but, all the same, I can't help but feel for her.'

'And so did I.' He shook her gently by the arms. 'I regret nothing. She did what was right at the time. It's no good looking at it with hindsight. She's showed us exactly how it was, and why she did it, and all of us – Mousie, Joss, you and I – we all accept her reasons.'

Emma sighed shakily and he helped her down on to a chair.

'Joss knows,' she said almost wonderingly. 'And Mousie. She explained to me before I read the letters and said that you were waiting until after the funeral to tell me.'

'That was how Joss wanted it.' He sat down opposite. 'She was afraid for you.'

Emma's eyes brimmed again. 'I thought of her just now. Opening them all alone that night. Mousie said she's been so brave. Poor Joss. What a tremendous shock for her, and then going up to find Mutt had died. Thank God that you were here, Bruno.'

'I do thank Him,' answered Bruno most sincerely. He hesitated. 'Perhaps we should have told you straight away. Mousie wanted to but Joss insisted that Mutt should be buried peacefully and you should have time to grieve.'

Emma managed a watery smile. 'Poor darling. That was sweet of her.' She put her hands to her face, massaging her eyes with her fingers. 'I can still hardly take it in. Is it wrong to say that I feel proud of her? Of Mutt, I mean?'

'You should be proud of her,' he agreed. 'She saved my life. You both did. I often wonder what would have happened if you hadn't turned up then. Can you imagine a small boy of four, left alone in Karachi during those times? Imagine the loneliness, assuming I'd ever made it home, with all my family dead. You and Mutt gave continuity to my life. We'd all been so close, you see. You *were* my family.'

She stared at him. 'We're not brother and sister,' she said slowly. 'I'm just taking that in. It's crazy but I still can't quite accept it. You aren't my brother.' She shook her head. 'It's . . . not believable, is it? I'm not Emma but Lottie. I asked you about Lottie, do you remember?'

He shrugged helplessly. 'What could I do? I'd promised Mutt.'

'Oh, I'm not blaming you,' she said quickly, 'but she called my name at the end, Bruno. She said it several times. Do you think she was remembering?'

'Probably. Who can say? After all, she remembered the letters that had lain hidden all those years.'

A short silence.

'If Joss hadn't read them, would you have ever told me?'

Bruno was silent for a moment. 'I would have kept my promise to Mutt,' he said at last.

She gave him a little smiling shrug. 'Well, it's no longer relevant,' she said. 'But if there had been some sort of trouble over the will, say that Ray had tried to force his plan to develop the boatyard, would you still have kept Mutt's secret?'

He made an odd snorting noise. 'I simply don't know. It would have become very difficult should Pamela and Rafe have been in any danger of losing their home. As it happens the problem doesn't arise. Mutt has left Paradise to you, just as we thought she would, and The Lookout, The Row and the boatyard are left to me. She clearly hadn't thought about Inheritance Tax.'

'Ray was worried about Inheritance Tax,' Emma said. 'He was hoping to find the will to see how things were left and how it could be paid.' She frowned, puzzled. 'I suppose Dan's arrival reminded her of the letters. Poor fellow. It's sad, isn't it, that after all his efforts he didn't get to see Mutt? So near and yet so far. But why ask Joss to find the letters? Why not you? Surely that was the obvious thing to do?'

'I have a theory about that,' answered Bruno. 'I put it to Joss that Mutt knew the time had come for the truth to be told but couldn't bring herself to face it. I think that, when she told Joss about the letters, subconsciously she was hoping they'd be read.' He laughed drily, remembering. 'God, I was angry when Joss told me. All these years of secrecy and all the time the letters had been lying there for anyone to find.' He paused. 'Joss has coped remarkably well, I must say.'

'George has helped,' murmured Emma with a rather wistful smile. 'I always hoped that Joss would have Paradise. Well, things have changed, haven't they?'

'I have great hopes that she and George will live at Paradise,' he told her gently. 'The way I see it, Emma, you still have rights, because of all that you and Mutt have done for us, and I hope to honour that. Put it this way: if our positions were reversed – if you were Hubert's child and I were Mutt's son – would you turn me out of The Lookout now? Would you feel differently about me or expect me, having read the letters, to assume that our shared past counted for nothing? No, I can see you wouldn't. But, if we're talking legally, then yes, things have changed.'

'Ray will have a fit.' She managed a little laugh. 'Never mind. He'll probably understand Mutt's motives. He might well have done the same in her position. So what will happen now?'

He explained to her how his grandfather's will could be re-proved so as to prevent paying Inheritance Tax twice and she listened intently whilst he explained his idea of giving Rafe and Mousie their cottages, to save future tax, and his wish to leave the rest of the estate to Joss and George.

'I look upon them as my children,' he told her. 'Anyway, I promised Mutt I'd look after Joss and I intend to do it if she'll let me.'

Emma looked at him with gratitude. 'I don't mind for myself,' she told him. 'I never wanted Paradise except for Joss. Bless you, Bruno. She'll be prickly about it, though, and what about Olivia and Joe? Won't they think it smacks of favouritism if George takes over Paradise, even with Joss?' She straightened in her chair, the whole reality of her new situation dawning upon her. 'They'll all have to know, I suppose?'

'I think so, Em.' He watched her compassionately. 'If only for Joss's sake, I think that the family must know. Pamela and Rafe will be her parents-in-law and you know how she hates subterfuge and lying.'

'Yes, I know.' She was remembering her daughter's face when she'd returned from her walk with George and the donkeys: that expression of joyous freedom after the strain of hiding the secret of her love for him for so long. 'Yes, you're quite right. Won't that make it even more difficult with the other children? After all, Joss has no legal rights at all, now.'

Bruno shook his head. 'I don't think it will,' he said. 'I've had an idea about it. Supposing George buys Paradise with whatever sum he raises on his house in Meavy? Nobody need know the figure, need they? It will between me and George, and any shortfall will be my wedding present to them. After all, it's not as if Joe or Olivia would ever want Paradise; at least, not to live in themselves. What do you think?'

Her eyes were full of tears. 'Bless you, Bruno,' she said. 'What can I say?'

Before he could answer they heard someone open the front door and shut it with a slam, as if it had slipped from nervous fingers; a short silence followed and then quick footsteps crossed the hall.

CHAPTER FORTY

Joss rushed into the kitchen, her cheeks flushed, her eyes bright with anxiety.

'Mum,' she said anxiously. 'Are you OK? Mousie caught me on the way home . . .'

Emma was on her feet, her arms wide, and they held each other tightly.

'Oh, darling,' she said, half laughing, half in tears, 'what a shock it was. We've just been talking it over and I'm still all of a tremble. However did you manage so bravely?'

Joss held her at arm's length, studying her. 'You're really OK?' She let out a great gasp of relief. 'Thank God, then. Mousie was right.'

'Mousie?' Emma looked puzzled.

'I was afraid you'd be really devastated but Mousie said that I was underestimating you and that you'd admire Mutt for her strength and courage and you wouldn't mind.'

'And she was right.' In her daughter's presence Emma was quickly regaining her composure. 'I think that Bruno might be right too in suggesting that subconsciously Mutt was hoping you'd read the letters and there would be no more need for secrecy.'

'Do you really think so?' Joss looked almost shocked. 'I wish I could believe it. And you really don't mind . . .?' She glanced anxiously at Bruno, wondering how much her mother had truly grasped.

'We've talked about re-proving the original will,' he told her, 'and we're all agreed on how we can go forward.'

'Dad will make a fight of it,' warned Joss. 'Oh, yes he will, Mum.'

'I think he'll accept it,' Emma answered quietly. 'He's a businessman first and foremost, and it's from that angle that he's always looked upon St Meriadoc. He can't help himself, dear old Ray, he sees everything from the standpoint of its financial potential, but we mustn't forget that he's always had our welfare at heart, Joss. Oh, I know his values are different ones, he can't understand the need for solitude or a desire for spiritual growth, but I think you'll find he'll accept the new order quite cheerfully once he knows the truth.'

She spoke with dignity and neither of them opposed her but remained silent, impressed by her calm defence.

'I hope that's true,' said Bruno at last. 'However, it would help enormously if we could find *Goblin Market* and the certificates. At least we can look now without upsetting anyone. I wish I knew where to start.'

'Oh.' Emma's eyes flew wide with the shock of a sudden realization. 'I bet it's in the parcel. Of course. So *that's* what's in it.'

Before their astonished gaze, she went to the dresser, took out the package and pushed it across the table to Bruno. He untied the string with difficulty, trying to control the trembling of his fingers. The paper cover was illustrated with strange Rackhamesque figures, its boards were hardly thicker than card, the pages were cut. He opened it carefully, first removing the envelope attached to the back cover with a strong paper clip.

'It's a first edition,' he said, examining it reverently. 'It cost five shillings. A great deal of money for a little girl to save.' He passed the book to them, opened at the title page so that they could read the inscription:

> To my sister Madeleine
> On her fifteenth birthday
> With my love
> Vivian

Emma turned the pages with gentle fingers, Joss watching over her shoulder, whilst Bruno read the letter that accompanied it.

> Paradise
> June 1948

My darling Bruno,

This is for you when you grow up because it is only fair that you should have the things inside it in case of some emergency in the future. I should have liked this book to go to Emma but I wouldn't be able to explain the inscription and so it might cause trouble. Keep it safe for me.

Please forgive me if I have done you any harm, my dear boy. I have only wished to make you happy but, as you get older, you'll find that we are all fallible and we damage others quite by mistake.

Thank you for your love, it means a great deal to me. I hope you know how much I love you in return.

Mutt

Deeply moved, Bruno stood up, smiling with some difficulty, folding the letter in with the other documents.

'I'm going to leave you now,' he said rather abruptly. 'I'd like to have a look at these documents, and you both need some time together. I'll come up tomorrow morning. Oh, and the book is for you, Emma. Mutt says so in this letter.'

He went out quickly whilst they stared after him.

'It's just as bad for him,' said Joss after a moment. 'Poor Bruno. All those memories.'

Emma turned back to the book, rereading the writing on the title page, and then picked up a photograph from the table. Together they looked at Madeleine and Vivian, smiling happily in the sunny garden, and then at each other.

'Oh, darling,' said Emma shakily, 'what a day it's been.'

'It takes an awful lot of adjusting to,' said Joss – but she looked happy, freed now from the need to dissemble. 'I think the worst is over, though, apart from explaining it all to Dad, and the miracle is that we're both still here, at Paradise.'

Mousie was sitting at her gate-legged table, watching the sunset. The wind had died to a gentle breeze and the western sky was scorched and stained with a vivid crimson fire that ran in flaming watery tongues along the horizon, dyeing the sea with brilliant colour. Dazzled by the spectacle she sat peacefully, reviewing the last few hours with a kind of contentment. It had taken Dan some time to understand Madeleine's story and Mousie had needed all her tact and authority to make the account true yet acceptable to him.

Still shaken by the turn of events, but trying to come to terms with this new light shed upon his great-aunt, he'd gone away with the hope that the result of his search was not the disaster he'd first feared.

'It was time,' she'd told him. 'Bruno was right about that. I'm sorry that you didn't meet Madeleine but that was her decision and I think she was right. You must read the letters, Dan. They'll tell you far more about her than I can.'

They'd talked for a while and she'd seen that his quest was

no idle whim born out of curiosity but, rather, a sincere desire to find out as much as he could about his great-aunt. As she'd grown older, his grandmother had told him a great deal about Madeleine, describing their shared childhood to him and revealing a hitherto hidden guilt that she had failed her sister when she'd most needed her.

'I meant no harm coming here,' he'd said remorsefully. 'Quite the opposite. I hoped I could go home with some positive news about Great-Aunt Madeleine, even though it was too late for Grandma Viv. I had no intention of setting the cat among the pigeons.'

'It was too late for both of them,' she'd answered, 'but not too late for us. You haven't done us harm, Dan, trust me.'

He'd muttered that Emma must be deeply shocked; it was clear that during their short space of time together he'd already grown fond of Emma and his anxiety for her touched Mousie.

'She's your cousin,' she reminded him cheerfully. 'She and Joss. That's a good thought, isn't it? You won't go back home empty-handed, after all, but with a whole new family. And, if I know Emma, she'll want to know all about you and Mutt's relations. What fun it will be.'

It was to his credit, she thought, that he didn't outstay his welcome but took his leave when enough had been said on either side and to delay further would have begun to be embarrassing. Evidently he had no desire to be present should any other member of the family arrive to discuss this extraordinary disclosure and Mousie was relieved to see him go, feeling strongly that Bruno might arrive before too long.

He came at last, knocking on the door and then calling her name as he entered the hall. She continued to sit at the table, waiting for him, and presently he laid the envelope in front of her.

'Emma had this all the time,' he said. 'She found it in the drawer where Mutt had put the letters but this was all wrapped up in a parcel and addressed to me. She was waiting until after the funeral in case it contained something that might cause trouble between me and Brer Fox.'

'Was *Goblin Market* with it?' Mousie did not touch the envelope.

'Yes, it was just as Mutt said. She'd written me a letter . . . Well, you can read it for yourself.'

He sat down, whilst Mousie took the sheet of paper and felt for her spectacles, resting his elbows on the table and staring seawards. He made no attempt to open the envelope either, but sat quite still whilst she read the letter.

Presently Mousie took off her spectacles and folded the paper, wondering just how difficult it would be for him to see those official reports of his family's deaths after so many years of denial. A long silence fell between them. The light was fading now, shadows gathered in the corners of the room, and one brilliant star hung low over the horizon. The sea poured in, the tide rising over the rocks, to break against the harbour wall and the encircling cliffs.

'It was a very terrible thing,' Mousie began gently, 'that you should lose your whole family in one savage blow. Yet, even out of such terrible tragedy, good can come. I think your work is such a positive result of it, don't you? Your childish instinct to blend fact and fiction, which was so necessary to your survival, released in you the gift of story-telling. The way you combine the dry bones of history with the colour and drama of fiction is a wonderful talent that brings delight to many thousands of people. Hubert would have been so proud of you.' She took the envelope and opened it, leafed through the certificates and put them to one side. 'It's right that you should have them, so that your grandfather's will can be re-proved without any fuss,' she said, 'but they have no further use. None of it was your doing; you had no choice. Let them go, Bruno.'

He looked at her. 'I think I've begun to do that. Up at

Paradise in the kitchen, while Emma was reading the letters, I saw the wedding photograph and realized that I could hardly remember them, or my sister, either. I felt as if I'd cut them out of my life deliberately. I tried to will myself to recall as much as I could, as some kind of reparation, and then Emma came in and, whilst comforting her, in some odd way I felt released from the guilt. It was odd because, although I *was* comforting her, she brought me comfort too, and I was reminded of Mutt appearing in that hotel room and how I felt then. I hope she knew how much I loved her.'

He took up the certificates, looking at them with a lingering compassion, and then put them back into the envelope, thinking of Mutt's words to her sister.

. . . There's something wise about Bruno, some grace which is far beyond his years . . . When he smiles at me, hugs me . . . I feel as if I have been granted absolution . . .

He didn't feel particularly wise but he was glad that he'd been able to give her such comfort in return for the stability and love she'd always shown to him whilst attempting to keep her promise to his mother. He remembered too the last sentence before her final farewell to Vivi.

Perhaps I am already an aunt, and Emma has a cousin she will never know and I shall never see.

That, at least, could now be remedied. He pushed the envelope aside and smiled at Mousie.

'So tell me what you think of Dan Crosby,' he said.

EPILOGUE

The May sunshine was hot, the drifting breeze scented with hawthorn blossom, and somewhere high above his head a lark was singing. The donkeys stood together in the shade of the tamarisk trees, heads drooped together as though they were sharing a secret, and he leaned his arms on the warm, rough wooden bar of the gate and smiled to himself.

He'd been to St Endellion, to pay his respects to his great-aunt Madeleine's grave, and now he was going to have tea at Paradise with Emma and Joss.

'After all,' Emma had said to him on the telephone, 'we *are* cousins. We need to get to know each other properly.'

He'd been reluctant to impose himself upon them, still guilty at being the agent of such a bombshell, yet the whole family had shown him nothing but kindness when he'd made a brief visit at Easter. Emma had given him his great-aunt's letters to read, suggesting that he should sit in her parlour at the desk where she'd written them, and he'd found the process a deeply moving one. That weekend he'd stayed at the same hotel at Port Isaac, determined not to take any advantage, but this time he was staying for two nights with

Joss and her mother at Paradise. The car was down in the quarry – he hadn't quite been able to bring himself to drive up nonchalantly to the front door – with his bags still in the trunk.

Dan shook his head at his own caution; it was as if he were waiting for something to help him across the invisible barrier that he imagined still lay between him and these people who had made him so welcome. As he stared across the sunlit grass he heard the arched wrought-iron gate open with a clang and saw a girl pass through, closing the gate carefully behind her. A flowery shirt was tucked into the long denim skirt and she wore a soft-brimmed straw hat that shadowed her eyes. The donkeys twitched their ears and flicked their bell-rope tails and she held out her hands to them so that they could take the carrots she'd brought.

He straightened up and Joss caught a glimpse of the sudden movement and glanced across the meadow. She raised a hand in greeting, walking over the grass towards him, smiling with delight. Gone was the air of wariness he'd first noticed about her and in its place was confidence and joy.

'You haven't been properly introduced to the donkeys, have you?' she asked as she came up to him. 'Rumpleteaser and Mungojerrie. They're rather elderly but they like to meet new friends.'

He laughed, letting himself into the field. 'The names sound familiar – but weren't they cats?'

She shrugged. 'Don't blame us. We just get what we're given by the donkey sanctuary. Are you ready for some tea? Mum's been cooking all morning so I hope you're hungry.'

'How is Emma?' He hadn't forgotten how drawn to her he'd been at their first meeting; that strange sensation of recognition and affection. 'Is she . . . coming to terms with things OK?'

She smiled at him, appraising him with something of her old uncompromising look, and nodded. 'She's getting used to adjusting to the truth,' she told him. 'We all are. Actually, it's rather liberating. We have you to thank for that. There's so much to talk about, and to remember, and we've read the letters over and over. She gets very emotional about it all – and sometimes very sad – but I've promised her that when George and I have our first daughter we shall call her Charlotte. Lottie for short.' She shot him a more mischievous glance. 'Or maybe Charlotte Vivian in memory of your grand-mother. What do you think?'

'Sounds a great name to me.' He couldn't resist her infec-tious happiness. 'Grandma Viv would have been thrilled at the idea.' He grinned, becoming bolder. 'Am I missing something here? I thought you told me you and George couldn't hope to be married until the autumn?'

'That's quite right and no, you're not missing anything,' replied Joss with a pretence of severity. 'I'm just doing a little forward planning. Perhaps you'll be able to get down for the wedding? After all, we *are* family, although we don't know you as well as we'd like to, Cousin Dan.'

'I'm sure that can be remedied, Cousin Joss.' He gave her a little bow. 'There's a whole raft of people out in the States who want to meet you and Emma. And George, of course,' he added quickly.

'And Mousie and Bruno,' she prompted him teasingly. 'And don't forget Rafe and Pamela and Olivia and Joe. You take one of us, you take us all; we're that kind of family.'

'I shall be honoured to.' He answered her with a quaint formality, yet with the oddly joyful feeling that the barrier was finally crossed. 'Thank you.'

They stood together – Madeleine's granddaughter and Vivian's grandson – smiling at each other for a moment in the sunshine, then she led the way across the meadow and he followed her through the gate into the Paradise gardens.

Marcia Willett was born in Somerset but now lives with her husband in deepest Devon. A former ballet dancer and teacher, she is the author of fourteen previous novels, including *The Children's Hour* and *The Birdcage*, both available in paperback from McArthur & Company.

www.mcarthur-co.com